Anna, Ann, Annie

D1372540

THOMAS TREBITSCH PARKER

Anna, Ann, Annie

A DUTTON BOOK

DUTTON
Published by the Penguin Group
Penguin Books USA Inc., 375 Hudson Street,
New York, New York 10014, U.S.A.
Penguin Books Ltd, 27 Wrights Lane, London W8 5TZ, England
Penguin Books Australia Ltd, Ringwood, Victoria, Australia
Penguin Books Canada Ltd, 10 Alcorn Avenue,
Toronto, Ontario, Canada M4V 3B2
Penguin Books (N.Z.) Ltd, 182-190 Wairau Road,
Auckland 10, New Zealand

Penguin Books Ltd, Registered Offices:
Harmondsworth, Middlesex, England

First published by Dutton, an imprint of New American Library,
a division of Penguin Books USA Inc.
Distributed in Canada by McClelland & Stewart Inc.

First Printing, May, 1993
10 9 8 7 6 5 4 3 2 1

 REGISTERED TRADEMARK—MARCA REGISTRADA

LIBRARY OF CONGRESS CATALOGING-IN-PUBLICATION DATA:
Parker, Thomas Trebitsch, 1943–
   Anna, Ann, Annie / Thomas Trebitsch Parker.
     p. cm.
   ISBN 0-525-93607-6
   I. Title.
PS3566.A6864A83   1993
813.54—dc20   92-36627
                           CIP

Printed in the United States of America
Set in Goudy Old Style
Designed by Eve L. Kirch

PUBLISHER'S NOTE
This is a work of fiction. Names, characters, places, and incidents either are the products of the author's imagination or are used fictitiously, and any resemblance to actual persons, living or dead, events, or locales is entirely coincidental.

For Gabriel

Vienna, 1927

Anna

Anna Moser is ten years old. Today she stands in the doorway of the third-floor bath and watches her father, Hugo Moser, the popular writer, trim his beard. His lips are pursed to whistle, but there is no song. He wears trousers, suspenders, a shirt without a collar. His sleeves are rolled to his elbows.

A flat, powerful winter sun from the lone window throws the objects in the nearly all-white room into sharp relief, prompting Anna to notice how pale Papa's arms are. He angles his chin to the mirror, stretches his neck, then snips at the errant hairs with a long, steel scissor. Tiny white bristles cascade into the wash basin and onto the marble floor.

When he finishes, he clears his throat, gazes importantly into the mirror, then returns the scissor to its leather case. In most instances a careful and fastidious man, Papa leaves the bristles where they fall. It is a habit that rankles Mama. Much older than she—nearly twice her thirty years—he has come to perceive all his quirks and mannerisms, no matter what their effect on others, as virtues.

"Aha, I see I've had an audience," Papa says as he passes Anna in the doorway and pads in his house shoes down the long dark hall into his bedroom. There he will put on a collar and cravat, a vest, a dark suit with a fine chalk stripe, shoes and spats, then walk down to the second floor to his writing room, where he creates his elaborate "science fantasies," a phrase Papa himself has coined to define his highly successful and imaginative musings about the future.

"Bravo, Papa!" Anna calls after his narrow back as he disappears down the hall. "Bravo," she repeats, eager to have him turn and perhaps raise a single, quizzical bushy eyebrow as only Papa can. The latch to Papa's bedroom opens with a precise click.

Still on the threshold, Anna is partially illuminated by the sunlight from the bath. She has thick, auburn hair worn in a single long braid, a small frame and delicate features, save for a somewhat broad and arching nose that complicates her face and gives her a whimsical, slightly bemused expression. It is Grandfather Leo's nose, she has been told. There is a photograph of him on the sideboard in the parlor, among a gallery of stern, posed relatives. He is sitting at a table, a bowl of soup before him, a spoon halfway to his mouth. He seems eager, his expression rapt, as if there were nothing more important in the world than the taste of soup. Anna likes everything about the photograph—its soft brown tint, the steam rising from the bowl, the intensity of Grandfather Leo's anticipation. About other things, however, she is less certain—Mama's eccentricities, her disappearances, her rages that drive Papa into his writing room and sometimes out of the house. Can't Mama see what she is doing?

Anna steps into the bath and moves quickly to the basin, where she contemplates collecting the bristles. That way, in the event of Papa's departure from the family—a departure she senses is imminent—she would have something of the essence of him. Not long ago she poured a small amount of his cologne into a vial and hid it in her dresser. Now she hears Mama approaching and rinses the bristles down the drain.

Skodagasse 14

The Mosers live at Skodagasse 14, a short distance from the ancient part of the city and quite near the Parliament. Their

three-story house is identical to the others on the street, made of
the same brown stone and plaster. It has a steep-pitched slate roof
worn and channeled by the elements, and its outer walls are
streaked black like a heavily made-up woman who has been
moved to tears.

The thick wooden front door is painted dark green with a
stylized brass number "14" on either side of the frame. Above the
door, on a stone ledge inscribed with the year 1641, is an ornate
casting of a sneering jester. Papa would prefer a more dignified
visage, and has twice negotiated a price to have the jester
removed. Mama, who was born at Skodagasse 14, will not hear
of it.

The door opens to the sharp, clear jingle of the entryway bells
and a tall woman with plaited silver hair wound like a tiara about
her head steps out onto the doorstep and into the chilly midafternoon. It is Mama's mother, Oma, holding a large, long-handled
dust mop. An apron covers her elegant, high-collared dress, and
she shakes out the mop with considerably more fervor than the
task deserves.

As she goes about the afternoon's work, she is at once angered
and pleased that Katrina, their servant of two decades, has left
them and moved to the country, and that a suitable replacement
has been impossible to find. It is the nature of the work that
irritates Oma: what pleases her is that she finally has tasks to
accomplish.

Holding the mop like a lance, she glances at the tarnished
brass street numbers. As she pulls a rag from her pocket to polish
them, a streetcar lurches past and stops at the corner. Stepping
from the car is Herr Sonnenabend, the piano instructor. He is a
florid man with a scraggly mustache, a stale odor and an unen-
dearing manner, all things of which he is aware and which please
him, for he knows that his skill with Vienna's young keyboard
prodigies has made him irreplaceable.

Sonnenabend buttons his cashmere greatcoat and looks at the
retreating trolley as if leaving it may have been an error, then
makes his way to the Mosers'. When he kisses Oma's hand she
notes his pockmarked neck where it extends beyond the coat's
Persian lamb collar and thinks once again that far, far too much

is being made of her granddaughter's talent at the piano, and far too little about anything else in the girl's life. Her mama pays her scant attention. And with so much time spent practicing, Anna has little left for schoolmates. The child needs girlish pleasures.

Piano Lessons

Anna loves the lessons, however, and the ease with which she can master the ever more difficult pieces of music Herr Sonnenabend teaches. She is even fond of Sonnenabend, which makes her unique in the household. But Mama, Papa and Oma have never seen the teacher at his best, when he takes the bench to demonstrate a new piece.

At first, he is predictably Sonnenabend. He massages his knuckles, takes countless deep breaths and gazes up and down the keyboard as if it were somehow of inferior quality. Then he bends to the keys, his ear close to his fingers, listening, it seems, to the stroke, the hammer on the string, the brief, ill-fated vibration. Music emerges whole and lovely, imbuing the parlor's delicate French furniture with grace and coloring the room's still air.

So perfect is the sound that even as it fills Anna with hope, it chills her, for it reveals how easily and deeply she can be touched. What amazes her is that she too can create such a sound out of the irregular clutter of notes on the page, that lately she can even sense a mistake before she plays it, at the very instant before the discordant note is struck. Perhaps, she dares to think, Sonnenabend's power might be hers, as well. And perhaps she can even use that power to dull Mama's dissatisfaction with Papa, to keep him nearer, longer.

One afternoon at the conclusion of a lesson, Sonnenabend asks that Mama and Papa join him and Anna in the parlor. Sonnenabend clears his throat twice, then a third time. When he is finally satisfied he has everyone's attention, he announces that Anna has the talent to become an artist of the first rank. "Believe me," he adds, "it is a rare occasion when Sonnenabend makes such a pronouncement. Indeed," he amends, "I have never before made such a pronouncement."

With one hand on the lid of the piano, the other vaguely indicating the ceiling, Sonnenabend glances quickly at Mama and Papa, who are seated at opposite ends of the parlor. Papa, in a large, stuffed chair, balances a cup of coffee carefully on a silver tray on his knee, while Mama sits cross-legged on the Persian carpet and smokes a small, gnarled Turkish cigar. The pronouncement gives them pause, for they too think themselves to be artists. But of the first rank? The question hangs between them.

Finally, they arrive at their unspoken answer. Papa concedes that his work, while pushing at the frontiers of literature, will (unjustly) never provide him the stature of a Schiller. Equally reluctant, Mama acknowledges that the Vienna Ensemble of Modern Dance of which she is founder and principal dancer will not soon be taken as seriously as the Vienna Ballet—*let it not be said, however, that she, Evelyn Moser, aspires to classical ballet.*

And so for Mama and Papa, that afternoon Anna is reborn, the vessel of a talent more readily understood than their own iconoclastic genius. In the months that follow, Mama fixes on Anna's physical well-being, particularly her hands. From the finest shops in the city, Mama brings expensive soaps, creams and emollients. She also takes special interest in Anna's diet, and in the absence of Katrina—damned, self-willed Katrina—instructs Oma to prepare only those foods with life-enhancing properties, primarily organ meats and vegetables in the cauliflower family. With the institution of this regimen, Papa ceases to take his evening meals at home.

Papa does, however, make Anna a marvelous gift: a grand mahogany Bösendorfer—the finest piano of the age, and said to have been once played by no less than Schumann (would that it had been someone *more* than Schumann, Papa thinks). The piano is installed in the rear parlor in place of the solid instrument upon which Anna took her first lessons and which has commanded the corner of the room for nearly a century. During the move, a workman breaks his leg. Papa pays for the fellow's physician and medication and at Christmas presents the man's family with a large holiday goose.

So pleased is Anna with the sudden attention from both

Mama and Papa that she is not even concerned over Papa's disappearance from the evening meal. On the contrary, Anna feels that somehow her talent has resulted in a rare compromise between her parents, in which both Mama and Papa get what they want.

In addition to Papa's interest in the instrument Anna plays on, he is concerned with her interpretations of the pieces Sonnenabend teaches. He urges Anna to stray from the orthodox and forge her own vision, further distinguishing herself from the teacher's other little geniuses.

One day, Sonnenabend takes Papa aside to suggest he not meddle in his daughter's artistic life. "You know nothing of music," Sonnenabend says.

Papa is furious. "Absurd. Outrageous. I am Viennese!"

"Your address and your heart may be Viennese"—Sonnenabend seems empowered by the remark—"but your taste and your ear are definitely Croatian." A small vein at Papa's temple throbs. How could Sonnenabend know that he detests Croatians? "Now, if your daughter were studying the concertina, perhaps your skill could be put to better use."

The man is nearly dismissed. Only when Anna absolutely insists he be kept on does Papa relent.

Now Anna practices her newest piece, a Schubert impromptu. Papa descends the stairs from his writing room to the parlor and stands at the foot of the piano. The massive lid is open, the gilded sounding board a path to his inexplicably open arms. As Anna picks out the notes, he hums the well-known melody—slightly off-key—coaxing her, slowing during the difficult passages.

When she finishes, Papa appears at her side, elegant, smiling, his finger wagging like a metronome. "I love it when you listen to me," she says. She even loves his flat renditions.

"Of course you do." Papa seems a bit embarrassed. "One plays to be heard."

She stands and puts her arms around him. He gives in awkwardly to her embrace. Still, the instant she feels his beard brush lightly against her cheek, things seem so perfect that all she knows is her fear of losing them.

In the Kitchen

Why, Anna wonders, has something as ordinary as baking suddenly become so pleasurable? Is it descending the stairs at dawn during that winter to find Oma in the high-ceilinged kitchen already at work with her long, thick rolling pin amid copper bowls, cake forms, wire whisks?

Is it learning more about Grandfather Leo and his love for food—hearing about his quest for marzipan on Oma's and his holiday in France, about the meals that he and Oma enjoyed when they were young, and the cakes and tarts she baked for him?

Or is it the eggs—truly comical, with a life of their own, sliding every which way? And what a marvelous froth egg whites make when they are beaten.

Flour is indeed the whitest and lightest substance on earth, closer to air than any solid.

And butter, well, that is something you can really get your fingers into. First lightly to see the distinct patterns each finger makes. Then press harder and make your fingers disappear completely.

The tarnished brass balancing scale holds a certain allure, the black weights with their denominations molded into them, some no larger than a thimble.

And there is always the yeasty, comforting aroma of the ingredients melding in the heat as Oma opens the heavy oven door to probe a tiny wood sliver into the crown of the cake to see if it is done.

But it is the recipes, Anna realizes, the recipes contained in Oma's ancient cookbook with its red-and-white-checked cover and stuffed with aging notes—recipes that Anna can return to from one day to the next, follow carefully, trusting their ingredients and their measurements, and be confident of the outcome— it is the recipes that please her most.

Ice Skating

One day, without mentioning her intentions to her daughter or son-in-law, Oma takes Anna on the streetcar to the frozen lake at the Stadt Park to teach her to ice skate. Oma shows Anna how to tie the laces of her skates together and drape them over her shoulders. The blades of their skates clink against one another with every jolt of the trolley.

Anna holds Oma's hand tightly as they first venture onto the ice. Others glide past, their skates kicking up fine chips that glitter in the afternoon light. Anna's fear is palpable. Though there are others her age and far younger on skates, she cannot imagine she will be able to do this. Still, as she feels the sensation of gliding so easily forward, she soon drops Oma's hand, finds her balance, and after some moments skates tentatively on her own. Quickly confident, she moves with purpose, first in circles, then to the farthest reaches of the lake, watching as the trees that ring its perimeter become a wash of gentle green in the high blue day; skating past and around the others until she finally returns to take Oma's hand.

"Ice skating?" Papa queries when he first hears of it. He repeats the words three times as if to better specify the activity in his mind.

"I'm very good at it," Anna assures him as Oma stares skeptically at this son-in-law of hers, only a year younger than she.

"Why shouldn't you be?" he says. "I too skated as a boy. And quite well, I might add."

Anna cannot imagine Papa on ice skates, nor can she imagine him as a boy.

"Nonetheless," Papa continues, happening suddenly upon the perfect sentiment, "your schoolwork and your time at the piano must take precedence over sport. For it is only through your lessons and your practice that you will be able to own your own life, like your illustrious Papa." He places his thumbs under his suspenders, fingers extended, to impress upon her his own personal title to life.

Exasperated, Oma puts her hand to her brow. "For heaven's

sake, Hugo. Let the girl enjoy these years. They're the best of her life." Anna is alarmed by Oma's remark. Certainly, it can't be true.

"She can do as she likes." Papa seems to relent. He shakes a finger at her. "Providing she does what is best." Then looking suddenly as if a matter of importance has crossed his mind, he quickly excuses himself.

And so it is settled, though to Papa's consternation it is skating Anna chooses. It is skating that brings her the greatest satisfaction—more than her lessons with Herr Sonnenabend and the attention her playing brings her, more than baking with Oma, and certainly far more than her tedious schoolwork. For out in the middle of the frozen Stadt Park lake—her eyes misting as she pushes purposefully through the wind, her tears freezing on her cheeks—Anna can sense the discrete power of her own frame, and has only herself to please.

Throughout that winter then, on the days when she does not help Oma bake, Anna arises before sunup and boards the street-car to the park. At first she skates as fast as she can for as long as she can, then slows to draw respectful circles around the thoughtful, mustached men in their tailored jackets—former lieutenants, Oma has told her, in the Kaiser's army, from a time not long ago when Vienna was at the very center of the universe.

Cybelle

Directly beneath the veneer of all Anna's activity that winter, she feels loneliness threatening to overtake her, like the sudden wave that catches bathers unaware and carries them out to sea. Then one spring morning, her teacher, Frau Schreiber, brings a helper into Anna's classroom; Cybelle Becker, a pretty, blond, pleasant-natured girl of thirteen—three years older than Anna—who attends the same school.

Cybelle's task that day is to assist the younger students with their penmanship. Seemingly aware of how much is to be accomplished in the little time she has, Cybelle kneels immediately at the desk of the student nearest her. Instead of bending to her own lessons, Anna watches the new girl—how confidently she moves from one student to the next, how certain she seems of her acceptance by the others. It is as if Cybelle possesses the very self-assurance that Anna once felt and senses she has lost fretting over Mama and Papa—lost, despite how well she plays the piano and the ease with which she has learned to skate.

When Cybelle arrives at Anna's desk and takes Anna's hand to move it with her pen across Anna's lesson book, Anna feels the pulse in Cybelle's wrist beat lightly against hers. Though Cybelle's attention is on the book before them, Anna lifts her pen from the page and looks at Cybelle's neck, at the fine, blond hairs that have escaped from her chignon. Anna is so close she can smell the soap on Cybelle's skin, hear the faint intake of her breath.

"Anna," Cybelle prompts, having read Anna's name at the top of the page. "Come," she urges, exerting a slight pressure on Anna's hand to bring the nib of the pen back to the paper. "Today, we write."

Writing that day with Cybelle—and in the days that follow—Anna feels that she has gained some of the older girl's confidence. Also, that her hand has somehow merged with Cybelle's, and that she, Anna, is now endowed with the skill to form the most careful and delicate cursive letters, letters that combine to create words that look elegant and serious on the page, like those on the commendations in Papa's writing room.

And later that spring, when Cybelle joins Anna's class on the soccer field, when the early June air is filled with the smell of fresh-mown grass, of the nearby flower gardens, and of sausages and mustard from the vendor's cart on the field's edge, Anna feels she owns some of Cybelle's bravado. She attacks the ball with a fervor that surprises her teammates, that pleases her, and that impresses even the unflappable Cybelle.

"But don't play better than the boys," Cybelle warns one afternoon when Anna has scored all their team's goals. "It embarrasses them." Later, as they walk from the field hand in hand, Cybelle confides, "It's true what I said about boys. They're all the same in that way."

"Yes, absolutely," Anna says. She is by now so seduced by Cybelle, by the aroma of her skin—like that of bedclothes left to freshen in the wind—by the pressure of the girl's delicate, soft hand on hers, that she will believe anything.

Fortunately, Cybelle seems equally taken with her, and the two spend many afternoons together that spring at the Skodagasse, spinning elaborate fantasies about their future. Cybelle's stories—because she is so much older and more worldly, Anna assumes—always involve lovers, men who will take her away from Vienna. These men are either extremely wealthy, roguish or cruel, often all three. Her stories inevitably end in a tragic death, either for Cybelle alone or along with her beloved.

The sad tale told, Cybelle stretches, then folds her knees beneath her on the Mosers' handsome inlaid wooden floors—they never go to Cybelle's because she claims it is too unpleasant there—looking again cheerful and self-possessed, as if she has not betrayed a thing by her telling.

At first, Anna's stories are much like Cybelle's. But after these initial tales of abduction, abandonment and untimely death, Anna recognizes that the sentiments are not hers, and in the weeks to follow she reveals her own vision of the future—to play the piano before royalty and receive flowers at the end of the concert, even from reticent Papa sitting to the Prince's immediate left; to skate for Austria in the Olympic Games; to travel on a holiday to America—about which she has learned in geography class—and peer unafraid down Niagara Falls, into the Grand Canyon and across the Mississippi River. Always in Anna's stories she is alone.

Not long after these afternoons with Cybelle begin, it occurs to Anna that perhaps Cybelle is not as untroubled as she seems. As quickly as the notion presents itself, however, Anna dismisses it. Still, she occasionally ponders, why Cybelle's tragic endings? And why has she chosen *me* to befriend?

One June afternoon, stories told, the two girls sit on the wooden floor in Anna's room. Usually by this hour Cybelle must go to prepare dinner for herself and her mother, but today she lingers, toying with the buttons on her embroidered blouse.

"Don't you have to go?" Anna asks, already feeling the void left by her friend's inevitable departure.

"I do," Cybelle says, "but today . . ." She stops and quickly unbuttons her blouse to her waist. "Today, I wanted to show you these." She pulls the blouse from her shoulders, revealing the two nubbins that are her developing breasts.

Anna turns away in modesty and embarrassment, but Cybelle touches her hand to Anna's chin, urging her to look. "Come, touch too," Cybelle offers.

"I'm afraid," Anna says, though of what she is uncertain. Afraid that she, herself, will soon be thirteen? Of becoming lost in her yearning for Cybelle? Or of something else entirely?

"What could you possibly be afraid of?" Cybelle asks, seemingly unaware of her effect on Anna. "Come," she repeats, taking Anna's hands. And as matter-of-factly as if she were helping Anna with her penmanship, Cybelle guides Anna's hands gently to her nipples.

After a few seconds, Cybelle rocks back slightly on her heels, smiling, as Anna withdraws her hands and rests them on her friend's bare shoulders. "See. Nothing to be afraid of. Nothing at all." And in that moment, in Cybelle's gentle yet compelling presence—and for the first time in recent memory—Anna feels perfectly safe and calm.

At the Prater

On a Sunday in June, Mama and Papa take Anna and Cybelle to the Prater, the city's famed amusement park. Mama wears a long blue velvet cape, a striped chenille scarf, and trousers tucked into high leather boots. She brandishes an imported cigarette in a long holder, gesturing with it expansively. Her attire is hardly the style of the day, certainly not for a woman, and the people stopping to stare make Anna self-conscious. She urges Cybelle— who has met Mama only once and is enormously taken by her— to fall slightly behind and watch as Papa and Mama part the crowd.

Papa holds Mama's arm and steers her, like a dispassionate attendant in a sanatorium, in the direction of the large Ferris wheel in the distance. In his other hand he carries a commodious picnic hamper made of tightly woven reeds. He is dressed, as always, in a suit, spats and cravat and seems aloof from the spectacle created by his wife. As they walk he stares ahead intently.

An eccentric, Mama is not without her following in Vienna. There are many in the city's intellectual and artistic community who consider Evelyn Moser of the Vienna Ensemble of Modern Dance a woman ahead of her time and to be taken seriously. It is precisely how Papa wishes to be thought of, but is not. His science fantasies, while popular among the masses, are considered lightly, if at all, by those he seeks to impress. No matter. Mama makes no distinction between her supporters and her detractors. She is bored by them all.

"Is your mama always so colorful?" Cybelle asks as she and Anna make their way through the press of onlookers left in Mama's wake. Nearby, two men on horseback guide their cantankerous mounts through the crowd, intentionally grazing those they pass with their boots and their steeds' flanks and rumps. The warble of a calliope can be heard between the strains of waltzes coming from the band shell. The air is filled with the smells of fresh coffee and steam. "Is she always so dramatic?"

"Yes," Anna responds with some energy, trying not to seem too overwhelmed by her mother's theatrics. More than ever she is confused about her parents; about what she has inherited from them, about which one she will be like when she is older. "Yes, always," Anna adds ruefully. "As far back as I can remember."

"Yes, well, I think it's wonderful. Fantastic!" Cybelle exclaims. She wears a cream-colored pinafore over a pale blue blouse. The heat and the excitement give her skin a pearlescent sheen and faint pink tint, like the inside of a seashell. "Women in this city have no color," she declares. "Vienna is dying and all the women are corpses."

It sounds to Anna as though Cybelle is repeating something she has heard elsewhere. In any event, she hasn't the faintest idea what her friend is talking about.

Suddenly, a spirited group of young men singing a German

folk tune, their arms locked together, passes between the girls and
Mama and Papa, and Anna loses sight of her parents completely
as she and Cybelle attempt to break free of the men. But it is
impossible. The young men jostle the girls, spin them around and
carry them like flotsam along the sea of their merrymaking. At
one point, the tallest of the group, a fellow with moist blond curls
matted to his forehead, cinches his arm around Cybelle's waist,
pulls her to him and, lifting her slightly, kisses her on the cheek.
"I love you!" he yells back as he and his comrades finally move
on, leaving both Anna and Cybelle a hundred meters from where
they last saw Mama and Papa.

"Are you all right?" Anna asks, touching her friend on the
cheek where the man kissed her. "Are you?" Anna asks again. But
Cybelle has yet to even notice Anna. Instead, she gazes at the
receding crowd of revelers, at the tall fellow who still glances back
at her.

"I'll survive," Cybelle suddenly announces, then laughs.
"Now, come on!" She tugs at Anna's arm. "Let's catch up with
your parents." But when they do—Anna relieved and Cybelle
still laughing—Mama and Papa pay them no notice. Instead they
continue to press steadily forward, unaware of the drama that has
just taken place.

At midday, the two girls sit across from each other in a
gondola on the large Ferris wheel at the center of the Prater. The
gondola, swinging gently, is stopped at the absolute apex of the
giant wheel's arc, over sixty meters above the crowd milling
below. Vienna—the old city, the two arms of the Danube River
and the woods beyond—fans out from where they sit like a world
in miniature, where everything happening is whimsical and of no
import. Though it is quite hot, a slight breeze cuts through the
gondola's open windows. Anna savors the breeze as she sits
poised, waiting for the wheel to turn again to transport them back
to earth.

"Do you think," Anna suddenly ventures, resting an arm on
the narrow window ledge in the small chamber, "do you think we
will always be friends?"

"Of course," Cybelle assures her. But ever since their experience with the revelers, Cybelle has been impatient with Anna, something Anna senses but feels helpless to influence. "What could come between us?"

"If you leave? Marry?"

"Well then . . ." Cybelle says. "Then we'll be correspondents. We'll write. Until the end." She states it with such certainty that Anna can see the letter, the envelope with the strange stamp, Cybelle's surprisingly plain and earnest handwriting. "Beloved Anna, you must come visit us now in Greece. Only in autumn . . ."

Then Anna recalls Cybelle's stories, and their ill-fated conclusions. Surely, somehow tragedy will be averted, she thinks. Perhaps even I will prevent it, arriving at the precise moment that . . .

The giant wheel creaks and the gondola in which the girls sit descends a few meters so that the next car at the wheel's base can be unloaded and take on new passengers. The sequence is repeated again and again and again, until finally the door to their car is opened and they are escorted out by the man with the small-billed blue cap and the impossibly large forearms who helped them on a few minutes before.

"Come back in a year or two and the two of us will have a real ride for ourselves, eh?" he says to Cybelle as he helps her out onto the concourse. Cybelle blushes as she pulls her hand from his. Anna cannot decide what to make of all these men with their kisses and their offers. What little she understands of desire intimidates her.

In the spot where Cybelle and Anna are to rendezvous with Mama and Papa, Mama is performing. She has removed her cape and leaps from one illusory boundary on the grass to another, extending her arms in homage to the sun; or so it seems to Anna and the others in the growing circle of onlookers. In the middle of the area where she dances, the picnic hamper sits open on a white cloth. Papa is nowhere to be seen.

Soon Mama's dance becomes even more spirited, and then after a final, athletic leap she collapses gracefully to the ground, folding her arms about her like the inwardly arching petals of a flower. Some in the crowd applaud. Others, however, think she is a crazy person, and laugh and nudge one another to indicate the pleasure they have taken watching a woman dressed as a male peasant make such a colossal fool of herself. Anna claps tentatively.

"I think she's fantastic," Cybelle asserts, loud enough for everyone to hear. "That was wonderful, Frau Moser."

Mama smiles, then arches her eyebrows and glares imperiously at Cybelle and Anna. Her face is flushed, her makeup dissolved to reveal the sharpness of her cheekbones. Her eyes glint in the sun like mercury. She looks like a goddess, some untouchable being, Anna thinks, certainly not a mama.

Presently, Papa materializes in the distance like a miniature, moving ever closer to rejoin the family. Anna wonders where he has been, whether he and Mama have had words or whether he simply left when she started to dance. Or whether in some way Papa drove her to it.

"Time to eat," he announces, taking his place on the white cloth and gazing into the hamper. "We've had our exercise. Now it is time to eat."

The Busk

In July, Papa has an idea. It comes to him on one of the infrequent evenings when he joins Mama, Oma and Anna at the dinner table. The fare, prepared by Oma under Mama's direction, is tripe and celery root. No one but Mama is eating. "Delicious," she says with her first bite. She chews slowly, carefully savoring the flavor. "Very refined. Very French. Très française." She flares her nostrils to appear French. The others watch. "Everyone," she suddenly demands, "mangez!"

Papa slices a piece of bread from the large black loaf at the center of the table, butters it thoughtfully, brings it to his mouth, stops and studies the others. "In Africa," he begins, "there are tribes that once a year take all their household goods and clothing and bring them to the center of the village. There, what is flammable is burned, what is not is destroyed by other means. This is called a busk."

"In Africa there are only savages," Oma submits.

"Big, beautiful, black savages," Mama adds, again trying to appear French, then continues eating.

"Why do the Africans ruin everything?" Anna asks, noting Papa's upset that his story is already under siege.

He turns head and shoulders to her, excluding the others. "Because, dear Anna, they wish to start anew. It is a symbolic act of rebirth."

Oma is studying the implements on the table. The china has been in her family for over a century, the silver nearly as long. She looks back up at her son-in-law and recognizes that alas, the discussion has not yet run its course. "Simple people destroy the past," she says, hoping it will close the issue.

"That is an old-fashioned notion," Papa insists, now turning back to Oma to engage her in an intellectual dialogue. "We hold on to the past because we are frightened of the future." The premise is the cornerstone of his "science fantasy" stories.

"Tell that to Herr Doktor Freud," Mama offers, entering the fray. She has finished her tripe and dabs gingerly at the corners of her mouth with a napkin. "Freud has some notions you might not want to totally ignore."

"The man is a moron," Papa says. "He's trying to make us all victims of his tedious childhood. Where is his imagination? His sense of adventure?"

"Not everyone, Hugo," Oma says, "thinks of adventure as riding off to the moon in a space vessel." She alludes (inaccurately) to Papa's recent popular success, *The Journey to Venus.*

Anna is quickly confused by the conversation. What does it all mean, she wonders? Are they arguing? Only ten, she still believes that everything adults say is sensible, that everything said is to be taken literally.

"I propose"—Papa suddenly interrupts Mama as she elaborates on the development of psychology from Freud to Adler to Jung, reducing it to a series of petty jealousies and spats among the principals—"I propose that we have our own busk. Right here at Skodagasse 14."

"Ridiculous," Oma says. She slams both hands flat on the table, causing the silver to shake and an empty glass to fall to the floor and shatter.

"Not"—Papa raises his fork—"an actual busk where everything goes into the fire. But one where we each take a few items we care about and sacrifice them to the pyre. A hat, a pair of shoes, a photograph . . ."

"It's one thing to have foolish ideas, Hugo," Oma continues, "and another to impose them on everyone else. Isn't that so, Evelyn?" she asks, hoping to enlist Mama's support.

But Mama has been uncharacteristically quiet. "My cape," she suddenly offers. "It would burn beautifully, with a cobalt flame." Oma is indignant. "Where shall it be done, Hugo?" Mama asks. She touches his hand and he looks at her. It is one of the few times Anna has seen tenderness pass between them.

"In the front. On the street. Out in the open." Papa is invigorated by her interest.

"So the world can see what idiots we all are," Oma sneers. She gets up from the table, her plate in her hand. "You're both children," she says. "Anna is more adult than either of you."

Anna hears this but it makes little impression. She concentrates instead on Mama and Papa. Mama has moved her hand from Papa's to touch his sleeve, his neck, his cheek. Papa looks directly into her eyes.

"Go," Mama tells Anna. "Go help your Oma." Anna hesitates. "Now."

When Anna returns from the kitchen, Mama and Papa are gone.

On the afternoon the Mosers are to have their busk, crowds surge through the Skodagasse toward the nearby Palace of Justice, where a massive demonstration is under way. Thousands of workers have gathered to protest the acquittal of the killers of two of their number earlier that year in a clash between Austria's conservative army and the liberal Social Democrats' Republican Schutzbund.

Papa, only marginally interested in politics, gathers the family in the front parlor. "It will be safer if we stay indoors today," he explains, "while these buffoons air their differences." Mama, however, has a rehearsal and leaves immediately, quickly becoming part of the throng out front.

Anna spends the day at the window in her bedroom, from which at first she sees the crowds dwindle. Next, men in small clusters swagger up and down the street yelling up at the residents of the houses to join them. Later, mounted police ride by, their horses' hooves making a tremendous commotion on the cobblestones. One horse slips on the trolley tracks, causing his rider to break ranks while the others, eyes forward, ignore him. Then the street is empty again, save for a servant girl who emerges from a neighboring house to peer after the retreating militia.

By midafternoon the street is unnaturally quiet. There are no streetcars, no women wheeling children in prams, not even the old veteran with one leg who always lurches up and down the Skodagasse on his crutches.

Suddenly, Anna hears a crack like the breaking of a branch. Then another and another, and after some time, the smell of smoke fills the air. Soon the street is again filled with men fleeing on foot, pursued by those on horseback. There are cries of outrage and fury. One man stumbles and falls. He tries to get up, but he is trampled by the men he runs with. Finally, he is grabbed by the shoulders by two others and dragged quickly away, his heels banging on the cobbles.

"Extraordinary," Mama exclaims when she arrives home hours later. Her face is smeared with dirt and makeup, her blouse torn and filthy. "To see it. To be a part of it. The power. The theater of the streets."

"Buffoons. All of them," Papa says. "You're fortunate you weren't killed."

"But to die feeling all that excitement, that energy. Now *that* is the way to die." Mama's eyes flash. She plucks Anna from the floor as if she were weightless and suspends her until they are face to face, only inches from each other. "Don't let *him,* don't let anyone ever scare the life out of you," she commands. "Remember me."

"Yes, Mama."

" 'Yes, Mama,' indeed," Mama repeats. "Extraordinary."

Vienna, 1931

The Recital

Anna opens her first public recital with a Chopin ballade. It is a difficult piece, one Herr Sonnenabend, who sits in a wheelchair in the first row, said should come later in the program. But Anna no longer feels tentative about her skill at the piano. She has honed it well, in order to own her life, as Papa instructed. Now the instrument is hers, an account from which she can freely draw after years of steadfast contribution—time spent alone in the parlor when often she wished she were elsewhere, with others, like her schoolmates whose lives, Papa warned, would never be their own.

Papa, however, has not come to hear Anna play in the small, slightly shopworn theater where the Vienna Ensemble of Modern Dance usually performs. He has, in fact, not heard Anna play since he moved from the Skodagasse two years earlier to take up residence in a suite at the Hotel Bristol. His absence from tonight's performance, he confided when Anna spoke with him at his private table at the posh Café Dolder, where he now writes and receives visitors, was to avoid the inevitable scene with Mama. "The woman is all emotions and no brains," he said, then apologized, not thinking it prudent to prejudice the girl against her mother.

"Still, I'd like you to be there. Very much so, Papa." Anna stood to go, kissing his cheek. Over the past year, she has also lost much of her tentativeness with him. Lately, she even bears him a small amount of anger for his desertion. "Very much, Papa," she insisted.

"I know," he said to her sadly. Were his eyes tearing? She studied him carefully. "But some things are impossible."

The ballade is a startling mix of melodies briefly discovered, then abandoned, bridged by delicate interludes. It is at once romantic and dignified, its emotions withheld, controlled, until the piano can no longer contain the accumulated notes and the music pours forth powerfully, charging the air.

Before the final note is struck, Mama stands. "Bravo, bravo," she cries. She glances behind her to urge on the others in the audience. Many of the two hundred or so in the hall are already on their feet, applauding. Anna intended to stand only at the recital's end, but Mama's bravos have created a juggernaut that leaves Anna little choice but to walk to the front of the stage and take a small bow. She shows a brief, broad smile, then stifles it. At fourteen, Anna is already wary of revealing her pleasure. Her once-whimsical expression has become more serious, and she has learned more about accepting less.

On the day that Papa moved from the Skodagasse, a pair of his valises rested atop a large, black steamer trunk in the vestibule. Mama roamed the downstairs, moving curios from one room to another and then back again. When Anna emerged from the kitchen with a tin of miniature pastries she had baked for Papa, Mama took her by the sleeve to a corner of the rear parlor.

"Nothing to worry over," Mama whispered dramatically, "this is a hoax. He needs me." And then, "Who would have thought he would actually go through with it? And at his age?"

Anna discerned a slight quiver in Mama's voice as she pulled her sleeve from Mama's grasp. "You made him do it!" Anna insisted.

Just then, Papa descended the stairs and Mama straightened, her voice full and confident. "I didn't *make* him. I *dared* him."

* * *

Unlike Anna, Mama spent little time ruing Papa's departure, and was soon seen on the arm of many of Vienna's bachelors and widowers, famous and infamous. Of note, the self-satisfied and contrary young opera critic, the astonishingly tall Negro dancer from London, the corrupt and amusing Minister of Public Works, and the vain, foppish and altogether unpleasant merchant who owned large woolen mills throughout Austria.

Cybelle—wise to Vienna's social goings-on—told Anna that Mama had become more notorious than ever, and that most or all of Mama's suitors had professed their love for her. "Yet she spurns them, each and every one," Cybelle said, a hint of triumph in her voice.

When, days later, Anna asked Mama whether she loved any of the men in return, Mama laughed. "I love only that they avow their love." And then looking Anna up and down as if for the first time, she added, "You'll see what I mean soon enough."

"I don't want to see," Anna called after Mama, who was already on her way out of the room. "I don't want their love. I don't want anything you want!" If Mama heard, she gave no indication.

As the applause in the theater diminishes, Anna returns quickly to the bench, and before the final "bravo," she plays the opening notes of her next selection, a Beethoven bagatelle. At that instant, the doors to the hall fly open and Cybelle rushes in. Though it is winter, she wears neither hat nor gloves. Her coat is unbuttoned. Her face is red and her long blond hair strings every which way. A tall, young, callow-looking man accompanies her. He has a proprietary hand at the small of Cybelle's back. They are quickly seated, lost to Anna's view.

Distracted, Anna begins the piece a second time. The bagatelle is light—yet not sweet—and Anna plays it purely, mathematically.

Cybelle, now seventeen, is a shopgirl at Lederer's, an exclusive store offering elegant women's fashions from Paris and soft, supple leather goods from Florence and Milan. The clientele are most often wealthy men shopping for their wives, or more likely, claims Cybelle, their mistresses. Cybelle has told Anna that she was given the position because her face—now refined, yet with a promise of illicit passion—has a definite attraction for these men. It was a look that Ilse Bauer, who manages the shop for Herr Lederer, recognized in an instant.

Cybelle's commissions provide her with sufficient funds to move from her mother's house, and she lives alone, not far from where she works. She and Anna are still friends. On some afternoons, Anna visits her at Lederer's, and on occasional Sundays they take trips to the nearby countryside. They never see each other in the evenings, however, for those are the times Cybelle keeps for the men who ask to meet her, if only briefly, at one of the city's more obscure coffeehouses.

"They are not lovers," Cybelle assures Anna, who cannot decide whether her friend is lying or not; and if so, why? "They would like to be, but they are not," Cybelle explains, seemingly amused about how flustered she leaves them. "I kiss them sometimes, but I never let them kiss me back."

Anna remains fascinated and excited by Cybelle, though the ease with which she seems to move through life bothers Anna. To have all that attention, and yet to have to do so little for it.

A second bagatelle, following right on the final note of the perfect first, is brief, concise—over so quickly that the audience sits mute for a few moments before breaking into applause. Again, Mama stands to urge them on, but Anna only nods in quick recognition before she returns to the keyboard and begins the Beethoven *Appassionata* Sonata. It is the most difficult piece of the evening, and Oma's favorite.

For a time, much to Anna's chagrin, Oma indulged Mama in her imbroglios, and would await Mama's return from her evenings with her lovers to listen to the intimate details. The discussions would often continue at mealtimes when Anna was present. Hoping at some point to make sense of what was being said, Anna cataloged every particular in a journal soon filled with descriptions of lovemaking and the shortcomings of men and their anatomy.

"Why do you wait up for her?" Anna asked one night as she and Oma sat before the coal stove in the front parlor. It was well past midnight.

"I suppose I'm bored," Oma offered. The photograph of Grandfather Leo about to eat soup was on the sideboard opposite from where they sat.

"Bored?" Anna was certain that boredom was not the reason for Oma's complicity. Oma always had some task under way, and lately had taken to reading scholarly books about history and the lives of famous men.

"Frustrated, then," Oma said. She slapped the arms of her chair, then fixed on the photograph. "It was unfair for him to leave me, to pass on, when we were both so young. Unfair. But"—Oma's voice softened—"you've already gotten a taste of unfair, no?"

Before Anna could answer, the key turned in the latch.

Anna guides the sonata to its stormy, agitated finale. Sweeping across entire runs, her fingers move so fast she can barely see them, though she knows they will land in the sequence she has practiced for hundreds of hours, and she gives herself to the power of the piece completely. She thinks of nothing, looks nowhere, only hears the music—furious and violent—and in a presto whirlwind of stretto, the sonata ends.

Now they are all on their feet, even Herr Sonnenabend, whom Mama and Oma help from his wheelchair. Anna sees them before her, offering thanks for being transported, touched—evident in their expressions, in their concentration on her alone. A perfect finale.

Still, Anna has one piece left to play, the Chopin A major prelude. It is a child's piece actually, one of the first Anna learned. But now, she toys with the familiar melody to show her precise control, she manipulates the tempo to prove her ability to surprise and delight, then brings the prelude to a close with a deli-

cacy of touch—more hush than sound—that reveals what her
ironic smile earlier suggested: that she will survive the confusion
of her life and the lives of those she has little choice but to love.
She will survive this and more.

Mama's Suitor

Tonight a man comes to the door dressed as a bat with a mask
that has a mouse-like false nose and whiskers. He introduces
himself as Herr Hartmann. Anna ushers him in and offers him
a seat in the parlor. She has never met the man before, but has
learned from the dinner-table discussion that he is a widower,
heir to a great fortune made in the import of cigars from Cuba,
and unable to sustain an erection. Anna is unsure precisely what
this last bit of information means, but in the telling of it Mama
was more amused than upset, so Anna assumed it to be of no
great import.

The fact is that Mama, while speaking candidly about many
aspects of sex, has not yet taken the time to explain the full
scope of things. And Cybelle, who, Anna expects, could by now
tell her as much about sex as Mama, has become increasingly
reluctant to discuss it at all, as if suddenly it has become her
duty to protect Anna's innocence. Oma, too, is mute on the
subject, further frustrating Anna, who has broached it with all
three of the women only to be rebuffed—or in the case of
Mama, ignored.

Herr Hartmann attempts to sit down but is confounded by the
stiff bat wings that protrude from his shoulders to his waist. Anna
watches as he moves about, seemingly flustered. Having developed some of Mama's nerve, she is about to ask him about his
unsustained erection when Mama appears.

"Evelyn!" Herr Hartmann bends to kiss her hand. He still
wears the mask. "Your costume is priceless," the man tells Mama
as he steps back to observe her.

Mama, however, having declared masquerade balls infantile,

wears no costume. She is dressed as she normally does, in a lavender double-breasted tunic, bright green silk pantaloons, boots and a broad red sash. Her only concession to masquerade is a brief black mask.

As Mama and Herr Hartmann are about to leave for the ball, Mama asks Anna to play something for them on the piano, but Herr Hartmann protests. They are already late and will miss the judging for the best costume. Mama insists. "The new Mozart," she says as the man reaches into his costume to produce a pocket watch.

"You see," he says indicating the time, "we are late. No Mozart tonight."

"He doesn't want to, Mama," Anna says. "Don't you see? He doesn't want to listen." Any of Mama's past suitors, Anna knew, would have readily relented, only too happy to do something to please Mama.

"Play the piece," Mama demands. "A few minutes won't make any difference."

"I beg your pardon, Evelyn, but it will. To *me.*" Herr Hartmann's wings flutter behind him like a hummingbird's. "Now, either we leave together this instant or I'll be on my way." He turns toward the parlor door.

To Anna's surprise, Mama, poised for a second in indecision, relents. As they leave the parlor Mama says to the man, "I only asked to make her feel good." The parlor door closes, and seconds later the entryway bells jangle.

Anna is furious. She has the impulse to call after them, "It wouldn't make me feel good. It wouldn't! What *would* make me feel good is . . ." and not knowing what indeed would, she says nothing at all. Instead, she moves to the piano and attacks the lower register with vengeance, making nonsense chords, then finally slamming the keyboard cover shut.

Having seen both Papa and Mama sulk, and determined to be like neither of them, Anna, still full of fury and energy, grabs a feather duster and dusts both parlors, then assaults the kitchen with rags and a mop, intending to scour it as it has never been scoured before.

At the Stadt Park

It is October and an autumn sun turns the dun-colored buildings at the northern end of the Stadt Park a blinding silver. Like
the blades of my skates, Anna thinks, pulling them on.

Out on the ice for the first time this fall, Anna soon experiences a familiar ache in her legs. The muscles in her calves feel
like cables drawn suddenly tight. But she will not give in to the
pain, knowing she can skate through it—that drawn ever more
taut, the cables will not snap, but loosen. Feeling the tightness
spread to her thighs and buttocks, Anna skates faster. She smiles
grimly, aware that skating deeper and deeper into discomfort, she
is also on the verge of feeling free.

Suddenly, she hears her name. Once, twice and then again.
She slows, the tautness in her muscles diminishes and she is left
gliding as a tall man skates alongside her.

"Don't you remember me?" he asks. He adjusts the knit cuffs
of his coat as he and Anna move in tandem. His breath makes
little puffs of steam they skate through. Though his skin is coarse
and his muttonchop whiskers don't match left side to right, he
is a pleasant-looking man, Anna thinks.

"No, I'm sorry, I don't remember," she says.

"A few months ago. I came to your house. To escort your
mother."

"A lot of people do that," Anna says matter-of-factly.

The man laughs. "I'm sure that is true. Your mother is very
much in demand."

The slight edge of scorn in his voice puts Anna off, but the
man laughs again, indicating that his tone is not to be taken too
seriously. Wrinkles around his green eyes suggest his amusement.

"We attended a masquerade ball, your mother and I. I left
without hearing you play. Mozart, if I am not mistaken."

"The bat?" Anna recalls the man's attempt to sit, thwarted by
his bat wings.

"Yes, the bat, indeed," he confesses. "I'm Herr Hartmann."
He extends his mittened hand for her to shake as they glide along
the ice. "I want to apologize for leaving so quickly that evening.

But, you see, your mother has a way of making people angry. Had you been Mozart himself, I wouldn't have listened."

"Nor would I," Anna confides. "She makes me angry, too."

They skate without turning and soon reach the southernmost end of the lake, where they leave the ice to sit on a wooden bench. Anna crosses her ankles and the man does likewise. For a few moments both stare self-consciously at their legs. He is like I am, Anna thinks, at least, how I'd like to be—amused and unruffled by Mama. Her legs hurt and she is afraid if she sits too long that they will stiffen and cramp. Still, she is comfortable with him, likes having him next to her.

"Your mama, you know," he finally begins, "has an astounding imagination. Genuine gumption. She is"—he pauses briefly—"quite a woman."

Anna nods, her eyes tearing from the cold.

"Of course," he goes on, "I knew that night your mama wouldn't wear a costume, but would wear precisely the opposite of what convention demanded. I also knew that her non-costume, whatever it would be, would be more original than anything my dull friends might have devised. Which, indeed, was the case."

"You even complimented her on her 'costume.' "

"True. And a risky business, that. For to do so, I knew, would place me in the category with the others your mama considers fools. But I, on the other hand, derived great satisfaction from knowing I had played the fool on purpose. Such was the elaborateness of the games we played that night, our third and last together. Suffice it to say, we had a miserable evening." Herr Hartmann claps his mittened hands, punctuating the finality of the relationship.

"But if you understood Mama's game so well, why did you bother to play it? Or ask her to accompany you even a second time?" What, she wonders, is the charm of the unconventional, of a woman who seeks only to prove men unworthy of her?

"Perversity, I suppose. And curiosity. I wanted to know why such a commotion was being made about Evelyn Moser, what everyone found so enchanting."

"And did you?" Anna moves to the very front of the bench and turns earnestly to the man. "Did you?"

He removes his mitten and touches her face. Her cheek is so cold, the faint pressure of his fingers against her skin leave a mark that quickly fades. "You really *would* like to know what all the commotion is about, wouldn't you?"

If only this sympathetic face were Papa's, Anna thinks, as Herr Hartmann considers the wisdom of telling the girl more about her mother. "It is not my place to be talking to you like this," he ventures.

"But if you don't tell me, who will?" Feeling suddenly desperate, she takes his hand and puts it to her face again, surprising herself. "Please, Herr Hartmann."

"Yes, well, I suppose if no one explains her allure you'll spend a lifetime trying to imitate her or avoid being like her or something equally ill-advised. So I will tell you what I think. But you are to repeat it to no one. Understood?"

Anna nods. "Understood. Besides, I have no one to repeat it to." Why the secrecy, she wonders? Why are adults so melodramatic, so certain that everything they say will somehow come around to bite them in the rear? "Really, no one."

"Yes, yes." Herr Hartmann appears to agree, then begins, "You know, of course, that your mother is her own woman. She is bound by no apparent rules, has little use for social graces or tradition."

"I know," says Anna, at once proud and rueful.

"Such a woman, such a rare and coveted prize as your mama, promises the male adventurer everything. A trophy who demands nothing more than tolerance, and in exchange provides her captor with a heightened sense of self-worth."

"But," Anna protests, "Papa left . . ."

"I imagine your papa was probably bored by her, if you can believe such a thing. But more importantly, as an older man, he was likely exhausted by her whims and vagaries. And finally, his vanity no longer required her presence. As it is, he will always be regarded by other men as a victor. One who even went so far as to reject her, thereby affording him the highest standing among those who now seek to repeat his success. Best of all, from old Moser's point of view, he gets to keep his peace of mind."

Hearing Papa described so makes Anna uncomfortable. She

feels she is deceiving him in some way, being unfaithful to him; though about Mama she has no sense of any deception. If Mama insists on being in the public eye, Anna thinks, she must be willing to pay the price.

"I admit," Herr Hartmann continues, as if reading her mind, "I am an imprudent and tactless man. The problem is we Jews learn justice before prudence . . . and tact last of all, if ever." He seems saddened by the admission, and for a few moments no one speaks, though Anna wonders if she too, as a Jew, is destined to learn in the same sequence. "But about Mama . . . ?" Anna urges out of the silence.

Again, Herr Hartmann hesitates, then continues. "The appeal of your mama is that while she promises everything, she gives virtually nothing. Promise and denial. Far more appealing than the woman who promises everything and gives everything. And, of course, far more appealing than the woman who promises nothing, but would give everything if she only had the opportunity. In any event, your mama's true genius, I believe, lies in how much she promises and how little she gives. It is an art form she has elevated far higher than modern dance, that is for certain."

Anna notes the unmasked disdain in Herr Hartmann's voice. Still, she would like to hear more, but before she can press him further, he says a quick good-bye and is off. It is near noon, the day is warming, the older skaters giving way to children and their mothers. The sounds from the skaters are shrill and high-pitched now as the children play and the women call to them. Skating in their heavy brown mouton coats, the mothers look like playful bears. Mama has no such coat.

Anna returns to the Stadt Park the next day and the next, hoping to learn more from Herr Hartmann. A week passes before they meet again, Anna finally finding him on the bench where she saw him last. The day is considerably warmer, and Herr Hartmann seems far more eager to talk.

"The most interesting thing about your mama," he begins with little preamble, "is this: and this is the part that is secret." Anna again vows secrecy. "I believe that your mother is on the very verge of acquiescing—and totally so, because despite her independent behavior, that is her nature."

"Acquiescing?" Anna is uncertain of the word's meaning.

"Giving in to someone. All the energy that has been used to create the Evelyn Moser you've known your whole life is going to turn to that one person. And everything else," he says quietly, "everything else will fall to the wayside."

Anna's first impulse is not to believe Herr Hartmann's pronouncement, yet what he has just told her seems so perfectly sensible that it feels suddenly as if he has revealed something she has known all along. At least, since the day Papa left with his trunk and two valises and little else; and Mama in tears for days, or so Oma told it, for Mama never left her room.

Now, Anna's own tears catch her by surprise. Surely, she can't be crying about losing Mama, for Mama has always been lost to her. Still, Anna concedes that recently she has been holding out the hope of Mama's repentance—of Mama's turning favorably toward her, as suddenly as she turned against the men who were under the impression they had won her over.

"I'm sorry," Herr Hartmann says after a while.

"For what?" Anna dabs at her tears with her mittened hand.

"For all of it. That which has been, that which is to come."

When they are again on the ice, Anna pivots on one skate and embraces him. The force of it sends them gliding along the ice together. "Thank you," she says and this time it is he who asks, "For what?" But she is already putting distance between them.

"You'll come visit?" he calls after her. "Come play Mozart for us sometime soon?"

"Yes!" she calls back, but it is lost to the sounds of the day.

"A son. Fifteen years old," Mama says when Anna asks who the "us" was Herr Hartmann referred to. "The man must have once performed well enough for his poor wife to conceive. No doubt it was the shock of it that finally did the poor woman in."

Araby

After a year as Mama's confederate, Oma gradually became annoyed, then angry with herself. She was distressed that she had so readily scorned the manners and morals she once held in such high regard. And the more she took part in her daughter's carryings-on, she realized, the more she lost something of herself, though she could not name what it was.

Now, by late 1931, Oma has lost all patience with Mama and her men, with news of the dance ensemble, and with Mama's schemes—the most notable and recent being Mama's redecoration of the front parlor, which for years has been done in the French manner, with elegant settees, antique tables, and gilt-framed mirrors that reflect curtains and coverlets made of quilted muslins in patterns of near-lifelike spring flowers printed in pale pastels. Also falling prey to Mama's scheme is the dining room, where a graceful mahogany table and chairs have long stood beneath a crystal chandelier trimmed with silver pendants, next to a gigantic, ornate sideboard that, even unadorned with Oma's silver and china, looks like a lavishly decorated cake.

But Mama has decided to turn Skodagasse 14 into a temple of the senses, into "Araby," as she puts it. According to her plan—which came to her in a vision—the parlor settees will give way to huge, fat cushions of red and purple. The ceiling is to be hung in multihued silks like a pasha's tent, rising to a peak at its center. Chests trimmed with embossed gold metal will serve as tables. Incense will burn on tiny silver plates. And in the middle of the room will be a large hookah, its base filled with rosewater, its bowl filled with hashish. In the dining room, the chairs will be replaced with flat, square velvet pads, the table with a squat, ivory-inlaid platform that sits only a few inches above the floor. Too large to move, the sideboard is to be festooned with small Persian prayer rugs, its sides swathed in colorfully printed cloth.

The day the redecoration is to begin, Oma retreats to what was formerly Papa's writing room. Mama directs the workmen hanging the silk that will transform the parlor into a bedouin's lair. Anna listens to the rustling of the material as it is hung, and carefully watches the anemic black-haired woman with the sewing machine stationed in the middle of the room making seams to Mama's order. The woman appears particularly nervous. She has never worked for a client like Mama; she, a master seamstress, has never sewn on demand, has never known anyone to grab material from her hands and yell, "Halt!" to examine the closeness of the stitching, then chastise her if something does not conform to some unspoken standard.

The commotion finally tears Oma away from what, more and more, she has been spending her days and nights doing—reading. No longer scholarly books, but journals and newspapers—at first only from Vienna, but then as she sees the tapestry develop, from Berlin, from Hamburg, from Frankfurt. Daily, she is more agitated by what she reads, yet she shares it with no one. Her daughter hasn't the patience or inclination to listen, and Anna . . . well, she cannot tell what she suspects to Anna.

Instead, on some mornings—as she did years before—she awakens Anna while it is still dark and the two of them descend the stairs to the kitchen. There, with her spectacles perched low on the bridge of her nose, Oma reads aloud from the red-and-white-checked cookbook as Anna mixes the ingredients for rich tortes, delicate petits-fours or airy meringues. But the elegantly decorated cakes, their steep sides like chocolate palisades, and the pastries arranged in patterns on cut-glass plates, sadden Oma, reminding her of a Vienna she senses is on the verge of being lost.

Now, Oma surveys the scene in the parlor, the partially draped silks, the beleaguered woman at her small stool suffering one of Mama's harangues. "Damn it, Evelyn! Let the poor woman be," Oma demands. "This instant!"

She has entered the parlor unnoticed and her outburst surprises everyone, particularly Anna, who has never seen Oma so angry. Slowly, without even looking at Oma, Mama retreats from the center of the room to confer with a workman on a ladder. The seamstress, unsure whether to acknowledge her savior, turns back to her sewing. Anna waits for Oma to say something more, something familiar. But she is gone.

One of the first visitors to the newly decorated parlor is the psychologist Karl Jung, a handsome Swiss with a gray beard. While he is not one of Mama's suitors, he seems nevertheless interested in her, and comes occasionally on rainy afternoons to spend an hour over tea.

Today, luxuriating on one large cushion, with Mama propped next to him on another, he asks that Anna and Oma join them so that he can read everyone's fortune in the tea leaves. "A specialty of mine," he claims, sitting cross-legged to face them. He moistens his lips with his tongue, takes his eyeglasses from their case, and carefully draws them on.

"The man knows so much," Mama declares.

"I look backward, inward, and forward," he concedes.

Oma has come from her reading room, carrying the hard-backed chair Papa used to sit in when he wrote. Anna, who has been practicing the piano, joins Jung and Mama on one of the cushions which, so much larger than she, threatens to toss her off. Her feet are out in front of her, her skirts ballooning.

Mama touches Jung's hand. "Now, this is the man," she announces, "the man who will someday eclipse the old doctor altogether." Could it also be, Anna suddenly wonders, the man to whom Mama will someday acquiesce?

Jung blushes. "You see," he says, "your mama also attempts to look at the future." He kisses Mama's hand as Anna looks on. Though he seems more charming than many of the men who come to visit Mama, Anna does not trust him.

"And now the tea leaves," he says. He fills the cups and urges everyone to drink. He then takes the cups one at a time, making a show of each reading. He begins by peering deeply into the cup, adjusting and readjusting his eyeglasses, then looking up at the owner of the cup and finally back into the cup again. Oma watches impatiently.

Having gone through the ritual with all three cups, Jung proclaims, "Amazing! The coincidence. The mathematical unlikelihood of it. Never in all my days as . . ."

"What?" Mama interrupts. "What is the fortune?"

Jung pauses, then presents Mama, Oma and Anna with what he assumes is his sweetest, most benevolent expression. "It is the same fortune for you all," he proclaims, throwing his hands up and surrendering to the ineluctable forces of the future. "A bright tomorrow. Happiness, success."

Mama clasps her hands rapturously while Anna stares at the man, who looks to the three women for a response. Anna can think of nothing to say and is about to go back to her practicing when Oma stands, one hand on the severe chair back.

"You have no right to attempt to seduce us with such prattle," she says.

"Right?" Jung remains on his cushion. With his pants legs raised nearly to his garters and the buttons on his vest straining, he suddenly looks to Anna like a small boy.

"Can't you see what is in the wind?" Oma demands.

"The wind?" It is as if he cannot understand images at all.

"Yes. And you know precisely what I mean." She glares down at him, at his balding pate. Sensing his disadvantage, he stands, upsetting two of the cups at his feet. Mama looks off into the distance.

"You know," Jung finally says, having fully regained his composure, "you know, I find interesting the paranoia of you people. And, how many of you react in such predictable ways." He straightens his glasses, then reaches to kiss first Mama's hand, then Oma's to bid them adieu. But Oma pulls back her hand, not allowing him his graceful exit. Not until he leaves the house does she pick up her chair and return to her reading.

When they are both gone, Mama, still on her cushion, begins to cry. Anna, never having seen Mama cry before except on stage, doesn't know quite what to do. She approaches Mama, and finally touches her face. Mama's skin feels surprisingly rough beneath her eroding makeup. Taking Anna's proffered hand, Mama holds it to her cheek, then puts her lips to Anna's open palm.

Is this the moment, Anna dares to hope—the moment when everything changes? She moves closer so that Mama's face rests against her skirt, then reaches to stroke Mama's hair. Suddenly Mama stands, letting Anna's hand go, and, using her own hands, rubs color back into her cheeks. After a few seconds, Mama clears her throat, glances quickly around the room, then finally at Anna. "Don't look so worried," Mama tells her, mistaking Anna's diminishing hope and her surprise at Mama's speedy recovery for worry. Anna feels trapped, deceived.

"You'll never see my tears again, I promise you," Mama says. "Now, pick these cups up," she orders in exactly the voice she used with Katrina before she fled, "and be off with you."

Ritual

It is sundown on a Friday in October 1931. Herr Hartmann produces four candles from a sideboard in the dining room of his large flat. "A special evening for us," he says. "Our first time together with Anna." He dons a yarmulke and gives one to Peter, his son. The room is darkening and everything in it is falling into shadow.

Anna, Peter and Herr Hartmann are clustered together at the head of the dining-room table as Herr Hartmann lights the first Sabbath candle. The flame flickers, then extends into the air like the shoot of a spring bulb. Soon there are four flames—two for the Sabbath and one each for Peter and Anna. Herr Hartmann draws his hands around the candles and toward his face. He then places his hands on each child's shoulders and blesses them in Hebrew, first Peter, then Anna.

During the ritual Anna fixes on Herr Hartmann's face, so oddly lit by the candles. It is particularly delicate and vulnerable, she thinks. His hands on her shoulders warm her, make her realize the chill she felt just seconds before.

A few minutes later the evening meal is served. Herr Hartmann places his spoon in his soup immediately, claiming he is far too hungry to even bless the bread and the wine. Peter mimics his father's ravenousness. Anna is also hungry and eats.

For some time little is said at the table and all that can be heard is the gentle scrape of silver on china. At one point, Anna looks up at the candles. They have burned down, but the four flames remain imprinted on her memory like the skeleton of a leaf fossilized onto stone. Transfixed by their soft light on this peaceful evening, she recalls another night—at the Skodagasse, when she was very young, no more than three, and was hiding under the dining-room table shrouded from Mama and Papa's argument by the cloth that covered the table and cascaded to the floor.

"Where is the girl?" Mama suddenly demanded of Katrina.

"I'll look," Katrina says. After a few moments she returned. "I can't find her." For once, Katrina sounded alarmed, though she was most often serene and even-natured, suffering Mama's tirades with great tolerance.

"This is ridiculous," Mama exclaimed. She stood up from the table and opened, then closed the pantry door. "Anna, Anna," she called, off in another room as Anna listened. Papa's legs, like columns holding up the table, never moved. Anna felt she should reveal herself—Katrina sounded afraid, Mama sounded angry. Yet the desire to remain hidden overrode everything. And so, as Mama, seemingly resigned to her daughter's disappearance, berated Katrina, Anna knelt, clutching her hands between her thighs, wanting only for all three of them to leave, thinking that perhaps then she could safely emerge, a butterfly in a summer world of flowers heavy with pollen, tufts of wild grass, and air—light, and filled with only the most delicate creatures.

Later over dessert, Anna asks Herr Hartmann whether he lights the candles every Sabbath. He admits that this is the first time in years. "And at your home?" he asks.

Anna recalls Mama once remarking favorably on their Jewishness during a rare civil dinner discussion with Papa in which Mama proclaimed that the Jews were remaking Vienna into a modern-day Athens—to which Papa responded that there already *was* a modern-day Athens. As for Jewish rituals at the Moser house, there were none.

"Never," Anna says in response to Herr Hartmann's question. And before he can press her for more about what happens at her house she asks why, if Herr Hartmann and Peter never celebrate the Sabbath, do they have the candles and know the prayers?

"My mother," Peter offers. They are the first words he has ventured in an hour, though Anna has caught him staring at her a number of times. "Before Mutti died, she did it all the time." He attempts offhandedness but a worried expression clouds his round, red face and a break in his still-changing voice betrays him.

Eating, watching Peter and his father watch her, Anna thinks that truly, Mama and Papa are odd people, so unlike everyone else, so unlike her. How then *did* it happen that she became their child? She has heard tales of waifs being taken in by wealthy families, and even once confronted Mama with the question of her legitimacy. For proof, Mama produced Grandfather Leo's photograph, then took Anna to a mirror. "These two faces are your answer," she said. With her hand on Anna's chin, she turned Anna's face in partial profile, then assumed the same attitude herself. Out of the corner of her eye Anna was shocked to see that she and Mama seemed cut from an identical pattern.

After dinner, Anna plays some Chopin mazurkas for Peter and Herr Hartmann, on an upright piano in a small reading room at the rear of the flat. Before she begins, Peter tells her that he will be a doctor. "In Vienna," he tells her. "I'll cure everything. No disease will confound me." Anna says that if he is a doctor and she is ill, she'll come to him for his help.

"And why not Mozart?" Herr Hartmann asks when Anna has finished playing. He is only half serious.

"I wanted you to remember me," Anna says earnestly.

"And . . . ?"

"And this Chopin I learned over the last weeks is something to remember."

"More to remember than Mozart?" Herr Hartmann whistles a few bars from *The Magic Flute.*

"I'll remember," Peter suddenly declares. They are nearly the same height, and Anna thinks for a moment that they may even look alike. "I'll remember because you played Chopin," he says with finality.

"And I'll remember," Herr Hartmann says, tamping the tobacco in his pipe, "because you didn't play Mozart."

When Anna has left and Herr Hartmann kisses his son good night, Peter tells him that he has fallen in love with Anna Moser, that they will marry.

Beatings

A few days after Anna's visit to the Hartmanns', she witnesses something unusual on the street. Two older men, both with long gray beards and wearing long black coats and broad-brimmed black hats, are being chased by a group of bullies. Anna recognizes the two men—one fat as a barrel, the other as slender as a barrel stave—as Hasids, a sect of mystical Jews of which there are very few in cosmopolitan Vienna. It was Papa who told her about Hasids after he and she happened upon a small group of them on a side street near the Skodagasse. It was sunset and the men were dovening, chanting prayers, seemingly oblivious to Anna and Papa. "Religion," he said, "when it becomes fanatical like this, it only leads to trouble. Better that fanatics are atheists. That way, at least, they are ignored."

The two Hasids are half-walking, half-running from the bullies, a crowd of teenage boys, some wearing short pants, though it is quite cold. The boys all have on identical caps and short-sleeved, open-necked sweaters, making it appear that they are members of a club. As the boys give chase they occasionally grab at the coattails of the men, slap at their hats or tug at their beards. It appears that on the boys' part, the attack is not vicious—almost good-natured, Anna notes, but for the fearful and confused expressions of the men, as if some terrible mistake has been made and they have become the unwitting brunt of it.

"Run faster," one of the bullies calls out.

Now the men are running as fast as they can, the barrel-sized one outdistancing his thinner comrade.

"That's it, you filthy clowns. Run!" As the Hasids flee, the boys slow their pace, stopping to catch their breath, laughing loudly.

"Did you see the spindly little legs on the skinny one?" one asks through his own amusement. "You could snap the bones like a twig, I'll wager. Like this, over your knee. He demonstrates while the others howl, one of them so convulsed with laughter that he falls to the street, holding his belly.

Just then a policeman saunters by, a truncheon in his hand.

He eyes the gang. "You there!" The gang stops laughing. "Two older gents," he says as the boys stare seriously at him, "two older gents claim you've been chasing them." A faint smile crosses his lips. "True?"

The gang's apparent leader asks, "Would these gents be hook-nosed and dressed in black . . . ?" ". . . with great, gray beards?" another chimes in, drawing his hand down from his chin to indicate the beards.

"Those are the ones," the policemen says.

"Not us," the leader proclaims. "Absolutely not us." The other boys nod in confirmation.

"Just as I told them. Viennese youth chasing old men? Certainly not."

"Absolutely not."

"You boys run along then," the policeman cautions, tapping one of them lightly on the rear with his truncheon. "I don't want any trouble out of you." On command, the gang disperses, heading off in different directions in groups of two or three, leaving the policeman peering keenly after them, as if he owned the place on which he stands.

"But they *were* chasing the two old men," Anna suddenly insists. The policeman has not noticed Anna, and is caught off guard by her remark.

"You actually saw this?" he asks.

"Yes. There were two Hasids with . . ."

"But," he interrupts, "the lads told me they hadn't chased anyone. Right here on this very spot they told me."

"They lied," Anna pronounces. "I saw them."

The officer looks at her sternly. "Clearly *someone* is lying." Then it comes to him. "You know," he continues, "you actually look like one of those old gents. Could it be perhaps that one of them is your papa?"

The accusation catches Anna completely by surprise. "No," she says. "My papa is famous. He'd never look like that."

"No, I'm certain now that one of those fellows was your papa, and he put you up to this lying. That's what this is all about."

"It isn't. It isn't," Anna insists. She is furious at the man, who now smiles broadly at her.

"If I were you, Fraülein, I'd go right home and pray to your God for forgiveness for the lies you've been telling."

"I'm not . . ."

"Quiet!" he demands. "I've had all the insolence I'm about to take from you." He raps his truncheon against his open palm. It makes a sharp slap that Anna can almost feel against the back of her legs. "Now go on, get out of here!"

"Oma!" Anna calls out, the entryway bells still jangling. Oma looks up from Papa's chair where she reads, her eyeglasses perched lopsided on the bridge of her nose. Though Anna has rehearsed the whole story—every detail, from the expression on the gang leader's face to the decorations on the policeman's chest—she collapses at Oma's feet, drawing the folds of Oma's dress to her face as she cries.

"My poor child," Oma says, "my poor child." The paper has fallen beside her and rustles slightly as Anna sobs. Oma strokes her face, the nape of her neck, rubs her shoulders.

When Anna stops crying she looks up. In that instant she recognizes how old Oma has become, how the energy seems to have been drawn from her face like vinegar tapped from a crock. Now powder provides serenity, where only a few years earlier it came from the sheer whiteness of her skin. For color she now wears rouge. But the change in Oma is most evident in her eyes, where a generous, forgiving expression has been sup- planted by a sharp, condemning gaze. Oma is, Anna realizes, one of those people who ages by losing her softness, rather than giving in to it.

When she finally tells Oma the story, Oma becomes more and more agitated, as if each word were pumice. When Anna is fin- ished Oma asks, "What is it that you want me to tell you, sweet girl?" Her voice is hoarse. "Do you want me to tell you not to worry? To ignore what you saw? That it will never happen again?"

Anna nods.

"Well, it will. And again. And worse and worse and worse." She grips the arms of the chair, then stands. "It is evident in every page I read," she goes on, gesturing to the stacks of papers and journals in Papa's former writing room. "They don't come out

and say it, yet it is as clear as the veins and bones in my hand."
Oma holds up her hand to reveal its skeletal superstructure and
the pronounced gray-blue lines that crisscross it. Anna stands
transfixed before her.

"Go," Oma suddenly urges. "Talk to your schoolmates.
Enjoy. Your Oma has become too cynical for a fourteen-year-old
girl."

Anna goes, walks up the stairs to her room. Uncertain what
to do next, she opens a book of photographs—of Papa, years ago,
sitting solemn as a duke; of Mama in an elaborate pose; of she
and Cybelle only three years earlier, Anna on Cybelle's lap, both
girls making faces at the camera.

Anna's school, like many of Vienna's buildings, is constructed
like a small castle, the classrooms facing an inner courtyard and
extending up four stories. One day, as Anna sits in her literature
class with twenty others reciting *Faust,* there is a commotion in
the courtyard. Though ordered to remain seated, the entire class
runs to the windows. Four stories below, three boys are being
pummeled by a number of others. Standing but a few feet away
is the athletics teacher, conversing with another boy. With the
windows closed, it is impossible to hear what is being said.

Presently the muffled action in the courtyard plays itself out,
and as the large group breaks away from the three, Anna can see
them lying in the cobbled courtyard. Their faces are bloodied,
their clothes torn. One of the boys gets up on his hands and knees
and screams up at those staring out the windows.

"Jews," says someone standing next to Anna.

"Serves them right," says a second voice.

The teacher, whose calls to order in the classroom have been
roundly ignored, finally grabs two of the children by the scruffs
of their necks and plants them at their desks. As Anna turns from
the scene down below she sees a few snowflakes materialize in the
teal sky. Sitting at her desk, she imagines what the new snow must
feel like on the boys' bodies and faces. At first the snow might
act as a salve. But if they lay there too long, it might cover them
over completely.

When class is over the boys are gone. Far later, Anna sees one of them walking down a corridor, his cap low over his eyes. He limps slightly, stopping to talk or look at no one. As he passes, others turn, watch, then turn again when he is out of sight.

At the Café Dolder

"We're not really Jews, are we?" Anna asks Papa. He sits at his table at the Café Dolder near the large fireplace, in the very heart of the baroque, high-ceilinged room, still lit by gaslight. The light, passing through dozens of small cut-glass chimneys, suffuses the room in a terra-cotta glow. The alabaster cloths on the tables are like white mushrooms in a darkened bower.

"Only in a manner of speaking," Papa tells her. She looks distraught. This makes him anxious, not so much out of paternal concern, but because it might affect his own measured equanimity. "Not really at all," he concludes, then rises to pull out a chair for her.

Anna is soothed by seeing Papa before the rich, ornate paneled hearth. It lends him a sense of calm and dignity, befitting her view of him. Before him on the table is his familiar long yellow writing tablet, filled with his carefully wrought, backward-slanting script. Anna knows that it gives Papa a sense of pride to have others see the impeccability of his manuscript—never a crossing-out or a scratching along the margin. For once Papa's words reach the page, they are the right ones.

Yet today, the perfection of Papa's page makes Anna think less of him, recalls the time he pointed out the Hasids to her near the Skodagasse, and earlier today, the look on the beaten boy's face in the courtyard.

"But Oma says we're all in the same tribe. And when they round us up we'll share the same compartments, the same bowls, the same beds, the same . . ."

Papa raises his hand. "Shhhhh," he tells her, putting a finger to his lips. He glances quickly around him. "Let's sit down before we go on with this." Anna sits but she is still agitated.

Papa looks quickly over her shoulder. "Herr Ober," he calls in the near-empty room, "some chocolate." Anna begins talking. "Wait!" he commands with the same tone he used to summon the waiter, much, much more loudly than he intends. "Wait," he repeats, softly as if to rectify the error.

Nothing is said as the tuxedoed waiter places the chocolate before Anna. Steam swirls about the rim of the cup. A separate dish holds whipped cream, and alongside it stands a glass of water, with a small, shiny spoon perched across the top. Papa gestures for Anna to drink. Only after she raises the cup to her lips does he speak.

"Now," he begins, "who is this 'they' who will be rounding all of 'us' up?"

"Germans, Austrians, bullies, Fascists, Nazis," Anna tells him, repeating what Oma has told her.

It brings a smile to Papa's lips. "Do you actually believe this nonsense?" he asks.

"I've seen it," Anna insists. She tells him about the Hasids and the beating of the boys in the schoolyard. Papa nods as he listens, bringing his hands to his vest pockets and leaning back in his chair.

"Incidents," he pronounces when she is through. "There have always been incidents. But to presume that something like this will take over all of Austria . . . ." Papa gestures with his left arm to encompass the coffeehouse.

"Europe, Oma says. All Europe."

"Come now, Anna," he says, suddenly leaning forward, looking right into her eyes, touching her chin. "I know and you know that Oma has become a bit soft in the head. Admit it."

"But I saw . . ."

"You saw what you saw. And what you saw might have less to do with 'us' than you might imagine. Young boys are always high-spirited. It's all that *energy*," Papa says, shaking his shoulders to indicate boyish energy.

"Now admit that Oma, the major source of your information beyond these incidents, has always been, shall we say, a bit on the eccentric side." Papa grins widely, revealing an abundance of gleaming gold fillings. "Well?"

Anna suddenly finds that she herself is grinning. And to admit that Oma's concerns are those of someone not to be trusted, to admit that what she herself saw was a mere display of boyish energy, would certainly soothe her concern.

Papa knows he has won her over. "So, how is it with the crazy ones?" he asks, taking Anna's hands in his. His fingers feel like parchment. "How is it?"

"Crazy," Anna says, finally giving in completely to Papa's good nature. She tells him of the redecoration of the parlor. As she does, Papa puts his hand to his head, rolls his eyes and laughs outright. "Araby!" he exclaims through his laughter. "Purple cushions. Incense. Marvelous!" And when Anna laughs with him, Papa suddenly announces—so loudly that all in the Café Dolder can hear—"I love you so much. So very much!"

Anna is so stunned to hear these words from Papa that for a moment she is speechless, then asks, "What?"

"What?" Papa repeats, raising a single eyebrow.

"What . . . what you just said," Anna prompts.

Papa's face turns serious as he tries to remember. Anna holds her breath, feeling tiny bubbles of perspiration form on her brow.

"Araby?" Papa ventures. "Cushions?" He looks to Anna for approval. "Still not right?"

"No, Papa."

"Well, give me another moment then. Your papa is not so old to be forgetting things. Not that old."

But Papa cannot recall his earlier words, and presently the perspiration on Anna's forehead dries and she breathes evenly again. Meanwhile, at the waiters' station, three liveried waiters, one smoking a cigarette, the other two with their small silver serving trays under their arms, look smugly over at the older man and his daughter. The one smoking inhales deeply, then says something that causes the others to titter.

When Anna leaves, she kisses Papa as she always does when their time together is over. Papa puts his arm around her waist. "It is not enough," he says, adopting a serious tone. It is an apology which Anna correctly assumes is for his absence these many years from the Skodagasse. "But what was I to do? Tell me."

Anna tells him he did the right thing, that she would have

done the same if she were he, and that she loves him, nevertheless. Now gracious and removed, he thanks her, as if for a small
gift or favor.

Outside, she looks through the door's thick glass panes, which
slightly distort the scene inside. But there is Papa, back at his
table, his pen poised, dreaming a future filled with science and
possibility.

Vienna, 1934

The Last Thing You'll Ever See

On a Friday evening in January, Anna, Peter, and Herr Hartmann travel on foot to the Raimundstheater for the opening of the Vienna Ensemble of Modern Dance's 1934 season: a three-act drama set to music and written by a young, consumptive-looking woman whom Mama discovered at a spa in Bosnia. Mama has left tickets for Anna and her friends at the door. She has promised a startling performance.

It is snowing. Like thick fleece, the snow swaddles the city in white. The air is dense with smoke from coal stoves. On street corners, vendors peddle roasted chestnuts from carts with cast-iron braziers, warming their hands over the open flames.

Anna, now seventeen, wears a heavy woolen skirt and sweater, and a loden green fur-collared coat, cinched at the waist with a wide red leather belt. Her red purse holds her wallet, fountain pen, a small diary and Papa's latest book, *Midst the Rings of Saturn*; also lipstick, rouge, powder and eye-pencil—to make her look "sophisticated," in Cybelle's words.

Earlier in the day, Cybelle helped Anna with her hair. She first formed it into a single, thick braid, then wound it on top of her head like a turban, exposing the strong nape of Anna's neck.

It is how Cybelle wears her own long blond hair, though she purposely leaves a few strands loose to suggest she is not as pristine as she might appear.

From Cybelle's flat, Anna went directly to the Hartmanns', where Peter answered the door. It was late afternoon, already dark, and the vestibule light appeared to radiate from around his head and shoulders like the light emanating from the saints and angels in the paintings Anna had recently seen with him at the city's art museum.

"You should see yourself—Signor Botticelli," she said, wondering why it was Peter who came to the door and not one of the Hartmanns' servants. "Where's Litzi?" she asked.

"I wanted to be the first to see you."

"You are."

Peter had not moved from his place at the door, and as she brushed by him, he touched her hair. "Very nice," he said. "Elegant."

Anna blushed. "Cybelle put it up for me. I suppose I could have done it myself but . . ."

"I have to confess," Peter interrupted as they crossed the threshold to the parlor, "that I am jealous of her, of the time you spend together."

Peter hadn't told Anna of his feelings for her, but they were obvious—from the golden ankle bracelet he had given her on her seventeenth birthday, to the flowers he often presented to her, for no reason. And now, in the last few weeks, Peter seemed always to find incidental ways to touch her hand, her wrist, her back.

"I don't see what you're jealous of. I really don't spend that much time with Cybelle. Not anymore."

"Well, then I'm jealous of the time you *used* to spend with her," he declared earnestly.

It was a sweet sentiment, typical of Peter. Still, Anna searched for the smile that might indicate he was joking—some trace of irony. But there was none. "Come," she finally said, leading him to the settee. "And don't be so serious. Besides, you have nothing to be jealous of."

This was not quite true—for, while she had been able to reconcile Papa's aloofness and Mama's disinterest, Anna still longed for the innocent intimacies she had once shared with Cybelle. Indeed, she had difficulty believing that those days were past, and was able sometimes to recall them with such vividness that for her they were not.

"Really, you have nothing to be jealous of," Anna repeated, aware that she was tacitly acknowledging his affections for her—and suggesting she felt something more than friendship for him, which she didn't. She was flustered by the complication.

"Well then, if that is the case, I'll be less serious," Peter declared, sitting down solidly on the settee as if a matter of great import had finally been resolved.

"No, you don't understand," Anna wanted to say. But things were already so confused between them, she simply let him believe what he wanted.

Now, Anna seeks out whatever untrodden snow remains on the cobbled walk, delighting in breaking through its icy crust with her rubber overshoes. She strays from Peter and his father, who walk in lockstep, and in a perfectly straight line, breaking stride only to avoid puddles. They are the kindest people she knows.

"Anna!" Peter suddenly calls. Anna turns to see that father and son have stopped for chestnuts. Herr Hartmann pays the vendor, taking the small bag from him and holding it out in Anna's direction.

"I'll peel one for you," Peter offers, already picking at the tough hide of the nut where it has been cut in a cross. Like his father, Peter is dressed in a handsome overcoat, but his knitted blue-and-gold cap makes him look boyish and eager—not like a young man about to begin his medical training.

Peter's innocence and the simple truths he holds—like the notion that medical practitioners will save the world—are not without their charm, Anna thinks. But she is aware too that though he is a year older than she is, she has already left him behind. Sweet, accepting and tentative, Peter is a version of her former self, when she was so worried about Papa's disappearance from the Skodagasse. And so, just as Cybelle once sought to protect her, she now feels protective of Peter.

Peter holds out the peeled, wrinkled chestnut to her on his

ungloved palm, his expression hopeful. The falling snow melts on the warm nut and in his hand.

"Not so serious, remember?" Anna says lightly, taking the nut from him. She closes his palm with her hand, then turns. "Now quickly Peter," she calls over her shoulder, breaking into a run, passing others on the way to the performance. "Hurry, or it will all be over."

The lobby of the theater is rich with the glow of gaslight, installed more than a century ago. Huge gilded, wooden-framed mirrors on every wall reflect one another; there is no end to any vista. From the complacent smile on Peter's face and the sudden, acquiescent look on Anna's, they appear to be lovers, though they have never even kissed. There are those at the theater who *are* lovers, Anna notes, having been told by Cybelle precisely what to look for: a man guiding a woman with a light touch to her elbow, a woman offering her profile to men other than her escort, chin raised, laughter like a freshet of gold coins. Joining Anna and Peter in the lobby, Herr Hartmann claps the snow from his gloves, unwinds his muffler and removes his hat.

In the theater, just beyond the first row where Anna, Peter and Herr Hartmann sit, musicians tune their instruments. The cacophony is familiar and oddly comforting to Anna, who, over the last year, has become chiefly a listener, going only occasionally to the piano—only for pleasure, and only when she is alone.

Initially, when Herr Sonnenabend took ill and had to forsake his teaching, Anna missed her twice-weekly lessons and redoubled her efforts at the keyboard in his absence. But the more intensely she worked, the more she sensed that the piano—the practice, the performance, the enormous effort required to feel certain of even a simple phrase—had worn her down, and over the years, had exacted a toll.

Then one evening, halfway through a Brahms rhapsody on the Hartmanns' upright piano, Anna stopped playing. Peter looked up from the book he was reading. "No more," she pronounced evenly, staring at the keys. The ivory on the old piano had yellowed; one of the treble strings had recently broken. "Enough." After all, what satisfaction did the playing bring her—now that Papa was gone, that Oma had retreated to her own room, that Sonnenabend was gone, that Cybelle—who always seemed too impatient to listen, anyway—was nearly gone. Certainly, she loved the sense of mastery and, of course, the music. But that evening at the Hartmanns', facing the keys and the blunt, dark wooden prow of the piano—facing away from so much else in the world—mastery and music seemed insufficient. Suddenly, she spun around on her stool, furious. "No more!"

"No more, today?" Peter asked uncertainly, then added, "I liked that, that . . . Brahms."

"Can't you understand?" Anna got up from the stool. Peter shrugged, then shook his head. "No. Of course not," she said, grabbing her jacket from the chair next to him.

"Is it my fault?"

"Don't be ridiculous. It has nothing to do with you." Yet his willingness to assume the blame—just as she once might have—further rankled her. "If it's Brahms you like so much," she called back, already in the hallway, "then buy a phonograph!"

Now, nine years after her first lesson, sitting in a theater and listening as the musicians prepare for their evening's work, Anna wonders what, if anything, will ever take the place of the piano for her—the instrument that Papa once told her would enable her to own her life.

Anna rarely entertains thoughts such as these, however. She broods little about her past and lives more in the present. Out of the material of her earlier life she has manufactured an indomitable goodwill and sense of possibility. And the cost has not even been that great, merely a matter of caring less—about Papa certainly, about Mama's antics, and even about Oma, who has spent long hours with Anna of late, recounting stories of her own childhood and young womanhood, urging Anna to write them down so that there will be a record. "Don't worry," Anna has said. "I will remember. Always."

* * *

One of Oma's stories in particular remains with Anna, comforting her and confusing her all at once. It is of the day that Mama was born—in the summer of 1897. Grandfather Leo is asleep in the room that will eventually become Papa's writing room. Oma is in the kitchen with one of the servant girls. It is very hot in Vienna that summer. The leaves on the trees turn brown in the sun as under a magnifying glass, the more delicate flowers wilt and die in the afternoons unless they are constantly watered. But Oma, carrying Mama inside her, has no sense of the heat—even when others complain of it. She feels, she says, light and cool, as if the child she is to give birth to is not made of the ordinary stuff, but of air, ether, and spun sugar. Perhaps she will be a dancer, Grandfather Leo jokes.

In the kitchen, Oma feels a twinge. The servant, whose name Oma can't recall, is a confident girl. "On the table," she says to Oma. And within moments, Mama is born—the labor, the birth, virtually without pain or effort. The girl cuts the cord, then swaddles Mama in dish towels she produces from a drawer. A fine patina of perspiration has broken out over Oma's brow as she lies on the table. The girl covers the red-and-white-checked cookbook with a serviette, places it beneath Oma's head, lays the baby next to her, then tidies up around them. The baby cries for a few seconds, then is quiet.

Presently, the two women make their way to the room where Grandfather Leo sleeps. Oma holds the baby, but feeling slightly dizzy on the stairs, she hands the baby to the girl. In the room, they place the baby next to Grandfather Leo. "Leo," Oma calls as she steps away from the bed, "Leo, it's that gift we've been waiting for." Grandfather Leo's eyes blink open. The room is dark, the shades drawn. "Gift?" he asks. Just then the baby cries. "Ah, the gift." He picks the baby up and holds her close to his face, then puts her down on the bed and opens his arms to Oma.

"I lay down next to him and slept for nearly two whole days," Oma told Anna, "and after that, the summer was as hot for me as for everyone else."

Anna replays the events of that day again and again—the baby's magical entry into the world, the heat, the knowing servant whose name has been forgotten, Grandfather Leo's gift, his arms extended to Oma. Anna believes every word of the story. Indeed, she is comforted by its detail and hopes that someday she will play Oma's part in a similar drama. What confuses her, however, is that the baby born without effort or pain turns out to be Mama.

The curtain opens. The giant folds of the material disappear swiftly, revealing a set that consists only of a few black benches placed before a painted, brooding, shadowed cityscape. Mama rises from one of the benches. She is incredibly tall and slender in a maroon caftan that covers her completely, save for her face and hands, which appear suspended in space, separate from her body. A single white spotlight tracks her insistently as she glides across the stage. Her gestures, always dramatic, seem even more so as she seeks to escape the light, leaping from its invasive beam. Her eyes are fierce, commanding the audience to remember her.

Anna studies Mama carefully. She leans forward, her elbows on the worn, padded brocade rail that separates her from the orchestra. Though she has seen Mama dance many times before, tonight she senses something different. Mama's expression seems genuinely alien, haunted, desperate. It is as if Mama has lost patience with everyone, as though tonight's drama will be her last.

Gradually, however, as the performance continues, Anna falls under the spell of the character in the caftan, and waits even comfortably for some sign from Mama—some indication of their bond. Certainly Mama can see her, sitting so near. Concerned she will miss the sign, Anna focuses all her attention on the stage and is only vaguely aware of Peter's hand stroking the back of her neck, of the conductor's arms rising in front of her, occasionally breaking her field of vision.

Late in the final act, Mama disappears into the wings and two other dancers, a man and a woman dressed as in a classical ballet, perform a stately pas de deux, a lushly lit and elegant pavane that seems part of another program entirely. Their appearance soothes Anna and she sits back in her seat, acknowledging Peter's hand

and noting that Herr Hartmann has fallen asleep only a few feet from the orchestra. He snores lightly.

Suddenly, Mama reappears. She looks even more haunted than before. Spying the man and the woman, she banishes them from the stage. A solitary figure in a darkening set, Mama moves feverishly. Without warning, she draws a dagger from the folds of her caftan. Gripping its hilt with both hands, she presses the dagger against her breast as she dances.

"Careful," Anna whispers. "Careful!" Just then the music shrieks. Anna jumps to her feet. And Mama, with a gesture as much of relief as pain, plunges the dagger into her heart, then falls to the stage directly in front of Anna. Still standing, Anna watches as the sign she has waited for comes, and unmistakably so. Mama looks directly at her, winks once, then shuts her eyes.

The spotlight is killed, the curtain falls. For an instant the hall is still. Then there is a scattering of applause, followed finally by spirited clapping and "bravos." The stage lights come up, the curtain is drawn, but Mama still lies where she fell. The other dancers take their bows seemingly oblivious to Mama, crumpled, her caftan covering her like a shroud. A murmur goes through the crowd. Anna's palms moisten. Could it be?

Just as the applause fades, Mama jumps up to join the others in the company, lifting her hands high in celebration. The audience is exhilarated by Mama as Lazarus. Anna, however, is caught off guard, trying to locate some meaning in Mama's revival, in her wink. She claps mechanically, feeling once again tricked by Mama in a way she cannot quite grasp.

"If I winked then there was something in my eye," Mama tells her the next day when she finally arrives back at the Skodagasse. "Some dust from the stage. Besides, you never blink when you are dying. You want to keep your eyes open as long as you can. To see the last things, the last things you'll ever see."

At the Zoo

By February 1934 there is civil war in Austria as Chancellor Dollfuss moves to suppress both the private armies of the Social

Democrats and the grab for parliamentary power by Austrian Nazis. Fought in isolated battles in the country, and in the city's farthest outskirts, the war is little felt by most Viennese. Occasionally, gunfire can be heard as the army under Dollfuss's command storms strongholds where caches of arms are known to be kept. But it is all distant from the Skodagasse.

"It is difficult for me to believe," Oma says one day, "that the Vienna of my childhood was such a happy place, full of music and pleasure, and the reassuring smell of cigar smoke when men would congregate. It was a time when everyone, everything, was so elegant." In the last few months, Oma has divorced herself completely from politics and moved back into her own youth.

"But, Oma," Anna protests, "there is still music . . . and cigar smoke and men . . ."

"No," Oma insists, "these times are different. What was will never be again. Not precisely so, with the winters so perfect like child's drawings, with my own mama and her songs, and the animals, the animals in the zoo, so good-natured, so proud, so well-loved."

To illustrate, Oma has Anna accompany her to the zoo, where Oma points out the lion's restlessness, its seeming dissatisfaction with all that hair. And the other cats—cheetah, lynx, panther, leopard, tiger—"they were once sleek and sly, their muscles thick and knotted, their coats glossy and perfect; spotted, striped, or black as ebon," Oma says.

"But now look." A huge abscess scars the side of a tiger. The panther is filthy, as if he has wallowed in dirt so long that his hair can no longer grow out black, but instead has turned a mottled brown and gray. Nearby, the impala, the gemsbok, the antlered elk silently traverse their compound, rarely looking up—pawing, searching, impatient.

At last Oma and Anna arrive at the elephant house, where Oma intends to show Anna the discouragement in the faces of the pachyderms. But the two resident beasts present only their colossal hindquarters, which are smeared with excrement and matted with dirt and hay. Nearby, a young boy heaves rocks at the elephants' posteriors. Suddenly, both creatures lift their trunks in unison, followed by two sharp, indignant bellows.

"Stop!" Oma commands the boy. He looks at her, laughs, then throws another stone. Oma turns back to the elephants. "They're so embarrassed for us and what we're becoming," she says to Anna, "that they can't even bring themselves to look at us anymore."

Lederer's

That spring Anna takes a position as a shopgirl at Lederer's, the posh specialty shop where Cybelle has worked for the last four years. The store is owned by the seventy-five-year-old Herr Lederer, who makes an occasional appearance, but is run day to day by Ilse Bauer, a thin, angry woman in her early forties with short hair the color of caramel. It was Ilse, Anna recalls on her first day at Lederer's, who hired Cybelle because she looked refined yet seductive, a combination, Ilse claimed, that would appeal to the shop's mostly male clientele.

Certainly, Anna thinks, studying her reflection in the fitting-room mirror, her own face holds no such promise. On the contrary, it is a plain face, at its best in a broad grin, where an inviting hominess gives her the appearance of a comfortable friend, a trusty confidante. Her attempts in the mirror at measured insouciance, at elegant reserve and ironic dismissal are, however, all a failure. The nose is the problem. While she has Mama's dramatic cheekbones, and her bottle-green eyes hold the promise of adventure, the nose is common, almost comic, definitely too wide. Still, she regards the nose as an ally—it is, after all, her only known legacy from Grandfather Leo—and thinks it gives her character. Her face would certainly be lonely without it.

Suddenly, Cybelle's reflection appears in the mirror behind Anna's. Cybelle, as lovely a woman as Anna has ever seen, has just turned twenty. Today she wears a rose-colored silk blouse, ruffled at the collar and sleeves. Anna blushes as she recalls touching Cybelle's breasts that afternoon long ago at the Skodagasse. Now such intimacy would be unthinkable. But then she thinks of the men who have enjoyed the same pleasure and excitement as she, and it angers her slightly. She turns from the mirror and walks past Cybelle to the front of the shop.

Lederer's is a large shop on a street of many smaller elegant shops, but unlike these establishments brimming with expensive goods, Lederer's has little merchandise on display. Rather, it has the studied look of a handsome salon, with settees of crushed maroon velvet, polished tables, lamps with cream-colored shades trimmed top and bottom with a braided golden cord, and thick rugs that cover much of the polished wood floor. Here and there are occasional pieces of clothing—a fine fur stole draped over the back of a chair, an elegant gown left out on a table, its layered crinoline underskirt giving the impression of an enormous meringue filled with whipped cream. At the rear of the shop are a few display cases that hold small leather purses, wallets and belts, the items seeming to have been placed there casually—here by a gentleman emptying his pockets before his next engagement, there by a woman's handmaid setting out her accessories as she performs her toilette.

"The rich," Herr Lederer has explained to Anna, "are not looking to select. They are looking for what no one else has. The less we show them, the more they will buy."

"Nothing I do pleases her," Anna whispers to Cybelle on her second day at the shop.

"It's because *he* hired you, not her," Cybelle whispers back. Nearby, Ilse runs her large hands down her hips to straighten her tight black skirt. She is always touching something, it seems—her earrings, the cluster of bracelets dangling from her wrists, the seams of her stockings.

"You, Moser," Ilse suddenly commands, "do something!" Anna, unsure what to do, repositions the sleeve of a fur coat lying on a chaise next to her. Ilse frowns. Cybelle steps away. Seconds later she reappears with a feather duster, which Anna accepts gladly, like a long-awaited gift. She is still an assiduous cleaner, still derives comfort from neatness.

"It's because," Cybelle repeats, following Anna as she dusts, "Lederer himself hired you. I knew he would, though. And she wouldn't have. That's why I had you talk to him instead of her."

Catching the girls plotting against her, Ilse glares. For a moment, Cybelle returns her gaze and the two are like duelists. But before either challenges the other, Cybelle walks away.

It is rumored, Cybelle tells Anna after her first week at Lederer's, that Ilse had an affair with Lederer twenty years earlier when his wife was still alive and his children were young, and that she blackmailed him into making her the shop's manager. True or not, in the tedious lull between customers, Ilse talks constantly about opening a shop of her own to compete with the "old Jew himself," often going on in detail about how her store will be superior to his.

Clearly, Anna thinks, Ilse bears Lederer—a kindly, heavyset man, nearly bald with tufts of gray hair over his ears—a resentment, and whatever transpired between them, the bribe of store managership was insufficient. When she mentions this to Cybelle, Cybelle responds with a short, bitter laugh. "The bitch won't be happy until she has it all."

To Anna's surprise, the shop's clientele is not as she anticipated—men who would rudely impose themselves on her. Certainly not the gentlemen she waits on, who are soft-spoken, courteous, and almost always gracious, like the men in the Vienna Oma remembers. Even the women who shop there treat her with only slight disdain. So the work, aside from Ilse's apparent dissatisfaction with her, is really quite pleasant.

Cybelle's presence makes it more so. She smiles at Anna from across the selling floor, or gestures to indicate that Anna has a hair out of place. They have again become confidantes of a sort, no longer speaking of their lives, but of the new fashions from Paris, Ilse's latest dictum, or the fortunes and habits of Lederer's male customers. If Cybelle meets any of them after work, she does not tell Anna, and Anna is quite satisfied in believing that she and Cybelle are alike in many ways—two young girls earning a living.

What satisfies Anna most about the work, however, is the quality of the merchandise Lederer's offers: the most delicate French satins, finely printed Chinese silks, pliant Moroccan leathers. To deal confidently with such goods, to sell only the finest, one must possess an inner quality as precious as the merchandise itself. Otherwise, would not a customer used to such quality walk away, reveal her to Ilse or Herr Lederer as a fraud?

Anna's success after only a few weeks at Lederer's suggests she is not. She seems able to convince others that she has the requisite inner quality to sell such finery. She cannot, however, quite convince herself. She is aware she has neither Papa's skill with language nor Mama's power to impress and entertain. How then, she wonders, is she able to fool Lederer's customers so readily? After some thought, Anna decides that it is her own high regard for the goods that accounts for her success—that, and her youth, which in a city full of middle-aged and old men, has its own unique currency.

One day, a finely dressed gentleman enters the store, leaving the French doors ajar. He is in his mid-thirties, quite tall, and seems agitated. "Where is she?" he demands of Anna as she closes the doors.

"Who?"

"Don't toy with me, little girl." He glances quickly around the shop. "The blond slut. You know the one."

Just then Cybelle emerges from the fitting room. "Eduard," she says. She is composed, cool even, as she looks at him. Her hands are on her hips. He moves toward her and grabs one of her wrists, pulling her to the back of the store.

"Don't you dare," Cybelle says evenly.

"I dare what I please." Ilse is off on an errand; there is no one else in the shop but the man and the two young women.

"Let me go." With her free hand, Cybelle slaps his face. When he refuses to let her go, she slaps him again, taking advantage of his surprise to wrench her other hand from his grasp.

"Out!" she says. "Now."

The man retreats, his hands at his sides, regaining his composure, the color of his rage gradually replaced by measured anger. "Don't for a moment think I am fooled by you," he says. "You and your kind. I know what you are."

"Do you, now?" Cybelle mocks.

He turns to Anna. "Leave her alone," Anna demands, the only thing she can think to say. The man has a slight twitch which collapses the right side of his face every few seconds.

"So you're part of her filthy little life, too, I see," he says.

"Get out," Anna insists. The man opens his mouth to speak, but then appears to think better of it. Instead he paces regally past her like one of the Lippizaner stallions at the Hofburg.

At the French doors, he turns and declares, "I know what you *both* are: second-rate. And when the time comes, there will be a sorting out. This, I promise." He strides by the front windows and down the street.

Anna turns to Cybelle. Cybelle's chin is set; her body quivers slightly. Her wrist where the man grabbed her is now poised at her hip, and seems impossibly delicate. Anna moves to comfort her friend, but when she puts her arm around Cybelle's small shoulders, Cybelle pulls away.

"Just leave me alone, you little idiot," she says. "And from now on, if I want your help, I'll ask for it."

Anna is stunned, but not offended. On the contrary. That moment she loves Cybelle more than ever: for her vulnerability, for her power. She would, she thinks, follow Cybelle to the end of the earth.

The Boarder

The lorry parked in front of Skodagasse 14 late one morning in June is being unloaded by two hefty men working bare-chested in the sun that slants between the two rows of houses flanking the street. The men seem nonchalant about their square hand-some faces, about the ease with which they move the sole posses-sions of Mama's new boarder, Eric Jacobi.

Jacobi, as he calls himself, stands to the rear of the lorry, overseeing the process. He is a fine-featured, worried-looking man in his early forties, of medium height and dressed far too warmly for the day in a double-breasted blue suit, spats, sweater vest and red butterfly bow tie. His face is pale, his hair long and thin and black, covering his ears and growing to his collar. He looks on sheepishly as the men heft his belongings, as if embarrassed that he must hire others to do his work. When the men seek to move the first of four huge, metal steamer trunks, straining even to slide it along the lorry floor, Jacobi calls up to them in apology, then studies the rear of the vehicle to see if he can gain access to help. "Don't worry," one of them calls out to him. Sweat streaks his back and chest. "We got it on. We'll get it off."

The thought of a man living in the house disturbs Anna, who on occasion recalls—though with guarded sentiment—the time of Papa's residence and her investment in his rituals. She remembers the smell of his cologne, how fastidiously he trimmed his whiskers, how he daily buffed the bottoms of his shoes to make them appear new. Another man in the house will surely eradicate the last vestiges of Papa, replace them with new odors, new habits.

Still, Jacobi seems like a nice enough fellow, and as she returns from a morning at Lederer's, she hails him and wishes him a good midday.

Jacobi is a historian—a famous one, to hear Mama tell it— who has come from Berlin to Vienna to research a book chronicling the history of civilization as revealed through the evolution of bread and bread-baking. The metal steamer trunks hold his earlier manuscripts, his notes and his books, the only possessions he deems valuable.

To make room for Jacobi's things, Mama removes the last of Papa's books from the study and sends them on to the Hotel Bristol, unaware that Papa no longer lives there, but at a far less grand pension near the Café Dolder. Interest in Papa's science fantasy has ebbed over the last years, and with it his considerable fortune. *Midst the Rings of Saturn* does not even sell out its conservative first printing. *The Sun's Core* languishes handwritten on sheets of Papa's yellow paper, like fruit left too long on the vine.

Papa leaves his accounts at the Bristol unsettled and when his books arrive from the Skodagasse, they are impounded. They are eventually destroyed in a massive housecleaning effort overseen by a zealous new manager from Munich.

Papa, as it turns out—not the Vienna Ensemble of Modern Dance or Oma's inheritance—was Mama's chief source of support, and thus she too has fallen on harder times. This, coupled with the fact that attendance at her performances has diminished, has forced her to move her troupe from the Raimundstheater to the far smaller stages of the cabarets recently established in Vienna that mimicked those enjoying success in Berlin. About the standard cabaret fare, Mama has pronounced, "Both the Germans and the Austrians share a common love for common entertainment."

To Anna's bewilderment, it is Jacobi to whom Mama now turns all her attention. He is, after all, so reticent, so uninterested in dancing and acrobatics, so unlike the important personages who were smitten by Mama, who escorted her to the finest entertainments in the city, who promised her land and possessions and security and wealth. By contrast, Jacobi possesses only a few shoddy pieces of furniture, two identical suits and the steamer trunks.

Besides, he seems to Anna so colorless and weak. Once even, when Mama, Oma, Anna and Jacobi are sitting together in the parlor on the worn cushions that remain from the time of Araby, Jacobi breaks down in tears. Mama jumps to console him. "What is it?" she asks, alarmed.

"I don't know. I can't help it," he says, reaching for her hand and bringing it to his lips as a parched traveler might a flask of water. He covers Mama's hand with kisses.

Anna is dismayed by the display. Jacobi seems to have no dignity. It is not like a man to show such weakness. "Why?" she asks Mama later. "Why him, and not the others?"

"Can't you tell?" Mama says. She wears little makeup, looks far less imperious. Mother and daughter are now the same height. "Don't you know quality? You, who works among all that finery.

Besides," she goes on before Anna can respond, "besides, if not me, who? You'd leave a man like that to fend for himself?" Mama is indignant.

Anna understands, for in the month that Jacobi has lived with them, it is clear that he is in need of *someone*. He runs a constant fever and is always suffering from one ailment or another. Scarcely a day goes by that Anna does not have to bring him a meal in his room, or rub his back—soft with slender bones like that of a large bird—or carry his bedding or underclothes down the stairs for Oma to launder. When she asks herself why she performs these chores for a stranger, she reluctantly admits she is still trying to please Mama.

"We're both children," Jacobi confided to Anna one day as she massaged liniment into his stiff neck. "I am a learned man," he began, "but I am a child." He turned, cocked his head and smiled back at her like a young boy seeking approval. She hated how successfully he manipulated everyone in the household, especially Mama. "You may be a child, Herr Jacobi," Anna said, turning his head forward and continuing her massage, "but I'm not."

"You'd leave a man like that to fend for himself?" Mama repeats.

"Well, what did he do before you? Us?"

This appears to amuse Mama. "And what do you think?"

"I don't know." Anna feels she should have an answer, but doesn't.

"There were others, of course," Mama says ruefully. "But not a one that knew how to please him, to give him what he needs to carry out his work."

"His work? You mean that *book*?" Anna says it as disdainfully as Mama did when talking about Papa's work, years before.

"That book, and more. You will see."

Anna tries to imagine what Mama means by "and more." When she can't she says, "But what about us? Our lives?" She means her own need to keep the house neat and clean in the face of Jacobi's slovenly habits—cigarettes lit and ignored, the litter of his pencil shavings, his inability to keep the bath clean. "Everything suddenly revolves around him. When Papa was here . . ."

"Your papa was already an old man who threw his best chances away writing nonsense. But *this* man, this man . . ." Mama gestures heavenward as Anna so often saw her do when she danced. "This man is something special."

"I doubt it," Anna pronounces. She turns from Mama, feeling that the money she brings home from Lederer's gives her some license. Mama grabs her by the shoulders and spins her back around.

"There have never been any rules because I never believed in their value. But now there will be and they apply to Jacobi only. I want him treated with respect. You don't know yet what he will do, what he will bring. But you will see and you will be proud."

Politics

What Jacobi brings to the Skodagasse is politics. A Jew, but not a religious man, Jacobi urges Mama to convert her parlor with its faded cloth canopy and worn cushions into a meeting place. The first meeting is attended by Herr Hartmann and many of Vienna's more influential Jews, a number of them Mama's former lovers. If she is embarrassed to have so many in the room at one time, she gives no indication. As the men attempt to gain purchase on the large cushions, Jacobi sits on a high-backed chair. Mama kneels on the floor at his right.

"We Austrians are hardly the ones to worry," says a heavyset, older industrialist, referring to recent events in Germany. He dabs perspiration from his thick neck with a handkerchief. A hot summer sun filters into the room through drawn curtains. Jacobi is perched on the forward edge of his chair. Anna watches from the partially open doors that separate the front from the rear parlor. Oma sits next to her, staring at Jacobi. Earlier that morning—the first time in years—she came to Anna's room to rouse her. "What can I say?" she said by way of explanation. "I like this fellow. Let's bake him some cookies." Now, in the parlor, it is difficult to tell whether Oma listens or not.

The large sideboard, which was once covered by Persian

prayer rugs and a menagerie of small, stuffed, multicolored animals, is today unadorned, stacked with pamphlets that Jacobi, with Mama's help, had printed on a small press set up in the former maid's quarters. Herr Hartmann picks up a pamphlet and leafs through it. It bears the title, "Defending Against the Nazi Threat."

"Isn't this somewhat alarmist, Jacobi?" Herr Hartmann says. The clandestine nature of the meeting makes him nervous. There is little hint of his usual good humor.

Mama stands, about to respond, when Jacobi restrains her. He seems to Anna like some cunning animal in the forest, sniffing at the wind to ferret out danger.

"And who, may I ask, Frau Moser, is our leader?" asks one of the men, his tone indicating that it is his nature to lead, not be led.

"Yes, and why does he get the only chair in the house?" adds another. There is laughter, then quiet. Jacobi stands—straight as some of the youths Anna has seen being drilled on the playing fields she passes on her way to Lederer's. It is difficult for her to reconcile today's Jacobi with the one who weeps for no apparent reason, the one who is befuddled by the task of changing his bed linen. Indeed, somehow he has turned his frailty to an advantage, his fine pale brow, the delicate bones in his face lending him a look of steadfastness.

"Eric Jacobi," he announces, "historian." No one appears impressed, but Jacobi seems unconcerned. "It is hardly necessary for me to be any more than that to justify my summoning you here. History tells us, particularly the history of our people tells us . . ." he says, then stops abruptly.

"But," he begins again, "I am not talking to fools here. I'm talking to some of the most astute men in Austria." A faint murmur of agreement goes through the crowd. Jacobi acknowledges it with a nod. "Now, in Berlin, my home, from where I have recently traveled . . ."

"That is precisely the mistake that is being made here," says the perspiring industrialist. "We are not in Berlin, nor are we Germans."

"The Germans have the disease," Jacobi says. "And a diminutive, mustached man, an Austrian as you well know, is seeing that the infection spreads. Let me just assure you that this particular disease is far more contagious than any plague. And just as surely, we shall feel the brunt of it. Unless we prepare ourselves, organize, take action, before the fact. *That* is what this meeting is about. And that is what I am for." Jacobi glances quickly around the room, then sits back down in his chair.

"By organizing we draw attention to ourselves," one man offers. "If anything, our organization merely forces their hand."

"Whose hand?" someone else asks, exasperated. "Are we already granting that a 'they' exists in Austria? Acknowledge a 'they' and you've already granted them power."

"There *are* sides, I'll have to admit," says Herr Hartmann, "and it seems that we aren't on any one of them."

" 'They'? 'We'? Can't you see what is happening here?" It is the exasperated man again.

The industrialist rises from his cushion. "Herr Jacobi, in all deference to your learning and the lessons of history, you are a German, not an Austrian, and have, therefore, a bleaker view of the world. I have absolute faith in our sovereignty—and in my safety."

Having made his declaration, the industrialist returns to his cushion. He lands too close to the edge, however, and rolls onto his back, his short arms and legs flailing.

Jacobi waits for the man to right himself and regain some dignity, then says, "Faith? Certainly the first three decades of this century must have dispelled that quaint concept from your vocabulary."

"Yes, but, Herr Jacobi," Herr Hartmann interrupts. There is a note of sadness in his voice. "We are not of this century. We are of the one before and can't be expected to dismiss what we were brought up to believe." Jacobi studies the man as he speaks. At least this one is less of a fool than the others.

Just as Jacobi is about to respond, Oma, who has been sitting and staring at him for most of the meeting, clears her throat. Everyone looks in her direction, and at Anna, who has her arm around Oma's shoulder. "So?" Oma says. She speaks clearly, without hesitation, like the Oma of a few years before, not like the Oma of the last months, who only reminisces. "You unlearn what you know. It is not that difficult. Particularly if your life depends on it. Particularly . . ." Everyone waits for her to continue, but as suddenly as she began, she is silent.

Just as suddenly, and to the consternation of those eager for debate, Jacobi calls the meeting to a close. "You will be back," he assures them.

Herr Hartmann is among the last to leave. He speaks quietly to Mama, who, much to Anna's amazement, has not ventured an opinion during the entire meeting. "I'm afraid he may be right," Hartmann says. "And if so, I wonder how much time we have. And how much we have to lose."

Jacobi, within earshot, says, "Everything. Count on it."

Later that evening, Jacobi comes down with a fever. Anna sits with him, placing cold towels on his forehead, going to Papa's bath every few minutes to rinse them with fresh water. "I don't want to die," Jacobi complains, again like a child.

"Don't be silly," Anna admonishes, wondering what he means—dying from the fever, or at the hands of "them," whoever they are. And if it were "they," where would they come from? Would they be a conquering army or would they be her former schoolmates? How many of them would it take? And how much would dying hurt?

Three days later, at two o'clock in the afternoon, Dollfuss, the Austrian patriot turned chancellor and peacemaker, is assassinated by a National Socialist on the floor of the Austrian parliament.

Tales of the Vienna Woods

The Sunday after the season's first snowfall, Anna and Peter board a streetcar near the Skodagasse for the ride to the Vienna Woods, the timbered hills on the city's distant fringes. They bring their skis for what Peter assures her will be a fine and simple day.

Anna senses otherwise. While she likes Peter—and has ignored the attentions of other young men—she has grown to resent his frequent gifts, his solicitousness toward her, his conviction that they will someday marry. After all, Anna thinks, the man I will marry will certainly not act younger than I, will certainly not be as simple as Peter. And, she acknowledges ruefully, his love for me will certainly not be as unequivocal.

But how to speak of her resentment to Peter, with his particularly endearing and disarming earnestness? Lately, unable to find words, Anna contrives to offend him in small ways, engendering mistrust, perhaps encouraging his disinterest: small, obvious lies, occasional insults. Her affronts, however, merely seem to intensify his interest. Anna recalls Mama's suitors of years before—how ardent they became when she ignored them—but cannot liken her situation to Mama's. After all, Mama derived pleasure from her manipulations, while she, Anna, grows increasingly frustrated by hers. Still, she accompanies Peter on this October day—precisely because he is someone who will never surprise or shock her.

It is still early morning and ice layers the windows of the streetcar, distorting Anna's and Peter's view. Children throwing packed snow at the stalwart red sides of the car appear impossibly rotund and clumsy. Shops and houses look short and squat, perched like toads on the hoary landscape. As Peter points to a tiny rainbow created by a prism of ice, he takes hold of Anna's mittened hand in her lap, quickly making her self-conscious.

"Can you imagine a finer day?" he asks.

"I suppose not."

He repeats the question, then goes on. "How clean the snow is as we move farther and farther from where all the people are."

Again, Anna is touched by his earnestness, his excitement for the day before them. "It's a lovely day," she admits. She squeezes his hand.

"It's what you deserve," he says. "Only the best days."

She is about to deny it, when quite suddenly tears course down her cheeks. They cool instantly, forming what feels like a mask on her face. She takes her mittens off to wipe away the residue.

"I feel," Peter says, looking full into her face, embarrassing her, "such a love for you. It is as if I were born to it."

Anna nods, though she cannot comprehend what he says. Who can be born to love? And why would she be the object of his affections? Certainly there is someone else who could provide what he seems to want from her. "Peter," she begins.

"Don't," he insists. "I know you'll only say you don't share the feeling. I don't want to hear it. Really. Really!"

His insistence, coupled with this rare moment of insight, charms Anna and she hears herself say, "Well, I do love you."

Peter blushes. Others sitting nearby look away. Anna wonders if her impulse is the right one, if it is to be trusted. And then as the streetcar lurches forward on the ice-slick rails, she thinks, if this is the talk on the way to the mountain, what happens afterwards, when we are both exhausted from our skiing, when we are flushed and hungry, allies drawn closer by our mutual exertion?

At the base of the mountain they strap their skis onto their boots with leather thongs. The sun is at their backs; the mountain sweeps upward before them. Evergreens break through the snow, their branches heavy with it, bending from the weight. Skis on, Anna and Peter sidestep up the slope in a jagged line along with dozens of other skiers. Off in the distance, church bells ring. An occasional breeze sends snow in billows around them. Finally at the top, they plant their poles and stare out at the vista before them; snow in bowls like powdered sugar, and the denuded trunks of trees like rows of matchsticks along the timberline. Again, Peter's gloved hand covers hers. Exhausted by the climb, their cheeks are flushed, their breathing forced.

And then they turn, separate and swoop down into the first bowl, skiing from sun to shadow and into sun again until they reach the bottom, breathless, exhilarated, their skis chattering on the frozen snow at the base. Then twice back to the top and down again. When the sun is at its peak, they find a small table at the base of the mountain. From his pack Peter produces two poppyseed rolls with sweet butter and sausage, and a small jug with cider. As she takes the jug and cants it to drink, she sees two deer in among the trees at the crest of the mountain.

"Look," she says, as much to herself as to Peter. She sets down the jug. Watching the deer as they gaze at the occasional skier, Anna longs to be able to see her life from a remove. She recalls once looking through the wrong end of a pair of binoculars, seeing the world in miniature—controllable and perfect.

Much later that afternoon, as they ski together into now fully shadowed bowls, Anna has the sudden sensation that she is descending into a darker world, a world of secrets like those Oma harbors, like those Jacobi discovers when he is moved to tears. Behind her, Peter calls out her name into the gathering evening. "Anna, Anna, Anna," it echoes. It scares her, seems like some invitation into the dark.

At the base of the mountain, she leans forward on her poles as Peter undoes the thongs that bind her to her skis. Stepping off them onto the snow, she feels incredibly light and unencumbered, as if capable of floating to the top of the mountain, which is now completely dark, visible only in outline against the night sky.

"Hurry," Peter says. "Our trolley." He points toward it and the other skiers who clamber aboard. A fading light marks the path. That same instant, however, the mountain is suddenly aglow with skiers carrying torches down its face, like a grand dowager adorned with a fine necklace that glimmers and sparkles with her every movement. Peter makes his way to the trolley, unaware that Anna has stopped to stare at the spectacle.

It is a beautiful moment, but for some reason it only heightens Anna's loneliness. She smiles a bitter smile, and before she knows what has happened, Peter blocks her view of the mountain and kisses her lips, the first time he has ever done so. The kiss is light, impossibly delicate and completely unexpected, a confusing pleasure that Anna acknowledges by kissing him back.

Nothing is said about the kiss. But on the streetcar home—as the lights from the emerging city appear themselves like tiny torches, quickly ignited, burning bright, warm and luminous, then disappearing, only to be replaced by others—it occurs to Anna that the feelings she has felt this day—confusion, pleasure, exhaustion, exhilaration and sadness—may have been love.

Papa

It is December. Papa's table at the Café Dolder is no longer in front of the hearth. Rather, it is near the waiters' station, some distance from the energetic fire that warms much of the café. The cuffs of Papa's fine blue suits are frayed, and his collars, while still stiff, are no longer as white.

But he is still Papa, and greets Anna with regal calm, though they have not seen each other for nearly a year—a year in which Anna has waited for him to make some overture to see her. He turns his bearded cheek to her for a kiss. As is his custom, he calls to the waiter to bring her a chocolate, but Anna tells him she drinks coffee now, so Papa hails the waiter to change the order. A few minutes later, the waiter arrives at the table with an empty silver tray balanced on his upturned palm.

"Excuse me, Herr Moser, but which will it be—the chocolate or the coffee?"

Sensing snideness in the man's tone, Anna says, "Neither."

"The coffee," Papa insists.

"It makes no difference," Anna says.

The waiter saunters off. Near the door to the kitchen he stops to exchange a few remarks with another waiter.

"There is no need to be rude," Papa tells her.

"I wasn't the one who was rude," Anna says. "He was."

"Now, why would he do that?" Papa wears a pleasant smile, one which she can tell is meant to smooth over the difficulty. The smile irritates her, reminds her of his smugness.

"Why did they move your table?" she counters.

"There were difficulties," Papa says with a slight wave of his hand, "but they have been resolved."

When the waiter sets the coffee down before her he is cloyingly gracious. "Here you are, Fraülein. I hope this meets with your approval." His smile is waxen. Anna notices that, though he is a handsome fellow, his teeth are slightly rotted.

"You see," Papa says while the man is still in earshot, "resolved." He puts aside his writing tablet to indicate he is giving her his full attention. His handwriting is still flawless.

When he asks about her progress at the piano, she tells him instead about Jacobi and of the many meetings at the Skodagasse. Gradually, his smile disappears and a small vein near his temple pulses.

"That makes me angry," he announces suddenly. "There's no need for plotting, no need for tracts, no reason . . ."

Anna has heard it all before—the dismissals, the arguments. Exactly the same as in the parlor at the first meeting. Since then, however, Jacobi's passion and logic and evidence have won over many of the doubters, Anna for one. But here is Papa, she thinks, obstinate Papa with all his pretensions. It angers her, so much so that she is surprised at the depth of it, and vows that this time she will not allow herself to be seduced by Papa's version of the future. She is, in fact, oddly elated by the prospect of goading him into losing his temper.

"But Papa," she begins, "you're wrong. There *is* ample reason. Every day it gets worse."

"Bah." Papa's face reddens.

"And Dollfuss? That meant nothing?"

"Less than you think," he insists. "Besides, everyone who is fifteen years old thinks that 'today' is the apocalypse, that never was the situation as grave as now."

"I'm seventeen, Papa," Anna says evenly.

"As if that makes the difference. It's the same self-centered, the same . . ."

"And Jacobi? He's well over seventeen."

"I don't know the man," Papa says, "but from the way you describe him, he's hardly a paragon of mature adulthood. The man is just like your mother from what I can tell. A flair for the dramatic, and not an ounce of insight. And you"—he glares at Anna—"you're turning out exactly like her."

Anna pushes away from the table and stands, shaking the spoon from the lip of her water glass. Her untouched coffee spills into the saucer and onto the tablecloth. Papa reaches to tidy it up. "Better than to turn out like you!" she tells him.

"Sit down," he commands, pouring the coffee from the saucer back into the cup.

"Absolutely not."

"Please, Anna." His voice is again quiet, measured. "I'm sorry. I've been foolish."

"All your life," she says. "Your entire life is foolish. And I'll tell you, I'd rather be like her. I'd rather be her than you with your nonsensical writing. What use is it?"

Papa glances at his writing tablet, then back up at Anna. He has regained his composure entirely. His face is flushed, the tiny vein in his temple back in place. "When you are older," he says, "I expect you will understand the value of art. Now it is all 'action' with you."

She grabs the tablet. "Art? Art! How can you call this stupidity art?" She reads a few lines aloud, then stops. Papa sits, palms down on the table, watching her, his head bowed slightly.

"Give it back, please." She hands him the tablet. "Thank you."

"I'm not sorry," she says, her own anger subsiding, deserting her, she feels. Where does it go, she wonders.

"No, I would not expect Evelyn's daughter to be sorry."

"I'm leaving now."

"As you wish."

Exalted and confused, Anna crosses the threshold of the Café Dolder, and moves out into an early winter Vienna evening, 1934.

Vienna, 1937

The Funeral

Anna and Oma walk arm in arm behind the horse-drawn hearse carrying Herr Sonnenabend as it makes its way to the Jewish cemetery not far from the Skodagasse. The cortege is small, made up mostly of former students. A number of dogs have joined the procession and trot solemnly to the cadence of the horses.

It is early spring, though a few thick banks of snow can still be seen—in the lee of a church, piled against random building fronts, and caught between the rungs of the wrought-iron fence encircling the graveyard. Snow also persists in the clefts created by the gravestones and the ground.

Passing through the cemetery gate, Anna feels a chill and pulls her coat more tightly about her. She has never before been to a graveyard for a funeral, only to visit Grandfather Leo's grave. Then, the cemetery seemed scenic—an odd landscape dotted with stones bearing familiar names, sprays of flowers, statues and small edifices. It was like visiting a tiny village, its populace condensed into neat, symmetrical rows.

A breeze rustles the branches of the elegant linden trees that surround the graveyard. Initially gentle, the breeze becomes insistent. The boughs of the trees begin to creak eerily, and Anna's hat is sent flying. Anna runs to retrieve it as it soars, glides and swoops like a gull, finally falling to earth at the outer fringes of the graveyard, where a small settlement of closely bunched houses abuts the iron fence. Here, a number of stones lie flat on the grass, scattered like dominoes. Looking closely, Anna sees a swastika scratched onto the surface of one of the stones.

Standing among the fallen stones, she feels exposed, alone, wondering where the perpetrator might be. She glances quickly at the nearest house and is uncertain if it is a shadow she sees or if someone has actually just moved from a window. She hopes it *is* someone, and not an illusion she fears. Continuing to stare at the window, she picks up her hat, then turns to rejoin the mourners.

At the gravesite, the mahogany casket is taken from the hearse and placed atop two wide belts suspended above an open grave. The casket is large and unadorned, and reminds Anna of a piano, evoking the image of her former instructor cracking his fingers, then filling the parlor with music.

The music in Anna's head soon drowns out the rabbi's prayers, and somewhat to her surprise, she suddenly feels far more moved by Herr Sonnenabend's passing than the perfunctory grief she has already allowed herself. The feeling comes in waves, as if from some inner cistern, bringing with it an indescribable sense of loss and sadness. Herr Sonnenabend will never again be able to touch her, or anyone else. Anna takes hold of Oma's hand and squeezes it so hard that her grandmother looks over at her, surprised.

The next day Anna returns to the graveyard, expecting to see the gravestone in place. Instead, she finds a mound of moist brown earth tinged a slight gray from the morning frost covering the grave. A month later the mound is flat and the gravestone sits atop a rectangular slab of granite. There is still no grass. But when she returns in late summer, the grass has grown, blending with that of the neighboring plot, and it seems to Anna that Herr Sonnenabend has always been here, and that the man she studied with, heard play, was someone altogether different, an impostor.

Closed Wednesdays

It is an overcast afternoon in April 1937. Cybelle and Anna are at work, the shop otherwise empty, when a half dozen young men—boys actually, no older than eighteen—saunter in. They are not in uniform, but each wears a dark brown leather jacket, broad at the shoulders, with sleeves that balloon to tightly knit wristbands. One of the boys wears an armband—an eagle whose talons grasp a swastika.

Anna turns quickly to Cybelle, who, much to Anna's surprise, has already fled to the rear of the store, her cheeks ablush with fear and excitement—the suggestion that all is lost. For reasons she will not question until later, Anna stands fast near the entry.

The boys have no interest in Anna, however. They brush quickly by her, shredding dresses on display, kicking in glass cases, ripping sconces off the walls, and splintering what furniture they can. Suddenly, two of the boys stop, eye the large front window, and without a word between them, grab a small settee and hurl it through the glass. With shards still falling onto the sidewalk, the boys regroup, dust themselves off, and saunter out. At the door, the one with the armband calls back, "Closed Wednesdays!" just as Herr Lederer arrives. "Understand?" Lederer looks at the boy, dumbfounded.

Anna is still at the precise spot where she was standing when the boys entered, and only Cybelle's sobbing causes her to move. "Look," Cybelle says when Anna and Herr Lederer try to console her, "there is glass everywhere." She moves from display case to display case. "Everywhere!"

"But we will clean it up," Anna says evenly, surprised by her own calm, wondering if it is real.

"Never, it will never be the same." Cybelle is ranting now, seemingly out of control, crying, then laughing, then crying again, as Anna and Herr Lederer try to create order.

"Can't you do anything for her?" he finally says as Cybelle stands shivering. Anna holds her, strokes her friend's face, her hair. It astounds Anna that Cybelle is so completely undone, and that she herself feels almost untouched.

Her arms around Cybelle's waist, Anna guides her friend out into the street. "Where are we going?" Cybelle asks. Women walking along the fashionable boulevard stare at them, neither wearing a coat on this blustery day, one in tears.

"To the Skodagasse," Anna says, hoping that Jacobi will be home. His presence has calmed Mama, changed her. Perhaps he will have the words today to calm Cybelle, as well. "There's a man there who will talk to you."

"A man?" Cybelle is dubious.

"Jacobi. I've told you about him. You'll see." It is quite possible that Jacobi will not be there, out instead talking to a Jewish merchant, speaking at a synagogue, or even lecturing on a street corner. "Time is short," he has warned Anna, "the danger real." One day he gave her two German children's books. In the first, a child is set afire for playing with matches. In the second, a child's hands are hacked off for not trimming his fingernails. "Think," Jacobi said, "if the children cut their teeth on stuff such as this, what type of adults they become."

As the two young women walk, Cybelle continues to sob. Gradually Anna's compassion turns to irritation, then disappointment, and finally anger. How can Cybelle, of whom she has been in awe for so long, be so easily victimized? "Quiet now," Anna says sternly. Cybelle falls silent, and only the slight shudder of her shoulders reveals she is still in a state.

Jacobi is home, not in Papa's study, surrounded by his usual clutter of papers, books and cigarettes, but in the kitchen. He wears a threadbare maroon robe that reveals a wedge of his pale chest. He sits with his feet in a shallow water-filled basin. His long black hair is disheveled and he leans forward at the table, a book before him.

"*That's* Jacobi?" Cybelle says, incredulous.

"I've told you about his aches," Anna begins, but Cybelle wrenches from her grasp and runs from the kitchen and out the front door. Anna starts after her, but stops.

Jacobi throws his hands up. "What was she expecting?" he asks. "Who is she?" Before Anna can explain, Jacobi asks in a pleading voice if she will add more hot water to the basin. "Otherwise . . ." and he points to his wet feet to indicate the difficulty of the chore were he to undertake it himself, "otherwise . . ."

Bringing the boiling kettle from the stove, Anna accidentally splashes some water onto her wrist and forearm. Ignoring it, she bends to replenish the basin. Her eyes, she realizes, are tearing, but she feels little pain.

Jacobi looks down at her gratefully. "It is important that someone does these things. I could never do them for myself, and then what?"

Anna studies his face, his small, frail bones, the dark little eyes, like those of a frazzled bird. "I don't know," she pronounces, thinking herself suddenly stronger than them all.

Two days later, after Anna tells Jacobi that Lederer has caved in to the vandals' demand to close Wednesdays, Jacobi appears at Lederer's dressed in suit and spats. Mama accompanies him, the first time Anna has seen either of them at the shop.

"We cannot bow to hoodlums," Jacobi insists. Anna notes how Mama studies him, as if trying to absorb his particular stance, his air of certainty about untrivial things.

"And what am I to do, Herr Jacobi?" Herr Lederer points to a nearby carton containing large glass shards. "Replace it all, only to have it destroyed next Wednesday? No. One day a week I'll grant them."

"And two?" Jacobi asks as Lederer turns. "Wednesday and Thursday?"

"Don't make it harder for me than it is, eh, Jacobi? I am not a political man."

"Hah," Jacobi pronounces. "Three, then. Tuesday, Wednesday, Thursday." Lederer walks away, refusing to face Jacobi again.

That afternoon Cybelle returns to the shop. She is composed, cooler than usual. "That was very stupid of me, the way I acted," she says to Anna. Anna nods. "I'm sorry, too, if I offended your uncle."

"Not my uncle," Anna begins, but Cybelle is already straightening jewelry and scarves in one of the surviving display cases, laboring to make things right.

Proposals

A few months later, one of Vienna's better-known bachelors, a wealthy thirty-year-old roué with a reputation for his conquests of young, eligible women and his subsequent dismissal of them, has asked Cybelle to marry him. She is uncertain about whether to accept his offer.

"I just don't know," she says to Anna, "whether I'm destined for marriage." Of late, Cybelle looks exceptionally radiant. Whatever confidence she lost in the raid seems to have returned, and in greater measure than before. The notion that a young woman not much older than she has sufficient power to choose her destiny renews Anna's interest in Cybelle, whose weakness in the face of the vandals now seems a temporary aberration. And so, as Cybelle considers her possibilities, Anna listens, as if for clues.

"Richard has charm, that is certain," she says, "but in certain ways, he is very, very young. I pity, in fact, all those girls he has supposedly deflowered. They probably think that 'this is making love,' perhaps never knowing how clumsily they've been had."

Anna nods, though Cybelle seems barely to notice. "How is it with you and Peter?" Cybelle suddenly asks.

Anna is embarrassed to tell Cybelle that she and Peter have not made love, but then thinks that perhaps if she confesses her chastity to Cybelle, her friend will confide in her even more. "Peter and I have not been intimate," Anna finally admits.

"You haven't? Really? You see each other so often and for so many years and you are still not lovers?"

"No. Not at all." In fact, Anna hasn't any plans for such an eventuality. "We are simply friends."

"Friends?" Cybelle stands and faces Anna, and places her hands on Anna's shoulders. "You're very sweet, Anna. I wish sometimes I could be so sweet, you know?" Cybelle kisses Anna, once on each cheek, then, much to Anna's surprise, on her lips. Even when the kiss is over and Cybelle steps away, Anna can still feel the pressure of Cybelle's fine lips on hers, the press of her hands on her shoulders. Anna blushes, aware at that instant that it hardly matters who is the braver or the sweeter or the more confident. All that matters, Anna realizes, is that years earlier when Mama was at war with Papa, and Anna felt she was free-floating in the dark—like Papa's ill-fated disabled rocket to Venus—Cybelle appeared full of light and promise to help Anna's hand across the page of her lesson book. And for that day alone, Anna now understands, she will always want to be near Cybelle—to smell her perfume, to see her perfect face, to witness her blush the moment a man enters the shop, and to watch her move to possess him under the guise of assisting him with his selection.

The following week, Cybelle is two hours late for work. Frau Bauer has been checking her watch every few minutes, then glaring at Anna, as if she were to blame. When Cybelle finally arrives she announces to them both that she has decided not to marry, but to leave Vienna altogether, to travel.

"Travel?" Anna asks. Her voice quavers.

"To England. To London, England," Cybelle says primly, affecting Englishness. She purses her lips and sashays around the store. Anna can barely stand to watch her, knowing she will soon be gone.

"Why London?" she asks. Frau Bauer has already abandoned them both.

"It's new." Cybelle continues her lyric movement about the selling floor, flitting from one garment to another, turning a sleeve here, touching a blouse, a bracelet.

"London? New?"

"Well, different, then." She stops, fixes Anna suddenly with her eyes. "It doesn't matter, don't you understand? It's away from here and from all the stupid people. Frau Bauer, for example," she says loud enough for her to hear. Frau Bauer turns and Cybelle sticks her tongue out at her.

"All right. Out then, you piece of trash," Frau Bauer threatens.

". . . and all this business with the Jews," Cybelle continues. "In London, England, they love them . . . us."

"Are you certain?"

"Out!" Frau Bauer insists.

"Gladly, you old witch," Cybelle pronounces as she passes in front of her, making for the door.

"I'll write," she says back to Anna. "I'll write and soon you'll come and join me."

Later that evening, Anna meets Peter and his father at their house for dinner. They have coffee in the parlor, and after he has finished his cup, Herr Hartmann claims that he is too tired for conversation and excuses himself. "That's fine, Papa," Peter says, "excellent." He stands as his father does. Anna, seated on the small chaise in the corner, notes that Peter seems particularly anxious this evening.

As soon as Herr Hartmann is out of the room, Peter closes the parlor doors, then turns on the radio, carefully tuning it until he finds a popular tenor singing a medley of love songs. "Tauber," he says, offering the tenor's name, "a wonderful voice." He joins Anna on the chaise. For a while nothing is said, and the only sound is Tauber's voice crackling over the radio's small, tinny speaker. Anna thinks it's funny that, singing about love, Tauber sounds as if he's in pain. She laughs.

"Funny?" Peter turns to her as the radio reception worsens. Their legs touch, and the next moment Peter puts his arm around Anna's shoulder and pulls her to him. "I want you to marry me," he says. Before she can respond, he kisses her. She kisses him back, but when the kiss is over, neither knows what to say.

Peter, now almost twenty-one, thinks it is because they are both so shy. It is not shyness, however, that keeps Anna silent. She has sensed this moment coming for years. Yet in all her rehearsed responses, she has never been able to find the right thing to say. First, because she has felt that anything she says that is true to herself will seem a cruel rebuff to a decent fellow. And second, because cruel is precisely what she wants to be—for there is something about Peter's tenacity, his fear of her rejection of him, his uncertainty about everything but the practice of medicine and his love for her—that makes her want to hurt him.

So now, Anna simply shakes her head slowly from side to side, watching Peter as he watches her.

"No?" he ventures, his face seeming to unravel before her.

"Not now, in any event," she offers, touching his cheek. He turns his mouth to kiss the palm of her hand, but she pulls it away. As she does the voice on the radio disintegrates entirely and static crackles through the room.

Peter takes a deep breath, then smiles. "Papa will be disappointed," he says.

"I'm sorry," she tells him, suddenly imagining Cybelle and Richard, how very different Cybelle's refusal must have been from her own which, Anna fears, has not yet run its full course.

"By 'not now' do you mean some time in the future, perhaps?" Peter is poised on the chaise, having moved away from her slightly. The room feels dank, though it is May and outside it is dry and hopeful.

"I don't know," Anna says. "Perhaps. Perhaps . . . perhaps . . ." And then it comes to her. "When I return from London."

"London?"

"It's new," she says, surprised that the solution would be so simple, "and they love Jews there."

"You're going to London?" Peter is stunned, never once having thought of leaving Vienna.

"Possibly. Cybelle will be there and . . ."

"Cybelle? Cybelle. Always Cybelle. Why? She doesn't care about you, about anyone."

"I don't . . ."

"She thinks she's so special," Peter suddenly lashes out, "when all she is is a whore."

Regretting it even as she does it, Anna slaps him. They stare at one another, then Peter stands.

"All right then," he pronounces. "All right then." And though he begins to say more, he stops and walks quickly from the room, leaving Anna, the radio now insistent with its static, the song altogether gone.

London

The following Wednesday, when Lederer's is closed, Anna goes to the huge library to read about London. She learns of its history, its architecture, and its commerce. But as she suspected would be the case, she finds no answers to her more practical questions. Then the very next week, much to Anna's surprise, a letter from Cybelle arrives.

Cybelle is now a domestic in a fine house owned by a man in the English financial community. She has her own room and shares a bath with the cook. As for English, it is an easy enough language to learn when you are "tossed into the kettle," as Cybelle claims to have been, "but there are also many girls who speak German to spend days off with in the lovely parks." The letter is signed, "I love you, Cybelle." A postscript in English reads: "Won't you not please in London, England come to me. C."

"Go," Jacobi tells Anna when she shows him the letter.

"Are you certain?" Anna has come to accept and even like Jacobi, though she still resents his whims and his whimpering.

"I'm certain. What awaits you here?"

It is not so much what does or does not await her in Vienna that concerns Anna as it is the thought of working as a servant in a strange city where she cannot even be understood. "I'm simply not certain," she ventures.

"Yes, yes," Jacobi says. "But in this instance, I am. Just as I am certain that you are not at all a fearful woman—as much as your mama has tried to intimidate you and both your mama and papa have ignored you. Believe Jacobi." And though he is sitting in his robe, a compress across his chest for his heart pains, his visage is learned, noble, and Anna is convinced he is right.

* * *

On Anna's next day off, she goes to the British consulate to inquire about working as a domestic in London. The woman she speaks with assures her that Cybelle is correct. A number of German and Austrian girls have emigrated to England, particularly Jewish girls. "So many," the tall, pale woman with the tortoiseshell-frame glasses says, "that I do little else, these days, but make these arrangements." The woman's name, according to a small wooden placard at the front of a desk filled with forms, is Ann Woodrow.

"Some, of course, don't like the idea of being servants, but then, considering what they may face here . . ." Miss Woodrow lets the thought dangle, then launches into another. "It's a new life, you know. A whole new life."

Anna smiles. Reaching for the form the woman hands her, she considers the possibility of starting afresh. The notion is intimidating, but also exhilarating. "My name is Ann, too," Anna suddenly announces.

"Oh? How nice." The woman seems genuinely pleased. "Now, is that 'Anne' with an 'e,' like the queen? Or just 'Ann'?"

"Just 'Ann,' " Anna says, beginning to fill out the form—that second deciding, for clarity's sake, not to reveal her new name to anyone in Vienna, but to remain her old self until she arrives in London. "Just 'Ann.' "

That evening, Anna tells Mama of her decision to leave Vienna. Though Mama is preoccupied with the logistics of Jacobi's upcoming rally of young Jewish men, to Anna's surprise, Mama turns from the papers she has been poring over at the dining-room table—which, along with its chairs, has recently been returned to the room.

"Sit down, then," Mama says. Anna hasn't a glimmer of what Mama may say. Anna holds firmly to the arms of her chair. "It's a new time, a difficult time," Mama begins. "Better, in a few ways, but far, far worse in the main."

Anna nods. She has seen Mama contemplative before, but always in response to something Jacobi has said. "I know," Anna finally says, not wanting Mama to own the conversation. "I just feel that if I had another . . ."

"You've been talking to Jacobi, haven't you?" Mama interrupts. A sudden hint of Mama's former, imperious self appears in her expression.

"Some," Anna admits, "but the decision was mine. I made it on my own."

"On your own," Mama repeats, as if considering the notion, then adds, "The man is amazing, you'll have to admit. He arrives here, a boarder, with his steamer trunks, then changes everyone and everything in the house, and now . . ." Mama stops, sounding both pleased and rueful.

"No," Anna insists, leaning forward in her chair to meet Mama's certainty full-face. "It was *not* Jacobi who put me up to this. And not Papa, not Oma, not Peter, not you." Anna's voice rises. "So please, Mama, for once, give me credit for having made my own decision—though Lord knows, with you as a mama and Papa as my papa, I've been making my own decisions forever."

It's all Anna wants from Mama now—for Mama to take her seriously. But then, staring at Mama from across the table, Anna suddenly realizes that she wants far more—she wants Mama to know that she no longer fears her, that she no longer wants Mama's withheld love, that Mama can no longer hurt her.

"And when I get to London," Anna announces—much to her own surprise—"I'll be called 'Ann.' " The instant she says it, she regrets it. Mama will find it silly, of course, she thinks, and find me foolish, as well.

At first, Mama says nothing, but looks carefully at Anna, as if expecting her to reveal something more. But when Anna remains silent, feeling she has already said precisely the wrong thing, Mama finally declares, "Well then, *Ann,* if you insist that going to London was your own decision, then it must be so."

And with that, Mama gets up from the table, goes to Anna and touches her hand to Anna's cheek. Anna feels a sob well inside her but compresses her lips to contain it, then looks up to see that Mama is crying. "Actresses," Mama says. "They can manufacture tears just like that."

Anna remains at the table long after Mama has gone. Slowly, the inchoate emotion that Anna feared might overtake her dissipates into tiny ripples that make her feel merely sad. She wonders if Mama will come back sometime soon for her papers, but she does not. Sitting there, Anna realizes how little she knows about her deepest feelings. Just when she thinks that Mama can't touch her anymore, she does. And just when it seems she won't miss Mama if she goes to London, Anna misses her simply when Mama leaves the room.

For Oma, the announcement of Anna's departure seems a tonic. Having grown quieter and quieter over the last months, she is suddenly energized. In the weeks before Anna leaves, Oma does dozens of small things for her—things of which Anna no longer thought Oma capable. Together they shop for clothes, secure a visa, buy a train ticket. One day Oma calls Anna to the kitchen. "This seems so solemn a gesture," she begins, "but perhaps you'll have use for this." She pulls the red-and-white-checked cookbook from the middle drawer of the baking table. "In any event," Oma continues, handing the book to Anna, "no one here will ever use it again. Cooking is over."

In the evenings, when Anna returns from Lederer's, she and Oma sit in the parlor, where Oma talks, almost without pause. Oma seems smaller to Anna. Her hands are still fine and pale as china, with delicate tracings of veins beneath, but her voice quavers as she recounts her stories: of her own youth, of a time when Johann Strauss was like a god, and the Kaiser was only a man; and of the chances she took—those that led to something and those that didn't.

"I regret little," she says one night, "except that year with your mama when she changed everything, and I just let it happen."

Another night—an exceptionally hot July evening, with the mercury hovering near the thermometer's apex—Oma confides that she wishes she had better understood what men—those she knew when she was young, and even kindly Grandfather Leo— really wanted from her. "I'm certain I was destined for trouble on that front," she says. "My own papa was weak, with a proclivity for the perverse. Virtually all my friends knew about his mistress, his regular visits to brothels. And my mama was fearful, always scared that the worst would befall us." Anna perspires as she listens to this talk of legacy, while Oma's face is as dry as stone.

"Perhaps, until your grandfather, I always met the wrong men," she concludes, "for I was quite pretty, and was courted only by handsome men, always part of a handsome couple. And from this I derived a sense of self-worth that I later found to be an illusion."

As the day of Anna's departure draws closer, Oma counsels Anna about the things she must heed: that she develop a sense of what she truly wants and not allow herself to be dictated to by others. Listening, Anna thinks that if it had always been this way with Oma, if Mama's tears had always been as real as those she cried at the dining-room table, she might not have chosen to leave. But now the decision is made, and she must. In mid-August she kisses Oma good-bye in the doorway to Skodagasse 14. Mama is not there, but with Jacobi on the train to Salzburg.

The Kiss

Two hours before her train is to leave, Anna, carrying a single valise, a purse, and a small sack of sweets, takes the trolley to the Café Dolder to wish Papa adieu. They have not spoken for over a year. She finds him still at his table, the one he was relegated to after his trouble with the management. "Anna!" He seems surprised, but pleased. "Going on a journey?"

"To London."

"Ah," he says. "An interesting destination. I've never been, of course, but there are stories." He gazes skyward as if to pull one from the air. "Sit, sit," he insists.

"I haven't much time." Anna is suddenly wary of Papa's graciousness.

"You would like something? A chocolate . . . no, a coffee." He beams. "You see, I *do* remember."

"Nothing, thank you." Anna wishes she were not so brusque, and yet feels that Papa invites it. Indeed, it is the only way he allows her to be with him.

"Are you going on a holiday?" Papa looks hopeful.

"Holiday?" Could Papa really be so dense as not to know they have little money, little time for frivolity? "No, to work. As a domestic."

Papa's expression darkens for a moment as he ponders this, then brightens. "It will only be temporary," he pronounces. "After all, you are a talented girl," he says, striking the tabletop with his fingers as if playing the piano, "there's a lot more in life than housecleaning for you."

Anna has told him that she no longer plays the piano and wonders if he has forgotten. She wonders too why this meeting is even more disappointing than those in the past.

"And the crazy ones?" He smiles broadly.

"I thought I told you that I didn't think they were so crazy."

"So my little Anna has finally become serious. A young woman, and all that. Well and good. Well and good. A good sign, I suppose, eh?"

"I suppose so." Her voice is hoarse.

"Well, I love you just the same. Every bit as much." He pats her hand. "And you'll come back and visit, of course."

"I'll try, Papa."

"Excellent, excellent." He continues to smile, and genuinely so, it seems to Anna, who at that moment realizes what she has come to loathe in him: that he truly basks in her company, but never himself seeks it out. Indeed, she would probably never have seen him since the day he left the Skodagasse had she not made the effort. No, Papa is a small, selfish man who behaves reasonably well when called upon, but only then.

"So, we'll see you soon then. You know where to find me." When Anna gives him her address in London—which she has written earlier on a small white card—he studies it with some concern, as if determining whether to hand it back to her. "You know what a poor correspondent I am. You'll be fortunate to get even a postcard."

"Please try." Anna stands, thinking how sad this moment is, but feeling only tired, disappointed. As she grasps the handle of her valise, Papa touches her hand.

Anna looks at his hand for an instant, then turns to the front of the café. "No kiss?" he asks.

"No, I'm sorry, Papa. No kiss." It is cruel, she knows. Good manners alone would dictate a kiss. She walks toward the door, thinking perhaps he may follow her. She pauses on the threshold and waits for a moment, ostensibly to reposition the valise in her grasp. But he doesn't come, and the door closes quickly at Anna's heels.

The Train to London

The old train station is thick with steam. Wheels creak as they begin to move along the rails. An incoming train brakes with a metallic screech, jolting passengers as its engine gives off a final gasp. Anna buys a sausage and some dense peasant bread from a vendor. He gives her a smile full of gold teeth as he takes her coins. Anna spreads hot mustard on the bread and as she takes her first bite, tears spring to her eyes. She thinks, perhaps this is the last thing I will do in Vienna, perhaps forever.

Anna crosses the concourse to her train, bound to London via Paris. She is dressed in a near-full-length green woolen coat with a mouton collar and a small green felt cap. Her auburn hair is in the style of the day—in broad waves and held by two tortoise-shell combs. Her lips are painted brightly, her face has good color. On the platform, a number of men offer to help her with her valise, but Anna turns them down.

The compartment smells of leather and smoke. The luggage rack above the seats is of polished metal, which Anna, gloveless, touches. Her fingerprint appears, then quickly disappears. It amazes her that her grasp is so ephemeral.

Already seated are a woman and her young daughter, identically dressed in light-brown fitted coats and broad black hats tied with a brown ribbon. They are still and prim, as if posing. Anna sits across from them and the threesome is quickly joined by a prosperous-looking man in his fifties wearing a black cashmere coat and a deep maroon cravat with white polka dots. He carries a loden hat with a large spray of feathers and a silver-headed cane. The man settles in his seat and crosses his arms. Waiting for the train to start, he beats his upper arms with his hands, smiling at

Anna when she turns to look. "Masochist," he says, then laughs a thick, jolly laugh.

The mother and daughter have not said a word when suddenly the girl jumps up to look out the window, surprising the mother, who looks distressed, ill actually. The child, by contrast, appears a picture of health. Just then the train lurches forward.

Moving purposefully through the outskirts of the city, the train is soon in the Austrian countryside—green, reborn, immaculate. Women in dirndls labor in front of farmhouses—fat, clumsy structures, white with dark brown trim, standing some distance from the tracks. Children play, run after the train for a few moments, then fall quickly behind. The whistle blows. Chickens scatter. Dogs bark. The cows are unmoved.

"You look like you are leaving forever," the woman says to Anna.

"Perhaps," Anna says.

"To Paris?" the man asks, his voice surprisingly high-pitched.

"London."

"We're going to Paris," the girl offers. "To the doctor." Anna glances quickly at the sickly mother.

"What will you do in London?" the man asks. He rests his palms on his knees, leans forward and turns.

"I'll be a domestic. At least to start with."

"No," the man announces. "No, you'll never do better than that. There is no opportunity for better. Unless," he adds, "unless you marry one of their little lords or something." His guffaw irritates Anna.

"I'll do better," Anna insists. How could it be otherwise, she thinks, barely twenty, having spent those afternoons with Cybelle and later alone, lost in her own imagination.

Presently, the discussion, the insistent jogging of the train, and her daughter's energy combine to undermine the woman's rigid posture and it appears that she may be nauseated. She leans against the side of the compartment. Her hat is askew and perspiration breaks through the powder on her face. She looks to be in her early thirties.

"Aren't you feeling well? Is there anything I can do?" Anna offers.

"No," the woman says politely. "No thank you. You are very kind."

Anna wonders what rare, unexpected disease has befallen this attractive woman, what Parisian doctors could do that the Viennese could not.

Soon the man and the girl are involved in a discussion about animals. "I can imitate the animals," he tells her, and without warning stands and lumbers around the compartment. "A bear," he announces. The girl laughs. The man imitates a squirrel. She laughs harder and the man joins her and in a few moments' time they are laughing so hard that the man's face turns a livid red, and his laughter dissolves into a sharp, barking cough. He reaches into his vest pocket for a handkerchief and coughs into it—once, twice, a third time. It is again quiet in the compartment, with the click-clack of the train's wheels on the tracks the only sound.

In Salzburg, the man leaves the train and walks up and down the platform, raising and lowering his arms with gusto. Another imitation? Anna wonders. The sound of yodeling fills the station. Vendors walking by the train offer small foil-wrapped chocolates and rolls filled with ham in waxed paper sacks. Anna buys a roll and two pieces of chocolate, one for herself and one for the girl. She hands it to her as her mother sits still slightly askew, paying little attention.

"Mutti, can I?" the girl asks. The woman looks startled at the intrusion, then says to Anna, "That was very nice of you, but I'm afraid she is not allowed chocolate."

It seems foolish, but Anna, deciding it is no business of hers, takes the chocolate and puts it into her coat pocket. The woman, having done what she felt necessary, falls back into her reverie.

After a while, the man, invigorated by his pacing and arm-flailing, reenters the compartment. Seated, he withdraws a pipe and tobacco pouch from his coat, fills the pipe, tamps down the tobacco and lights it. At once, silvery, aromatic clouds drift through the compartment and up to its ceiling.

Suddenly the little girl turns pale and gasps for air. Before Anna can react, the girl throws the compartment door open and runs out. Just as quickly, her mother follows. The man looks to Anna for explanation, then at the pipe in his hand, which he now extinguishes by tapping its bowl on the window ledge and empty-ing the tobacco and ashes on the platform. When the mother and daughter reappear, the girl has recovered her good cheer. The mother, however, looks worse than before.

"I'm sorry," the man says. "If I had only known . . ."

The woman nods. Known what, Anna wonders, as the train leaves the station to make its way over the Alps, climbing higher and higher. Thousands of feet below at the bottom of the pass, Anna sees a river flowing like a fine blue vein, surrounded by jagged rocks.

At the border passports are checked. The Swiss guards are efficient, dressed in green and gray uniforms. The medallions on their caps catch the alpine sun and throw reflections which alight here and there like elusive multicolored insects. One of the guards asks Anna and the man what their final destination will be, whether they will be stopping in Switzerland, what the reason for their journey is. The man is traveling to Paris on business. As the guard checks the woman's passport, the girl sticks her head out the window and calls, "Mutti, look!"

"To Paris," the woman says, handing him both her passport and her daughter's. "My little girl is dying," she explains, looking quickly from Anna to the man, "and perhaps in Paris . . ." The guard claps both passports closed and hands them back to the woman.

The sound is like a slap across Anna's face. How little she knows. How easily fooled she can still be. How, she wonders, will she ever survive the new world she is about to enter?

Later, as the train roars open-throttle toward Paris, Anna cannot bear to meet the child's innocent gaze, fixing instead on a gold button on the young girl's coat.

London, 1937

Ann

To Ann's surprise, her primitive English—most of it learned in the few weeks before her departure—works. She engages a taxi from a queue of identical black vehicles in front of the train station and is soon on her way to Kensington and the home of the Petersons, the family for whom she will work.

The summer air in London is thick—filled, it seems, with something heavier than air, like ashes. The buildings she sees out the taxi window are stalwart and drab, without the whimsy or decoration of those in Vienna. And though only centimeters from Ann, the unshaven taxi driver with his soiled tweed cap and macintosh, who carries on an extended conversation with himself, seems as remote as China.

Still, Ann refuses to be daunted by this new place. Instead, she imagines her reunion with Cybelle, to whom Ann wrote as soon as she knew she was coming to England. But the time between posting the letter and Ann's departure was so short, she didn't expect a reply—and there was none.

We'll meet in a park, Ann thinks, unable to picture Kensington, or what a coffeehouse there would look like. The park she imagines is reminiscent of one she has seen in a painting by

Seurat. Its colors are muted, trees and shrubs well trimmed, pale flowers restrained to manicured little beds. And—aside from the two young, energetic women running hand in hand, holding their hats to keep them from flying off in the breeze—everyone in the park is proper and formal, everyone carries an umbrella in the event of a sudden downpour. Ann can feel Cybelle's hand in hers as surely as she did more than ten years ago during her penmanship lesson. She is less sure, however, what they will say when, breathless from their run, she and Cybelle find a bench, then face one another for the first time in months.

As Ann frames her first words to Cybelle, the taxi passes a park—not at all like the one she pictured. Though the day is overcast, the colors in the park are vivid—the grass an intense green, the small pond as blue as indigo, the myriad flowers bright yellow, orange, violet and red. And in place of the proper men and women with their umbrellas, elderly nannies dressed in black-and-white uniforms stand like sentinels next to black, chromium-trimmed perambulators holding their charges.

As one of the nannies bends to lift a baby from its pram, Ann recalls the story of the day Mama was born. Now, hundreds of miles away from Mama, Ann dares to imagine what it would be like to have a child of her own—a "gift," as Oma called the infant she placed next to Grandfather Leo. Ann remembers being once handed a newborn to hold—how near-weightless he was, and how he gripped Ann's thumb so tightly that the knuckles of his tiny hand turned white. Ann supported the baby in the crook of her arm, resting his chin on her shoulder. Soon he fell asleep, his breath swirling gently in her ear.

Another time, Ann recalls, she sat next to a mother in the Stadt Park as she laced up her four-year-old son's ice skates. When the boy stood, his mother buttoned his coat beneath his small chin, touched the red blush of anticipation on his cool cheek, and asked whether he had his mittens. He held up his hands to indicate he had. A few minutes later, when the boy stumbled and fell on the ice, Ann picked him up and set him back on his skates. He looked up at her and told her his name: "Gerhardt Josef Samuelsohn." "That's an important-sounding name," she said. "I know," he agreed solemnly, and shuffled off on his skates to his mother, who waited with her arms outstretched. I would wait as patiently, Ann thinks now. I would be the most patient mother in the world.

The taxi slows, then stops before a tall Georgian house on a narrow but handsome street. A single, elegant automobile is parked in the distance. The houses on the block are all large and relatively close to one another. Each has a small front yard with a waist-high, black wrought-iron fence defining its perimeter. On the sidewalk in front of each house stands a slender sapling tethered to a taller stake and planted, it seems—judging from the loose earth at the base of the one marking the Petersons'—only recently, perhaps today. Ann smiles. "Yes," she says in English, "today."

Valise and purse in hand, Ann climbs the small flight of steps to the Petersons' front door, where she is greeted by a large, black woman wearing an even blacker dress. A tiny white hat like a serviette perches on her head, pinned to her thick, coiled hair. "I'm Carolina," she announces in what Ann incorrectly guesses is an English accent, "and you're Ann."

In a Name

After three attempts in three days to telephone Cybelle, Ann finally reaches a man who claims to be a plumber. "I only picked up because I thought you were my super," he explains, reporting that the Swift family is on holiday and won't return for a month. When Ann asks if there is any way to get a message to Cybelle Becker, the housekeeper, the man pauses, seeming to give the notion some thought. "I would say, no," he decrees after a few moments.

"How long have they been gone?" Ann wonders whether Cybelle has even received her letter.

"Days," he says contemplatively, "days and days."

At the end of Ann's first week in London, Amelia, the Petersons' thirteen-year-old daughter, knocks on the door of Ann's room to tell her that "Pater" wants to see her in his study. Ann wonders what the occasion might be. Certainly not to criticize her work, which she has done well, she believes.

Mr. Peterson is a squat, heavyset man, not much taller than Ann, with a round little head that appears lost perched on his bulky shoulders. His arms are short and when he talks, his small hands flutter. He looks like an enormous bumblebee, Ann thinks. She finds it impossible to take him seriously—no one else in the household does, though he is her "master," as Carolina has informed her, sneering at the notion. Now in his study, he stands before his desk, the feeble light from the single desk lamp behind him throwing his face into shadow.

"You're not 'Ann,' " he accuses as soon as Amelia closes the door. "You're '*Anna.*' "

Ann is so struck by the contrast between the dramatic setting and the inconsequence of Mr. Peterson's accusation that she laughs. "No," she begins, "Anna is what I once was . . ."

"I'll have you know, young woman, it's not funny," he warns, pointing a finger at her. Mr. Peterson is "something of a journalist," Amelia has told Ann, and he has professed to have a linguist's interest in language. Indeed, he has more than once corrected Ann's English, and just yesterday when Ann announced there was a "train coming through the window" when what she meant was a "draft," Mr. Peterson assembled the entire family—wife, son and daughter—and had her repeat it. Later, when she looked up the English words "draft" and "train" in her German-English dictionary, she found they both translated to the single German word, "zug," so her error was not as ridiculous as it was made out to be.

Now Mr. Peterson riffles through some papers on his desk, finally producing a document from the Austrian consulate. "This," he says, wagging the paper in front of her, "this is how I found you out." He indicates her name on the page where, indeed, it is spelled "Anna." "Now, is 'Anna' your name or is it not? This is what I am asking." His fingers drum on the sides of his trousers.

Ann peruses the paper and hands it back, refusing to give in to Mr. Peterson's consternation. "My name was 'Anna,' " she says, articulating each word carefully in her new English, "but when I arrived here, I changed it."

"You changed it! Why . . . how . . . what, what legal avenues . . ." Overwhelmed, he cannot go on. Instead, he moves to his desk, sits down in his huge leather chair and leafs through the papers over and over, all the while speaking to himself, attempting to bring reason to what he has just heard. Then quite suddenly, he looks up. "You know," he begins, "you know, it's not as catastrophic as I originally thought."

Aloud, he tries the name "Anna," then shakes his small head. Then he tries the name "Ann," and nods his head. "Anna . . . Ann, Anna . . . Ann," he repeats, finally concluding, "No, it's not so catastrophic for you to make a small change. Besides"—he brightens—"saying 'Anna' would require an entire extra syllable for us. For *each* of us, each and every time we say it."

"Yes," Ann says. "I'd never thought of it that way."

"Well," he offers, "sometimes a new *perspective . . .*" He stops, not wanting to belabor the insight. "Well, sometimes it can . . . can make all the difference."

The Petersons

When the heaviness Ann felt in the air her first afternoon in London persists through the next weeks, she asks Carolina about it as the larger woman oversees the cleaning of the Esquire's—as she calls Mr. Peterson—bedroom. Carolina, who is too old for heavy work, according to Mrs. Peterson, has been relegated to light duty, which involves answering the door and the telephone, serving meals, and little else. The rest of Carolina's day is spent either roaming around the house or in the pantry gossiping with another black woman also named Carolina, an old friend from the West Indies. "Big Carolina"—as she is called because she is even larger than the Petersons' Carolina—arrives nearly every morning in a large white Rolls-Royce driven by a liveried black man who remains in the car reading tabloids and smoking cigarettes. Ann finds it all somewhat amusing, though she hasn't the faintest idea what to make of it.

"It tisn't actually the air itself that's so heavy," Carolina pronounces, going through the Esquire's commodious vest and trouser pockets, retrieving coins, which she drops into the deep cleft between her bosoms. "It's all them 'tut-tuts' these people say. You know, the 'tut-tut this' and the 'tut-tut that.' " Carolina lets out a big laugh, her single gold tooth with the silver crescent moon on it glinting in the rare sun filtering through the Esquire's window. "That, and all the wind they break." Carolina laughs even harder as her huge bosom heaves like that of the opera singer who visited the Skodagasse one day.

There are seventeen rooms in the Peterson house, which Ann is to clean six days a week. She begins each day by breakfasting in the small kitchen with Carolina, then climbs the stairs with a carpet sweeper, broom, mop and bucket, rags, and a feather duster to begin work.

For her first two weeks on the job, Ann wears one of Carolina's huge old uniforms over her own clothes, cinching the belt twice around her waist and pinning up the hem. Then one day Carolina brings her two new black dresses from a shop called "Wilhelmina's Well-Dressed Domestics." Sitting at Mrs. Peterson's mirrored vanity, Ann is surprised to find that not only do the dresses fit her perfectly, but she also looks the part of the well-dressed domestic: young, foreign and slightly mysterious.

Ann wonders how, of all people, she, with her comical nose, can look mysterious, then quickly decides it's that she possesses a separate vocabulary, a wholly unique way of expressing herself, that the English, the Petersons, can't understand. Continuing to gaze into the mirror, she says a few words in German, then a sentence, then recites a few lines from Schiller. Doing so makes her all the more eager to see Cybelle. But when she telephones, there is no answer.

Except for Amelia, the Petersons generally ignore Ann. Following the "Anna/Ann" discussion, Mr. Peterson has said little to her. He seems, in fact, uninterested in women in general, a trait that does not go unnoticed by Mrs. Peterson, who is frequently called on by handsome, younger men arriving in their own automobiles.

As for Mrs. Peterson, she occasionally pays Ann a small compliment about an exceptionally well-scrubbed floor or a perfectly polished piece of furniture. This alternately pleases and irritates Ann. As she has for years, Ann derives satisfaction from the simple task of cleaning a room or bringing up the luster of a long-ignored table finish, but the thought that she is now being measured solely by such tasks rankles. In any event, Mrs. Peterson's perfunctory manner makes it clear she has little use for Ann. ("The trick," Carolina offers, "is to make them realize you got even less use for them.")

Harold, the Petersons' son, is almost as tall as the door frames that he stoops beneath as he passes through. He has a small, wispy mustache, fine blond hair darkened and slicked down with pomade, and a conspicuous lack of chin which accentuates his prominent Adam's apple. Harold is twenty-five, has no profession, and is engaged to be married in April, eight months away. Most days he wanders through the large house, reading aloud from books of poetry.

"He's an artist," Amelia tells Ann one day as Harold perambulates wraith-like through the parlor. She is an overly sincere but likeable girl with uninteresting brown hair that won't hold a curl. Occasionally she'll dare a smile, but then, as if fearing to be censured, will stifle it.

"He's trying to decide between poetry and fine art," Amelia continues. She finds everything in the household tedious except Ann's work, and has taken Carolina's place following Ann from room to room as Ann cleans, often insisting that she clean and Ann watch.

"Don't you think he's very handsome?" Amelia asks as Harold vanishes from the parlor.

"Do you?"

"Oh, no. I'm his sister." She blushes deeply, making quick passes at the furniture with the feather duster to hide her embarrassment.

"And what are you going to be? Or do?" Ann asks. "Marry, as well?"

Amelia averts her eyes and peers out the window. Ann wonders what she is looking at. "Pater says we're going to war," Amelia confides. "Otherwise I would like to go to Paris and study design."

Ah, she is gazing at Paris, Ann realizes. "Design? What kind of design?"

"Interior," Amelia says as if sharing a dark secret.

On Ann's third Sunday in London, she accompanies Carolina to her social club, the West Indies Maids, Orderlies and Charwomen's Society of London. Ann is dubious about going, but Carolina insists. "Time to get out of the house."

"Will I be the only white person there?"

"Absolutely," Carolina chortles.

"You're not making me feel comfortable. If I go, I'll want to feel comfortable," Ann says, half joking, half serious. "I'll want to feel at home."

"Poor baby," Carolina says, "when's the last time you felt 'at home'?" She lumbers over to Ann and hugs her. Carolina's face next to Ann's smells like flowers, her white dress like bleach.

"Well, what do I wear?" Ann asks.

"What we all do . . ." Carolina points first to Ann's maid's outfit, then her own. ". . . the *uniform*," she declares gravely.

The West Indies Maids, Orderlies and Charwomen's Society of London is located in a storefront in a part of the city populated almost entirely by black people. Carolina holds Ann's hand as the two of them step from the bus. "Nothing to worry about," the larger woman assures her. Music emanates from the Society's storefront. Closed, brightly patterned drapes cover the windows, and a heavy wooden door bears an elegant brass sign with the Society's name. On either side of the storefront are shops—a tailor's and a market with bins out front heaped with fruits and vegetables, many varieties of which Ann has never seen before. Carolina buys a mango, asks the greengrocer to cut it open for her, then hands it to Ann.

She bites into it, and the juice from the fruit drips into her palm. "Why?" Ann asks, unsure what to make of Carolina's gift.

"Someone has to pay you some attention," Carolina says. "Besides, I like foreigners. Providing they aren't English." She imitates a stiff walk, an interrogatory glare. "Guess who?"

"Mrs. Peterson," Ann laughs, amazed at how Carolina— weighing easily twice what Mrs. Peterson does—can create an almost identical effect.

The social club is no more than a large open room with a coal stove at one end, some card tables and chairs at the other, and in between, a sitting area furnished with tattered twin settees, a low table and three large, mismatched stuffed chairs. As promised, there are no white people and everyone there—all women— wears either a black or a white dress. In the sitting area, a half dozen women chatter in a language that sounds almost French. Every few seconds, one of the women reaches to take a handful of nuts from a bowl in the middle of the table.

Another woman, incredibly tall and blacker than anyone Ann has ever seen, stands near the coal stove, drawing languorously on a cigarette that is black as charcoal. The woman's exaggerated manner and her black cigarettes remind Ann of Mama.

"Carolina brings her friend from the Continent," the woman suddenly announces, sweeping toward Ann, who still stands on the threshold of the storefront, the door not yet closed behind her. Carolina steps between Ann and the approaching woman.

"Oh, just let it be, Saramanda," Carolina says. The woman stops, then smiles. Her teeth are stained a dull red.

"Well now." Carolina turns to Ann. "Feeling at home yet?"

"Not yet." Indeed, Ann feels she has just set foot in another country right in the heart of London.

"Didn't think so. Just give it a bit more time, though," Carolina says. "Things have a way of turning around."

Much to Ann's surprise, Carolina is correct. After Saramanda's retreat, five other women emerge from a door at the back of the room, sit down at one of the card tables, and invite Carolina and Ann to join them. One of the women pulls a deck of cards from her bosom. The others go through their pockets for matchsticks, which are divided up between the players and used for wagering.

The card game is a relatively simple one of matching cards by remembering their location as they are spread first face up and then face down on the table. Complicating the game are dozens of rules that—it is soon obvious to Ann—are made up on the spot. "Pick up a Jack, put him in your belt," one of the women calls. "All sevens back on the table," calls another. Throughout the game, too, the women playfully shove or tap one another.

Ann does well on the matching and likes the play. After about a half hour, when she has amassed a few pairs, she calls her own rule: "Queens to the bottom, Kings to the top."

"Queens?" Carolina echoes, dismayed.

"Queens," Ann laughs.

"But I just got queens." Carolina gives them up reluctantly, then chucks Ann under the chin. "Last time Carolina's going to take you *anywhere.*"

One day Mrs. Peterson walks into the kitchen to find Amelia on her hands and knees scrubbing the kitchen floor with Ann. "Amelia! Whatever are you doing?" Amelia glances down at the floor and then at the scrub brush in her hand as if she hasn't the faintest idea. Ann continues to scrub as Amelia gets to her feet and walks away. She does not see Amelia for a few days and assumes their odd sisterhood has come to an end, but after a week, Amelia appears in the kitchen as Ann and Carolina eat breakfast. "From now on," Amelia says, ignoring Carolina's rolled eyes, "I'll only work when Mater is out. If that's all right with you?"

Later that day as Amelia helps Ann clean the "loo," Amelia asks, "Ann, do you have people back there?"

Ann recalls the muddle of the recent past: Mama off with Jacobi to some rally, Oma sitting in the parlor lamenting a lost age, Papa undaunted, forging the future at the Café Dolder, and Peter—if his letters are any indication—still waiting patiently for her. "Yes," Ann says, "I have people."

"So you'll go back, then? If there is a war," Amelia goes on.

"I mean, you'll go back to be with them. In their time of need."

Returning to Vienna has not occurred to Ann—and the fact that it hasn't makes her feel, suddenly, in the face of Amelia's question, as if perhaps she has been too single-minded in her quest for a new beginning. To start over, she decided she would have to put them all out of her mind—and she has accomplished this so far with some success. But now, partly not to disappoint Amelia, Ann says, "Yes, of course. In their time of need."

Amelia considers Ann's response. "It *is* the proper thing to do, after all, isn't it?" She puts a finger to her brow for a moment as if in deep thought, then continues. "Yes, I'd do the same. Yes, *absolutely,*" she insists, just as Ann realizes that if Amelia ever escaped the Petersons and survived the first months, she would never, never return. The realization strengthens Ann's own resolve to remain in England. She has made the choice to leave Vienna, to take on a new name, to speak a new language. She will stay where she is.

The reaffirmation is a tonic. From that day on, her tasks become more pleasurable, the Petersons less foolish, the air easier to breathe, and the rendezvous she has finally been able to arrange with Cybelle—after being in London nearly a month— filled with possibility.

Sybil

"What a marvelous idea!" Cybelle says when Ann tells her she has changed her name. "How very clever."

At Ann's urging, they meet at a park not far from the Petersons' to which Ann often walks after work. It is nothing like the park Ann had imagined for their reunion, but more like the one she saw on her first taxi ride to Kensington—verdant, with a thick swath of close-cropped grass surrounded by healthy old elms dense with leaves, and huge beds of primroses bordering gravel paths.

"You know," Cybelle continues—she insists they speak only English—"you know, I could do the same. With my name, that is. I could call myself 'Sybil.' " She laughs. It is reminiscent of

Cybelle's unfettered laugh of ten years past, though tinged with a slight nervousness.

"Sybil and Ann," Ann says.

"Quite British."

"Quite."

Holding hands, the two young women walk along a path to find a spot for their picnic. Cybelle's palm is much cooler than Ann remembers. Ann has brought sandwiches and two bottles of lager, Cybelle a white cloth and napkins, which she carries in a tattered cloth sack.

"No, seriously," Cybelle says, "from now on it's 'Sybil.' Agreed?"

"Yes. Agreed." Spreading the cloth on the grass with Sybil, Ann is amazed at how like an Englishwoman her friend appears, how little like the vibrant Cybelle of only months before. Her face is paler, her hair bobbed, the blue mysteriously gone from her blue-green eyes. Most remarkable is the way she moves—not with the familiar, easy grace that pleased and confounded her Viennese beaux, but with measured care, as if not to break a thin, transparent shell surrounding her.

"Cucumber sandwiches?" Sybil asks when she pulls one of the small white rindless tidbits out of a waxed paper bag.

"Ever so good!" Ann mimics an expression she has heard at the Petersons'. "They were left over from yesterday's tea and . . ."

Sybil has already finished the first sandwich and begins eating a second. "I hope you don't mind, I'm famished," she says.

"Aren't you getting enough to eat?" Something is not quite right about her friend, Ann is now convinced. Not only has she changed, she seems to have lost her grip in some way—too much laughter, too much effusion, poorly masked by moments of unconvincing calm.

"Enough to eat? Oh, plenty," Sybil insists. She lays her second sandwich on the cloth and withdraws a cigarette from a pack in her purse. After she lights it, inhales deeply and lets the smoke stream upward into her nostrils, she offers a cigarette to Ann. "Who do I remind you of?" Sybil asks.

Ann tries the names of a few film actresses she has seen in the tabloids left at the Petersons' by Big Carolina's driver.

"No, you silly," Sybil interrupts, "I look like Evelyn Moser." And when Ann doesn't respond immediately, Sybil prompts, "Remember her?"

Without warning, tears form in Ann's eyes. "Really," Sybil says, touching Ann's cheek to wipe them away. "Really."

Finishing her cigarette, Sybil leaps to her feet. "Don't you just love it here?" Ann is not sure what Sybil means. "I mean, being out of *there*. That stuffy old city. And those people."

Ann says that the only people she has met so far—aside from Carolina and her friends, who are not English—are the Petersons, and she hardly sees them as an improvement over the people she knew in Vienna.

"What?" Sybil demands. "Could it be that you're a true-blue Viennese? Who ever would have believed it?"

Ann starts to protest, but stops. Instead she says, "I suppose I just haven't gotten out and around enough yet."

"Well, we'll see to that, won't we." Sybil rises and holds her hand out for Ann, who is still sitting cross-legged on the white picnic cloth. "We will simply just have to see to that."

The rest of the afternoon, Ann and Sybil decide, will be spent on a bus tour of London originating at Westminster Abbey. To get there, however, they must first catch another bus at the far end of the park.

"Hurry now," Sybil says, starting to run, distancing herself from Ann, who is still gathering the picnic cloth and the bottles and wrappers they have left. "We really haven't much time before the bus leaves," Sybil calls out.

Ann bundles everything in the cloth, slings it over her shoulder like a washerwoman, and runs after her friend. As Sybil looks back to urge her on, a little girl, no more than three, crosses Sybil's path. The next instant they collide, sending both Sybil and the girl sprawling. The girl wails while Sybil sits on the ground stunned, her skirt grass-stained.

By the time Ann reaches them, Sybil is on her feet, but the little girl is still on the ground, crying even louder. Ann drops her bundle to pick the girl up, but she spins away and redoubles her cries. Off in the distance, a heavyset nanny strides toward them.

"Let her be," Sybil commands in German. "We'll miss the bus."

"I just want to see"—Ann again reaches for the little girl—"to see if she is all right."

"Of course she is," Sybil insists. "Come on now. Besides," she indicates the approaching nanny, "she'll have more help than she needs in a moment."

"Sybil, wait!" Ann demands.

"Wait? Wait!" Sybil is furious. "All I've ever done is wait. I'm through waiting. Through!" And with that Sybil is off, on her way to the bus, alone.

In the days that follow, Ann tries to call Sybil, but Sybil refuses to come to the phone. "I'm cross with her," Ann once hears Sybil say to another servant who has answered the ring. When a day later it is Sybil who picks up, Ann quickly demands, "Why are you cross? What have I done?"

"Done? You've not done anything. It's just that you're so . . . so damned *thoughtful,*" she accuses. "And it makes me feel simply terrible, makes me feel like I'm . . ."

"Does that mean we can't be friends?" Ann interrupts, holding the phone tighter to her ear. She feels suddenly so desperate at losing Sybil entirely that, while having heard the word "thoughtful," she has not registered its meaning. "Does that mean we can't meet again? Does it? I promise not to be thoughtful if we do," Ann pleads.

To Ann's surprise, Sybil laughs. "You're so very silly," she finally proclaims. "Of course, we'll meet again. We're both in England, aren't we?"

"Oh yes," Ann says, relieved, "yes." Still, when she returns to her room and considers Sybil's accusation, her relief is tinged with anger.

The Party

Carolina and Ann sit beside each other in the back seat of Big
Carolina's Rolls-Royce, sent to fetch them to the party. The car
drifts through the traffic like an ocean liner plying its way among
a clutter of boats as it nears a port. Roderick, Big Carolina's
driver, is at the helm. When Ann asked why Big Carolina had
invited her, Carolina explained, "Because I asked her to. And
because ever since you seen your friend, you been sad-looking as
old vegetables. Besides, a good party never hurt nobody."

For the occasion, Carolina wears a silky red dress that
stretches across her bosom and bottom like the spinnaker sails
pulled taut against the wind that Ann remembers from the boats
on the Danube. Carolina's legs, sheathed in silk stockings rolled
to above her knees, look the color of cocoa. She has brought a
bottle of whiskey, which she now pulls from a gargantuan purse,
a "clutch," she calls it. "I'd offer you some, but then there
wouldn't be any for the trip back." Also from the clutch she
extracts a small silver cup bearing the engraving "Amelia Prescott
Peterson, 6 lbs, 12 oz, September 14, 1924." Ann recalls dusting
it many times.

Carolina has offered little by way of explanation about the
party or about Big Carolina. Just that Big Carolina was working
in Barbados as a maid to an English couple and the man's wife
died, drowned while they were on the island. "And before that
little, pink man had dried his big tears, he'd taken up with Big
Carolina. Just like that." Carolina snapped her fingers. "He asked
her to come back with him and here she is, married and gone to
heaven without ever having to die."

"They were lovers? Big Carolina and the little, pink man?"
Ann tries to sound nonchalant.

"Of course," Carolina replies with a significant shrug. "That's
the way of the world."

Ann catches Roderick's eye in the rear-view mirror, and for
a moment they stare at one another.

"The way of the world," Carolina repeats, pouring herself
another cup of whiskey. "Imagine that Mrs. Esquire," she says,

changing the subject, "she puts a little mark on each one of these bottles, so she knows how much there is"—Carolina starts laughing, jostling Ann with her shoulders—"and how much there isn't. And she going off every afternoon with those *boys.*" Suddenly Carolina stops. "Just about there," she announces. She spins the top back on the whiskey bottle, drinks down what remains in the silver cup, wipes it out with a tiny handkerchief and puts everything back into her clutch.

The large white automobile, having left the main roads some time before, now moves through narrow country lanes bordered by birch trees, white as milk, and by heaps of stones, painted white. Ahead are fields awash in fall wildflowers, and in the distance, a slight bend in the road and an open iron gate as tall as the Rolls-Royce and topped with fat finials that remind Ann of a Buddha.

As they pass through the gate, Ann sees the house. It is a mammoth U-shaped structure with rounded, turret-like towers at either end and a grand entrance at its center marked by a dark blue-and-white-striped awning supported by white pillars. So white is the house in the peculiar light of early evening that it looks as if it might have been carved from soap.

"Big Carolina lives here?" Ann asks.

"Lady of the house," Carolina says, sounding both proud and irritated.

Big Carolina's husband—indeed, a little, pink man, of perhaps sixty—is standing next to Big Carolina under the awning. The couple remind Ann of a dark Gypsy organ-grinder and his albino monkey she once saw at the Prater. When Roderick opens Ann's door, Big Carolina comes to greet her, then turns her attention to Carolina, still extracting herself from the limousine. For a moment, the two Carolinas eye each other like pugilists, and then the Petersons' Carolina guffaws and the two women embrace, kissing each other's cheeks.

On a raised area nearby, four black men with white hair sit on small chairs and play jazz, music that Ann has heard Carolina play on the Petersons' gramophone. At each corner of the stage gigantic sprays of autumn flowers emerge from huge urns, and covering the dais itself are more flowers woven into a lush carpet. The fragrance is so powerful that for a moment Ann feels over-whelmed, reeling slightly as Carolina guides her in the direction of her host.

"Ann," he says, moving toward her, "I'm Thedy." He grasps her hand. "It *is* Ann, isn't it?"

Big Carolina hands her a glass of champagne and puts her arm around Ann's waist. "Yes," Ann assures the man, "yes." But breathing the cloying odor of so many flowers, hearing the jazz and, from a distant room, a Chopin mazurka artlessly played, and suddenly surrounded by a half dozen newly arrived guests, Ann is not certain whether she is Ann—or even Anna. Away from home now for nearly three months, she never has felt so com-pletely adrift. "Yes, 'Ann,' " she repeats.

Thedy—a foreshortening of his first name, Theodore—con-tinues to hold her hand, patting it absently as he looks about him at the others. He is as pink as the inside of a rabbit's ears, Ann notes, sipping her champagne; particularly the top of his head, which she can see clearly as he bends to kiss the hand of a woman arriving on the arm of her husband. "Ah, the Pearls!" Thedy exclaims. Fixing on Thedy's silver-rimmed eyeglasses and his white goatee, Ann hardly notices the couple, nor that they are speaking German with a Viennese accent. And when it finally does register, it is as if she is waking from a dream.

Before she can say anything, however, the man and woman have drifted into the house. Holding her champagne glass before her like a torch, Ann walks toward the stage, where the four musicians, who have stopped playing, are leaning forward in their chairs, bending over their instruments and passing around a slender cigarette. One takes the cigarette and inhales it deeply, throwing his head back as he does. He holds his breath for one, two, three, four counts, then exhales slowly—barely any smoke escaping at all. The ritual is repeated until one of the men, noticing Ann, offers the cigarette to her.

Suddenly Carolina is standing next to her. "Don't go getting lost just yet," she says. She takes Ann by the arm through the foyer and into a large salon, where perhaps a dozen people sit on sofas and deep chairs. There is a grand piano in the far corner, at which the man who artlessly played the Chopin now assaults Schubert.

"How did Thedy know my name?" Ann asks Carolina.

"From Big Carolina, I suppose. She probably told him all about you."

Ann is about to ask her what Big Carolina could have possibly told him when Carolina, having delivered Ann into the salon, joins a conversation with two young men who are so fair and pretty that Ann is uncertain whether they are really young men or young women. Nothing, in any event, is as it first appears, here at Thedy and Big Carolina's.

Presently, the Schubert is over and the man at the piano stands. He is wearing a tuxedo and pulls at his shirtfront and his cuffs, then covers the keyboard with a long maroon velvet cloth. Another tuxedoed man, as elegant as a count, walks over to Ann—she assumes to engage her in conversation. Instead, he plucks the empty champagne glass from her hand and replaces it with a full one. "Oh, thank you," Ann says, far too loud, for others in the large room turn, among them the man and woman who have been speaking German earlier, the Pearls. As quickly, they all turn away, save for the woman, who continues to study Ann as she moves from the archway leading into the salon to a point nearer the piano. The woman's gaze follows her. She is an older woman, petite, and wearing a blue dress whose bodice shows traces of the powder she has liberally applied to her face and neck. Her eyes bulge slightly. Suddenly she pulls at her husband's sleeve. He is tall, pale, and saturnine, with thick sideburns that thin quickly to uncombed wisps of white hair.

"Nathan," she insists as he continues his discussion with a Chinese man. Unsuccessful at gaining her husband's attention, and aware that Ann is watching her, she mouths the word "come" in Ann's direction. Ann, not knowing what to expect, does.

"I never forget a face," the woman says in English. Then she repeats the words in German, more dramatically, this time prompting her husband to turn. "It has been six, maybe more, years," the woman continues, pleased with herself, "but I never, never forget a face. I am certain."

The husband is gracious but accustomed to his wife's feats of memory, and seems impatient to have the identity of the person in question revealed so that he can go back to his conversation.

"You're the Moser girl," the woman proclaims. "Correct?"

Ann nods.

"Ah," says the husband, "uncanny. My wife is uncanny." He pats her head as if she were a large dog. "What a memory!"

"But *you* remember, too," the woman goes on. "Evelyn Moser's daughter. Evelyn Moser," she repeats.

Ann has been mute during the entire exchange, almost, in fact, since she arrived at Big Carolina's. But now she feels she must say something. "Yes," she offers in far better English than either the man or woman. "Evelyn Moser. The dancer. I'm Ann . . ."

But before she can say anything more, the man adds, "Of course, of course . . . the pianist."

Ann blushes. Mama is a dancer and Papa is a writer, but never would she presume to refer to herself as a pianist. "I studied with Herr Sonnenabend," she offers. Over the man's shoulder she sees Carolina, champagne glass halfway to her mouth.

"You'll play for me now?" the man asks as Thedy appears.

"Certainly she will," Thedy says, softly taking Ann's hand, his fingers tickling her palm as he leads her like a dancing partner toward the piano. Big Carolina seems to materialize at the far end of the keyboard. She snatches the maroon velvet off the keys like a magician.

There are a dozen reasons why Ann cannot, will not play, but the excuses she is looking for in English fail her. Instead, she finishes the champagne she holds in her other hand and sits on the bench.

"Chopin," it says across the familiar ecru frontispiece of the book of music. "Polonaises."

"How can I?" she asks herself, but an impulse stronger than protest has her turning to the sixth polonaise, the grandest, the one she once played as she was convinced Chopin intended it to be played—not romantically, as was the style of the time, but martially.

Pearl stands next to her. When the first measures don't fail her as she expects they will, she essays the next, and when she reaches the bottom of the page, Pearl turns it for her, then the next, until he realizes that she is not reading the music any longer. About a third of the way into the piece, Ann's uncertainty finally overtakes her and she stops. Immediately, she feels the man's hand at the nape of her neck.

"What is clear," he whispers in her ear, "is that you have played little if at all since I heard your recital. And that you play even better now."

Ann is confused by what has happened; by the champagne, by the overwhelming scent of the flowers, by the four jazz musicians she now sees at the far end of the salon, by Big Carolina with her arms around her diminutive husband, and by what the man, Pearl—whose hand now rubs the back of her neck—has whispered in her ear. She rushes from the room.

Carolina finds her in the loo. "Something good always happens when Big Carolina throws a party," she says. "And it's always a surprise."

Ann remains at a distance from the party for the rest of the evening, sitting on a bench in the gardens, watching wisps of clouds scud across the face of a huge, orange moon, listening to the odd anarchy of the jazz, and catching the sweet scent of the cigarette the men share every so often.

Finally, Ann returns to the salon to find Carolina. Most of the guests are gone, disappeared without the sound of automobiles. Perhaps they are elsewhere in the house, Ann thinks.

The couple from Vienna remain, however, the man ensconced in a deep purple chair, with his feet propped up on a table on which he has placed a newspaper. He puffs on a large cigar. His wife naps on a small chair in the corner, tight and closed as a tulip. There is no sign of either Carolina or Thedy.

"I'm sorry," the man calls in German when he sees Ann. "My asking you to play was not meant to embarrass you." Ann moves toward him, slowly. "But you touched me once. And I was hoping you might again. And you did. You did." He reaches into his coat for his billfold. "Here," he says, holding out a white card. It is long and narrow with scalloped edges and bears the name "Nathan Pearl," and beneath it, the word "Impresario."

"We're living in America now. And if fate takes you there, you must be certain to call."

The Fight

The day after Big Carolina's party, Ann asks Mrs. Peterson if she can use the telephone—the new procedure in the household following Mr. Peterson's decree that the phone be kept free for important communication. Weighing Ann's request, Mrs. Peterson declares her desire to speak with Sybil about Big Carolina's party "insufficiently pressing."

Two more days pass before Ann has the time to walk to the public phone adjacent to the park where she and Sybil last met. Standing in the large red windowed booth, she waits for the connection. The phone rings a number of times, but no one answers.

At first Ann is disappointed, then relieved. What, after all, would she tell Sybil? Something about playing the piano, perhaps, but what? That for a few moments she felt as if she owned her life, as Papa had promised? That she would take up the piano again. That everything was, indeed, still possible.

No, Ann realizes as the ringing continues, her beautiful self-centered friend would not be interested in any of these things; only in the magnificent white house, the various and odd guests and their mysterious disappearance, the dissonant music, the ride in the Rolls-Royce, and perhaps, just perhaps, the Viennese she met.

The very next day Sybil telephones Ann at the Petersons', saying she must speak with her. She barely makes mention of their first meeting or their last phone call—now nearly a fortnight ago—except to say that she has been under some strain. "Please," Sybil says with such intensity that Ann imagines she feels her friend's breath in her ear.

As Ann holds the heavy black receiver of the parlor phone

close to her mouth to reply, Mrs. Peterson walks by. "For good-
ness' sake, who is on the line?" she demands, holding her hand
out for the receiver.

"A friend," Ann offers. "My friend." Mrs. Peterson's hand
falls to her side, but she remains standing next to Ann. Ann
wants to ask Sybil what the nature of the strain is, whether things
are better now, whether they will ever be close again. But it is
impossible with Mrs. Peterson standing next to her. Instead, she
listens as Sybil instructs her as to when and where they will meet.

A few days before the rendezvous, Ann asks Carolina to
perform her assigned duties. Carolina is amenable, claiming, however, that she has recently been diagnosed as allergic to both dust
and water. "What it really is, though, is that I'm dead tired of Big
Carolina going on about the good life—that's what I'm allergic
to," Carolina confesses. "But don't you fret over it. You just go
on out. I'll put little Lady Amelia on the job."

Setting aside her recent frustrations with Sybil—recalling instead their earlier times together—Ann anticipates their meeting.
We'll talk about the strain she is under, Ann thinks, and I'll help
her with her problem, whatever it is.

Ann arrives ten minutes early at the restaurant where Sybil
has suggested they meet. It is a tiny, squalid place with stained lacy
curtains in the window and a half dozen tables covered in faded
yellow oilcloth. Odors of sour milk and rancid meat contribute
to the overall unsavory impression. Ann wonders how Sybil has
learned of this place, why she would choose it for their meeting.

The owner, an Indian wearing a turban and soiled white shirt
and trousers, is, however, quite gracious, and as Ann waits for
Sybil—ten minutes, twenty, an hour—he brings her tea in a glass,
bowing as he refills it a half dozen times. When finally Ann stands
to leave, the Indian refuses to take her money.

"You will accept my hospitality," he says, removing the glass
from the table, "and you will return."

Without thinking, Ann says, "No, no, I will not." She drops
a handful of coins on the table and rushes out.

Big Carolina's Rolls-Royce is parked in front of the Petersons'
when Ann returns. Snow falls lightly, making the scene of the

limousine, the street and the houses before her appear as if seen through a delicate scrim. For the briefest moment Ann recalls skating in the Stadt Park on a day like this, a chauffeured phaeton driving by at the very edge of her field of vision.

Now as she approaches the car, Roderick eyes her. He rolls down the window. "We could go for a ride, you know," he offers, "and you could sit in the front." He pats the seat. But Ann says nothing, walking to the back of the house to enter through the pantry.

Confronting her in the kitchen is a most astounding sight. There on the floor on her back is Big Carolina, and sitting astride her is Carolina, her hands on Big Carolina's throat, choking her. Big Carolina grabs at Carolina's wrists, pulling away one, then the other as Carolina collapses over her, and their faces touch with a slap.

"You bad, bad bitch," Big Carolina bellows, as she kicks her legs to throw Carolina off her. Carolina crashes into a table as Big Carolina climbs to her feet.

"Carolina!" Ann yells, stepping between them, just as Carolina is about to sink her teeth into Big Carolina's ankle. Ann pushes her away. "Carolina!"

Big Carolina uses the break in the battle to retreat to the far end of the table, standing hunched over it, her knuckles on the chipped ceramic tabletop, trying to catch her breath. On the table is an assortment of whiskey bottles and two of the Petersons' Waterford highball glasses, one broken.

Panting hoarsely, Carolina tries to get her legs under her, grabbing hold of the icebox. Halfway erect, she slips and sprawls heavily back to the floor.

"What are you doing? Are you both crazy?" Ann demands. "I don't understand *any* of this, any of you." She wants to cry but cannot.

At that moment, Mrs. Peterson appears at the kitchen door. She takes in the scene—Big Carolina pulling down the hem of her mauve beaded dress, the broken and the half-filled glasses on the table, and Carolina still on the floor. "You'll leave now," she says to Big Carolina, "you'll leave now and you'll not return."

For an instant it looks to Ann as if Big Carolina will lunge at

Mrs. Peterson, so intently does the larger woman glare at her. Instead, she extracts her coat and purse from under an overturned chair and huffs out the door, whispering angrily.

By then Carolina is standing. She straightens her black dress, ripped below her arm, finds her tiny white cap under the table and pins it to her head. "Sorry, Madam," she says to Mrs. Peterson, then charges past her toward her room.

"And *you* . . ." Mrs. Peterson says to Ann, who remains rooted to the spot where she first pushed Carolina, "what, pray tell, is your role in all this?"

Standing next to Carolina, who sits on her bed, her head in her hands, sobbing mightily, Ann tries to console her. "What is it about?" Ann asks.

"About feelings," Carolina confesses after a while. She stops sobbing. "It's damn unfair, is what it is."

"Unfair?" Ann is uncertain what Carolina means, for "unfair" suggests that rewards are in some way commensurate with effort, a dynamic certainly not in operation in her own life.

"You know each other for years," Carolina begins, "and then you don't." She repeats it twice.

Ann sits on the bed next to Carolina and puts her arm around her. She can feel the throb of Carolina's heart coursing through the fabric of the torn black dress. It is the first time, Ann realizes, that she has embraced anyone in a long while. It makes her suddenly, incredibly sad.

Not until she is back in her own room does she think about Sybil, wondering what has befallen her.

"Nothing," Sybil insists when they finally reunite, weeks later. "It was just a mix-up, the wrong address," she explains, "and I've certainly never heard of that horrid restaurant." It is late December and they meet in a tearoom, a small house actually, where they serve tea and sweets all day. Again, Ann arrives early, Sybil, nearly an hour after they have arranged.

"You're such a fussbudget," Sybil says when Ann points out that Sybil is late, feeling she must comment on her friend's rudeness. "Such a fussbudget," she repeats, staring beyond Ann into the hearth at a fire burned down to embers.

"Something is wrong," Ann says. "I know it." She reaches for Sybil's hand, which Sybil pulls away. "I know you," Ann continues. "What's wrong?"

Sybil repeats, "What's wrong?" with an exaggerated English inflection, making it sound as if it were truly a silly question. "What's wrong," she goes on, now irritated, "what's wrong is that I'm pregnant. That's what's wrong." She puts both hands on the edge of the table, as if she is about to push it over. "So"—she suddenly smiles—"how is it with your friends Amelia and Howard? And your Negro companion? Still hunky-dory?"

Ann tries to find some resemblance to the Cybelle with whom she played soccer, who rode with her on the Ferris wheel, who kissed her so sweetly once, who dreamed of men coming to take her away with them. Of that girl or that time, there is no trace. Even the language is different—"hunky-dory." "Is there something I can do?"

"No."

"Something? Anything?" Ann seeks warmth from the cup of tea before her, but it has turned cold.

The man won't marry her, that is certain, Sybil says. Besides, he might even be married himself. There is no way to hide it from the Swifts, the family she is working for. No way of having the child, then securing another post. She will have to return to Vienna.

"Can you just imagine," Sybil begins, "going back to that bleeding city filled with the stink of Nazis? And pregnant. Perhaps Ilse will have something for me," she jokes grimly.

"I've heard it isn't so bad with the Nazis," Ann says, recalling Peter Hartmann's letter, received only two days earlier, asking whether she might return.

"Not too bad." Sybil stands and puts her hands on either side of Ann's head. "Ann. Dear, sweet Ann. Use your head." Ann feels Sybil's moist palms cover her ears, and the increasing pressure Sybil exerts. "Use . . . your . . . head!" Ann pulls Sybil's hands away.

"Are you certain I can't . . ."

"I told you, no!" It is said as if accepting Ann's help would be the last insult Sybil could bear. Sybil pulls on her coat, taking her gloves from her pockets. Her hands shake so, however, that she cannot put them on, so she throws the gloves on the table. "You," she pronounces, "you take them, then."

Ann watches through the open-shuttered window of the tea-room as Sybil climbs to the second level of a double-decker bus. Taking on more passengers, the bus remains at the curb for a few moments, and though Ann cannot be certain, she thinks she sees Sybil's face in the bus window, and Sybil's bare hand, waving tentatively.

London, 1938

New Year's Day

On New Year's Eve, 1937, Carolina is fired following a dinner at the Petersons' during which she repeatedly spills food and drink on the guests, once on the trousers and spats of an important acquaintance of Mr. Peterson's. An elegant woman's diamond brooch is either misplaced, lost or stolen.

"Carolina has been let go," Mrs. Peterson tells Ann the next morning, "so you'll be expected to take on a bit more until we replace her."

"Is she already gone?"

"Gone. And," Mrs. Peterson adds, "she won't be back. I can assure you of that."

Ann cannot imagine that Carolina would leave without a farewell, or at least a few final hard-bitten words of advice. Ann was, after all, in her room the entire evening, right next to Carolina's. Certainly she would have heard her packing. Distressed, she goes to Carolina's room now, and is surprised to find it completely intact. Carolina's large, colorful dresses hang in the dark wardrobe like friendly flags. Her odd-smelling powders and perfumes are scattered on the dresser top.

Ann opens one of the drawers filled with Carolina's underthings. Her stockings are wadded into a huge ball held in a rubber swimming cap. Opening a second drawer, Ann finds a few familiar blouses and one with tropical fruits printed on it which Ann has never seen. Not knowing why, she puts it to her face and inhales Carolina's perfume. Perhaps it is only suggestion, but the blouse smells like fruit. Ann laughs. She will miss Carolina.

In the bottom drawer, Ann finds a few empty whiskey bottles, a silver flask engraved with initials that are not Carolina's, though not any of the Petersons' either. There are, however, Mr. Peterson's missing pocket watch, and, judging from their size, a pair of his trousers. Finally, there are some letters, all in envelopes bearing stamps from Barbados.

Ann is curious what they might contain, but decides against reading them. It is strange enough being so intimate with Carolina's clothes. Finding a box-like suitcase bound with cords under the bed, she gathers Carolina's clothes and letters and packs them carefully. The last item she puts into the case is the red dress Carolina wore to Big Carolina's party. Ann recalls sitting with Carolina in the Rolls-Royce, Carolina's face in profile as she stared at the great white house ahead, her cheeks shiny and brown as burnished brass. What did she see? Ann wonders. What did she hope for? Ann is certain the answer is in the letters, the first thing she packed.

She closes the case, ties the frayed cords and sets it down at the foot of the bed. If Mrs. Peterson is correct about Carolina never coming back (and given the missing brooch, this is most probably the case), then Ann will have to find her.

Trying to find Carolina, however, quickly becomes frustrating. All Ann knows is Carolina's last name: Waters. She does not know Big Carolina's full name, nor Thedy's, and hasn't an inkling where the great white house is. Ann's best hope is the West Indies Maids, Orderlies and Charwomen's Society, but when she takes the bus to the section of the city where she remembers the social club to be, she cannot locate the storefront—nor has anyone she speaks with ever heard of the club. And when, as a last resort, she asks Mrs. Peterson where Carolina might be, she is told, "I don't know a thing about those people."

Finally, one morning, Ann walks into Carolina's room and finds the suitcase gone. Amelia tells her Big Carolina's driver picked it up days ago. A satisfying conclusion, Ann thinks, picturing the two women together again.

The Note

As winter draws on, Ann finds little time to leave the house. No replacement for Carolina has been found, and Ann has been called upon to serve at mealtimes as well as to clean. She no longer has Sundays off, and she isn't free in the evenings until nine o'clock or later.

Also confining her to the Petersons' is the weather. While not as cold or as snowy as the Viennese winters she has known, the London winter is exceptionally windy and severe. When snow does come, it is shoveled or plowed into drifts that melt partially during the day, forming huge puddles that freeze in the night. The roads, too, are covered with a sooty slush that passing lorries splash through, splattering everything in their wake. Still, when it is February and Ann does not hear from Sybil, Ann travels by bus and on foot to where Sybil works, rather than try to reach her by phone.

It is the first time she has seen the Swifts' house, and she is surprised by how much less impressive it is than the Petersons'. She recalls the flat in Vienna where Sybil and her mother lived, and where she almost never visited because Sybil was so ashamed of it. Ann rings the bell, and after some time a middle-aged man appears at the door—not a servant, as it turns out, but Mr. Swift, who introduces himself after Ann tells him her name. "I would like to speak with Sybil."

"I see," he says. He is pale, like most of the English she has met, but has an improbable spot of high color on each cheek. His expression, however, is somber. "You're looking for Cybelle."

"Sybil," Ann corrects. "It was Cybelle, but . . ."

"I know," the man says, amusement flickering briefly across his face. "I recall the day she asked Mrs. Swift and myself to call her that. She'd come in from an afternoon off, all excited about this idea of a new name . . ." The man stops. "In any event, we never did—never called her Sybil, that is. I mean, we simply couldn't imagine anyone changing her name just because she'd come to a new place. Perhaps, though . . ." He stops again, and asks Ann into the parlor. They both sit. He takes a cigarette from a gold cigarette case on a small side table, starts to light it with a large, silver lighter, then stops. "This is difficult," the man begins.

"Difficult?" Ann tenses.

"Of course," he goes on, "we would have liked to have gotten in touch with you, but I simply didn't know how." The man stands, goes to a desk and picks up a small envelope. "I can only imagine she must have been quite distraught when she left this— he holds the envelope out to Ann—not to have given me an address or a telephone number where I could reach you." A solitary lamp in the corner throws a dim yellow light. Outside it snows.

Ann takes the envelope. It bears her name, nothing more. She lets it sit on her lap for a moment, trying to imagine the precise words it contains. "She went back to Vienna?" Ann ventures, certain this is not the case.

Mr. Swift returns to his chair, this time lighting the cigarette. The flame makes odd patterns on his face, ages him. "No, I'm afraid not." He snaps the top of the lighter closed with a click. "Cybelle," he says slowly, "took her life last Saturday. Sleeping tablets. We have no idea where she even got them."

"I see." Ann studies the envelope on her lap. Her fingers are numb as she opens it. She tries to recall Sybil—or Cybelle—that last time, getting on the bus. Was that her face Ann saw in the window? Did she actually wave? Why? As Ann unfolds the note on her lap, her eyes fill and it is difficult to read.

The note says little, in any event—that Cybelle was sorry she had been "cross" with Ann, and couldn't she see it was the best thing to do under the circumstances? She had no choice.

When Ann finally looks up, Mr. Swift sighs. The sigh is faint, but significant, and Ann knows its meaning. Cybelle had enchanted him, as she had Ann, and so many others.

"As I said," he begins again, averting his gaze, "we would have liked to have gotten in touch with you about the funeral, but . . ." he stops. "The family liked her, you know . . . Cybelle. She could be so lively. Particularly when we were all together on holiday. At the seashore, only last summer—how many months ago, three? Five?" Again, Mr. Swift pauses.

"I understand," Ann says softly.

"Do you?" He glances briefly at her, then down at the cigarette between his thumb and forefinger.

"Yes. Believe me, I do."

"It's not what you think," he suddenly blurts, his voice rising.

"Really," Ann says, "I understand."

"The children," he adds quickly, "she was quite good with children. They liked her a great deal."

"Good with children?" she repeats, surprised.

"Yes, playful, like a child herself—when she was with them." How little I knew of my friend, Ann realizes, wondering whether she or Cybelle was to blame for that. "In any event, we're all terribly, terribly sorry." The man stands, and Ann assumes it is an indication for her to leave. "No, no, no," he says. He puts his hand on her shoulder.

"Took her life," Ann says to herself, wondering precisely what it means, translating it back into German. Taking had nothing to do with it at all, did it? She feels the pressure of the man's hand. Why couldn't Cybelle have stayed on here? Certainly, Mr. Swift—who, Cybelle must have known, loved her—would have understood. Or why didn't she go back? Surely, what might have happened to her in Vienna could be no worse than what she had planned for herself here.

Ann finally rises, just as the lamp in the corner of the room flickers. For a moment, the winter storm buffets the house and it seems as if the electricity will fail. But there is a resurgence of power. "Thank you," Ann says.

"Yes, well, we have her belongings. We telegraphed her mother, but there was no reply." Mr. Swift leaves and returns with two suitcases, then walks with Ann to the front door. "These are difficult times," he pronounces, "and I'm very, very sorry. It's no solace, I know. I know how it is with friends." Ann thanks him again and leaves the house.

Back in her room, Ann places the suitcases on her bed, trying to decide whether to open them. She knows that every item of clothing will evoke a memory—but to what end? Immensely sad and frustrated, she also feels the glimmer of something else—a feeling she is now far too ashamed to acknowledge. It first came to her on the bus, two hours earlier when, well before her destination—a suitcase propped against each leg—she reached behind her to pull the cord to signal her stop. Hefting the suitcases, she descended from the bus to the sidewalk. The storm had eased, and the widely spaced streetlamps each illuminated their patch of the newly fallen snow. For an instant she just stood, inhaling deeply, feeling the chill penetrate to her lungs, then out through her mouth and nose. The air smelled fresh for the first time in a long while. Then, without another moment's thought, she turned to make her way back to the Petersons', kicking at the powdery snow with her black boots, crying at times, laughing at others, as the suitcases she carried became lighter and lighter.

March

In mid-March, Hitler annexes Austria. Not a shot is fired. His triumphant entry into Vienna is supported by a national referendum. Within days, Ann hears over the Petersons' radio that racial laws have been imposed. Jews are banished from universities. Shops are looted, synagogues defaced and closed. A week later, Ann receives a cable from Mama. "Jacobi arrested. Oma no longer speaks. All is lost! I love you, Mama." Ann is distraught by the news, perplexed by the closing. In this, Mama's clearest communication ever, Ann attempts to discern motives, hidden meanings. Is she asking me to return?

With Harold's wedding less than a fortnight away, the entire Peterson household is in a state. Mrs. Peterson, still unable to find a suitable replacement for Carolina—or so she claims—accedes to Amelia's wish to let her help Ann with the housework. The next day, however, the cook gives notice, and Ann—having once told Mrs. Peterson she knows how to bake—is given responsibility for the cooking and serving, as well as special preparations for the wedding reception, which is to be held at the house.

The red-and-white-checked cookbook weighs less than Ann remembers, but the recipes are as easy to follow as they were more than a decade before, the results just as predictable. Cooking from the book is no more difficult than baking, and the first meal that Ann prepares for the Petersons—cucumber salad, sauerbraten with tiny dumplings, and a seven-layer cake with a hard sugar glaze—is a qualified success. Skinny Amelia even asks for a second helping, ignoring her mother's comments about keeping her figure.

"It's nice that you prepared something familiar to *you* for your maiden meal, as it were," Mrs. Peterson says in the kitchen after the dinner. She spies the open cookbook on the table, notes the German words as if they were hieroglyphs. Fingering the cover, she closes the book. "In the future, however, I think we'd all prefer something more familiar to *us.*"

With the wedding so close and Mrs. Peterson still dubious about Ann's ability to prepare "good English fare," Mrs. Peterson bows out of her private social scene to oversee food preparation and other wedding arrangements. One day, guiding Ann through the particulars of the evening meal, she suddenly asks, "Are you planning to marry?" It is said as if Ann's marriage would be a lesser union than hers with Mr. Peterson, or Harold's with his bride-to-be—an adorable match to be observed with some condescension.

"I have been asked," Ann replies, "but I turned the proposal down to come to England." She recalls Peter's desperation that night, his anger and jealousy—not unwarranted—toward Cybelle, the crackly tenor on the radio. "Really?" Mrs. Peterson seems genuinely surprised, and makes a quick show of touching the oven, the table, the icebox, the china cabinet, as if to demonstrate that she knows what goes on in a kitchen. "A young man from back home?" she finally asks.

"Yes, of course."

"And his vocation?"

"He was a doctor. He *is* a doctor," Ann corrects herself.

Now Mrs. Peterson stares directly at Ann, one eyebrow raised, as if to discern whether she is lying. "A doctor? And you turned him down? Why would you have done that?"

"Because," Ann says, without thinking, "I was in love with someone else. Not exactly in love, but . . ." She stops. It surprises her that she has said it, and to Mrs. Peterson, of all people. Even more, however, it astonishes Ann how her love for Cybelle has changed over time—and in just the last month, since she learned of Cybelle's suicide. For years captivated by her perfect friend, Ann now feels truly free—for the first time in memory.

"And that 'someone else'? Do you still love him?" Mrs. Peterson asks.

"Oh, yes," Ann says. "Oh, yes."

"Love," Mrs. Peterson snorts as she leaves the kitchen. "You mark my words, young woman. You'd best be wary of love, or you may end up having a very lonely time of it."

That night Ann cannot sleep. A constant flow of lorries and buses travels the generally deserted street before the Petersons' house. Shadows appear on the walls. There are voices, dogs barking, even a siren. On the nightstand next to Ann's bed are Mama's cable and Cybelle's note. Ann has read them many times. They are both so brief, like the Japanese poetry called haiku Papa once told her about—so brief that as the night draws on, Anna must create her own images to fully grasp their meaning.

First, Mama's cable: "Jacobi arrested . . ." Jacobi weeping over a small blister on his foot or a coffee stain on one of his beloved books, yet confronting a half dozen young fascists at the café when they sneered at him. "Oma no longer speaks . . ." The day she and Oma jokingly jousted with mop and broom from kitchen to vestibule and right out onto the steps of Skodagasse 14; the perfect whiteness and flawless lace of Oma's wedding dress wrapped in tissue paper in the attic; how polished and smooth Oma's skin was when Anna kissed her last. "All is lost!" The house, the piano, the Stadt Park. "I love you, Mama." Oh, Mama.

And Cybelle's note: "I am sorry I have been so cross with you . . ." Cybelle's sudden anger at the boy they met at the films who wouldn't leave his friends to sit with her; the winter day they went to Cybelle's flat and there was neither coal for the stove to make tea, nor wood for the fire for heat; Cybelle, late for the recital, her black coat open, her lovely hair in disarray, the flush of the cold or of lovemaking on her face, the young man's hand on her back. "I have no choice . . ." Cybelle, totally undone by the vandals at Lederer's, unable to stop crying.

Why didn't I see it coming? Ann laments. Certainly if I were a better friend . . .

The following afternoon, her preparations complete for the evening meal, Ann returns for a second time to that part of the city where she remembers the West Indies Maids, Orderlies and Charwomen's Society of London to be. This afternoon her instincts are true and she finds the storefront immediately.

Carolina, her back to the door, sits at one of the tables, playing cards with her friends. Putting a finger to her lips to shush the others sitting with Carolina, Ann walks up behind her and claps her hands over Carolina's eyes. "Guess who," she says, disguising her voice.

"Too easy," Carolina teases. "Amelia Peterson."

"How did you know?" Ann kisses Carolina's cheek.

"Before I saw black, I saw white," Carolina says, pulling a chair from a neighboring table. "Sit. We'll deal you in next hand."

The game is the same one Ann played last time—the same women are playing, and there is still the good-natured jabbing and shoving, the improvisation on the rules. "What surprises me," Carolina says when it's her turn to match the card in her hand with one of the ones face down on the table, "is that you're still there."

"And where would I go?"

"I suppose"—Carolina turns, gesturing with her cards toward the women at the table—"to be with people you know. Maybe you and your friend," she offers, "both of you together go back home."

Before Ann can respond, Carolina asks what is happening with the Petersons. She takes great delight in Ann's report, laughing so hard about Harold's fiancée's hives, that she tumbles off the small folding chair. Carolina is still laughing when Ann and two of the other women help her back to her seat and the game continues.

"All aces are kings!" Ann proclaims a few hands later, finally certain of her next step.

Gloves

On the eastbound train at the French-Swiss border, a Swiss soldier, no more than eighteen, wearing a uniform he has yet to grow into, enters the compartment Ann is sharing with an older woman. He studies Ann's passport, compares the photograph to the young woman before him. "Please, Fraülein, if there is an alternative, take it. I have seen too many like you come the other direction relieved by their good fortune." Ann thanks him for his concern. She knows her choice is reckless, but feels confident.

"He doesn't say a thing to me," the older woman laughs when the soldier is gone. She has a wide mouth, and her teeth are fine and even like pearls, perfectly set. "The young look out for the young." Ann objects, but the woman holds up her hand. "Who can blame him?"

As they travel through Switzerland, the woman confides that she is a Gypsy from Yugoslavia who has married above her station and lives in Vienna with her husband, a manufacturer of women's gloves. She has just come from Paris, where she went to show their wares.

"*Those* are certainly fine gloves," she says at one point, noticing Ann's. They are actually Cybelle's, the ones she threw at Ann at their last meeting, a slightly shopworn pair given her as a going-away gift by Herr Lederer. Ann tells the woman that she once worked at Lederer's.

The woman seems pleased. "Ah," she says, "then you will understand." She takes her sample case from the rack above and opens it next to her on the seat. It contains dozens of pairs of gloves, each wrapped in cellophane that vibrates like a pulse with the movement of the train. There are long gloves made of the most delicate kid and dyed in myriad colors, shorter gloves that come to the wrist, where a tiny row of buttons runs to the palm, gloves of leather and wool, soft and rich-smelling.

"Here," the woman urges, removing the cellophane from a short green pair, "try them on."

Ann is reluctant, but the woman insists, taking the cellophane from pair after pair. Drawing on the pair that the woman tells her are the most expensive, Ann has a sudden recollection of Cybelle using her gloves—not simply for warmth and fashion, but to entice a man. As she leaned forward to speak to him, she'd touch the man's hand with a soft, pliant glove, a touch that suggested elegance as well as the mystery of the woman whose hand lay inside.

"These gloves are exquisite," Ann says, holding both hands to her cheeks to better feel the softness of the leather.

"I know," the woman who married above her station responds, "which is why you must keep them. That very pair. The best." Ann protests, but the woman is adamant. Later, as the train stops at the Austrian border, the woman wakes from what appears to be a restful sleep. "I will die in Vienna," she pronounces without preamble. "It is my intention. But what about you?"

Just then, a soldier wearing the Austrian eagle on one sleeve and a swastika on the other enters the compartment and demands passports. He looks at Ann's and hands it back. "Have a pleasant journey," he says, then turns and leaves the compartment, taking the older woman's passport with him.

"Come back here with that," she demands as she stands, but another soldier appears in his place and with two fingers to her chest pushes her back into her seat. Ann watches as the woman blinks once, twice, then as tears suddenly course down her cheeks, dissolving the color and powder that lent her her aristocratic veneer. The tears fall to the green and gold embroidered yoke of her dress, discoloring it. Once again the woman tries to stand, but the soldier, gazing placidly out the window, merely raises his hand and pushes her back down. "Why me?" she implores. "Why here?"

As the tears continue to erode the woman's face, Ann imagines she can see the woman's life unravel before her. With each moment she seems less like the woman who valued the finery she offered, and more like the sly child who had finagled her way out of Yugoslavia to marry and have a better life. When Ann can no longer bear to watch, she says to the soldier, "Can't anything be done?"

"I assure you, Fraülein, that something will be done," he says, his tone even, contained. He persists in looking out the window, his expression half hidden from Ann.

"What . . ." They are standing so close, she touches his arm to gain his attention. ". . . what, what will be done?"

The soldier wheels, furious as he pushes Ann's hand away. "Touch me again, Jew, and it will be your passport next!"

"Leave it," the woman suddenly interrupts, pulling at Ann's sleeve. "Leave it be!"

Ann, more shocked than afraid, retreats, sitting down and putting her arm around the woman, who shivers, though the compartment is warm. After a few seconds, Ann looks back at the soldier, who has again assumed his placid pose before the window. Surprised by her own calm, yet curious about what interests him so, she too looks out the window. Just below the level of the glass are three soldiers in conversation. Aside from that, she sees little of import: tiny red berries, like rubies, grow from bushes half buried in snow at the platform's edge. Somewhat farther off is a guardhouse built to look like a chalet, its brown and green trim standing out before the rise of the Alps behind it.

Suddenly, a train comes from the other direction, slows, then stops, blocking the view to the mountains and leaving Ann to look into the compartment across from hers. In it, it appears, is a family of five—a husband and wife and their three young sons. When a soldier enters the compartment, the father hands him his papers eagerly, obsequiously. When after a few seconds the soldier leaves, the children cheer, but they are quickly hushed by their mother. Perspiring, the father wipes his brow with a handkerchief. He then stands, kisses his wife and each child, and returns to his seat.

At that instant, the soldier who took the Gypsy woman's passport returns. "Would you please come with us, Frau Meckle," he orders.

"Why?" the woman asks. Ann tenses.

Before another word is spoken, the second soldier grabs the woman and pushes her out of the compartment. Ann is stunned, not knowing what, if anything, to do. That moment too, the train next to theirs moves, and out the window all she can see is the featureless side of a green baggage car. Glancing quickly around her, she spies the woman's sample case. Without thinking, Ann grabs the case and runs down the corridor with it, hoping she can still find the woman. At the end of the corridor is another soldier, leaning against the side of the car, a rifle dangling from a strap on his shoulder.

"The woman with the green dress," Ann says. "This is hers. She needs it."

He looks around at her, amused. "Really?" he asks. "Did she forget it?"

"She didn't have a chance," Ann says. "It happened too quickly."

He seems sympathetic, and takes the case from Ann, assuring her that he will take it to the woman. "The one with the green dress, correct?"

"Yes."

Back in the compartment, Ann touches her hand to her heart. She expects it will be beating wildly, but it barely beats at all. Strange. She touches her forehead. It is cool. "It makes no sense," she says aloud as the westbound train pulls away, again affording her the view of the guardhouse. There is not a soul in sight. Suddenly her own train lurches and moves forward slowly. Searching for the woman, Ann can find no trace of her at first, but then on the platform, not fifty meters ahead, she sees the case, splayed open, and scattered along the tracks are dozens of pairs of fine leather gloves.

Vienna, 1938

"Wien, Wien, Nur Du Allein"

In Vienna, Ann steps from the train onto the platform. She has traveled with Cybelle's two suitcases as well as her own. When it becomes too clumsy to carry all three cases, she leaves one of Cybelle's at the entrance to the station—having had no real plan for her friend's possessions other than to bring them to Vienna. Immediately, someone calls her attention to the abandoned case, but she leaves it where it is.

Not until the incident on the train with the woman did Ann realize how foolish and filled with risk her return may be. Still, Carolina was right, it was time to return home—certainly time to leave the Petersons'. Besides, there was nowhere else Ann could think to go.

The city she returns to, however, is quite different from the one she left just seven months earlier. Men and women no longer stroll the broad boulevards, but stride as if moving toward a defined goal. There is something more purposeful too about the conversations she overhears as people pass. Where once Viennese was the most melodic of the German dialects—spoken in waltz tempo—the language now sounds clipped. Even the clothes people wear seem more fitted, as if to reveal more of the physique, the person underneath. There are still coffeehouses, of course, and the air in their proximity is still redolent of roasting beans. But men and women no longer idly leaf through newspapers—instead, they lean forward in serious discussion.

At the flat where Cybelle once lived with her mother, Ann is told that Frau Becker has left the country, that she has left no forwarding address.

Uncertain where to take the remainder of Cybelle's belongings—or whether to simply leave the second suitcase on the street as she did the first—Ann finds herself in the vicinity of Lederer's, already some distance from Cybelle's mother's flat. Perhaps it is the two-day journey from London, the events of the train ride, or returning home to an unfamiliar city, but Ann feels like a somnambulist. She recalls thinking just a few days before that somehow the easy commerce among the card players at Carolina's club could be hers if only she were with those she knew. Already she realizes that she had deluded herself.

Two large yellow Jewish stars are posted on Lederer's window. Herr Lederer and Ilse Bauer are conferring at the rear of the store as Ann walks in.

"I'm sorry, Fräulein," Herr Lederer says, "but we are closed today. Perhaps next week." Before Ann can respond, he recognizes her. "Anna! You are back?" He approaches her, opening his arms.

"Cybelle's things," Ann begins, indicating Cybelle's suitcase, the lighter of the two she carries.

"Yes?"

"I've nowhere else to take it."

"Yes?" Herr Lederer repeats. He does not comprehend, but he has already accepted the suitcase from Ann.

"She died, you know," Ann says. "But, of course, how could you?"

"Ah!" murmurs Herr Lederer. "How sad." And then, "How inevitable." He puts the suitcase down and turns to look at Ilse, who stares at her fingernails. When finally she looks up, she pronounces, "All for the best, I'm certain."

"Why haven't you fired her yet?" Ann demands.

"Also for the best," Ilse says.

"If she stays on, I've been told," Lederer offers, "they'll allow me to keep the doors open . . ."

"So he thinks," Ilse interrupts, not even bothering to whisper. She places a hand on the diminutive man's shoulder. "The fact is, he won't be able to hang on, and then it will finally be mine."

Not far from Lederer's, Ann passes the gallery of an art dealer named Rottkraut, well known for his shrewd business dealings. It is usually a sedate place, but today a line has formed outside. A sign in the window proclaims, "Jews! Excellent Prices Paid for Art." Those in the line carry paintings, pieces of sculpture, antique silver tea services. There is little talk as people wait their turn. Occasionally, someone emerges from the gallery, embittered and furious.

"Anna!" she hears. She turns to see Herr Hartmann standing in the line, a large painting under each arm. Having called to her, he now seems embarrassed to have drawn attention to himself, and moves so that he is partially hidden behind a large woman holding a gilded bird cage. Ann joins him in line. "I'd embrace you, but . . ." and he indicates the two paintings.

Ann leans to let him kiss her cheek, then kisses his forehead. "It's so good to see you," she tells him.

"So, you *have* returned," Herr Hartmann says, "just as Peter expected." He lowers his voice. "You know about Jacobi, of course?"

"Yes," though Ann is certain there is more to know.

"Jacobi was right. We were foolish, and now . . ." He stops. The line ahead of them moves. A pair of soldiers walks by. The one with the truncheon pokes a few of those standing in line in the ribs. "Don't block the way," he commands. "People must pass."

"In two weeks Peter leaves for America," Herr Hartmann says quietly so that the others in line can't hear. "It is all arranged. Visas for him . . . and for you. Only yesterday he wired London to tell you," he begins, "and already you're here." He taps his brow at the marvel of it.

"A visa for me?" Ann cannot believe that anyone could be so tenacious, so certain as Peter. Never once in her brief letters to him did she give him any indication that she would return.

"Yes," Herr Hartmann continues, "he is an extraordinary young man, actually. I didn't think he had the aptitude to become a doctor, really, but he proved me wrong. Though all they let him do now is work in a small clinic an hour from the city. And about you, well, he never had any doubt. How do you explain?"

"But I didn't come back to leave with him," Ann insists.

"No? Why then?" Herr Hartmann is incredulous. "Why would anyone . . ."

"I've come to be with my mother," Ann proclaims, thinking it now the only reason anyone could possibly believe—the only reason that she herself can believe.

But Herr Hartmann has become too pragmatic for sentiment. "At this point, that is far, far too great a risk," he says. He has propped one of the paintings against the side of the building housing the gallery, and holds Ann's elbow tight. "Your mama is every day at the Gestapo headquarters begging for Jacobi's release. No one understands why they haven't taken her as well, although there is conjecture. She is, after all, a very handsome woman. But when they finally do take her, for whatever reason, they'll take your grandmother, you, anyone, be assured."

Angry at herself now, at her foolish decision to return, Ann repeats, "I haven't come back to leave with Peter. No."

"Come by tonight," Herr Hartmann insists, as if part of a conspiracy that stationed him at Rottkraut's just as Ann walked past. He is now the next in line to enter the gallery. "Tonight," he urges, "we'll expect you." A woman holds open the door as he disappears into the building, carrying his paintings.

At the Café Dolder, no one seems to recall Papa, not even the waiter who was so rude to her the day she left for England. How long has she been gone? Only seven months. That so much has changed seems impossible.

Not far from the Skodagasse are three men and two women on their hands and knees, scrubbing the cobbled streets with brushes. The men are dressed in dark suits, their hats resting in a doorway. The women are also well dressed, one in dark green, the other in blue. They are all middle-aged and each wears a yellow armband. They work without speaking.

As Ann approaches, three soldiers emerge from a nearby coffeehouse. Two are younger than she. A third, their obvious superior, is in his late thirties. Like the soldiers on the train, they wear armbands with swastikas. At a distance, Ann tries to make out their features, and surprisingly, they all have pleasant faces, friendly even.

The man on his hands and knees closest to Ann looks up for a moment, sees Ann and, with his scrub brush, points to the horizon. "Get away," he whispers. But there is something so curious and outrageous about the whole scene—the small, old street, the amiable-looking soldiers, the occasional bird alighting to observe—that Ann stands her ground.

"Fräulein, does what you see interest you?" It is one of the younger soldiers. Smiling, he approaches her slowly, his rifle hanging from its shoulder strap.

"You've just returned from a journey, I see," the other younger soldier says. He indicates her suitcase. "Or perhaps you are leaving?"

"Passport, please," the older soldier says. Ann reaches into her purse for her passport, but before she can produce it the officer turns his attention to those scrubbing. "Who told you to stop your work?" he demands.

One of the younger soldiers kicks the man who warned Ann.

"Alas," the other young soldier says, "we have no more brushes." He guides Ann by the elbow to where the other two stand. "You'll have to come back tomorrow."

"Clearly, this one has other talents useful to the Reich," the officer says.

"Clearly." They all laugh.

"Who then?" questions the officer. "Who then will be given the chore?" The two young ones engage in a mock argument, as it dawns on Ann what they intend.

"Don't worry," the older one says to her confidentially, "neither one of them has the equipment to do much damage."

The first soldier still has hold of her, but as he argues, his grip loosens. Seizing her opportunity, Ann pulls away from him and runs down the street with the two young soldiers in pursuit, still laughing and arguing. Rounding a corner, Ann knocks a stunned old man to the ground, feeling as she does her strength, the power of her gait. Before her is a familiar coffeehouse and she rushes for its white-curtained glass door. The next instant, however, one of the soldiers lunges at Ann's legs and she collapses on the sidewalk, knees and elbows banging sharply. One soldier holding each arm, they escort her back to where the scrubbing continues. Her knees can barely support her.

"It's time to settle the argument once and for all, Fraülein, no?" the officer says. Ann's body has never hurt in so many places. She says nothing. "Ah, you've forgotten. The argument about which one of us will have the honor of your company in our local offices."

Ann cannot imagine how she can possibly avert what is about to happen. Besides, the pain in her arms and legs is so overpowering, she can barely reason through it. Still, she tries. "I've never done it before," she says. "It will be no pleasure for you. None at all."

The three look at one another, as if stupefied. "That you should have told us earlier, Fraülein," the officer finally asserts, "for then there would have been no cause for argument." The two young ones nod in assent. "None whatsoever."

Before Ann can register the officer's meaning, he wraps his arm around her waist. She has run once already, and will not, cannot again. She thinks to scream, but does not as the man guides her to a boarded-up storefront. He opens a door half off its hinges. There are a few chairs in the room, a desk, a lamp, some newspapers scattered about and a portrait of Hitler.

"Sit down," the man commands, unslinging his machine gun and propping it against the door. Ann stares around the room, then sits in one of the chairs. As she does, the pain in her knees abates and she experiences a brief moment of relief—overriding even the fear, the disgust she feels. The next instant he is standing before her, his trousers unbuttoned. His underwear is stained, his penis a white stem.

"So?" he says, pushing her face into his crotch. Again, she

thinks to scream, but cannot summon the breath to do so. She pleads with him to let her go, but he counters each plea with what he imagines is a persuasive argument. "So?" he repeats over and over again. She feels his flesh against her chin, and finally does as he wants.

Later, on the floor, no longer with the energy or will to plead, the officer on top of her, she gazes over his shoulder at the machine gun. Surely it will fall and surely it will fire and surely she will die, but what of it, she thinks. She already feels dead.

Moments later she is back out on the street, where the men and women still scrub. No one looks at anyone else, no one looks at her. The officer, approaching the two soldiers, gazes stiffly toward the sky as he adjusts his hat.

It is true. Oma no longer talks. Nor does she listen, it seems. Or even register Ann's arrival. And Mama is nowhere to be found. So Ann goes to the Hartmanns', where, following Peter's relieved greeting, she tells him that she will marry him. But only if they can leave Vienna immediately. Now!

New York, 1938

Spring

"Mason and Hamlin," it reads in gold block letters on the open keyboard cover of Ann's newly acquired piano. It is an old, secondhand upright, black and scarred. The ivories are stained a light dusty brown, and the round stool squeaks when Ann depresses the pedals. But the instrument's tone is wonderful. Ann has removed the panel revealing the action, the hammers, the strings and the sounding board. Though the piano is no Bösendorfer, "Mr. Mason and Mr. Hamlin," as Ann refers to the piano, are extremely good, hard workers.

She and Peter found the piano through an advertisement in the *Herald Tribune*. It belonged to an elderly woman whose hands had become too arthritic to play any longer, and seeing the piano in her living room had become too difficult for her to bear. They paid fifty dollars for it, and found a piano mover for ten dollars more. The man was slight and did not appear particularly strong, but knew everything about balance and physics—he was at once a magician and a contortionist. Alone, with no tool other than a crudely carpeted dolly, otherwise bearing the weight of the piano on his back, he delivered it to their fourth-floor apartment. "I love America," Ann told him when she gave him the ten dollars, Abraham Lincoln twice.

Ann also loves their furnished Riverside Drive apartment with its tall ceilings and large rooms. On the polished wooden floors are thick rugs woven with a floral design. The furniture is simple, made, it seems, to last rather than impress or decorate. The kitchen is small, and painted a cheery yellow, with glass-fronted cabinets where Ann keeps dishes she has bought at Woolworth's and the canned goods she gets on Broadway, two blocks east. There is a small icebox with a motor and fan on top that hums much of the day. A tiny freezing compartment holds a single metal tray with ice in cubes and a container of coffee ice cream. On the kitchen table is a red-and-white-checked oilcloth cover—like Oma's cookbook, which Ann keeps on a counter next to the sink, like the tablecloths in the Italian restaurants she passes on her walks. The bedroom has two identical beds separated by a nightstand and a dark green rug which is especially soft.

From the window next to the piano, Ann can see the trees along Riverside Drive, the gentle hillocks and green expanse that runs between the boulevard and the river, the shimmering Hudson, and beyond that, the Palisades of New Jersey. On some days she can see ocean liners like the one she and Peter were married aboard on their way to America only a month before. On other days she sees pleasure boats, occasionally even a warship. She particularly enjoys watching the variously colored tugboats pushing their charges—something so small moving something so large!

Today, having practiced the Chopin polonaise she played the night of Big Carolina's party, she decides to call Nathan Pearl, the man who had whispered in her ear. "Why not?" she thinks, gazing out at the Palisades and the rickety-looking roller coaster directly across the way. She produces the man's card from her wallet, precisely where she left it that night six months earlier. Pearl's phone exchange is familiar, "Murray Hill"—she has heard it on radio advertisements—and without any thought of what she will say if he answers, she dials the number. Mr. Pearl is abroad, she learns, but will return in the fall. She leaves her name but not her number.

Later, Ann leaves the apartment and walks the width of Central Park to an area on the east side of Manhattan called Yorkville, populated largely by Germans and Austrians, and crowded with restaurants and shops offering delicacies from the "old country." It was where Peter wanted to live, until Ann found the apartment from which she could see another state. Hurrying across the undulating greensward of the park, Ann enjoys the feel of the afternoon mist moistening her cheeks. A black, horse-drawn hansom driven by a man dressed in morning coat and top hat slowly crosses her path. The man snaps his whip and the horse picks up the pace.

At a large delicatessen with a high, embossed tin ceiling, Ann eats slices of fresh rye bread with goose fat. The taste of the soft bread laced with caraway and the smooth, glistening, transparent fat spread from crust to crust is magnificent.

Sitting at a small table at a far corner of the establishment, she listens to the German being spoken, hears the name "Hitler" mentioned by those waiting at the counter and in front of the display cases. Jews also are a topic of conversation, yet when the most overbearing of the speakers sees Ann alone at her table, he turns quickly away, muting further conversation. It is Grandfather Leo's nose that marks her, Ann supposes. Even the Negro superintendent of her building has asked her if she is Jewish.

The newspapers too, left on the table by previous diners, are filled with stories about the power Hitler is amassing. President Roosevelt insists that America will not become involved.

Since arriving in New York, Ann has written to Mama and Oma a number of times—on onionskin paper that folds with a disconcerting crackle. Ann uses carbon paper to make copies of the letters so that she will have a record of what she has written. Her correspondence leaves her hands blue with ink from her leaking fountain pen, black from the carbon paper. But the feel of the writing tools is reassuring—just as the smell of New York has become—old, alive, quickly familiar—and Ann wakes up eager for each day, never certain where it will take her.

Back in the apartment, Ann assembles a simple meal of cold cuts, rolls and potato salad she brought from the delicatessen. "You shouldn't have to cook for me," Peter once told her, holding her hands to his lips, "it's time you stopped working for others." Talk like this upsets Ann, who already feels guilty about marrying Peter for reasons he will never know.

Another time, when Peter returned to the apartment before she did, she found him waiting for her on the sidewalk in front of their building. It was dark out and raining; his jacket was drenched. "Why," Ann asked, sheltering him with her umbrella, "why didn't you wait inside? In the lobby, at least?"

"I just wanted to know you were safe," he insisted. "After all, we've come such a long way. And we have such a long way to go together." Ann heard the words, assumed them to be true, but could not, cannot accept them.

Now, in the kitchen awaiting Peter's return from the hospital where he studies and works to gain his license to practice medicine, Ann pulls at the ice tray frozen solid in the icebox's freezer compartment. When she cannot dislodge the tray with her hands, she chips away at the frost surrounding it with a fork. Suddenly, the fork glances off the ice and breaks through the skin on her forearm. It's not painful, but blood flows from four small punctures. Ann goes to the sink and runs cold water over the wounds, diluting the bright red blood until it swirls pale pink down the drain.

Just then, Peter walks into the kitchen. "My God," he says, dropping a bouquet of spring flowers on the counter, "my God, what's happened?"

"Nothing," Ann insists, "I cut myself with a fork . . ."

Peter grabs her hand, looks at the punctures, then takes a dish towel and wraps it tightly around Ann's arm. "You call that 'nothing'?"

"Please," she says, pulling her arm from him, holding on to the dish towel with her other hand. "I'm all right. Okay."

"I just wanted . . ."

"I know," she says quietly, moving to the table, where supper is laid out. Most probably—if what is said about Hitler in the papers is true—Peter has already saved her life. But though she tries, she is unable to manufacture affection out of gratitude. And his solicitousness, his care, only make her feel more beholden, more resentful of him. "I know what you want," she says, "but I'm all right."

Over supper, Peter tells her of a new opportunity that will enable him to qualify for his license sooner. It will require a move to Florida, though, in July—a month from now.

"You mean leave New York?" Ann asks. She has come to feel at home here.

"We'll be back," Peter assures her, noting the alarm in her voice. "In a year. Nine months, even. Maybe"—he tries to appease her—"you could even stay in the apartment over the summer, then join me in the fall."

Later, they make love, but all Ann can think of is the pleasure of spending the summer alone in New York. Still later, when Peter is spent, lying quietly on his back beside her, his arm over her shoulder, she recalls the first time they slept together—a quiet night at sea, the moon visible over the water through the porthole in their tiny cabin. "I'm here, but you're not," Peter offered when he had withdrawn from her. Could he guess what had happened in that boarded-up storefront just a few days before? "It's just all so new," she told him. "Of course, of course," he reassured her. "I'm certain it will happen in time." He kissed her a dozen times on her cheeks, her eyelids, her nose. But all Ann could smell was the ocean and the odd metallic breath of the soldier. And all she could feel was the steady thrum from the liner *George Washington*'s propellers, the tedious swell of the Atlantic, and the blond stubble on the soldier's jaw rubbing across her face as he came inside her.

Now, however, long past midnight, she thinks again of the summer, and of being free in this safe, new place.

July 4

One evening, a few days after Peter has left for Florida, Ann sets off for Yorkville to a delicatessen that remains open all night. It is the end of a hot day, a holiday actually, the Fourth of July—of which Ann has been only vaguely aware. The second she sets foot on the street, however, it impinges on her. The air is filled with the smell of something like gunpowder, originating, Ann realizes, from the fireworks people are setting off in the park across the street. Just then a splendid display begins to crackle from a barge on the Hudson, colors bursting into the sky to form magnificent multihued flowers that bloom for an instant, then burn themselves out, too beautiful to survive.

Ann walks to the corner, then heads east. As she waits at the light along Central Park West, dozens of cars stream past her, mostly taxicabs painted yellow with a stripe of black and white checks from front fender to rear, moving past her like a continuous, undulating snake. When the light changes, the taxis' taillights dissolve into a red blur.

In the park Ann stops to watch a family with its own small cache of fireworks. At one point the young son, maybe two years old, holds what looks like a reed up over his head. His father lights it and it sparkles, emitting tiny pinpoints of illumination. The little boy's face glows in the sputtering light as he stares in wonder at the sparkler until it is spent, and he looks crestfallen. Ann has the impulse to hug the boy, assure him there will be more, more light. She does not, of course. Instead she continues through the park. A pair of mounted policemen ride along the path, reminding her of the day she, Cybelle and her parents spent at the Prater eleven years before.

There is sawdust on the floor of the delicatessen and there are tables covered with white butcher paper. Sausages are strung like necklaces from hooks in the ceiling, and meats and cheeses are stacked to form mountains, with tufts of parsley representing foliage surrounding the topography in the display cases. Two men yell across the room to a woman smoking a cigarette while bending to straighten the seam of her stockings. Two more men argue about a chess move that one of them has just made. A man and a woman sitting across the table from one another feed each other bites from an enormous sandwich, laughing loudly as they chew.

The only quiet in the place surrounds a man who sits at the end of one of the longer tables farthest from the door. His shirtsleeves are rolled up, his tie loosened. On a plate before him is a smoked pig's knuckle. Using a pocket knife, the man meticulously carves small strips from the knuckle, placing the slices on a thick piece of rye bread that he has spread with butter. From where she stands, Ann can see his face only in profile.

Still slightly overwhelmed by the noises of her first Fourth of July, she sits with her barley soup and sausage at the table next to his, at the fringe of his quiet concentration. He looks up as she touches her soup spoon to the rim of the bowl. His eyes are a pale blue like faded ink, his light brown hair considerably longer than the trim style of the day, his soft cheeks boyish and vulnerable. He is perhaps twenty-five, certainly no older. He reminds Ann of one of her schoolmates when she was twelve—also of a boy Cybelle once spent time with, and of others Ann knew in Vienna. But familiar as he seems, this man, who now dares a slight smile, is a stranger.

"Good?" she asks him in English, surprised by her boldness. She gestures with her spoon at the man's plate.

He looks down at it, jokingly trying to get the pig's knuckle to respond. "Like home," he replies, "only better."

Ann discerns an accent, not German but not quite Viennese. "Better than home?" she hears herself saying. "How can that be?"

"Because here everything is still possible, and that makes every bite delicious. Here," he offers, cutting another perfect slice from the knuckle and holding it out to Ann on the point of his knife, "taste." Ann takes the meat from the knife and chews it slowly, thoughtfully.

"You're right," she says.

"I know I'm right, but tell me your name."

"Tell me yours first," Ann counters.

"David Green," he says. But noting Ann's disbelief, he raises his hands in surrender. "All right, formerly Greenberg."

That settled, she tells him her name and then, not knowing what else to say, returns to her soup. David pulls a folded newspaper from his back pocket and makes a show of reading it. Finally he turns back to Ann and says, "Viennese?"

"Yes." Ann feels that his question and her answer have now bridged the gap between them, far more so than when she accepted the slice of meat.

He too is from Austria, from Linz, but knows something of Vienna from working there with his brother in a factory that manufactured men's shoes. David offers the names of two coffee-houses, a restaurant, and the street on which he lived. None of the names is familiar to Ann.

"How did you get here?" he asks. "You have people here?"

"A husband."

"In New York City?"

"In Florida."

"I see," he says, going back to his newspaper for a moment. "Florida?"

Ann tells him of her impending move to Florida, of Peter's medical school. After she finishes, he goes to the counter to get them both a beer. As he pours it into pilsner glasses, the copper-colored beer forms a head and spills over the side. *"Prosit!"* he says, raising his glass, the foam cascading down his hand and wrist. Ann picks up the second glass. It is ice-cold in her hand, like touching metal on a freezing day, and the white froth feels light and ephemeral like the seafoam left by waves on the shore.

Later he tells her that his brother, who immigrated a few years before, has established a leather goods business in Manhattan. "It's going to be a great success," he claims. "Believe me. Now that I'm here to help him."

"I believe you."

"No, really."

"Really, I believe you." They both laugh, so earnest is their conversation.

"Let's drink to that as well," she says. "To great success!"

Outside again, walking with David to catch his bus to Queens, Ann smells the fireworks, now blending with car exhaust, the sweet blossoms of the trees that grow along Fifth Avenue.

"I'll see you here again?" he asks, waving as he steps aboard and hands his coins to the driver.

"Maybe," says Ann, so certain of it that it frightens her.

David

Over the next few weeks, Ann and David meet at the same delicatessen a dozen times. Then one night after they have enjoyed dinner and shared a few bottles of beer, Ann suggests that tomorrow they meet at the movies instead. "Just for a change," she offers, aware of the significance of the change even as she proposes it.

For some reason, David glances at his wristwatch. "Tomorrow, early I'm supposed to . . ." Ann reaches across the table and covers the watch with her hand.

"Going to the movies has nothing to do with tomorrow morning," she says. "It has to do with tomorrow night. Besides, your business and your brother and even America will wait for you," she says, "just this once."

He sweeps his hand through his thick hair and laughs. "You think I'm all work, don't you?"

"I think that you think you are."

"Then"—he reaches down to touch her hand where it still rests on his wrist—"I think you're in for a surprise."

The next evening they meet at Times Square. Ann spots David standing under the unnaturally bright light of a theater marquee. Red chaser lights surround the name of the feature film, reflecting off every metal surface. Everything is bright, unreal— even David, who looked so familiar across from her at the delicatessen the night before. "David," she calls, and before she can even register that it has happened, he has her hand in his.

They decide to go to a comedy—in it a pair of handsome, well-to-do bachelors are involved in a deliberate mix-up of identity, with each man trying to charm the woman to whom the other has been betrothed. David continues to hold Ann's hand throughout the movie. But when the "Movietone News" chronicling "Hitler's Growing Forces" and the "Axis on the Rise" comes on between features, Ann pulls her hand away. Sometimes the newsreel features Hitler in light conversation, kissing pudgy blond babies, or joking with his confederates. Other times, he is addressing what looks like hundreds of thousands of soldiers who goose-step in perfect unison, saluting as one.

After the second movie, Ann and David go to the Automat. It is a ballroom-sized restaurant with an entire wall of small glass-faced chromium compartments behind which is the largest, most varied selection of prepared food Ann has ever seen. Walking quickly past the compartments with David, she sees roast beef and roast turkey, macaroni and cheese, spaghetti, hamburgers, frankfurters and baked beans, and—near the wall's end—dozens of wedges of cake pointing at her like purposeful little ships.

"I like it much better here than the delicatessen," David confesses after he has made his selection, something called "Yankee Pot Roast." Ann chooses the same. "It's faster, it's cleaner," he goes on, "it's more like where we are."

"Where we are?"

"Like America." He indicates the Automat's rows and rows of tables filled with hundreds of moviegoers. "As for that other business," he says, "the Germans, the Austrians, the 'old world' as they call it here, I'm tired of it. That's done."

"But you kept coming to the delicatessen . . ." Ann begins, wishing to fully share his sentiment. Yet she cannot.

"I went back because I knew, or at least I hoped, I'd see you there. Otherwise, maybe I'd go once in a month, but no more." About this he seems uncharacteristically resolute, Ann thinks, then remembers how he talks about the business.

"There's just something comfortable," Ann begins, "comforting in hearing the old language, in . . ."

"So, why did you leave, then?"

Ann blushes. She recalls searching the faces of the goose-stepping men in the newsreel for the one who took her into the ramshackle room in Vienna—and finding his likeness in every soldier she saw. "Things were not good there," she tells him.

He waits for her to continue, and when she doesn't, he asks, "And here, are things good here?" There is nothing boyish or vulnerable about him now as he leans toward her, gesturing with a teaspoon.

"Here is better, much better," she finally agrees, impressed by his fervor, by the constant ebb and flow of people in and out of the Automat, by the compartments filled with food behind David's back.

"Here *is* much better," he repeats. "And all the rest is history."

Not much later he tells her that tomorrow is another early day for him, that he must go. She is not surprised that it is his work that prompts him to leave. "I thought I was 'in for a surprise,' " she jokes.

"The surprises are all yet to come," he assures. It is past midnight, and though he insists she take a taxi, Ann refuses.

"I'm not afraid," she says to him as he boards his bus. "I'll take my chances on foot."

The next morning a letter arrives from Peter saying he has moved out of his rooming house and found a perfect place for them to live in Florida, and that she should join him as soon as possible, within the week, in any event. So timely is the letter's appearance that Ann has the irrational sense that she is being watched.

That afternoon she calls David at work to arrange a final rendezvous, though she does not tell him that this is the reason for her call. He suggests they have dinner in Yorkville, at "their" delicatessen.

"I thought you said you only went once a month."

"It's a new month," he reminds her, "August."

The night is particularly hot and humid. Men sit on benches in the park, shirts half unbuttoned, shirtsleeves rolled. They fan themselves with newspapers. Only slightly more decorous, women unbutton the top buttons of their blouses and fan themselves with their hands.

"Florida?" David asks, with the same inflection as on the night they met. In the interim, their shared knowledge of Ann's imminent departure has been tacit. Little of Peter and nothing of Florida has ever been mentioned. "Well," David goes on after Ann explains that she will leave within the week, "I wish you luck." He takes his hand from his beer glass and extends it to Ann, who does the same. In the dense August air, leavened only slightly by a nearby electric fan, their hands touch, cool and damp with the condensation from the glass. His hand is softer than Ann remembers.

"Do you mean that?" she asks. She does not withdraw her hand.

"About luck?" David seems as uncertain tonight as he was certain the night before.

"About luck, about anything," Ann says, confused about what she wants from this man, even about who he is—the industrious businessman, the spirited American who has already forgotten everything of the past and urges her to do the same, or the flustered, unsure man who now sits across from her? He takes his hand from hers, sweeps his hair from his brow, then touches his fingers to his glass, though he does not drink.

"We're both a long way from home," he says finally, "and quite frankly, I have no idea what I'm doing here with you . . . what I've *been* doing with you . . . Mrs. Hartmann."

Ann casts her eyes to the table. The beer is flat in the glass. Her food is untouched. "No idea?"

"Oh, certainly, some idea. But I should have my head examined. During the day I should be working and not thinking about whether you will be here or not, or whether we'll meet. And at night I should see other women, and not be imagining, imagining . . ." His frustration getting the better of him, he gesticulates with his hands. ". . . imagining Florida," he concludes darkly.

"And what is it that interests you, that you'd even give Florida any thought at all?"

"You're as new as I am," he says without pause.

"New?"

"To here, to possibility."

"And American women? Certainly they're newer. Newer to you, at least."

"Well," he admits sheepishly, "I've tried. But I can't quite give up everything that's familiar."

Ann smiles. She cannot imagine a more perfect answer. "You'll come and visit me then?" she asks. She writes down her new address and phone number.

"Only if there were some promise. I mean, I can't just go down to Florida . . ."

"There will be promise," Ann insists, certain of it in the abstract, but without a notion of how "promise" might play itself out.

As they walk to the bus stop, the bus approaches in the dark, humid night, slowly, as if emerging from under water. Nothing comes easily, Ann thinks. When the doors open, a young girl alights, far too young to be out alone so late. She looks cool, fresh, and full of hope as she half walks, half dances along the sidewalk. Both David and Ann watch as she disappears into the park. At that instant, David turns Ann to him, embraces her, kisses her on the cheek. She touches his face, traces her fingertips over it and kisses him on the lips. "Promise," she says.

Florida, 1938

A New Life

When Peter meets Ann's train, he is wearing short pants cut to his knees, a blue shirt with multicolored fish on it, and sandals and socks on his feet. He has on sunglasses. He looks so radically different from the way he has ever looked before, Ann feels she has taken a journey like those in one of her father's books. Florida does little to convince her otherwise. As they travel by borrowed car to the house Peter has found for them, Ann sees low-slung, pale-colored buildings with flat roofs, few taller than a single story. Palm trees pop up into the sky like parasols.

At one point the road narrows considerably and bisects a dense grove of orange trees that goes on for miles, cutting off much of the sun, the branches occasionally brushing against the passenger window. After a few moments passing through the grove, Ann feels queasy. Her hands perspire, though her forehead is cool, and air rushes through the open windows of the car. She looks over to Peter as he drives. The little light that filters through the trees creates a continuously changing pattern on his face and arms. His sunglasses are off and he smiles. This certainly is as far from Vienna as I will ever come, Ann thinks. Just then Peter glances quickly over to her and says, "I thought you'd like the outfit." He brushes his fingers along her forearm, and to Ann's amazement his touch feels familiar—surprisingly good and safe.

Masking the view of their house from the street is a huge, comical plant that looks like a palm tree without a trunk. Enormous pale green fronds sprout directly from the ground. It is, Peter tells her, a century plant that blooms just once every hundred years. He indicates what appears to be a large sac at the end of a thick stalk emerging from the very center of the plant. *"This* year," Peter announces. "A new life."

Flanking the entranceway to the small white stucco bungalow are two flamingos serving both as decoration and as brace to a meager overhang that creates a patch of shade in front of the green-painted door. "I can't stay long," Peter says, as he opens the door into the living room and sets down Ann's suitcases. The drapes in the room are drawn and it is dark and close. When Peter opens them, Ann is astounded by the intensity of the light. Perhaps it is her imagination, but the air smells like citrus.

The house is furnished, the living room dominated by a blocky tweed sofa. A radio the size of a bureau sits off in one corner. "Even a piano," Peter says, taking Ann into a small room off the living room. Ann brushes her fingers along the keys and plays a single note, the highest "C." "Does it please you?" he asks.

"Yes," Ann says, again surprised, this time by how easily, how quickly she has let go of New York, its pleasures and its dangers. Perhaps, she thinks, I really do want things to be simple—just that and nothing more.

"To tell the truth," Peter says, "I actually bought the piano from the people who lived here before."

"I'm glad." Ann caresses his cheek, also familiar, reassuring. "You've done exactly the right thing."

He puts his arm around her waist. "Come," he says, and leads her through the rest of the house, opening curtains and blinds, turning the small, shadowed chambers into bright, hopeful places.

In the bedroom, a few moments pass before anything is said. Ann sits before the vanity and looks purposefully into the mirror, trying to locate some sense of herself. She does not usually like mirrors, because the person she sees is never the one she is expecting. When she feels certain, she looks tenuous; when she is most afraid, she looks dauntless. Now, in the overarching brightness, she looks warm and accepting—*exactly* how she feels, exactly the opposite of how she thought she would feel. Peter places his hands on her shoulders and gently kneads the muscles of her back and neck, tense from the moment she entered the orange grove.

"Feels good," she says.

"I can't stay long," he repeats, bringing Ann down with him onto the bed.

In the citrus-filled air in this incredibly bright little room, their union is sweet and pleasurable. In the final moments, Ann bends her back like an archer's bow, feeling the string pulled more and more taut, then fluttering mightily with release. When suddenly Peter withdraws from her, she is startled by his absence, and pulls him to her again, her hands on his narrow back. He pulls away gently, kissing Ann's arms as he lays them across her breasts. "Really," he says, "I can't stay long."

For that instant Ann cannot believe her good fortune. It is as if, in the minutes that have just passed, their history—all of it—has been just washed away. And in its place, a new life, after all.

Women in Deck Chairs

Most mornings Ann takes the bus to the beach, carrying with her a blanket and a folding wooden deck chair she has found on the back porch of the bungalow. The wood has been bleached near-white by the sun, and the striped canvas sling is faded. With her on the bus are other women with their deck chairs; and sometimes too with their children. At the beach, the women each claim a patch of sand some distance from one another, lay down their blankets, unfold their chairs, then light cigarettes.

The beach is where Ann writes; letters mostly, to Mama, Oma, to Herr Hartmann, reporting what little is taking place. In this new life of Ann's, there is no drama, something which makes her feel more thankful than disappointed. She has made the decision not to write to David, to forget their brief flirtation—which, as it turns out, is far easier than she expects. Indeed, she can barely remember his face, even confusing his image once with that of Cybelle's.

Occasionally, Ann writes other things. Once she attempts to construct a story around her experiences in London, beginning with Carolina's greeting, "I'm Carolina, and you're Ann," and ending with Ann's final visit to the West Indies Maids, Orderlies and Charwomen's Society. A number of other times she has tried to describe the rape, but her writing never reflects the outrage or shame she expects she should feel. Instead, the tone is flat, clinical, as if the entire experience happened to another person.

Today Ann arrives at the beach later than usual, having this morning received a letter from Mama. It is as perfunctory as the cable Mama sent Ann in London: "Moser died recently in pauper's hospital. Oma still mute. Jacobi God knows where. I toil every day for his release." Again, the letter is closed, "I love you, Mama."

Ann rereads the line about Papa, feeling the same intake of breath she did the first time she read it. Though she easily imagines Papa out of her life, she cannot imagine her proud, vain papa dead, or even dying, and certainly not in a pauper's hospital. She bites her lower lip to stave off the tears she expects, and they do not come. After a while, she folds the letter and calls Peter at the hospital to tell him what has happened. "Horrible," he says and offers to come home. But Ann tells him no, they'll talk about it later, though she cannot think what she might say.

Now, the letter and her writing implements in a striped beach bag slung over her shoulder, her deck chair and blanket in hand, Ann walks down the wooden stairs that lead to the sand. The other women are already in their chairs. The sun is past its apex and it is possible to make out the red-glowing tips of cigarettes as the women draw deeply on them, then drop their hands languorously to their sides. Children building sandcastles run into the sparkling water to fill their buckets, then scurry from the surf.

Ann has decided that today she will write about Papa, but sitting in the sun for over a half hour, she cannot find a story to tell, or even the place to begin. Finally, she just drops her pad to her lap, and lets both hands fall to the hot sand to sift the fine granules through her fingers.

After a while, somewhere between reverie and sleep, the memories finally come as photographs, imprinted onto her by the sun like darkroom images onto paper—photographs, not only of Papa raising a single quizzical eyebrow, or of his shaving ritual, or of the jokes he could tell that would make even Mama laugh, but photographs of all those Ann has left behind. Her tears are hot, coursing down her cheeks and onto her neck as she imagines breathing life back into Papa with her long-withheld kiss, unfolding the dense blanket that Oma has wrapped herself in, extracting Jacobi's whereabouts from the very soldier who raped her.

Later, Ann sits up, shading her eyes from the glare off the sand. Before her, an incoming tide washes closer to her blanket, but she knows, like wise Canute, it will not reach her. Others, positioned nearer to the encroaching waves, have moved elsewhere, leaving Ann closest to the ocean. A small, blond boy—no more than five or six—bucket and shovel in hand, approaches the water as a wave builds in the distance. He moves forward and drops his bucket into the backwash of the prior breaker as Ann watches as the no longer distant swell continues to build and as the little boy skims his bucket along the water's surface. Then, just before the huge breaker is upon him, the boy turns toward the shore—for no reason that Ann can discern, save to escape the full brunt of the enormous swell. It envelops him instantly, sweeping him up like a rag and heaving him seaward.

Ann is in the water the next moment, thrashing with her arms at the spot where she last saw the boy. When he is not where she expects him to be, she pistons her legs high to carry her farther forward until she sees him, adrift in a briefly realized harbor between the flowing and ebbing sea, face down, enveloped in froth. She pulls the boy to her and carries him to the shore. Exhausted, she drops him on her blanket where he coughs up water that flows onto his neck and chest. The boy's eyes open as he attempts to grasp what has happened. The moment before he does, the look of absolute surprise on his face is the most beautiful expression Ann has ever seen. It is gone as quickly as it appears, however, as the boy dissolves into tears, and as his mother lies down beside him, strokes his forehead, kisses his face.

So moved is Ann that she is unable to watch, and instead looks at her writing tablet lying on the blanket next to the boy. It has been soaked by the breaker, and not one word that she had written the last few days is legible.

Later, the mother, holding the boy in her arms, walks with Ann to the bus. When she asks, Ann tells the woman her name, and that she is from Vienna, a refugee. "My husband is a reporter," the woman says, "so watch the paper."

Indeed, the next day, there is a small story about Ann saving the boy from drowning, which Ann cuts out and translates, then sends both clipping and translation to Mama. Not a week passes before someone from the paper calls her, this time to do a feature article about her and Peter. It bears the headline, "The New Americans," and includes a picture of Peter in his white laboratory coat and Ann wearing a white blouse, posed before the century plant, now in full bloom.

Patients

Much has changed in the three months Ann has been in Florida. Jokingly referred to as "Freud" by his associates because of his Viennese origins and accent, Peter has taken a sudden interest in the man and in the diseases of the mind. He even grows a beard and strokes it thoughtfully when talking to patients about their physical symptoms.

"Who can say how these things happen?" he says to Ann, referring to his sudden interest in psychiatry. He sits at the vanity, amused and pleased at his reflection in the mirror as Ann trims his beard. "What begins as silliness becomes deadly earnest," Peter laughs, as he grabs the hand with which Ann holds the scissor.

"Careful!" she says.

"I've been much too careful. For much too long."

Ann kisses his cheek. "And what makes you so brave all of a sudden?"

"You, I suppose." He blushes. "Us, finally." He pulls her to his lap. "Yes?"

Ann nods. "Maybe. Maybe so."

And so it is settled. Next summer, when they return to New York, Peter will become a psychiatric resident, and will go into psychoanalysis himself as part of his training. "Who knows what I might discover?"

At first, Ann finds it difficult to reconcile this more introspective, probing incarnation of Peter with the far simpler, more direct man she assumes her husband to be. Initially, she attributes his transformation to the unexpected death of a patient he was treating—a man who had come to him complaining of a slight burning sensation in his foot. But she soon realizes that laying the motive for Peter's adoption of this new persona solely on the unfortunate patient's demise is incorrect. Peter has, indeed, changed.

But how? Is it possible, she wonders, to change your essence by growing a beard, by asking more questions? Traces of his old self remain, of course—his dogged belief in lives lived happily ever after, his trust that medicine will eventually cure every illness, the methodical manner in which he dresses, fastening his shirt so that the buttons form a perfectly straight line with the snap and zipper closure of his trousers. Nevertheless, Ann is willing to be captivated by this new fellow. And though she still doesn't love him, she becomes interested in his contradictions—and increasingly seduced by his kindness, his attentions.

One day, Ann alters her routine of cleaning house, practicing the piano, and going to the beach to write. Instead, she packs a lunch for herself and Peter and brings it to the hospital, to the small office he shares with a dozen other interns. In the office, Ann sits across from Peter on a folding chair. The bag containing their lunch is on the wooden desk between them. Peter is surprised and a bit confused by her unexpected arrival and tells her

so. "But don't be hurt," he adds quickly, "I just think it important that things be said, that they"—he taps the desk—"be put
on the table."

"Yes," she says, embarrassed by how little she has told him,
how much she withholds. "Absolutely."

"I'm always amazed we're here, together," Peter says, as the
two of them walk to the small park across from the hospital to
eat. They sit on a low stone wall that seems anomalous in this land
of sun-washed stucco. The fronds of a palm tree overhead flutter
in a slight breeze.

"Me too. Amazed," Ann repeats, knowing that Peter means
their being in Florida, while she means their being married.

"Tell me," Peter suddenly begins, then falters. "Tell me what
happened that day in Vienna? The day you came back, met my
father?"

"What makes you think anything . . ."

"Please"—he holds up a hand—"please, no need. But sometime. When we have more years, when you are more certain. Just
promise me you'll tell me then."

Ann hasn't any idea how to reply, so surprised is she by
Peter's directness, so quickly is she overtaken by the memory—
not of what happened in the room with the soldier, but of the
painful fall to the pavement that came before it.

"Promise me?"

"Yes," she finally stammers, "sometime."

A few nights later Peter returns from the hospital with news
of an exceptional coincidence. "Nathan Pearl," he announces.
"Nathan Pearl with food poisoning, traveling through Florida on
his way to New York," he says. "Can you imagine? It was just luck
that I saw him and not one of the others." Peter presents the story
as if it is a gift. He even has the man's phone number at the hotel
where he is staying. "Tell your wife to call me," he has told Peter,
"and assure her that it is not every woman I pursue."

"Well?" Peter asks. "Do you call?" He is like a boy again,
rather than a psychiatrist in training.

"I'm not sure I can," Ann says, recalling Pearl's voice, the aroma of his cigar, the promise of his words. Peter hands her the slip of paper with the phone number. That evening as Peter sleeps, she gets up and goes into the living room, turns on a small light. She holds the paper with the number up to the glowing bulb, as if to see through it for the answer she seeks. Some time later that night she decides she is not ready for Nathan Pearl, whatever his plan for her, and tells Peter so in the morning. She has not slept at all.

As always, he is understanding. "Perhaps when we return to New York. Perhaps then."

We are such adults, such a *couple,* Ann thinks, feeling comfortable with the knowledge. And early that morning when Peter kisses her good-bye, she has the impulse to tell him everything— about Vienna, about anything he wants to know—but he has no time now for talk. Maybe later.

A few minutes before noon the telephone rings. It is David.

Temperature

Having listened for the car, Ann is already at the door when David rings the bell. When she opens the door and sees him with the century plant behind him, she laughs. She is that nervous. They shake hands and she invites him in. Set off by his white linen suit, David's blue eyes seem darker, more intense than she remembers. He looks purposeful, eager for what is to happen. "So, this is Florida?" he says. The screen door slams once, twice, behind him.

Ann offers him the beer she hurriedly bought at the market after inviting him to come by. But before he can accept, she is chattering about the house, taking him from room to room. Not until she reaches the bedroom does she even realize what she is doing. Seeing her nightgown laid on her bed, she quickly closes the door, leaving the two of them standing in the small hallway.

He puts a hand on her forearm. "We can't stay here," he says. Ann wonders if he can feel her body vibrate like a harp string. "We have to go somewhere, if only to talk."

"Of course," she says, steering him back down the hallway to the living room. "We'll go to the beach." A safe place, she thinks, out in the open. She goes back to her bedroom, puts on her bathing suit and her clothes over it. When she rejoins him, he is at the piano, picking out the melody to a popular song. Before leaving the bungalow, Ann hands him Peter's deck chair and hers to carry.

"I should show you," he says as he opens the rear door of the car and slides in the chairs, "what brings me to Florida."

"Not me?" Ann jokes lamely, instantly wishing she hadn't.

"You know me better than that," David says, half serious. "Business first, then maybe some pleasure."

"I should have known."

David lifts the lid of the deep trunk to reveal three wooden trays, each holding about a dozen women's purses, made of crocodile and ostrich and seal and snake and calf. David picks one up and hands it to her. "Go ahead, touch it." The purse is snakeskin, dyed black and trimmed in gold. When Ann doesn't take it, he opens the purse to reveal its elegant silver moiré lining, the leather-edged mirror and tiny compact in their separate compartments.

"It's lovely," Ann finally says, still not touching the purse.

"Yes." David returns it to the tray. "I know it's boasting, but about these purses, I'm very proud." He hands her another, smaller purse in red kid.

It is somehow less intimidating, and Ann takes it in her hand. "Like butter," she says, running her thumbs along the leather, recalling precisely the feel of butter between her fingers when she and Oma used to bake.

"I'd give it to you, but . . ."

"Oh, no," says Ann, handing it back. "Oh, no." From the house next to hers a neighbor peers out a window. "We really should go."

In the car, Ann asks whether he made the purses himself. "Mostly," he tells her. "Not the stitching, though. My hands are too clumsy for that." He takes his hands from the steering wheel to show her. His hands look substantial, not clumsy. "Ah," Ann says.

As Ann sets up the two deck chairs, David puts on his swimsuit in a small cabana near the water. He emerges, pale, lean and somewhat muscular, with a sparse growth of hair at the center of his chest. "I'm embarrassed," he says, noting Ann's tan. He holds his arm up to hers. "Compared to you, I'm one of those chickens in the market." Ann offers him her suntan lotion, and he takes the bottle, rubbing the oil over his body until he gleams.

Finally they sit next to one another. It seems to Ann that the day is exceptionally bright, so much so that opening her eyes to take in the scene is painful. Still, she does, sees a sailboat in the distance, its creamy white sail luffing in the light breeze. And on the horizon, a dark gray ship with three funnels, moving slowly, if at all.

"What do you do here?" David asks. Ann cannot understand how he can be so calm.

"I write letters, most often."

"I don't," he says. "I used to. To the consulate, to my parents, to my relatives, but"—he brushes some sand across his legs— "but I never hear back. And you?"

"Once in a while." She tells him of Mama's last letter.

"There's nothing we can do," he concludes. "Read the papers and worry. Or make a life for ourselves." His tone reveals no hint of loss.

"Nothing," she agrees, wishing she could be as certain.

In the quiet and the heat that follow, Ann remembers a photograph she saw in school the year she met Cybelle—of two lions in the sun. The female sat sentinel-like, ears pricked, paws slightly tensed, yet delicate before her; the male rested on his side, face and mane flat on the dusty ground. David rubs some oil on the tops of his feet, then offers the bottle to her. She takes it from him simply to touch his hand.

Minutes later, David stands and, without a word, runs into the surf. Emerging from the water, the sun glinting off the droplets on his back and shoulders to form miniature rainbows, he looks sleek and magical. Before returning to the blanket he holds his arms out to the sky, then closes them about his body as if to grasp the sun. "This is the best!" he pronounces.

The water looks delicious, but Ann remains in the deck chair, feeling the sun scorch her image into the faded striped canvas sling. In the growing heat, she looks at David in the chair next to her, tries to recall Peter, but cannot. Their house, their experiences, everything that has happened between them from the day they met at Herr Hartmann's seem a dream, lost in the brilliance of the day, in the perspiration that falls hot and salty into her eyes. Is it really so unbearably hot?

After the beach, Ann and David go for a drink at a bar made to look like a tropical hut. Overhead fans create slow-moving shadows like a succession of animals on the small tables crafted of seashells and flotsam. At the far side of the room is a young couple. The woman laughs. The man leans over the table and kisses her. Could this be us, David and me? Ann dares to wonder, recalling how David showed her his hands to demonstrate how clumsy they were. In his white suit, he looks incredibly cool. When he leans to sip his drink, his chin brushes against the thick knot of his green necktie.

"What happens now?" David suddenly asks.

"Now?"

"Yes, now." He looks at his watch. "We're together for a few hours, we don't talk much, but for me it feels like it was just yesterday I saw you last out in front of the Automat."

"The delicatessen," Ann corrects, "the delicatessen was the last place . . ."

"It doesn't matter," David interrupts, then adds softly, "does it?"

Ann nods. "I'm really afraid," she finally says.

"Who isn't?" David asks. "I go into a buyer's office, I know I have what he needs, I know I have better than he has ever seen, but my voice still cracks. What can you do?"

Ann wants to smile at David's odd comparison, even at his impatience—he is at once man and boy. Instead, she looks worried, thinks about the decisions ahead. "I don't know," she says, "what can you do?"

Gradually the heat diminishes, the afternoon slips by and early evening comes, unexpectedly cool. David drives her home. She turns down his offer to walk her to the door. Instead, she runs from the car and lets herself in quickly, closing the front door behind her. Alone in the living room, she cannot recall a single thing they have said.

Not much later, Peter returns from the hospital. It is not until he is inside the house, in the room next to her, in the same proximity to her as David was only hours before, that she realizes how truly dangerous her life has suddenly become. Then Peter too touches her forearm, and she slips quickly away into the kitchen.

"I never got to the store," she says, opening the refrigerator, closing it the instant she sees the two bottles of beer.

"It's all right," Peter tells her. "We'll go out. Besides, I have to go back to the hospital tonight."

Back in the living room, Ann sits on the couch. The feel of the fabric against her hot skin is irritating. Peter touches his cool hand to her brow. "You look flushed," he says to her. "Are you not feeling well? Is there something wrong?"

The dinner out is long. Since his decision to become an analyst, Peter's questions to Ann have become incessant. "How do you feel? Why do you think you feel the way you do? Do you feel that your feelings are typical?" Why won't you leave me be? she thinks, recalling the red purse, the patterns created by the slow-moving fan.

When finally Peter goes off to the hospital and Ann is alone again in the house, she tries to sleep. Images of the day and of New York and of the boat ride across the Atlantic Ocean all blend together, devolving to flashes of colored light.

When the taxi drops her at the hotel, she does not hesitate. Nor is she surprised to see David as awake as she is when he answers her soft knock at his door. She is not embarrassed that he is in his boxer shorts, nor is she embarrassed to kneel before him and take him into her mouth as she has only one man before. But this time it is her choice, and she makes it without reservation.

"You wanted promise," she says when he is hard, then stands and takes off her clothes. "Is this what you meant?" Ann is breathless, excited, aroused, more so than ever before, she realizes.

"Better than I meant," David says. "Different." In the room, he looks far less pale than earlier, even when his body is next to hers.

"Are you disappointed?" she asks. The room is small, the door only a few feet from the bed, and when he embraces her, his arms surprisingly strong, she pushes him back and onto it. "Are you disappointed that it was so easy?"

"No, but surprised."

"And pleased?"

"And pleased."

For the three days that David remains in town, Ann lies guiltily and easily to Peter about her day's activities, the long walks she takes in the evening. In the elevator on her way to David's room, she anticipates his touch—but far more, the way he can touch her.

Once, riding in the car on a small road alongside the water, all the windows open, the wind billowing around them, he hums the sweet melody of a familiar Austrian children's song. Another time, he brings two huge inner tubes to the beach, so that he and Ann can bob far offshore together, and look back at the women in their deck chairs. And when air begins to hiss from under the red patch on Ann's tube, David props her on his, then pulls her powerfully to the shore.

"Children!" he exclaims after they make love later that afternoon. "Of course! How could we not have children? The only question is, how many?"

"Two," Ann answers after a moment, "so that neither would ever be alone." In Florida, a thousand miles from New York, thousands more from London or Vienna, Ann, without seeking it out, finally discovers what Cybelle was searching for.

Ann and David agree it is best that she not leave with him, but that she remain in Florida for a few months until he completes his cross-country sales trip and the business becomes better established. But living in the little bungalow with Peter and his constant questions about her distraction, and listening to her own incessant lies, quickly become untenable.

Then one day, with Peter not a half hour out of the house, Ann decides to leave. She is making his bed, turning the coverlet down and putting the pillow into place, when she simply reaches under the bed and pulls out her suitcases. Packing quickly, she calls a taxi, locks the front door and goes to the hospital.

Peter is speaking with another intern when he sees her, suitcases in hand, in the corridor. "I knew it," Peter declares, directing the comment as much to the other man as to Ann. "I knew it."

In his office, Peter sits back in his chair and strokes his beard. "What is it?"

"I thought you knew 'it,' " Ann says, surprised at her rancor when she thought she felt only guilt and sympathy. "I thought you knew it, just like you knew I'd be back to marry you, just like you know everything."

"Is it this place, this, this"—Peter raises his hands to encompass the room—"this Florida? Because we'll be out of here soon enough."

"No," Ann says, suddenly aware that she will miss the beach, her deck chair, her time in the sun. "No."

"Me then? I could understand," he says, more to himself than to her, "I could understand that. If it's me, you have to give me more of a chance. I could be home more, we could be together more. Just tell me what it is, what you want?"

"You're the one who wants to be the analyst. *You* tell me."

"Ah," he says, as though given a chance to make everything right if he can only come up with the right answer. "The inclination to make mistakes . . ." he begins.

"Mistakes? How can you know whether I'm making a mistake? You met me ten years ago and told your father you'd marry me. You don't dare make mistakes. There is no room in your life for indecision. You don't know the first thing about how I feel, what I want."

"And this is my fault?" Peter backs away from the desk that separates them.

"No. Mine. But it doesn't make any difference. I'm going!"

"Ann. Anna! I love you. I love you!" He pounds his fist on the desk, his face red where it is not covered by his beard.

Ann grabs her suitcases, and crosses the threshold. "Love," she declares evenly, "love is not at all what you think." She starts down the corridor.

"This is not fair," he yells after her. "I brought you here! I saved you!" Others in the corridor stare at him, a short, bearded man in a long white coat, waving his fist.

New York, 1939

The Honeymoon

Ann and David stand at the very edge of the observation point at the head of Niagara Falls. David holds Ann tightly to him, his other hand grasping the slender iron railing that traces the helter-skelter perimeter of the rocky ledge overlooking the cataract. They are both soaked from the spray. David concentrates on the flat and placid-seeming water just before it tumbles over the edge, while Ann watches an excursion boat at the base of the falls make its way toward a small rainbow that has appeared above the water's surface. Some of the passengers have cameras, others wave. When the boat is precisely at the center of the rainbow's arc, Ann pulls David even closer to her. "Look!" she yells over the roar of the falls. David glances down at the boat. "I see," he yells back, kissing her twice, and then again. "Beautiful!"

It is April, two months after Ann and David were married by a justice of the peace in a small anteroom in the New York City Hall. David's dapper, sophisticated brother, Hans, and one of Hans's women friends were witnesses. The woman was very slender and quite exotic-looking, wearing a brief dress festooned with green and black rhinestones, along with bright green high-heeled shoes and a bright green coat trimmed with a white fur collar and cuffs. "She's about to become a fashion model," Hans explained when the woman excused herself to use the powder room after the ceremony.

Leaving the building, hand in hand with David, Ann was struck by the perfection of the scene before her. The day was bright, clear, cool. A man at a kiosk at the corner sold a newspaper to a woman in a red coat. Children played tag in grass lightly dusted with snow. A tall woman in a yellow hat wheeled a baby carriage. An old man stood on the steps, tamping down the tobacco in his pipe. Just then, David stopped to take it all in. "Haven't we seen this movie before?" he joked. He squeezed Ann's hand and she could feel his ring, the wedding band that matched her own.

Later that evening, Hans took them all to an elegant supper club where, at one point, he commandeered a telephone to make a call from their table. Toward the end of the meal, a woman with a large camera came by and took their picture. The photograph is mounted in a leather-edged frame that sits on an end table in Ann and David's apartment. Hans's expression is expansive, his arms outstretched behind Ann and his date. The exotic woman looks bored and slightly worried; David seems to be peering at something behind the photographer; and Ann is dazzled by the flash.

Ann and David leave Niagara Falls early Sunday to arrive back in New York City for a lunch meeting that Hans has arranged with an important buyer from out of town. The used Chevrolet David recently bought has overheated a number of times on the trip, and now, in traffic only a few blocks from their apartment, the car has become balky. David notes the steam escaping from beneath the hood, then glances at his watch. Up ahead, the light changes to green, but the cars in front of them remain at a standstill. Ann wishes she could do something to speed the traffic, to put him at ease as he was a few hours before.

"I don't understand," David says, exasperated, "Sunday morning, who's on the road?" Just then, a pair of policemen walk by, chatting amiably. "What's going on?" David yells out the window.

"Easter," one of the policemen says. "Parade," adds the other.

"Easter parade," David announces grimly back to Ann. Though it is warm in the car, she is pressed as tightly against him as she was on the observation point.

"You go," she offers, suddenly realizing the simple solution. "I'll stay with the car." He's given her several driving lessons after buying the Chevrolet.

"Really?" David smiles as if unable to believe his good fortune. "On our honeymoon?"

"That was yesterday," Ann laughs. "Really." She turns the ignition off and reaches across David's lap to open the driver's door. "Go!"

Halfway out the door, he leans back in and gives her a quick kiss. "You're the best!" he says, and is off.

It is nearly an hour before the traffic clears, plenty of time for the car to cool down. Stopped for a red light on Fifty-fifth Street, Ann can see down Fifth Avenue. The broad thoroughfare is still closed to traffic, and families dressed in their Easter finery stroll from curb to curb, kicking up the confetti which covers the street like huge, pastel snowflakes. Some of the flakes land on the Chevrolet's hood and windshield, and when Ann reaches out the wing window to brush them away, the confetti clings to her hand.

"Beautiful parade," someone walking by remarks.

"It's the most beautiful parade I've ever seen," Ann replies, the small multicolored flakes now adrift in the car like those in the clear glass ball with the winter scene which Ann suddenly recalls from a time even before Papa left.

The following Sunday, Ann and David walk the nearly sixty blocks to Washington Square, where David is challenged to a game of chess by an old blind man who makes a show of playing and beating a half dozen opponents on a half dozen boards simultaneously. On another Sunday in late May, they go to Jones Beach, Ann fixing their new beach umbrella in the sand, like

Columbus planting the flag of Spain. And in June, they spend a Saturday driving from farm to farm in New Jersey, eating fresh Italian bread and tomatoes that are deep red, ripe and enormous.

The Woman Upstairs

The woman in the apartment upstairs from Ann and David's, Erna Bamberger, was once an opera singer, and by her own admission never quite good enough for a starring role. Though she has retired, she occasionally still sings in the opera chorus. One day, she shows Ann a picture of herself as a Valkyrie in *The Ring of the Nibelung*. It hardly looks like Erna, who is now at least sixty—though she claims no more than fifty—and whose slender arms clearly reveal veins, what is left of muscle and bone. Erna's face, while disproportionately fuller now—retaining a hint of the soft-cheeked handmaiden to Odin—is far more complex, less, less . . . " 'Innocent,' is the word you're looking for," Erna says, as she takes the picture from Ann. She is originally from Munich, having emigrated to America before the First World War.

They are sitting in her apartment, filled with memorabilia from her singing career. Everywhere are inscribed photographs of famous tenors dressed as clowns and rogues and kings, caught mid-note, one open hand extended; of huge divas, playing the coquette in dresses the size of tents; of groups of singers, musicians and stagehands sitting around a table, the singers in their street clothes yet still with traces of makeup that, not hours before, transformed them into Egyptian slaves. In an umbrella stand near Erna's door is an array of spears, scepters and staffs. On the coffee table before them is a jewel-encrusted crown, and next to that is what looks like a large vase filled with carrots and celery stalks. Erna is a vegetarian.

"An odd word, 'innocent,' " Erna continues, "because of its opposite: 'guilty.' Lose your innocence, in other words, and what are you left with?" Erna gestures vaguely in the direction of her photographs with a celery stalk. "So it is with language," she concludes. She chews the celery on the right side of her mouth where her teeth are better, lending her face a slightly disquieting lopsidedness.

"And me," Ann asks, "which do I look? Innocent or guilty?" She is certain she looks guilty—for leaving Vienna when she might still have been able to help Mama, for abandoning Peter, for whatever she didn't do for Cybelle, for not finding the breath at least to scream, and then later on the floor, for not resisting.

"Hah!" Erna exclaims. "Your face is still so innocent, it does not even reveal how it might someday change. With most your age you can at least see that, but with you there is not even a hint."

Erna shambles into the kitchen, identical to Ann and David's, and returns with an enormous bowl of fruit. Grapes drape down its side, and the leaves of a pineapple serve as its crown. It looks like a prop from the opera. A few small flies cluster around the bowl when Erna sets it down on the table.

"I've bought too much, as always," Erna says, "so you must eat it with me." She has a small paring knife which she uses to cut into the pineapple, plucking a piece from it like a cork from a bottle, then eating it down to the rind. She winks.

"So tell me, my friend from 4C, what do you think makes you less than innocent?"

"Have I said I was?"

"Not in so many words." She hands Ann an apple, first breathing on it, then polishing it on the brown velvet collar of her dress.

For an instant they both look at the apple and laugh. Then, as if reading Ann's mind, Erna says, "Understand, you cannot be made less innocent by something that has been done to you. That loss must come from your own heart." Erna stops, touches her heart with her slender hand, then suddenly begins again, "A woman loved me once, and I loved her. More than I would ever dare tell her. And yet, I set out to hurt her, I cannot tell you why. And I did, and I changed who I was because I never wanted it—to love someone like I did her—to happen to me again. And it hasn't, and now I am . . ." She reaches into the air for a number. ". . . however old I am. Do you understand?"

There is an element missing in this too easily told story, Ann thinks, though she cannot quite determine what. Nevertheless, not wanting to appear foolish, she says she understands.

"So then, next topic of conversation," Erna insists.

"Nathan Pearl," Ann suggests, curious about the man and aware that Erna knows him.

"He has a reputation."

"A reputation for what?"

Erna takes a photograph from the wall. It is one of those of a group, post-performance. "See, here." She points to a woman who may be herself. "This is me, and *this* is Pearl."

"And . . . ?"

"And he may disappoint you, and he may not. Just keep in mind that in the small world of performers and pretenders with enormous needs, everyone knows everyone and everything. And if he whispered in your ear, there is already someone besides you and he who knows what he said. Now"—Erna pats Ann's arm— "since you didn't understand my first cryptic confession, do you understand this?"

Ann nods as she blushes, not certain if it is because Erna seems to see her so clearly, or because of the impossible coincidence that Erna has recently spoken to Pearl, and that he indeed has told her what he whispered in Ann's ear.

Encore

When Ann tells Erna she needs a part-time job to help pay the bills, Erna knows just who to call. So now every weekday afternoon—following a morning of housework and practice— Ann walks the few blocks from the apartment to the Steinway & Sons showroom, where she demonstrates and sells pianos.

"I'm so tired of these Juilliard types," Erna's friend, Mr. Steinweg, the showroom manager, confided to Ann the day she came in for her interview. He was a diminutive man in his late sixties, bald, with exceptionally large hands and tufts of gray hair growing out of his ears. "They're all just passing through. No desire at all to build a career." He looked Ann up and down after he had taken her through the piano demonstration she would be required to give. "How about you?" Steinweg arched his back and rubbed an imaginary distended belly. "Any buns in the oven?"

The small man mimicking a pregnant woman in this elegant establishment seemed so contradictory that Ann was not even embarrassed or offended. "Not for quite a while," she assured Steinweg, recalling the decision she and David had made to wait to have children until the business was on its feet.

Three others work with Ann at Steinway: Victor Vulturski, a rangy, imperious ghoul of a man who glides in oversized black shoes across the showroom floor without making a sound; Arabella, a large, voluble woman with a double chin and small hands and pudgy fingers, who claims she can span as many notes as Rubinstein; and Herbie Bixby, a former Juilliard piano student down on his luck who, having heard of Steinweg's dislike for his kind, told him he was self-taught, never had a lesson in his life. About Steinweg, Herbie tells Ann that he is a bastard son of old Steinway himself—the missing son of "& Sons." But Erna assures Ann that this is not the case. "If he's a Steinway," she says, "then I'm a Romanov."

There is no conversation to be had with Victor or Arabella. When the showroom is empty of customers, Victor either retreats to the back room, pulls on his wire-rimmed glasses and reads a Polish newspaper, or sits as still and straight-backed as a mannequin at one of the pianos in the showroom window. And when, on her third day at work, Ann asks Arabella her last name, she sneers at Ann as Mama might have at the Philistines who didn't understand her modern dance.

"Just 'Arabella,' " Herbie says to Ann. "You know, I made the same mistake, but the babe claims to be from some no-last-name tribe of Gypsies, if you can imagine it." Herbie is Ann's age, twenty-two, and has a maniacal laugh that is so infectious that Ann often finds herself laughing along with him.

After one such outburst, Herbie accuses her of not taking life in the Steinway & Sons showroom seriously enough. "It's not me," Ann insists.

"Oh yeah? Who *is* it then?"

"It's me imitating you."

"Wrong. I think it's you having a good time," he counters.

"Maybe so," Ann says, "maybe so."

When customers do come into the showroom, however, all quickly becomes solemn and businesslike. Victor's sixth sense brings him from the back room and Arabella moves toward the door, her arm extended like a diva about to deliver a tragic finale.

"There goes the Vulture and Lady No-name," Herbie says, launching into a giggle, then, like a mime, passing his hand across his face and wiping on a serious expression. Steinweg stays at the rear of the showroom, and because Ann is the most junior of the salespeople, he has requested that she remain there with him. "Wait and watch," he instructs. "You've been hired to handle the overflow."

One day, Steinweg learns from upper management that Rubinstein himself is coming in to select a piano for a friend. When he hears the news, Victor becomes noticeably animated, leaning to whisper again and again in Steinweg's ear. Arabella, in a rare show of domesticity, dusts every piano on the floor. Herbie is unfazed, and Ann is simply eager to see what the man looks like. Steinweg decrees that Victor will accompany Rubinstein from piano to piano to answer any questions he might have, but that only he, Steinweg, will speak to the maestro about money.

Rubinstein is to arrive at three o'clock, but does not. Other customers come and go. Victor even sells a grand piano to an elderly woman in a wheelchair who has asked specifically for him, but he seems distracted as he writes out the delivery instructions.

"He's scared to death Gypsy will get Artur, and that she'll make him show her how many notes he can span," Herbie observes, then starts in on his laugh.

"Don't!" Ann commands, but it is too late. Herbie's high-pitched cackle is already caroming around the showroom, and Ann, helpless in its wake, has no choice but to join him.

Just then, Ann hears, ". . . and who, Victor, is this young lady?" She turns to see Rubinstein, not ten feet from her. He is shorter than she expects—not much taller than her five and a half

feet—and his narrow face, small, sharp eyes and large nose remind Ann of a fox. Rubinstein smiles. Behind him is his entou-
rage of three men and a woman, along with Victor, who glares
eagerly over the maestro's shoulder. "The young lady's name,
Victor?" Rubinstein asks again. When it is clear to Rubinstein
that Victor doesn't know Ann's name, she provides it for him.

"And what, pray tell, Ann," Rubinstein continues, "what was
so amusing?"

Ann tries to remember, but can't. Instead she reaches out to
shake Rubinstein's hand. It is much like Arabella's—small, with
short fingers. To Ann's surprise—though it is well known that
Rubinstein is a flirt—he raises her hand to his lips and kisses it.

"Victor," Rubinstein demands playfully, though it is obvious
that he expects little help from Victor, "what more can you tell
me of this woman? American?" He takes a short, theatrical step
backwards and studies Ann for a moment. "Absolutely no," he
declares. "Married?" He still has her hand in his and rubs his
thumb across Ann's wedding ring. "Absolutely yes. But"—he
turns to a craggy-looking man behind him in a severe black
suit—"it's the eyes more than the ring that give it away, don't you
agree?" The man laughs and is soon joined by the others, Victor
included. "And talent?" Rubinstein asks. It is suddenly completely still in the showroom. Ann spots Herbie on the periphery,
Steinweg looking worried. "Now there's a secret that can only be
revealed in one way."

"Come," he says to Ann. "My friend here"—he indicates the
man in the black suit—"wants to purchase a piano for his mistress. More a woman's piano than a man's, in other words. So it
would be pointless for me . . ." He stops. "Come."

Ann remembers being led to the piano at Big Carolina's party
to play for Nathan Pearl. Then, she hadn't played for years, but
now, a year and much practice later, she is more certain of her
skill. Steinweg gestures to the largest of the grand pianos on the
floor. It is black, and so highly polished that Ann can see her
reflection as she purposefully approaches it.

"Do you require any music?" Rubinstein asks. Ann shakes her
head.

"Well, then . . ."

At the conclusion of the Chopin ballade, Rubinstein touches his hand to his heart. "There is a man," he begins, even as the last chord resonates through the room, "there is a man with whom you simply must speak."

Last Chance

Erna accompanies Ann to Nathan Pearl's Upper East Side office. They go by cab, though there is little money for such extravagance. But Erna insists, producing a five-dollar bill from her large purse. "He'll smell the subway on you," Erna says of Pearl, "and right away, he'll think he can own you, control you."

"But isn't that what I want from him? Don't I want him to take over a part of my life?" Now that Ann is finally to do this, she wants to do it right.

Erna looks surprised. "I thought you knew. You with your crazy mama. There is no such thing as a part of your life. It's either yours completely, or someone else's."

In the cab, Ann takes out her compact and studies her face in the mirror, then dabs on some powder. Erna pats Ann's leg. "I know you think this is your last chance, but at twenty-two, take my word, you have many more." Ann returns the compact to her purse. Erna is right about many things, but wrong about this, Ann is certain. She can give part of her life to Pearl, just as she has given part of it to David. And it *is* her last chance.

Pearl's office is actually a handsome Fifth Avenue penthouse across from the Metropolitan Museum of Art. Dominating the room where Ann, Erna and Pearl sit on a small sofa are two ebony grand pianos, facing each other so that the person playing one can peer over the highly buffed lids at the person playing the other.

"There's no time to lose," Pearl insists, after tea is brought to them by a black woman with an accent like Carolina's. There is no table, so delicate cups and saucers are balanced on laps, and any movement results in the clatter of china. "I say 'no time to lose' because every day adds a new layer of experience, and if the foundation isn't solid and broad, after a while it cannot sustain your growth or whatever you call it, and you end up trying to re-create what you've once done, or even sadder, playing Strauss waltzes by ear."

Exactly, Ann thinks, and looks quickly at Erna. She does not, however, seem to have heard what Pearl has just said. Instead, Erna peers at his profile as if trying to find something she has lost. It is suddenly clear to Ann why Erna suggested she accompany her, why Erna made a point of telling her that Pearl's wife had left him, why they took a cab instead of the subway. Ann smiles. Where once she was distressed by what she didn't know, Ann now loves the intricacies that unfold before her.

"Let's begin, then," Pearl pronounces. He stands and calls to another room. From the same doorway through which the maid brought them their tea emerges a young, tall, slender man with a boyish cluster of freckles on either cheek, set off by a sharp, regal nose and close-set, raven-black eyes. He wears a white silk shirt with loose sleeves that balloon to his wrists. "Jorge," Pearl offers by way of introduction as the man takes his seat at one of the pianos.

"We'll start with the Polonaise in A-flat major, since I am certain that is a piece she knows," Pearl says to Jorge, then indicates the second piano to Ann. "No time to lose," he repeats. Ann rises, puts her cup down on the floor and approaches the bench.

Before she is even seated, Pearl says, "Now, Jorge, the first eight bars." He plays them, but less martially than Ann likes. "Now you, Ann," Pearl says, "exactly the same way." When she does, he smiles. "And that is how you will relearn the Chopin."

"And the interpretation?"

"Jorge's," Pearl says. "It's romantic. It's what they like in this country. Besides, it is more or less just as your friend Artur plays it"—Pearl puts his hand to his heart in imitation of Rubinstein—"and that should be good enough. At least for the time being."

Ann looks at Pearl questioningly. This is certainly not what she expected. "I know, I know," he says. "You thought I was that nice, encouraging fellow you met in London. That was merely a ruse to get you here, playing again. But now it is time to go to work. Jorge!" Jorge plays the next eight bars; then, like a conductor, Pearl points to her and she plays the same eight bars.

Later, after the lesson is over and Jorge is out of the room, Pearl says, "Who knows, maybe after a year or two of this, at a cost we will determine, we may have something, the two of us, and you may be a pianist, after all. We will see."

On the subway, Erna, usually so talkative, says little, jostling gently against Ann as the train clatters over the tracks and the light in the car flickers on and off, on and off. Abstracted, Ann looks down at her hands, recalling only the pleasant feel of her warm fingers on the cool white keys.

New York, 1941

Confidence

"It is a matter of confidence," Pearl says to Ann, greeting her at the door of his studio one January day after she has worked with Jorge a little more than a year-and-a-half. She is surprised to see Pearl; he is rarely there. Usually it is Jorge who greets her. "The talent," Pearl goes on, "the skill—one of which you have, the other of which you are gaining—make little difference unless you feel certain you own the piece." She follows him into the room with the two grand pianos, cradling her music with both arms across her chest like a schoolgirl.

"I believe that," she says, placing the music on the piano she usually plays, "and I believe I'm becoming more confident."

At Pearl's request, she plays the first movement of the Beethoven sonata she and Jorge have been working on. Having learned each phrase by rote, she has no need for music, no need for any thought at all, and she concerns herself only with the sound and the feelings it evokes—her own interpretation, after all.

When she is finished, Pearl is at her side. "Yes, I can see that the confidence is there—growing, in any event, at least. Growing . . ." he repeats.

"Where's Jorge?"

"No longer with us." Pearl looks solemnly at the second piano. "Not to worry, however," he goes on, brightening. "There are many Jorges. This city is filled with excellent technicians, excellent. They come . . . and they go." Pearl rearranges the music in front of Ann. While seemingly trying to decide between Debussy and Chopin preludes—opening one book first and then the other—he continues, ". . . but here's another thought, before it flees my mind." He looks at Ann for a moment, then back at the music.

"Yes?"

"This is not a requirement," he says. "And whatever the outcome, it will not affect our professional relationship in any way—in no way, this I promise . . ."

Ann knows what is coming, having sensed it really from the moment when Pearl whispered into her ear at Big Carolina's party, though at the time she could never have articulated it. "You're right," she says, "it is a matter of confidence, and I am confident"—she takes the book of Debussy from his hand and opens it—"that your proposal is not really even what you want." She begins to play, then stops. "I'm sorry," she says, embarrassed that maybe she has misconstrued his intent, after all. "I'm not really that confident."

"No," Pearl says, "you aren't. But you are right about my offer—an obligation, really, to my ego. A young woman, alone in my studio." He sits at the second piano. "There was a time, twenty years ago, when I might have insisted, but now it's just something done out of habit, I suppose. I hope you won't think . . ." He does not finish, instead plays a Debussy prelude himself. It is short, lovely, perfect. "There," he says, rising. "Do you think you can do it precisely like that?"

"You know I can," she says. And for the next months, she works only with Pearl, though she soon learns that his two other protégés take lessons from Jorge's replacement.

One day in late spring, at the beginning of a lesson, Pearl tells Ann that her introduction to the world is not too far off. "A year, perhaps two." It surprises her, for Pearl usually prefers to deal only with the present, with the piece they are currently working on, and rarely looks ahead to the next.

"Do you mean my 'debut'?"

"Call it what you like," Pearl says, dismissing any more talk with a wave of his hand.

But Ann cannot get the notion of her professional debut out of her head. And while the words "introduction to the world" strike her as a bit pompous when Pearl first utters them, by the time her lesson is over, she is totally captivated by the idea. Indeed, except for her desire for David—that first day in Florida, when he opened the trunk of his car to show her his purses—she cannot recall ever wanting anything more.

Later that evening, when she and David are in bed and she is about to tell him of the debut, he suddenly asks, "Tell me, how good does that old man make you feel?"

"He's not old," Ann says.

"Even worse," David jokes, "but how good?"

"Very, very good," Ann confesses.

"As good as I can?" He brushes his fingers lightly over her breasts. He has been moody lately—distant, actually—and Ann has assumed it has to do with business, with Hans's insistence that they expand, take their considerable profits and move to larger quarters. Now, for the first time, Ann considers that David's extended silences, his preoccupation on their Sunday outings, has something to do with her. "Really, tell me," David repeats, propping himself on an elbow, "does he make you feel as good as I can?"

"Sometimes," Ann answers warily, "but in a different way, of course."

"Of course."

"You're not jealous . . ."

"No, no," David says. "No. I love it that you play the piano, really. And I even love it that an ancient, old man, an old grandfatherly fellow can make you so happy. Really."

Ann pulls his head to her breast. "I don't know whether you're joking or not."

"I'm serious." He nuzzles her. "But just remember, I'm only

a leather worker, a businessman. What I know, I know well, but I can only understand so much."

To the Future

It is early fall—though still exceptionally hot—the day that Hans is coming to the apartment to celebrate the opening of the new factory on Canal Street, near the waterfront. Ann and David sit at the table in the kitchen, where a large fan in the corner provides the only relief from the heat. Ann is as nervous as David about the large loan the brothers have taken for the factory rather than using their profits—Hans's idea—and tries to engage David in conversation. As is lately more and more the case, he is reluctant, says little.

"What makes him so much more certain about this loan business than you?" she asks.

"I'm certain about making purses," David says, "Hans is certain about making money." Wistfully he adds, "I thought I was an American, but it turns out I'm only an American's kid brother."

"Why not then pay off our part of the loan with what we have . . ."

"Please," David insists, wiping perspiration from his upper lip with a handkerchief, "no more talk, no more suggestions. It's too damn hot."

It is so quiet in the apartment that when Erna arrives she assumes no one is there and lets herself in with the key Ann has given her. She rarely rings the bell, in any event, claiming that bells make bad neighbors. Bringing a bowl of fruit into the kitchen to rinse it, she is surprised to see Ann and David. "What kind of celebration is this?"

David reaches out to touch Erna's forearm. "It's been a quiet day."

"True?" Erna turns to Ann.

"Actually, I have plenty to talk about." Ann looks across the table to David.

"Please," he says again.

Erna transfers deep purple plums and fat yellow peaches ablush with red from the bowl to a colander and runs water over them. "For some," she declares, "big occasions leave them speechless, for others . . ."

Just then the doorbell rings. Ann gets up to answer it. Hans wanted them all to go to Sardi's to celebrate, but Ann insisted the celebration take place in the apartment. For the occasion she has made Yankee Pot Roast, modifying a recipe from the old red-and-white-checked cookbook. When Ann opens the door, Hans is in the middle of the hall, arms extended like a crooner, a bottle of champagne in each hand.

"Room service," he announces, crossing the threshold. On this hot, hot day, he looks cool in his beige double-breasted suit and his thick blue silk tie with a red-and-gold diamond pattern. In the new factory, it has been decided that David will oversee the workers and the machines, and that Hans will run the swank outer office, seeing to the needs of the customers and handling the books. The arrangement seems fine with David, but Ann does not trust Hans, and has urged David to at least take some interest in Hans's activities. David says he will, but Ann knows that even with all David's confidence in his work, as Hans's younger brother, he dares not.

"Everyone in the living room," Hans commands. Ann takes off her blue apron, smooths her flowered dress, and brings four glasses from the drainboard. They are not champagne glasses, but regular, thick tumblers, water glasses. Erna sets the fruit bowl down on the coffee table, plums and peaches speckled with drops of water, heavy and clinging. David is the last to leave the kitchen.

Hans clears his throat dramatically as the cork pops and the champagne gushes from the bottle into the four glasses. When everyone has a full glass in hand, Ann reaches out to touch David's free arm.

"To the future," Hans pronounces. David smiles a shy smile. His face is hopeful, open, untarnished. "To the future," David repeats, followed by Ann and Erna in perfect unison, as if rehearsed.

"You bet your boots," Hans says. The glasses clink together and they drink the champagne down.

The New Factory

One morning, after David leaves for work, Ann calls in sick to Steinway and visits the new factory for the first time. When she phones to tell David she is coming, he assures her she'll be bored; she insists she won't be, and besides, she's almost never seen him at work.

Arriving early, Ann walks along the nearby waterfront to the huge piers of the Cunard White Star Line. Standing where the esplanade meets one of the piers, she gazes down twenty feet into the green, brackish water. Droplets of oil create small, slick circles that glint in the sun. A single shoe floats by. Curious to see more, Ann moves to the very edge of the pier, stepping out onto the massive, weather-beaten wooden cross-member that stretches between two pilings. For a moment, she remembers how lonely she was as a child on the Skodagasse. Then, off in the distance, in the yellow, slightly diffuse light, she sees a liner on its way to sea, white hull, blue decks, three blue-and-white stacks emitting identical slender streams of smoke. Now, all that is left of Vienna for her are the tall, thin headlines in the *New York Times*, the narrow columns that she follows from the front page into the heart of the paper. Ann searches for Jacobi's name, but it never appears.

A few minutes later she and David are in the elevator going up to the factory on the fifth floor. The elevator is a crate-like contraption with wooden slats for sides exposing greasy cables and pulleys. Sixty feet above is a skylight made of translucent glass reinforced with wire mesh. A dull light filters through, illuminating the shaft and throwing shadows of the moving cables across David's face like scars. "Say something," she commands quietly, but David can't hear above the clatter of the elevator. He docks the car on the top floor, a few inches below the landing. "Watch your step," he says, taking hold of her hand.

In the office, Hans is on the phone, his double-breasted suitcoat open, his legs up on the desk. Clamped between his teeth as he talks is a cigarette in a slender tortoiseshell holder. When he sees Ann, he pulls his feet from the desk, buttons his coat and waves. David opens the steel door to the factory floor.

The factory is not large—it employs about sixty workers—though in David's description of it to Ann, it is a gigantic enterprise. Large windows run along three walls, and near the tall ceiling is a system of motor-driven belts, gears and pulleys connected to various machines that create a significant racket.

Expecting the same sweet, slightly corrupt aroma of leather she smelled when David opened the trunk of his car in Florida, Ann instead smells something akin to gasoline, comforting yet astringent. "Rubber cement," David tells her. "It holds everything together." Picking up a gallon can of it, he paints a small amount on her palm, blows on it until it dries, then rubs it off with his own hands, forming tiny black balls that fall to the floor. Ann holds her palm to her nose. The smell remains, though faint.

In the far corner of the factory, four men work at stamping machines, iron leviathans with huge curved armatures like elephants' haunches. Elsewhere, a crew of women with black hair held in check by floral bandannas work with brushes and cans of rubber cement, gluing leather to leather and leather to silk, then passing the items to shirtsleeved men at large black sewing machines. A pretty young woman runs a machine that punches holes and a wily-looking man with a small goatee sits at another machine which, fed by a continuous paper-thin roll of gold, embosses the completed purse or belt with the name of Hans's and David's company: "Green Brothers."

Soon the noise of the machines, the smell of the rubber cement make Ann dizzy, so she sits down on a stool not far from the door leading back to the office. David is off helping the man with the embossing machine. Odd, Ann thinks, here at the factory she can sense David's presence more than she can when they are in bed.

After sitting a few moments, Ann realizes that she is actually at the end of a long table where a few feet away a dozen women work, assembling women's compacts—one puts on the hinges, another the mirror, another inserts the tiny powder puff, all the way to the far end of the table, where the last woman puts the completed compact in a gray velvet sleeve. Unlike the rest of the workers, who have given in to the clatter of the machines, these women seem undaunted by it, creating instead their own cacophony—a constant, melodic, high-pitched chatter, as on street corners in Puerto Rican neighborhoods. Next to each woman is a bin that holds the materials necessary to do the job. At the table's end larger bins hold the completed compacts. Circling around the table, refilling and emptying bins, is a clubfooted man, seemingly in perfect rhythm with the women—never an empty bin, never one that overflows.

As Ann watches, soothed by the process, the chatter suddenly accelerates; then one of the pieceworkers stands and screams at another. The man with the clubfoot looks up, holding the bin he is about to replace. Work comes to a standstill as another of the women yells and walks away from the table. Before Ann can even register what has happened, David is at the place of the woman who left, taking up her work, gluing a mirror into a compact, then another, then another, mimicking her rhythm exactly, slowly, hypnotically, transfixing the others. Watching him, one by one, they all start to work again, quietly. And when David begins to sing—not in Spanish, but in German—they resume their chatter. A minute or so later, the woman who left the table returns, and David relinquishes his stool. "Good, good," he says, standing behind her. And in a few moments, everything is as it was before.

Ann is amazed. Before David can return to the embossing machine, she goes to him. "I love you so much," she says. He touches her cheek softly with the palm of his hand. It smells like rubber cement.

For lunch they go to a nearby Italian place David has told her about. It has long tables with checkered cloths and benches where people eat sandwiches and spaghetti served on red-painted pie tins. Ann and David buy a loaf of the tawny-crusted bread, baked to near black on the bottom, a slab of cheese and a half pound of mortadella, sliced thin. They share a large, cold bottle of beer and tear off chunks of the bread, pieces of the crust falling to mingle with the sawdust on the floor. People yell at one another. A man with a huge mustache that looks like a whisk broom beneath his nose snores in the corner. Two other men sitting across from one another puff thoughtfully on cigars, a tumbler of Chianti before them. Yet another man works a mathematics problem in a three-ring binder.

"Let's never leave here, never leave New York," Ann says. "A deal?" She extends her hand for David to shake. But just that moment David looks out over Ann's shoulder to the street. "What do you see?" she asks. She turns to look for herself. "Something I don't know about?"

"About me, you know everything," he says, and touches her arm.

Later that afternoon, David suggests they leave the factory early, do something new, go to the planetarium. Sitting in the dark, their profiles caught in the projected light that creates other planets and galaxies, Ann and David look like children transfixed by a vision—David, especially as he follows the paths of the stars across the dome, as night accelerates and the sun emerges from the far wall of the round room. Ann's eyes remain fixed, however, at the apex of the dome. "Directly overhead," the deep, reassuring voice of the narrator has revealed only a few moments before, "the constellation of the stars is one and the same as that seen by our friends in Europe, where it is already night."

"Oh, Mama." Ann wishes she could just see her again, spend a few more hours with her, thinking that maybe now things could be set right between them. It is December 6, 1941.

New York, 1943

Selective Service

As promised, Pearl has arranged for Ann's introduction to the world, the debut to take place less than two months from today, in Minneapolis, Minnesota, nearly as far from New York as Vienna. Since Jorge's departure two years ago, she has worked only with Pearl, has given that part of her life over to him completely. Pearl has chosen the program she will play, specified the piano, accompanied her to Bergdorf-Goodman to buy a long black gown. Occasionally, he jokes about the fact that through all this they have not become enemies, lovers or both.

Occasionally, too, Ann considers the possibility of crossing the simple threshold that separates the room with the two pianos from the one where Pearl sleeps. After all, Pearl has waited for Ann at the beauty parlor while she has had her hair done for her publicity photographs, has taken her to lunch at elegant restaurants, has even come to Ann and David's apartment to oversee the tuning of the Mason & Hamlin. Such fine comrades, why not lovers? Ann wonders, mostly after she and David have made love and lie together in bed, his arm around her shoulders as he gazes quietly out the window, as far from her as Minneapolis, Minnesota.

Sometimes, she asks him what he is thinking. If he reveals anything, it is usually about business. When it isn't going well, he worries about why; when it is going well, he frets about the possibility of failure. Ann thinks to ask what has happened to his confidence, but she already knows. He has developed a refugee's addiction to success in his new world, and nothing else, it seems, can nourish him—though Ann is uncertain whether it is America or David's own idea of success that has so seduced him.

One night, however, David tells her that he is lonely, that something is missing in his life.

"Missing?" David's silences, his growing distance over the last year or so make her feel tenuous, desperate—in contrast to her excitement about the upcoming concert. Bitterly, she sometimes thinks she is about to lose what she loves, just as she is about to gain what she needs.

"Just that," David says softly, as if he has already said too much.

"Maybe a baby," Ann offers, remembering the families strolling along Fifth Avenue the Easter Sunday she and David arrived home from Niagara Falls. "We always said," she goes on, unsure where this talk may take them, "we always said we'd have a baby when . . ." Twice now, it has been put off; first until the business succeeded, then until after Ann's debut.

"Maybe," David says into the dark, "maybe it's you I miss."

Ann knows precisely what he means, yet feels compelled to make him say it. "You mean Pearl? The concert?" Where seconds before she felt uncertain, now she feels anger.

"Maybe . . ."

"No," she insists. "It has nothing to do with that."

"No? What then?"

"I don't know. But you're the one who's missing, not me. You're the one who's gone seven days a week, the one with . . ."

"You're right," he interrupts, "it's me." He switches on the bedside lamp. He looks tired and much older than when we met, Ann realizes. "I'm sorry," he tells her. "You should do what pleases you. And I . . . I'll be different, you'll see."

"And us?" Ann asks. Couples have problems, "rocky times,"

she has read in magazines. Now in the soft, conspiratorial yellow light from the single lamp, she cannot imagine that these last years have been anything more than a difficult stretch for them. And that after the concert, and after the loan is paid back, things will be more normal. And when the war is over, she and David will have a baby, move to a house, settle in. Still, she asks a second time, "And us?"

"We'll be fine," David assures her.

Today, an unexpectedly temperate February morning, Ann practices a Beethoven sonata—Opus 111, his last. Pearl has selected it for Ann's program because of her enchantment with a piano "rag" they once heard at a jazz club that he had taken Ann and David to. "I'll teach you a piece you can play just like that," Pearl said, as the three of them listened to the gray-haired Negro with a baggy suit and pearl-white fingernails.

Absorbed in the Beethoven, Ann is momentarily disoriented when the apartment buzzer sounds. It's the postman, downstairs with a registered letter. In the minute it takes him to bring the letter up to 4C, Ann steels herself. She has no doubt the letter concerns Mama, that Mama is dead. Ann tries to imagine what she will feel when seconds from now her conviction proves true, but cannot. The letter is not about Mama, however, or even from the "other side." It is from Washington, D.C., and though it is addressed to David, she opens it. It's a draft notice, instructing David to put his affairs in order and report for training in three weeks' time. The notice lies open on the telephone table near the front door where Ann forgets it in her rush to the factory, to tell David face to face, to prove that she can be there when he needs her.

"Impossible," he says, though it has been rumored that recently naturalized citizens may be taken. Ann and David are alone in Hans's office, David in his brother's chair, Ann sitting on the edge of the desk next to him.

"I simply can't go back there," he says, hitting the desk with his palm. Ann puts her hand on the back of his neck. The day has turned even brighter, and the sun, streaming through the dusty windows, catches them momentarily like specimens under a glass.

"You know I can't go back there." He takes her other hand and puts it to his cheek. "You *know* that," he insists.

"I know," she says, feeling the slight stubble of his beard. No one has worked harder than David to cut himself off from the past. He never speaks of it, nor will he read about the war in Europe in the papers or listen to the radio programs. He refuses even to try to make contact with those he left behind, and the only time in recent memory when Ann has heard him utter any German was at the factory, when he sang to soothe the piece workers. Going back, Ann knows, would be his undoing.

"I simply can't," David begins again slowly; then, as if suddenly overtaken by some memory or image, he puts his head in his hands, elbows on the desk, and cries.

Ann kneels next to him, cradles his head in her hands. "I know," she repeats, wondering if, as Mama did—and is maybe still doing—for Jacobi, she will be able to do what needs to be done.

Dr. Peter Hartmann

Peter will only meet with her at his office—as it should be, Ann thinks, for though she has not told him the purpose of her visit, it is his professional help she seeks. She has heard of Jewish refugees, naturalized citizens like David, escaping conscription into the army by having their wives declared unstable. "The perfect Viennese response," Pearl has said. He has cautioned her not to go to her ex-husband on David's behalf. "You say David is growing distant," Pearl has said. "Do you think this will bring him back?"

Ann has no doubt that it will. She believes, in fact—and guiltily so—that the draft notice is a godsend, and that it will enable her to make the single grand gesture that will break through David's silences and reveries, bringing him back from wherever they take him.

Peter's waiting room is filled with toys, children's books and puzzles. Odd for a psychiatrist, Ann thinks. On the walls are pictures of clowns and jugglers. As she escorts Ann into Peter's office, the receptionist tells her that Dr. Hartmann specializes in the treatment of young people.

"Why children?" Ann asks Peter. Compared to the waiting room, his office is surprisingly spare—a rather severe chair at the head of a small couch, a desk with a blotter and pen and pencil in an onyx base, a few books on largely empty shelves. Next to the chair is a small table with a writing tablet and a photograph of Peter and a woman, outdoors. Though they are wearing ski clothes and their skis are planted next to them, they look serious.

"My wife," Peter says when Ann's gaze falls on the photograph.

"Why children?" Ann repeats.

"Because I think they are still curable."

"And adults?"

"I'm less certain about adults." He offers a thin smile. His beard is long and red, his new mustache redder yet. "I know it's sacrilege to say such things even as we're trying to legitimize the profession, but . . ."

Ann waits. It is difficult to believe that she was married to the man, he is such a stranger.

". . . but I am a simple man, as we both know." Ann sits on the couch, Peter on his chair. Though they look at one another, both face the same direction, like passengers on a train.

"I never thought . . ." Ann begins.

"Please, don't patronize me. Tell me instead what brings you here, what it is you want me to do for you." He picks up his writing tablet.

Ann knew it would not be easy, that she would have to pay a price for the visit, though she was uncertain what it would be. "I know you're still angry," she says.

"Don't flatter yourself." He looks at his wristwatch. "Let's just get to it, all right?" He sets down his writing tablet, knocking the photograph over in the process.

"All right," Ann says, as Peter replaces the photograph. "You saved me once before," she goes on, remembering the words he called down the hospital corridor in Florida.

Peter makes a steeple of his fingers and studies it. "I don't recall thinking of it in those terms."

"Well, I'm sorry about it all. Very, very sorry."

"No need to apologize." His voice cracks slightly. "Now please, what is it you need?" There is something almost plaintive in the request, and though his beard is professional, his certificates on the wall impressive, Ann recognizes the boy who would do anything to please. Hard as it is to believe, he still loves her, and in the same way.

She tells him about her upcoming concert, but he seems uninterested. So she says, "David has been drafted."

"And he wants no part of it. Who can blame him? To go back . . ." Peter stops. "I don't know what I'd do if I were in his situation."

"But you're not."

"No, no. Wife, child, poor hearing." Peter claps his hands to his ears. "Can you imagine it, Anna? I'm to make my living listening to people, and I can barely hear out of one ear." He laughs, less for the irony than for the nervousness he feels. "In any event, I'm here for the duration, yes."

"And your father?" Ann asks. "Do you hear from . . ."

"And from me you want?" Peter interrupts.

"If I were unstable, if someone were to declare me unstable, you see . . ."

"Of course, of course. Simple as that, 'someone' like me." Peter stands and walks to his desk. "I've actually heard about these things. A false suicide attempt, a few weeks at a sanatorium . . ."

"Are you certain?"

"Certain?"

"About the steps you have to take. *I'll* have to take." It is far, far more than Ann has anticipated.

"Exceptional times," Peter shakes his head, "require exceptional steps. Otherwise," he goes on, "how would it look? Your husband is drafted and a few days later you see a psychiatrist. No. Far too obvious. They, whoever *they* are, will be wary of that, and of the physician who makes the diagnosis. You'll simply have to be more devious. Certainly you understand that? Deviousness?" Peter tears the top sheet off the pad.

"I told you I was sorry."

"Yes." Peter holds out the paper. "A prescription. For sleeping tablets. You needn't actually take more than three and then throw away the remainder. Then have David call me. I'll see to the rest."

Ann is reluctant to ask. "The rest?"

"The ambulance, the emergency room. And later the arrangements at the sanatorium. It will be done correctly, as always. You can count on me."

Ann cannot discern whether Peter's wan smile is one of self-pity, commiseration or victory. "And another psychiatrist?" she dares to ask. "He would tell me the same thing?"

"Ah, I didn't know you knew another. And so well that he would be willing to bend the law." Peter stands. "You should definitely ask him. Get a second opinion."

"And my concert?" Ann hears the desperation in her voice.

"I cannot imagine an unstable woman could give a concert. Could you? No, I think that would have to be put off."

They are standing together in front of the couch.

"You knew I didn't love you," Ann says. "But still you absolutely insisted."

"True." Peter nods.

"Well, what did you expect?" Ann suddenly says, far more loudly than she intends. "What . . . did . . . you . . . expect?" There is silence. Then a knock on the door.

"Your next patient," the receptionist says.

Just as Ann turns to leave, however, Peter reaches out and touches her hand. "Please, before you go," he says, "one more thing. A question."

"What?" She expects he will ask her about love, what it is in David that she loves so much that she will do what she is about to do.

"That day in Vienna," Peter begins, "the day you came back from London. What happened?"

"Why?" Ann asks. "What difference could it possibly make?" Oddly, those few moments in the boarded-up storefront with the soldier are among the only memories Ann never revisits since being with David, no matter how many times they make love, no matter how many times she dreams.

"Because I understand everything else about us but that," Peter says. "And I need that . . . that piece of the puzzle to complete the picture."

"So, that's the price? The price I have to pay for your professional help?"

"No. You've already paid that price by coming," Peter says quietly, his voice tentative, like that of the young man who peeled her a chestnut on the way to the theater, who asked her to marry him knowing that she would turn him down. "Please," he says.

And so she tells him, providing details only when he asks. And when she is through, he thanks her, regains his professional bearing, puts his arm solicitously around her shoulder and guides her to the door. "It would be better," he says as he turns the knob, "if you take the pills during the week, while I'm in the office."

Peace and Quiet

"Unacceptable," Pearl decrees when he hears of Ann's decision to cancel the concert. She tells him before they sit at the twin pianos.

"It's my life," Ann insists, throwing her music on the small couch.

"Then live it." Pearl paces the room, hands in his pockets.

"I do. I have. I've risked everything. I've left everyone."

"Nonsense." He stops his pacing. "Save for the husband you never wanted to marry, they all left you. And your current husband, from what you say, he's on his way as well."

"That's not true," Ann counters, though lately she is less certain. Still, she is convinced that her plan, her grand gesture, will keep David. She cannot tell Pearl this, however, for she knows he will mock her.

"Besides," he goes on, balancing on the sill of a closed window and looking out, "it may be your life, but it is my reputation. I do not cancel concerts. Not even for the great ones. So tell me, Frau Green"—he turns back to her, his voice soft, cajoling as it was on the night of Big Carolina's party—"why should I cancel for you?"

In the instant she has before she must answer or leave Pearl's apartment forever, she sees Pearl, not as he sits regally peering out his penthouse window, but on the delicate pink upholstered chair at Bergdorf-Goodman, surrounded by clothing on racks and on the carpet, while a half dozen saleswomen and tailors tend to Ann's gown. "Yes, lovely," he says, as the hem is pinned, the waist pinched. "That one."

"You will cancel the concert," she begins, certain what she is about to say is true, "because you love me," then adds, "though I honestly do not know why."

Pearl throws up his hands in a gesture half comic, half despairing. "There is still time," he says. For what, Ann does not ask.

The evening before Ann is to take the pills, she lies on her back, unable to sleep or even to close her eyes. She has told David about seeing Peter, about her plan. At first, he objects. "It's too much," he says. "And to give up the concert . . ."

"Not to give it up," Ann corrects, "but to do it at a better time. When we're both happy again."

"Ah, happy." David's smile is bittersweet.

Now, David comes to her in her bed. "After this is done," he begins, when they are under the covers, "I promise . . ." Ann puts a hand to his cheek, his lips. She has come to mistrust promises, even her own. Slowly, softly, they fall into their lovemaking. At first it is as familiar as the shadows she sees cross the ceilings on the nights she cannot sleep, and yet tonight there is something different. And when passion overtakes tenderness, her body feels as lithe and limber as Mama's must have when she danced. Ann's heels and elbows dig into the soft mattress, her back arches and rises to meet David's fall as if he were weightless. And when he comes, which is soon and sweet, she feels they are closer than ever before.

The following day—as planned—an hour before David is to return home, Ann takes three of the sleeping tablets with a glass of water. She has already composed her note and has placed it beside her on the bed. "If I lose this, I lose the last thing I have." The tablets are bitter, and she goes to the bathroom for more water, carrying the remainder of the pills to dump into the toilet. Before she does, however, she looks into the mirror. Odd, she thinks, I've never looked happier. Could it be so? Will the doctors be able to tell? And before giving it any further thought, she swallows six or seven more pills, then throws what is left in the toilet and flushes them down. "There," she says aloud.

Back in the bedroom she glances at the clock: 6:15. David is usually home by 6:45. Earlier, she has called Peter to tell him that today is the day. She looks again at the note. "If I lose this . . ." This, what, she wonders? Is it clear? She writes another. "If I lose you, David, I lose everything." She crumples the note up and throws it into the small trash container next to her vanity. Looking at the solitary, crumpled-up paper at the container's bottom, she feels the first hint of drowsiness. More dizziness than drowsiness, actually. She stands, feels behind her for the bed, then sits on the edge, her head in her hands. Seeking vivid memory, she is disappointed that everything that comes to her is bleary, cast in gray. The fire in the fireplace at the Café Dolder when she last saw Papa is burned out, there is no life in Mama's eyes when she picks Ann up as a little girl, and Cybelle—Ann cannot imagine Cybelle at all.

"What did you do?" David asks. His hand is on her shoulder, he is pale, his voice quavers. His face is the first thing Ann sees when she awakens in the hospital room. "Three pills. You were only supposed to take three pills. Are you really crazy?"

Ann tries to form the word, "No," but her tongue is too thick, her mouth filled with a foreign taste, all the bitterness of the tablets and more.

The sanatorium on Long Island to which she is discharged is a large brick building trimmed in white with impressive white pillars ringing a semicircular entranceway. Ann's room is equally white, impressively clean, and the sheets of her bed smell of soap, starch and fresh air. Fearing an institution full of raving lunatics, Ann is instead confronted by a genteel set of women, some as young as fifteen or sixteen, others in their eighties. They are not dressed, but pad around the wide, daylit halls in slippers and robes.

"I'm not here for long," Ann says to a woman her own age whom she meets in line for breakfast, which is served in a large common room with dozens of tables. "Actually, I don't belong here at all."

The woman smiles sweetly, but says nothing. There are bandages on her wrists.

Ann remains in the sanatorium for three days, doing little with her time, thinking little, the episode with the pills and the aftermath providing her with hours and hours of peace and quiet. She sleeps, eats a little, doesn't even miss the piano. No one visits by order of her doctor.

When her stay is over, David picks her up. He brings her clothes to wear, a bowl of fruit from Erna, and a gift from Tiffany's—a large golden brooch in the shape of a butterfly.

"You needn't treat me like an invalid," she says, as he opens the door for her and helps her in. "I'm perfectly all right, you know." Inside the car, he kisses her on the forehead, on the cheeks, and on the lips.

"It's done," he says.

Ann smiles and settles back into the seat. He pulls out of the arching circular driveway, then once on the road he asks, "And that's all you ever intended?"

Ann is sleepy. She studies David's profile as he drives.

"Of course."

He takes her hand and kisses her palm. "Then everything is fine."

Pearl

The day following Ann's return from the sanatorium, Pearl comes to the apartment with a bouquet of roses. "The spring equinox," he says, by way of explanation, "and your rapid recovery." Standing at the door holding out the flowers, he looks boyish, bashful, not at all the noted impresario. She cannot decide whether she likes him better this way or not.

"Why do you care so?" she asks, as he watches her snip the bottoms of the stems and place the roses in a vase.

"I told you."

"Did you?"

"Yes. In London. I told you that you touched me once."

"But certainly others . . ." She carries the vase into the living room, and he follows. ". . . others have touched you."

"What can I say? Not in the same way."

Ann is mystified that she can affect some men—as disparate as Peter and Pearl—and not others. "Truly, though," she says to Pearl, "what is it I do or have? What touches you?"

"Youth, possibly. A chance to begin again, through you." It rings false.

"If I knew what it was," she declares, "I would stop it."

"Don't," he says. "Whatever it is, I like it too much."

"And we'll go on as we have?"

"Absolutely. As I promised years ago." No longer proffering flowers, Pearl once again becomes the eminent teacher. "There'll still be lessons. And, of course, the concert. Minneapolis, same time, next year." He puts on his homburg, kisses Ann on the cheek and is gone.

There is to be no concert, however, not next year, in any event. Ann is pregnant.

Will

Though it is contrary to the medical practice of the time, Ann decides to have her baby without anesthesia, an idea that comes to her in a dream not long after she learns she is pregnant. In the dream, the baby's birth is accompanied by a colossal rush of freedom, a purging of all that has gone wrong in the past, a cleansing away of the guilt Ann feels for those she abandoned and those she couldn't save. So real is the feeling that when she awakens, she knows her pregnancy cannot result in any other outcome.

When she tells her obstetrician of the plan, he cautions against it, claiming no hospital will allow it. So Ann goes from doctor to doctor until she finds one, an older woman, also a refugee, who will attend the birth, which is to take place in her office.

The air that New York summer has a peculiar quality, like steam, singeing the nostrils, making it difficult for Ann to breathe. Her hands perspire, her shoes no longer fit—the very opposite of Oma's experience with pregnancy.

Studying herself before the mirror, Ann often thinks of Mama, her dancer's body, and tries to imagine how she must have looked carrying Ann, now twenty-seven years ago. Since Ann has never seen Mama naked, it is difficult to picture, and all Ann is left with is Mama's face, never soft, almost always certain. She wishes she could be with Mama now, if only for a day—though with the stories in the newspapers about Jews being mistreated in work camps, Ann has grown afraid to imagine where that might be.

As much as Ann has changed, however, it is David who seems most affected by the pregnancy—or perhaps by her grand gesture to save him from the army. It is a rare evening when he does not return from the factory before six. Weekends are spent going on expeditions together, sometimes extending to three days or four. David has even bought a camera, and once a week he photographs Ann's growing belly, though it is uncertain whether the Kodak company will develop the film.

"How can this be?" David exclaims one day after he has snapped the picture and Ann lets her nightgown drop.

"What?" she asks, happier than she can recall. "How can what be?"

"You know. That we can be together again when . . ."

" 'When' what?" she taunts. She wants him to say it, whatever it is.

But David cannot find the words. "It's good, no?" he finally offers.

"Yes." Ann nods. "Yes."

* * *

The moment of their son's birth is exactly as she has dreamed it. And when their baby cries and the doctor hands him to her, she cannot remember whether she has hoped for a boy or a girl, or even that the boy's name she and David have decided on just the night before is Will.

New York, 1946–47

Winter

In early December Ann takes Will, now three years old, to see the Christmas windows at Macy's. They could go by subway, but Ann prefers to walk, carrying Will or holding his red-mittened hand in her gloved one as she matches her pace to his. She loves the pressure of his four small fingers in her palm, the faint impression of his thumb on hers. Crossing the larger avenues, she grips his hand tightly. She wonders if she loves him too much, if such a thing is possible.

Sometimes, too, she wonders how he has come to be her child. His hair is blond, his eyes are a soft blue, like looking into an aquarium, his nose a delicate little nut. Except for his eyes, he looks nothing like her or David or anyone else she is related to. His nature is also foreign—open, untroubled, he rarely cries. And in the morning he often awakens laughing, as if from the most pleasurable sleep.

"What did you dream about?" Ann asks. He refuses to say, though she is certain he knows, understands the preciousness of his reveries, and is afraid to destroy their power by revealing them. He is a gift, she decides, a visitation on her life. Then one night when he falls asleep in her lap as she reads him *Peter Rabbit*, it comes to her—the faint blush of his cheeks, how good, how important he makes her feel. She has been given Cybelle's child.

Snow falls in occasional flurries, driven by sudden drafts, dusting the Manhattan sidewalks like flour. On the streets, where automobiles and taxis bunch at a light, then travel in droves to the next, the snow turns instantly to slush.

At Times Square, an officer on a huge chestnut-colored horse directs traffic. Though cars stream around him not two feet from his flanks, the horse, protected from the weather by a dark blue saddle blanket, stands his ground, his strong legs like stanchions. Will sees the horse before Ann does, and urges her closer. They are about fifteen feet away, at the head of the intersection where the horse stands, when suddenly there is a loud pop. The next instant, a policeman's whistle sounds and the horse carrying the officer rears, its forelegs churning in the air as an automobile passes nearly underneath.

"Stop!" someone yells from the crowd. A man pursued by a policeman on foot rushes past Ann and Will, pushing them aside as he does. Trying to keep her balance, Ann loses hold of Will's hand, though she quickly regains it. But the panic she has felt the instant before persists.

"What happened?" Will asks, seconds later.

"I let go of your hand," she confesses. "I didn't mean to."

"No. What happened to the horse?" He is earnest, serious. Ann smiles, and lifts him to her shoulders so he can see the horse, now off in the distance. She wants to give him so much, she cannot even imagine what she will give him next.

In the largest of the Macy's windows is a group of mechanized elves on ice skates, dressed in red and green, skating along a frosted pond in the center of a winter landscape. Of course, Ann thinks, and buys skates for Will and herself.

A few weeks after Will was born, David was late returning home from work. At eight, Ann called the factory, at nine, Hans. An hour later, she called the police, spoke with the Missing Persons Bureau. "Probably nothing to worry about," she was told. There had been a spate of "wanderers" lately, businessmen staying out at night, "blowing off steam." The woman on the switchboard suggested Ann wait until at least noon the next day before calling back.

Early the next morning, on the vague cusp between dark and light, Ann heard a key in the lock, the click of the latch, the familiar squeak of the heavy wooden apartment door on its hinges. She was awake, as she had been all night, now sitting in the green wingback chair feeding Will—a pleasure offset by her fear that nothing would ever be quite the same again.

"David," she said quietly.

"Yes." He sat down on the couch. She reached to turn on a lamp, but he cupped his hand over the switch. "Don't, please." His features in the early morning gray were as ephemeral as the light itself. "I'm sorry," he said after a while.

"For what? Where were you? What happened?" Will had fallen back to sleep.

"Just out," he said.

"But where?" Ann heard a pleading in her voice that reminded her of Peter.

"Nowhere in particular."

"Blowing off steam?"

"What?"

"Were you alone? By yourself?"

"Mostly."

"Mostly?"

"Please," he said. "I'm sorry. Enough."

Ann laid Will down beside her and refastened her nightgown. "What happens now?" she whispered, her voice barely carrying the distance between her and David.

"I don't know," he said. Then, after a few moments, he stood. "Nothing will happen," he assured her, "things will just work out."

Catching a glimpse in the dim room of the photograph taken at the supper club the night of their wedding, Ann thought, Of course, of course things will work out. She could not even imagine the alternative.

David opened the door to the bedroom. Light streamed into the living room where Ann sat, and she could once again make him out clearly. His hair was disheveled like a young boy's in a schoolyard; his face looked as if he had just been roused from a deep sleep. "Don't worry," he said, smiling wanly as he half closed the bedroom door behind him, "I won't leave."

The morning after Ann buys the skates, she, Will and Erna walk to the skating rink in Central Park. It is still early. Men stand at street corners, checking their watches, searching for their buses in the approaching traffic. Coffee shops are full, their windows clouded by steam from shiny, squat coffee urns. There are few women on the street, and only a single pair of skaters—a teenage boy and girl practicing a carefully choreographed routine—at the rink.

"Why did we have to come so early?" Erna claps her hands together in the cold to keep warm. The black limbs of the trees are silhouetted against the morning sun, barely visible on the eastern horizon.

"Another time," Ann says, speaking in the code she and Erna have created to refer to events that took place in the past.

"Ah! That explains any craziness." She finds a patch of sun to stand in while Ann takes Will to the edge of the rink. He stares out at the two balletic skaters, clearly awed by their twists and turns.

"Mama, look!" he commands, as the boy lifts the girl shoulder-high and, hands on her waist, swoops the length of the rink. "Like acrobats." His tone mixes pleasure with concern.

"Don't worry, Will. We won't have to skate like that. Not today." On the ice, he is timid, no surprise to Ann. It took him a year longer than the other children to essay the tall metal slide in the playground—only when he was confident that he could do it perfectly would he dare to climb the rungs leading to its apex. Now, Ann stands before him, holding both his hands in hers to form a circle. Her own skates lend her height. Will's blades are still turned sideways. "Come on, Will, skate with Mama," she urges. "Not today," he declares; then, not wanting to disappoint his mama, he adds, "the day after tomorrow."

Finally, standing behind him, her hands under his arms, she lifts him onto the blades and, holding him between her legs, she skates the short distance to the edge of the rink. When she steps off the ice, Erna takes Will's hand, but coaxes Ann to stay on the ice and skate alone.

At first Ann is reluctant, but when Will says, "Go ahead, Mama, let me see if you can," she relents. Then, within moments, as if it were yesterday when she skated at a respectful distance from the proud, taciturn soldiers of the Kaiser's army, she is propelled by the spring of her muscles, the smooth pump of her legs. For a minute or so she skates fast—recklessly, even—briefly losing sight of all around her. Through for the day, the two teenage skaters watch, not without interest.

When Ann feels the pain of her muscles stretching to accommodate her movement, she slows. Erna and Will play in the snow. In his black boots and royal-blue snowsuit, he circles around Erna while she stands like a maypole, her colorful hat festooned with imitation flowers. Soon other children join in the revelry, yelling back and forth to one another. How quickly the time has passed, Ann thinks. First steps, then words, and now ideas and opinions. About his papa, Will has said, "He's always going away."

"Only to work," Ann reassures him. But it is more than that, she has recently come to understand, though she will occasionally allow herself to be fooled—by the camping trip to the mountains early that summer when she and David went canoeing; by the nights when he brings home cold cuts and lays them out on platters for a family feast; by the plan to move across the Hudson River into a house with a fenced yard and a swing set.

Now, on the path leading away from the skating rink, Ann puts an arm around Erna, while holding firmly onto Will's hand. Slung over one shoulder are both pairs of skates, laces tied together, their blades clinking dully against one another. Ann wonders what it is about her that causes those she loves the most to disappear.

Jake Weigel

On Christmas Eve, Jake Weigel, Hans's lawyer friend from Massachusetts, drops by the apartment. The year before, he helped the brothers collect from a customer in Boston who, going through tough times, refused to pay for the goods he'd ordered. "Just passing through," Jake now says. He is a tall, blocky man in his fifties, with a shock of thick black hair and the residual good looks of a matinee idol past his prime. He wears a dark suit but, though it is nighttime and quite cold, neither an overcoat nor a hat. His hand is so large that Ann is startled by how it envelopes hers when she shakes it. Quickly, she looks back up and into his blue-black eyes. Though he smiles, there is something tough and unforgiving about his expression, reminding Ann of the smooth crime bosses she has seen in the movies.

"I like European women," Jake says to David. "There's something about them I just like." He continues to look at Ann, who eventually averts her eyes.

David stands across the room, tearing the cellophane wrap from a bottle of scotch he bought after Jake called to say he was coming. The scotch is Jake's favorite, very expensive.

When Will enters the room, Jake walks right up to him, picks him up, and holds his face against his, cheek to cheek. "How are you, fella?" he asks. Will doesn't answer. "Kids don't understand me. I can't figure why." Jake looks quickly around the room, like a large animal finding itself suddenly caged. When he sees the small, sparsely decorated Christmas tree in the corner he says, "Oh, do you folks celebrate Christmas? You should have said so. This must be a bad time."

"Only for the boy," David begins. But Jake has already taken a seat on the recliner, tilting the back until his feet are raised.

"Talk, talk, talk," he says. "Doesn't anybody drink anymore? And you," he says to Ann, bringing the chair back down, facing forward with his feet flat on the floor and his hands on his knees, "don't you talk at all?"

Ann has never met anyone so direct. It disarms and befuddles her, and before she can answer him, he just waves her away, saying, "I'm just kidding, Annie." And then to David, "Women don't understand me either. I can't figure why."

David hands him an old-fashioned glass, half filled with scotch, no ice, no water, which Jake quickly drinks down. "Well," he says, getting up, "I don't want to ruin your Christmas Eve." He walks to the door and turns the knob. "I was just in town and thought I'd meet the family. Be sociable."

"But Jake," David says, "stay for dinner."

"Really?" He is already halfway out the door.

"Really," Ann pronounces, surprised at her conviction.

Over dinner, Jake tells Ann and David about his stint as state attorney general, about his zeal for exposing swindlers and racketeers. "Once," he says, "they even tried to take me out. Got me in the leg." He pushes away from the table and rolls up his pant leg to show them the scar. His skin is pale, hairless, and there is a deep gray indentation halfway up his calf. From his wallet he produces a newspaper clipping chronicling the event. There is a photograph of Jake on crutches with a quote as a caption: "It takes a lot more than a punk to slow down Jake Weigel." Ann hands the clipping to David, who looks at it, sputters, laughs, and can find nothing to say.

Done with his story, Jake eats fast, checking his watch every few minutes. "Plane to catch," he says. With dinner he drinks three more scotches.

"Well, what do you think of our Robin Hood from Massachusetts?" David asks. Will sits on his lap.

"I didn't like that man," Will offers.

"Not you." David tousles Will's hair.

"I can't even imagine his life," Ann says. The hour with Jake went by quickly. "It's like he lives in another world entirely."

"He seemed able to imagine you," David says, his voice slightly ragged.

"He's just a flatterer."

"You know," David says somberly, "you know what would scare me?"

Ann puts her hand over his as he strokes Will's hair. "What?"

"To somehow have him turn on you. To suddenly find he's not on your side any longer."

"Now that," Ann agrees, "would be unpleasant."

Mama, Again

The doors of the enormous barracks-like building that extends along the pier are open, the four gangplanks leading down from the red-white-and-blue ocean liner, empty. Inside, the structure is open and airy, a single room. Birds perch atop the girders that make up its skeleton. Ann stands at the Customs area where blue-uniformed clerks go through the suitcases of the arrivals from Bremerhaven.

At first, Ann cannot pick Mama out from the crowds of new immigrants waiting in lines. There are so many, and they cluster so close together, emerging from the group only when the Customs clerk signals it is time. And then they proceed quietly, almost reluctantly. Many are camp survivors, Ann knows, though like others who escaped the horror before it became day-to-day and real, she cannot imagine it—nor could she bear to look at the photographs or films of the liberation of the camps. And now, searching among the refugees for Mama and Jacobi, Ann is embarrassed by her relative self-assurance, by her health, by her survival.

Finally, Ann sees her. And though prepared by the actual appearance from Europe of some of the relatives of friends, the woman Ann recognizes in the crowd is not the Mama she expects, but an old woman—though Mama is barely fifty.

"Mama," she says, as much to herself as to the apparition before her. A half dozen women look up, hopeful. But Mama does not hear, or so it seems; she is concentrating instead on undoing the twine from around a cardboard box. "Mama," Ann repeats. Suddenly Mama stands upright, a foot taller than the others owing to a feathered hat. A mesh veil covers the upper part of her face, which is heavily powdered and rouged. She gazes quickly around her, like a bird of prey, sensing another predator, and then her gaze fixes on her daughter. "Anna!" Ann runs to her, to the consternation of the nearby Customs clerk, who moves to intercede but then thinks better of it. These refugees are creating havoc with the rules.

Ann and Mama embrace for only an instant before Mama pulls back and holds Ann by the shoulders at arm's length. "Let me look at you," Mama says. Ann cannot imagine what Mama sees, whether she looks any different to her mother than she did years before. For now, in Mama's arms, Ann feels exactly as she did then—proud, intimidated, confused.

Up close Mama looks even older than from afar. Her makeup has been applied haphazardly, her lipstick extending well beyond her lips to cake in small crevices on her skin, her rouge creating bright red blotches on her cheekbones. Indeed, it looks less like makeup than a disguise for a role Mama is playing.

"I'm so sorry," Ann says, when she can think of nothing else. Before Mama can respond, Jacobi appears at her side. He is another man entirely. He has lost several inches in height, and his back is humped. Jacobi's eyes are bloodshot and too large for his face, which looks caved in, deflated. His lips are thin and pale; his white hair grows to his shoulders and is streaked flaxen, though Jacobi was never blond. Still, his clothing—a beret and an ascot visible under his tweed overcoat—affects a jaunty air, Mama's doing, no doubt.

"See," Jacobi says in careful English. "Now, aren't you glad you left?" He has no upper teeth.

"You can joke about such things?" Ann is incredulous. Humor is the last thing she expects.

"I have from necessity become a comedian. Your mama, however, she is less amused."

Mama insists on carrying the two cardboard boxes tied with twine that hold their belongings, the single large feather on her hat fluttering with her steps and the swirling crossdrafts in the building. Ann walks between them, her arm around Jacobi. He is only a few inches taller than Will, she realizes, wondering if Jacobi still possesses his simple, direct power, or if he has been completely diminished.

At the furnished apartment that Ann and David have rented for Mama and Jacobi, Ann and Mama sit on the couch, Jacobi on a straight-backed chair. He breathes deeply to get sufficient air. Jacobi has made a few jokes about their journey, Mama has laughed, and now there is silence.

"What happened?" Ann finally dares to ask. Jacobi's face, frozen into a sweet, meaningless smile, suddenly fills with reproach and he shakes his head.

"About that, we do not talk."

Later, as Jacobi naps on the couch, Ann joins Mama in the bedroom, watching as Mama unpacks Jacobi's belongings and hers. "Believe me," Mama says in German, "I know little about what happened with him, with his back—anything." As she speaks, Mama places the few clothes they own gently, reverently, on hangers. She strokes the back of Jacobi's suit, adjusts the shoulders on the hanger, kisses the lapels. She smoothes the wrinkles in her dresses, running her hands the length of them again and again, shifting what little nap is left on the black velvet one that Ann remembers. "Sometimes, though, he'll awaken in the middle of the night, sit up in bed and relate a single event in the sharpest, most horrific detail. But in the morning, he has forgotten."

When Mama hangs the last dress in the closet, she shuts the door and turns back to Ann. Ann notices that Mama has a slight twitch on the left side of her face. She stands to put her arms around her, determined that this time Mama will not push her away. Mama allows it, and as Ann holds her, she notes how thin Mama is, how sharp her ribs are, like steel bands encircling a slender barrel.

While Mama puts her last few possessions into the bureau and her back is to Ann, Ann asks her how she avoided being taken by the Nazis all those years. "Don't ask," Mama says quickly. "It is enough to know that I never caused anyone else any harm." Then she turns, smiling, catching Ann by surprise. "It's over, and not worth dwelling upon. Time for us to go on."

"That simple?" It is David's sentiment exactly, and Ann, unwilling and unable to completely forget past times, wonders whether letting one's memories go is, after all, necessary to survive.

"It has to be," Mama says hoarsely. "What are the choices?"

"What happened to them all? To Oma?" Ann asks.

"Gone," Mama pronounces, "died at the Skodagasse the day before they came for her."

"And Papa?"

"I told you in the telegram. He died in the hospital."

"For certain?"

"Probably not," Mama says, relenting, "though it's certain he died. As for where, they needed the hospitals for their own. I have no idea what really happened."

"And you never thought about him?" It sounds like an accusation, Ann realizes, and she wishes she could take it back. It is just that Papa was Papa, whatever his pettiness, and she cannot rid herself of the images of him watching her practice, or later even, at the café, trying to maintain his dignity as it was being stolen out from under him.

Mama fidgets with a small vial of medicine. "For me, there were other, more important things to think about. Once, maybe, I cared about him, or mistook him for my own papa, or found him charming, but all that passed."

Ann nods. She is confused by her feelings about Papa, and about the others Mama's return evokes—Oma, Herr Hartmann, Peter, Grandfather Leo.

"And you?" Mama suddenly asks. "Are you happy now? You were such an unhappy child."

"No," Ann protests, "I wasn't unhappy, just lonely."

"Well, then, I had it wrong. I tried, but I simply didn't understand you."

"But," Ann begins, unsure whether to go with Mama's sudden revision of that time, "that's not what happened. What happened was . . ."

"I was excited about my life," Mama interrupts, "and there you were, so quiet always, like you were passing judgment. You always seemed so, so, so . . . dissatisfied."

"How can you say that? And besides, if I was, I had good reason."

"You were born to it," Mama says, with some finality. "It was your temperament. There was nothing I could do. I won't be blamed."

"But I'm not blaming you," Ann insists, her sadness for Mama's fate, her guilt for her own escape, quickly evaporating, leaving only anger. "Well, maybe I *am* blaming you. But now that you're here, I want you to understand what happened back then."

"Ah, *understand,*" Mama mocks. "You think that after what happened there is anything about human behavior that can be understood? It's all a terrible perversion. There are only victims and survivors. And those little family insults and slights, they are nothing. Nothing." Mama sits down at the vanity and studiously applies some rouge.

Ann realizes that she has once again deluded herself that this Mama, so many years older, caked in makeup and sentimental about Jacobi's suit, would be any different from the one who so confused and ignored her over the years. Hoping that now things would not be the same, Ann is furious that they are, furious at her gullibility, and disappointed that she cannot forget Mama's earlier slights and accept her as she is—particularly after what Mama has been through.

As if he has been listening all along, Jacobi suddenly calls out. Ann follows Mama into the living room where Jacobi has been napping on the couch. A blanket covers the slight outline of his body. He sits up, wiping sleep from his eyes. Ann recalls the time when he whispered to her in confidence that they were both children. Of Jacobi, it seems even truer now than then. Mama smooths his unkempt hair with her fingers and kisses his cheek.

"What have you two been talking about?"

"Nothing." Mama casts Ann a warning glance.

"Nothing?" Jacobi's face suggests disbelief.

"Nothing important," Mama says. "I'll get you something to eat."

"Excellent." He smacks his lips. "I am famished for my first American meal." He mugs for Ann to indicate his enormous hunger. Behind him she sees Mama in the kitchen, going through the cabinets to examine what Ann has bought for her, opening the refrigerator, taking things out, putting them back in.

"Anna." Jacobi grabs her arm and whispers urgently. "We've done you no favor coming back here. There can be no satisfying outcome for you with your mama." He gauges her reaction. "Or perhaps you know that already."

Ann nods.

"She's bitter. She's angry, angrier, if that is possible, than I. She blames everyone."

"Me?"

"You. Everyone. No one acted as he should have . . ." He stops, then declares, his expression taking on the authority it sometimes would back at the Skodagasse, ". . . and I need her more than ever."

"Then why did you come? Here, to New York?"

"The job, the money," he says sadly, referring to a teaching position offered him at Columbia University. "I've yet to find out whether it's charity. But these days, I'll gladly take charity. Gladly. Gladly."

"What were you talking about?" Mama asks, as she returns carrying a large plate full of lettuce.

"Nothing," Jacobi says.

"Nothing important," Ann adds.

Much later that evening, Ann explains the day to David. He listens for a while, impatient with the details. Finally he says, "Your mama is right. The only answer is to move forward, leave things behind, change."

"So you've said." Ann nods, less and less certain precisely what "moving forward" means for David—or for her, for that matter—and how it will play itself out.

The Debut

What a strange and beautiful place for an "introduction to the world," Ann thinks. She stands on the crest of one of the winding paths leading to a small natural amphitheater in the foothills of the Berkshire Mountains. Before her lies a lush valley in the shape of a shallow bowl, stepped gently from its rim to its base, and thick with blue-green grass and clover. At its center, on a raised circular wooden stage, is a piano.

After Will was born, Ann stopped going to Pearl's studio. She had left Steinway & Sons months before, and rarely played the Mason and Hamlin—the last trace of her marriage to Peter—following her return from the sanatorium. But by the war's end, when it was clear that giving up her playing would bring David no closer, she called Pearl once again. "But I'm so old now," he joked over the phone. "Only three years older," Ann assured him the afternoon they made love for the first and only time. "As perfect and delicate as the second movement of Brahms's First," she told him as he fastened his cufflinks in front of a full-length mirror. Still in bed, Ann saw herself reflected in the background, Pearl's trousers on the floor next to her. She felt satisfied, but looked troubled.

"Brahms!" Pearl exclaimed. "You know that he's only my fifth favorite, if that." He turned, saw that Ann was about to speak. "I know. Don't even say it. We can't do this again."

A year after they began working together again, Pearl was paralyzed by a stroke. Now, only a week after Pearl's funeral, Ann is about to complete what was set in motion at Big Carolina's party nearly a decade before. Though she has told no one, Ann knows that her debut will also be her swan song, for it was Pearl's confidence that made tonight possible, not her own.

An hour before the concert, torches are placed at the head of each path leading into the amphitheater and in a circle along the stage's perimeter. Couples and families emerge from the woods carrying picnic hampers and blankets which, spread out on the grass, form an enormous patchwork quilt. David and Will and Erna will be there, as will Mama and Jacobi. The others—and she has been told that there will be a few thousand, for this concert is part of a popular festival—are all strangers.

Still standing at the rim of the verdant bowl, Ann smells a sudden sweetness in the air—of flowers, and more, it seems, as if their petals and leaves and stems had been crushed to create an intense perfume. Looking out into the amphitheater, she can see fireflies where the light from the torches does not reach, the occasional glow of cigarettes like tiny lanterns in the dark. The crickets are so loud, she cannot imagine anyone will be able to hear a note. And instead of walking the distance to the piano, she feels as if she could float. Then, a tap on her shoulder. "Now, Miss Green," someone whispers.

It is difficult to make them out—Mama and Jacobi, Erna, David and Will—in the torchlight, which twists and flickers with the faint breezes, illuminating their faces with serpentine streams of orange, red and gold. So evanescent and deceptive is the light, in fact, that sometimes Ann sees others in their places—Papa, Cybelle, Pearl—gazing at her like schoolchildren gazing upon a teacher, their mouths just slightly open, their expressions expectant.

She gives them Bach and Mozart, but their expressions do not change—Mama, expecting to be exonerated; Jacobi, hoping for a more just world; David, wishing for fewer questions; and Will, wanting love, simply that. Only Erna seems satisfied.

So she gives them Beethoven and Scriabin, but Papa grumbles in his grave—if he was even given one—seeking acknowledgment. And Cybelle still searches for the perfect lover, or more likely, perfect love—uncorrupted and unequivocal.

As for Pearl, all he ever really wanted was for Ann to touch him again. So she gives him the Chopin polonaise she played for him the day they met. It was to be the "centerpiece"—as he put it—of her program, though in his memory, she saves it for last.

She wants to touch them all, if she can, to give all the families on their blankets the best she has to give—deeply felt moments, persistent images, shadow-images, inexpressible feeling—and, of course, the music.

Seconds before her third and final encore ends—Chopin again, a nocturne—she strikes a note so singular and so high it seems to have nowhere to go but up, lofted by currents into the comforting, starlit, dark blue sky.

New Jersey, 1950

Old Farm Knolls

Ann, David and Will now live in a ranch house in New Jersey, in a development called Old Farm Knolls, built on what was once a small dairy farm. The few mature trees left on the property look anomalous on the newly landscaped lots—slightly contoured patches of dirt with a few promising shoots of green. Men carpool to work in Manhattan, women stay at home, migrating from house to house to have coffee and cigarettes with one another. David rarely carpools, however. Most often he rides by himself, taking the Chrysler and returning home late. Ann knows the business is doing well, that David has more and more to do.

At night, after Will goes to bed, she watches television. Sometimes she calls Erna.

During the days, there's a chain-smoking neighbor who calls herself Doody—the joke being "Howdy, Doody"; a talkative milkman named Jack; salesmen selling vacuum cleaners and encyclopedias; misty snow and test patterns on the TV. The Mason and Hamlin is downstairs in the finished basement, and Ann sometimes plays while she waits for the washing machine to go through its final rinse.

At 3:45, the school bus drops Will off. She marvels at the ease with which he leaves in the morning, his nonchalance upon his return. There are days when she actually gets into the Ford wagon and thinks to pick him up early, drive with him lord knows where, just to make sure he is safe, that they are together. Stubbing out a cigarette, Doody tells Ann she knows exactly how she feels.

When Ann tells Mama of her concerns about Will, Mama takes it as a personal affront, an attack on her own more laissez-faire approach to motherhood. Only Jacobi seems to understand. The rare times they are together, he and Will play like the best of friends. "You know what Grandpapa told me?" Will says one day. "That we are both children."

Ann smiles. "Imagine that."

One Saturday morning, Hans and his new wife come to the house for brunch. Her name is Shirley and she is from Iowa and looks exactly like Dinah Shore or Patti Page—Ann is not sure which, she always gets them mixed up. Shirley wears a pleated black skirt and white blouse, cinched at her tiny waist by a huge flat belt. Brunch consists of cold cuts that Ann buys from a German refugee who comes around in a Plymouth station wagon every Saturday, the back of the car filled with cheese, rolls and sausages.

It is odd seeing Hans, who was always in the company of fancy women, with Shirley. He is rarely more than a few feet from her; they are constantly touching. When he puts his arm around her shoulders, she nestles compliantly in the half-circle of his embrace. Ann finds it difficult not to stare.

At one point Hans and David excuse themselves to sit in the breezeway. It has recently been screened in to offer some privacy, and the men huddle over two huge ledgers and a box of loose papers. Ann and Shirley are in the kitchen, sitting at the red Formica table. "How do you take it?" Shirley asks.

"You get used to it," Ann says, uncertain what Shirley is talking about and reluctant to ask. Ann hopes it has to do with David working so hard, coming home so late. She recalls the thirty-one matched purses and shoes in her closet, the four different colors of one style called Haymakers.

"I could never get used to it." Shirley smiles. It is a warm, guileless, Midwestern smile, and in that instant Ann understands Hans's attraction to her. "Don't get me wrong," she says. "I'm not criticizing. Everyone lives their life the way they choose. I know what you've been through. And it's sure no worse than what you've already experienced." She offers a serious nod.

Ann feels the need to change the subject. "Well, at least the business," she begins, "at least that's doing well." The kitchen is bright, the floor white and clean, the counters red, the appliances spotless. No, there's an odd black smudge on the face of the oven. Ann gets the Ajax and a sponge.

"The business?" Shirley says, when Ann's back is to her. "He hasn't told you about the business?"

Later that afternoon, David assures her that Hans's leaving the business to start a new venture will not be a problem. As for the money he is taking with him, there's plenty in the bank left over from better times.

"Better times?" Ann is astonished. "I thought we were *in* better times."

"Last year," David says. "This year it's worse times."

"But why didn't you tell me?" She waits to continue their talk until they are both in their beds, the time when she feels they are the closest, though a night table separates them. David's back is to her. His pajamas, a birthday gift from Will, have sailboats on them. A harvest moon fills the room with unreal orange light. She cannot believe how easily, now in her mid-thirties, she can still be duped. She has thought somehow that she has learned to read the signs. "Why didn't you tell me?" she repeats.

"Because it's a passing thing, because there was no need for us both to worry." Though it is said with little conviction, it sounds like his last word on the subject. Still, she asks him to turn and face her. He does so grudgingly, reshaping the pillow and pounding it twice to form a nest for his head. "You like this better?" In the light he looks like a specter. Sitting on the edge of the bed across from him, she imagines she must look the same to him, so she clicks on the lamp on the night table.

"It's almost midnight," he complains.

"Do you remember the purses?" she suddenly asks.

"What purses?"

"The ones in the trunk of the car. In Florida?"

"Of course. But that was a different business back then. Just a few of us."

"I'm not talking about the business. I'm talking about the time. Do you remember the time with the purses?"

"What are we talking about?" David is impatient.

"I'm talking about what do we have to do to go back to that time?"

David sighs heavily.

"No, really." Ann catches her reflection in the mirror beyond David's bed. "There must be a way."

"How can you even think like that?"

As always, Ann's reflection surprises her. Expecting to see herself tired and worried, she looks quite awake, vibrant, in fact. "Is it the way I look?"

He opens his eyes. "No, no, of course not," and then after a few moments, "you know, you're still very dear to me."

"But not dear enough to make love to?"

"We could make love," he offers.

"What about my nose?" she asks, putting her forefinger to its tip and pushing it back to transform it from Grandfather Leo's nose to Shirley's—to what the shampoo commercials call "pert." "What about changing it to something like this?"

David joins her on her bed, puts his arm around her. "That looks cute," he says, looking into the mirror with her.

"Really?"

The Nose Job

Before the doctor administers the anesthetic, his nurse asks Ann to sit down in front of a plain wall painted a pale blue. All the other walls in the small anteroom hold before-and-after photographs of his patients. One of them, a famous movie actress, once had a nose that looked exactly like Ann's. "Look natural," he says, as the flashbulb pops and blinds her. She hopes she hasn't blinked in this, her last opportunity to look natural.

The doctor has told her that after the operation her face will feel something like her shin might had she smacked it against a coffee table. That is exactly how it feels—an intense ache that radiates through her entire face, extending even to her neck and shoulders. Her eyes, where visible through the bandage that covers much of her face, are black and swollen. Two small holes define her nostrils. She can hardly move her mouth, finds it difficult even to drink with the curved straw the doctor's office has provided.

"How does it feel, Mama?" Will, now seven, asks. He has come with David to pick her up, and studies her bandaged face carefully from every angle. David's look is more cursory.

"It's okay," she says, with a pronounced adenoidal twang. She tries a smile, fails. "Really." Will is concerned about what to tell his friends. Now that he sees her, he decides, "Car accident."

The bandages stay on for two weeks, and by the fifth or sixth day her face hurts less, though it is still impossible to eat anything other than ice cream, which Will feeds her using the small silver spoon she used to feed him when he was a baby. She wants to hug him while he does, but is afraid to jostle things under the bandage. Twice a day, she uses Q-Tips dipped in hydrogen peroxide to keep her nostrils free from scar tissue.

On the day the bandage is to come off, David drives her to the doctor's.

"Excited?" he asks. Actually, she is more curious than excited. The changes in her life that she had already wrought were largely irrevocable. Her old nose, she figures, she can always get back as long as she has the pictures. "Are you?"

David glances quickly over at her. Since her decision to have the operation, Ann has sensed his renewed interest in her. Once he even touched her cheek exactly the way he had in Florida.

"Are you excited?" he repeats.

Just as she is to answer, a car cuts in front of them, then speeds away. "Sonofabitch," David says. He steps on the gas, and for the next five minutes chases the car through the highway traffic. The big Chrysler heaves mightily with every lane change. Ann grabs onto her armrest to keep from sliding along the front seat. She is scared for her new nose, still tender and not fully healed under the bandages—even more so, she is scared by David's fury.

"What's the hurry?" she asks. But David doesn't seem to hear. Finally, he is right behind the car, a low-slung black Lincoln, only a few feet from its bumper.

"I'm just going to tap him," he says. There are bubbles of perspiration near his temples, on his upper lip.

"Tap him? Are you crazy?"

David closes the distance between the two cars, then accelerates slightly. Ann awaits the contact, feet braced on the floorboards, hands on the dashboard, but the contact never comes. Instead, the Lincoln lunges forward and to the right, cuts onto an off-ramp, and is gone.

David watches the car disappear, looking for a way off the highway himself. When he cannot find it, he slows, pulls to the right shoulder, and slumps forward, head on the steering wheel, and facing the driver's door.

"I've never seen you . . ." Ann begins.

"I'm leaving," he says softly. "It's the only thing I can do."

The Unveiling

"The show must go on," Doody insists about the party she is giving in mid-December to unveil Ann's new nose to the neighboring wives. The operation is still sufficiently rare that the interest level is exceptionally high. Friends of friends have RSVP'd from as far away as Pennsylvania. The fact that all these strangers can see of Ann's old nose is a copy of the photograph taken in the doctor's office and a few other photographs of Ann seems immaterial. "It's an excuse for them to make the trip," Doody says, "get out of the house."

In the week that passes between the time the bandages are taken off and the party—time for Ann's eyes to lose the black circles around them, and for the swelling to go down—Ann studies the nose constantly. She knows she should be more concerned about her life and Will's without David, but somehow she simply can't get around to it. The moment something comes to mind about the future, or of the past, she is at the mirror. It is the oddest thing—not only her behavior, but the nose, which looks like an interloper on her face. At other times, the nose seems like a diminishment of something that once was, the trace left behind by the thief who makes off with the valuables. At still other times, it looks like something on loan for a special occasion—a borrowed silk dress that doesn't quite fit.

Also, she is not certain whether the surprised expression she confronts each time she looks in the mirror reflects her surprise at her new self, or whether it is permanent, the result of the mix and match of her old features and her modern nose. Sometimes she leaves the mirror smiling. At other times, she can only gaze at it for so long before she must offer up a look of reproach for having done this to herself.

David has said he will stay on through the holidays, until Will goes back to school. Ann tries to make something of the concession. Is he giving them another chance? Is there something she can do in the meantime that will change things? But she soon realizes it is only a matter of convenience for him, since he leaves early, comes home late, doesn't really spend any time with her or Will. Nothing is said to Will about David's leaving, but he knows anyway. Where only a few days before he would anticipate his time with David—if only to wake up as early as he, sit with him while his coffee percolated—now Will hides in bed under the pile of blankets he has asked for the night before.

"Are you so cold?" she asks. "I could turn the heat up more." No, he prefers the blankets. As he sleeps, she watches, pulling the blankets down from over his head.

In the days before the party, the weather turns "mean," as Doody calls it. She appears daily in a large pea-green anorak, a fur-trimmed hood covering her hair. The wind whips at the aluminum screen door when she opens it. "David ought to take this thing down before it blows away," she says, stamping the snow off her boots in the entranceway.

"David who?" Ann says.

Doody puts her hand to her mouth. "Whoops!"

Ann always has one of Doody's Chesterfields with her coffee. She hates the taste, but loves watching the smoke mingle from the two cigarettes as they sit in the ashtray, their tips tinted with two shades of lipstick. One day, Doody arrives with a bottle of Cointreau. "You like oranges?" she asks, coming up the walk, holding out the bottle, trying to keep her footing on the ice that has formed in the night. Doody laces their coffees with the liqueur. After four such refills, Doody is on her way, leaving Ann at the kitchen table with the empty bottle, the dishes, the ashtray filled with a half dozen butts.

When Ann stands to put everything into the sink, she realizes she is tipsy. Still, she goes about cleaning up, but at the sink, looking out the window past the sweet potato propped by toothpicks growing in the jar on the sill and into the blowing snow, she becomes dizzy, disoriented. She reaches behind her for the chair and, locating it, sits back down heavily.

"How can this be?" she thinks. "Why is this happening?" And for the first time since David said he was leaving, she cries.

The morning before the party, Mama calls from Manhattan to announce that she and Jacobi are coming for a visit. It has been nearly six months since Ann has seen them. As estranged as she felt from Mama when they lived together in Vienna, here Ann feels even less of a connection. Mama and Jacobi are a pair of eccentrics, embracing suddenly on the subway, stealing the salt and pepper from shakers in restaurants ("If it's on the table, it's ours to keep," Mama declares by way of explanation). Long-haired Jacobi entertains schoolchildren on the bus with a fiddle bought from a pawnshop. Ann recalls Cybelle's pronouncement of twenty-five years ago—"The women of Vienna have no color"—then thinks of Mama's dramatic feathered hats and her outrageous dresses, each of which she has retailored to create a special effect. Some are slit nearly to the waist on the back or side, others reveal her shoulders. "There is no need to get old," Mama has told her.

In fact, Ann thinks, Mama's costumes make her look older than her fifty-three years. They make her look as if she is impersonating someone young. Finally, however, Ann knows that the rancor she feels toward Mama has nothing to do with the way she acts or dresses, but with Mama's never having loved her, and Mama's refusal even now to acknowledge that.

Mama turns down Ann's offer to drive to Manhattan and pick them up by car, and says they will take a cab instead. The extravagance of it makes Ann wary. What could they possibly want? Feeling she must match Mama's extravagant gesture with one of her own, Ann bakes a cake, a Sacher torte from Oma's old cookbook. It is satisfying work, particularly smoothing the slick, bittersweet chocolate icing over the raspberry glaze. When it is finished, the cake looks professional, complete with a script chocolate "S" on the top which Ann creates using a pastry tube.

So concerned is she with determining the reason for Mama's visit, she forgets the obvious: her new nose, about which she has told Mama over the phone. Of course, it is Mama's vanity that brings them, her curiosity about plastic surgery and what it might offer in her own campaign against age. Realizing this, Ann goes about her cleaning early that afternoon with a sense of victory, of excitement even.

"David called," Mama begins, after barely acknowledging Ann's nose. The three of them sit in the living room. Jacobi reclines on the BarcaLounger, his spats pointed skyward. At the mention of David's name, he gazes out the picture window. The snow of the last few days has melted, and only patches remain on the wet grass. "David called and said he was leaving."

"Why would he do that?" Ann looks at Jacobi, who refuses to look back at her. The thought that David has been talking to Mama, to anyone, behind her back makes her furious.

"He thought maybe that we could help . . ."

"That's ridiculous. He must know that."

The twitch in Mama's face has gotten worse.

"Mama, you've never helped. Never in all these years."

Mama sits straight as a schoolteacher, saying nothing, bearing the onslaught.

"I can't tell you how many times a word or two from you, something, anything, could have made a difference, but never . . ."

"I told you," Mama finally interrupts, no longer able to keep silent, "it was your temperament."

"How would you even know what my temperament was?" Ann throws up her hands, exasperated. "You never spent the time to find out."

"Oma told me," Mama pronounces. "She told me everything."

"What?" Ann tries to imagine the discussion, Oma's and Mama's, about her temperament. She cannot. Oma was her confidante, never Mama's. "You're lying."

Mama lets out a surprised laugh. "The wisdom of children," she sneers. "Always able to interpret the true meaning of things, eh?"

"As well as most adults."

"And you still believe it?" Mama gives a patronizing nod. "I think that must be the charm you hold—correction, you *held*—for your husbands."

"Enough!" Returning the BarcaLounger to the upright position, Jacobi pitches forward like a large doll. "You," he addresses Mama, "you should once, just once, let her have her say. She is, after all, still yours, your responsibility."

"Never mine," Mama insists. "His!" Ann winces. It is so unfair that this is happening to her now, of all times. "I'm leaving," Mama announces. "Someone call a taxicab." She goes to the closet, puts on her coat.

Ann is desperate. "Tell me one thing, Mama." Mama adjusts her hat in the foyer mirror. "Tell me just that Oma didn't betray me."

"I'll leave that for you to determine in your infinite child's wisdom." Mama opens the front door and steps out onto the porch. The wind swats at the tails of her coat as she stands, stalwart, her back to the picture window.

"We're leaving anyway," Jacobi says, "tomorrow, to Switzerland, by aeroplane."

"And this is it?" Ann indicates Mama, who peers out into the street as if to will a taxi to materialize. "Our last time together?"

"Perhaps," Jacobi says, "but Anna, you knew this about your mama from years back. She has nothing for you."

"But you came. What for?"

"David said he was scared. He told us about that thing with the pills."

"You came because of *that*?"

"It was a compelling gesture," Jacobi says.

"But that was nothing, an accident."

"Well, then," Jacobi says, pointing to his own coat in the closet, "we leave you not in the best of times, but also not in the worst." He holds his arms out to her, but before she can lean down to kiss him, he withdraws the embrace.

"It's not all your mama's fault, you know. I was her co-conspirator, so there's no need to kiss me. I'm not even a relative."

"But"—Ann touches his shoulders and kisses his cheek—"at least sometimes you tried."

When Ann asks Doody where she has gotten an actual veil and sari, Doody just smiles and says, "the inscrutable Orient." She adjusts the outfit until she is satisfied. "Look demure," she instructs.

"It's hard to breathe."

"Twenty million Indian women can't be wrong. Or is it twenty million Indian men?"

In all, a dozen women show up, most coming from the neighborhood; others, as Doody has promised, from as far as Pennsylvania. Some, unable to find babysitters in the middle of a school day, bring their children. Doody shepherds the youngsters to Will's room, where he, home with a cold, is assembling a parachute jump with the Erector set David has given him the day before—without any explanation, though it was bought as a Christmas gift and Christmas is still a week away. Little men with cotton parachutes dangle from strings from a series of struts at the top of the five-foot-tall structure. Ann thinks it looks more like a hanging than a carnival ride.

Back in the living room, the women chat with one another,

passing around the "before" photographs Doody has provided. Doody serves coffee; Ann has baked another cake, just like the one she made yesterday for Mama. Most of the women smoke, though only Doody inhales, then exhales in long, continuous streams, like Lauren Bacall. The others cough out the smoke in nervous little puffs.

With her sari and veil, Ann glides around the edges of the gathering, unable to smoke, eat or drink. No one, for some reason, not even Doody, addresses her directly, referring to her as they look at the pictures as "she," "her," or more rarely, "Ann."

Finally the moment has come. Ann stands in the middle of the living room while the women sit on the couch and the chairs brought from the dining room. Doody has put a baroque fanfare on the record player. "Ta da!" she announces, pulling Ann's veil off like a magician. Ann feels absolutely ridiculous, particularly in those first moments, when everyone just stares and no one says a word. Suddenly, one of the women stands and begins clapping. She is immediately joined by all the others, now converging on Ann. "Look, but don't touch," Doody cautions.

With her veil off, Ann is now included in the festivities. She even partakes in a game of Doody's devising: "Pin the Nose on the Housewife." Halfway through the game, Doody asks, "Does anyone like oranges?" and produces three bottles of Cointreau.

One of the women says that her husband hates it when she drinks during the day, and takes the key to the liquor cabinet with him to work. Doody assures her that Cointreau is not liquor, but liqueur, with none of the same debilitating side effects. Ann takes a bit of it in her first cup of coffee, and also her second.

Not long before everyone has to leave to get home in time for their husbands, the Chrysler pulls into the driveway. Doody is the first to notice. "David, King of Kings," she says, sidling up to Anna, "home early, of all days."

He comes in the side door, through the breezeway and kitchen, and goes into the master bedroom, where Ann waits.

"I didn't mean to interrupt," he says. Ann hears the front door open and close, cars start. As they drive away, she becomes aware of how dark it has become. She clicks off the light.

"I have to go now," David says softly, opening the closet.

"But you just got here." Ann feels a twinge in her belly like a small animal inside her taking an exploratory bite.

"No," David continues. He pulls a suitcase down from the top shelf. "I have to go, *now*. I can't come back here anymore."

"Really?" Ann has resigned herself to his leaving, but not until after the holidays as they planned. She looks down at the suitcase and then at her sari. "But what about our arrangement?"

"I'm sorry," David says. "It was a bad arrangement." She knows he is referring to everything: the marriage, the house, perhaps even Will. She imagines she hears the Erector set motor pulling the parachutes to the apex of the structure, poised for their leap.

"Was it something I did? Could have done?"

"Ann, we've been through it already, how many times?" David is exasperated. "I had hoped I could just get in and get out while the party was going on."

"Would you have left a note?"

"Don't be so melodramatic."

"No, really," she says, moving forward, seeking to engage him. Just then, however, she feels the twinge in her insides again. It makes her think she might be sick, so she tells David, "Excuse me," and goes into the bathroom, locking the door behind her. She sits on the closed toilet, waiting for the tears to come, or the nausea, but neither does. Instead, she feels a slight chill go through her, though it is extremely warm in the house.

She looks at the uncurtained bathroom window over the tub. It is a small black rectangle. She goes to the medicine cabinet. There are a dozen or so bottles of pills, all left over from Will's childhood ailments. Also mouthwash, deodorant, aspirin, Geritol. "For tired blood," it says on the bottle. Ann tries to imagine it, tired blood. Pale red, slow to flow from a wound. She picks up David's razor, a silver Schick double-edge. Twirling the base of the handle, she opens the hangar-like flaps to reveal the blade. Ann holds the blade between her thumb and forefinger, flexing the thin metal. She puts it back into the razor. Dangerous business, this blade. Could she really have had too much Cointreau?

As she closes the medicine cabinet, there is a knock on the door.

"What are you doing in there?" David asks.

"Nothing," Ann answers. As she does, however, there is a slight catch in her voice, and suddenly she feels tears course down her cheeks, over her new nose. At the sink she turns on the cold water.

"Come on," David urges at the door. "Come on out."

"In a minute." But Ann can't imagine coming out in a minute. There are too many things to attend to. The tears, whether or not she is allowed to blow her nose, the sick feeling in her stomach, the dizziness she feels every time she stands. "In a few minutes," she amends.

"Why don't you come out now?" He turns the knob, finds it locked.

Ann thinks to list her reasons, but stops.

"Please." He tries the knob again. Ann watches it jiggle as she sits again on the toilet.

After a few minutes of silence he says, "Don't make me mad. I don't want to be mad."

David, mad? Ann thinks. She has rarely seen him mad, never directly at her. That is one of the amazing things about David—he has always been so even-natured, except that one time in the car. Other than his actually not being there, there has hardly ever been a clue that he did not want to be.

"Ann!" he says sharply.

She thinks now she will open the door soon, but really must compose herself before she does. After all, there is Will to think of. She doesn't want him to worry. Of course, he'll worry when David leaves. She can imagine Will's confused and slightly pained expression when she tells him. She should probably have told him earlier. Now it will . . .

"Ann!" David pushes against the door.

"Just a few more minutes." She opens the medicine cabinet and takes out the mouthwash, unscrews the cap.

"Don't do anything you'll be sorry for."

She studies the mouthwash, the small, white mouthwash bottle, "ODOL." She unscrews the tiny black lid, runs some water in her toothbrush cup and adds a few drops of the ODOL. She is about to gargle with it when there is another rap on the door, softer, less insistent.

"Mama, come out. Please."

"Will?"

"Please."

"I am. I will. What's all the fuss?" She gargles once quickly, wipes her face with her washcloth, thinking as she does that the three of them will sit down now and David will explain why it is that he is leaving. Will David use the same words to tell Will that he used with her? "Someone else." No name, so mysterious.

"Just tell me who," Ann demanded.

"It doesn't matter." True, David was never mad.

His refusal suggested someone she knew. She scoured her memory for every woman she had ever seen him with. In her wildest, half-asleep fantasy, she imagined it was Cybelle, not dead at all, but tracking her back to Vienna, to New York, Florida, New York again, and now New Jersey.

"Mama!"

Ann opens the door. The hall is dark. Will puts his arms around her waist and buries his head in her sari. Ann looks toward the bedroom, and then toward the living room.

"Where is Papa?" she asks, her voice small.

"Papa?" Will says it as if it were a word quickly fading from his lexicon. "Papa's gone."

"Ah. And he told you . . ."

". . . that he would be gone."

She hears the garage door close. "Come," she says, "don't you want to go to the window? And wave?"

"No."

But Ann does. Not to wave, but to watch. I must be crazy, she thinks, standing before the picture window in full view of the neighbors, in full view of David now backing the station wagon out of the driveway. She flicks on the small lantern-shaped light at the end of the driveway. It illuminates his face as he swings the car out onto the street. He looks worried, as if perhaps the station wagon won't make it. Why was he so sure there was nothing she could do? There must always be something.

Ann feels Will's small hand on her back.

New Jersey, 1953

Annie

Jake Weigel leans forward on the nubbly green sectional sofa, legs spread, hands on his knees. His fingers form a steeple on which he rests his chin. He is larger than Ann remembers, out of scale with the furniture, the rest of the room. He looks uncomfortable in his dark suit. An untouched highball sits on the glass coffee table before him. The glass sweats in the waning, humid September afternoon. "I'm told that I'm irresponsible," he says. "Not about the law"—which, with his Boston accent, he pronounces "lore"—"but about everything else."

"What do you mean?" Ann asks. He has been in her living room less than ten minutes and she is already confounded by him. As he did on that Christmas Eve seven years ago when he arrived as suddenly and unexpectedly as a storm out of season, Jake flatters her, talks too fast and seems certain about everything. Not like Peter, Ann thinks, who was certain about abstractions, or David, who was certain about a small part of the world. No, Jake Weigel's certainty extends to the whole of life and his mastery over it.

The broad expanse of Jake's shoulders in the black suit brings to mind an anvil. The occasional lapse of his animated face into an expression of cold assessment recalls the photograph of Mount Rushmore in the civics book Ann studied for her citizenship examination. "What do you mean, irresponsible?"

"It means"—Jake puts a finger under his collar as if chafed by the question—"it means I get into things with people, and I don't know how to act." He looks up at her like a chastened child, unable to help himself. "It's true. But what can I do?" He picks up his drink and gulps it down, then sets the glass back hard on the table. "Actually, it's worked out pretty well so far."

"Are you warning me?" Tonight will be the first time Ann has been out with a man since David left, three years before.

Jake laughs. "Warning you? You might say that." He seems relieved to have gotten it out of the way, as if, having explained himself, he can now do whatever he wants.

"What makes you think I'm interested?"

Jake looks hurt. "Listen," he explains. "I don't have much time for this sort of thing. I met you a few years back and I liked you. I still do—don't ask me why, because I don't know that sort of thing. So, if we hit it off, well, what the hell, let's make it into something."

Will walks into the room. "Hiya, fella," Jake says, holding his hand out to the boy. Will, at ten, with no memory of the man he said he didn't like, pumps his hand in return. Ann marvels that her son has become cheerful, outgoing, seemingly unscathed by David's departure, by anything.

Jake takes Ann to see *South Pacific*. In it, Emile de Becque, a late-middle-aged South Sea Island plantation owner, and Nellie Forbush, a young navy nurse, fall in love. Jake is captivated by the performance. When the rest of the audience chuckles, Jake laughs uproariously. During scenes of tenderness, Ann looks over to him and sees him cry. And when the entire company, as a navy crew, turns out to sing "There Is Nothing Like a Dame," it is as if Jake is a member of the crew himself, tapping his feet to the beat of the song, conducting the music with his hands.

Afterwards, in the cab heading for dinner, Jake insists he's like Emile de Becque, and that Ann is his Nellie Forbush.

"Meaning I'm supposed to fall in love with you? And you with me?" Going through the park on a moonless night, Ann can barely see Jake, though she can feel his bulk jostling against her in the turns.

"Who knows, Annie. Maybe sometime. Not now maybe, but soon. You wait and see."

The more he calls her "Annie," the more she likes it. Unlike "Ann," which was cool and reserved and ultimately didn't serve her well, "Annie" sounds familiar, fun, perhaps even exuberant. Ann smiles at the possibility.

"From now on you can always call me 'Annie,' " she says as they get out of the taxi.

Jake gives her shoulder a squeeze. "Was there ever any question?"

At a small French restaurant on the Upper East Side, Jake's favorite New York eating spot, he greets the maître d' with a hug. Dancing the man away from his station like a bear, Jake winks at Annie, who is still standing in the coat-check area. "Roland is crazy about me," he announces to her and to most of the others in the place.

Jake and Annie's table is isolated somewhat from the rest of the dining room, surrounded on three sides by a mahogany partition. There is a small vase on the table with a single white rose, its stem leaning slightly from the weight of the bud. Overhead is a crystal chandelier.

When the tournedos of beef Jake orders are too well done, he insists that Annie accompany him to the kitchen to oversee the broiling of the next batch. The two of them—Jake carrying his plate, a napkin still stuck in the waistband of his trousers—walk through the restaurant past solemn diners. In the kitchen, Jake makes an incision in the offending beef for the chef, whom he also seems to know.

"Once more, with a little less feeling, Henri, if you please."

"But of course," the man says, with a disingenuous smile. It looks to Annie that the faint stain where his toque meets his brow is growing, though Jake does not seem to notice. "And who is the lady tonight?" Henri asks.

"Annie," Jake says. "Annie Forbush, Registered Nurse, U.S.

Navy, retired." Henri claims it is an honor to meet her, then butterflies another piece of filet and places it under the broiler. He also places a fresh piece of salmon on the grate—Annie's entree—so that her dinner will be ready at the same time as Jake's.

"This time I'll do the hollandaise," Jake announces, grabbing an apron from a hook. To Annie's amazement, Jake is wearing a gun in a holster beneath his coat, fastened under his arm. With the tails of his tie flying and his thick black hair falling over his face as he whips the egg yolks and butter wildly with a whisk, he looks like a madman. "You can't make a grand hollandaise without sweating," Jake declares, as perspiration soaks his shirt. When it is done, Jake carries both entrees back to their table.

"Is it always this way?" Annie asks.

"Like I said, I don't really know how to act. I suppose I could have just sat here and made a fuss about things not being right, but why? See what I mean?" He looks at her, his fork poised with a large piece of beef and some peas balanced on it. One or two fall to the table.

Ann searches for a reason, but they are all connected to some notion of propriety or good manners, things that Jake Weigel clearly does not concern himself with. "Yes," she finally acknowledges, "I see what you mean."

"Thank God," he jokes, putting the fork in his mouth, having waited for her answer. "Now eat up before it gets cold."

"One more thing," Annie says.

"What?" Jake's mouth is full.

"The gun . . ."

"Protection," he assures her. "I haven't used it in years."

Later, Annie and Jake face each other in the yellow-tinged light emanating from the two small fake lanterns at Annie's front door. When he asks her whether she has enjoyed herself, she admits she has. "And do you like me, do you think of me as Emile de Becque?"

"Possibly. I'll have to think more about it." It is late. Annie takes her keys from her purse. She is certain the babysitter is asleep.

"Then why don't I just come in and spend the night," Jake

suggests. "I haven't got a hotel room, and it's a long way to Boston, so what the hell."

Annie's hand is on the doorknob, her shoulder against the door. It feels solid. Beyond it is the small foyer, and then the living room and the familiar couch on which she sat so much of last year and the year before, watching TV until, one by one, the stations signed off for the night, leaving only a tiny pinpoint of light on the screen that persisted long after Ann turned the set off. Except for Will and the few piano students she had taken on, there were not many people in Ann's life. Even Doody had stopped coming by.

Worst of all were the late afternoons when, after the divorce, David would come in the other woman's red convertible to pick Will up for dinner. The top was often down, and standing behind the drapes, Ann could see David at the wheel and the woman close to him, her blond hair in a kerchief.

Ann hated herself for watching, but felt compelled to. Each time she saw them, her hands perspired, and she could feel a pulse beat at her temple. When Will was finally in the car and they drove away, the sensation would fade and Ann would feel merely embarrassed. One time, however, she recognized that it was not embarrassment she felt, but pleasure—as if she were witnessing what she had coming to her.

For what? she wondered. What had she done to deserve this? She sifted through all the obvious possibilities until she arrived at the only one that made any sense at all—that day in Vienna, the German officer, and the fact that she didn't even scream.

Jake is serious. "I know, Annie. Your mother wouldn't approve. Still, I think it's a fine idea." He puts his hand over hers on the doorknob.

"You're wrong about that," she says, "about my mother not approving." Yet even about that she is not certain, Mama having changed so.

As they make love, Jake's long, thin penis sheathed in a prophylactic—a "safe," as he calls it—Annie tries to give herself to the moment. But she can't—not quite—though she is pleased by how she is able to arouse him, and touched by how long afterward he keeps his arm around her, his head resting on her shoulder.

The next morning Jake shows Annie and Will that his nose is like rubber, with no cartilage in it at all. "I had it broken so many times when I was a kid on the South End, the doctors just gave up. Worked out okay, though. I had a paper route, and my boss used to shake us down every day by holding us by the heels. But me, I could keep my pennies in my nose."

"Really?" Will asks.

"Is that really so?" Annie can't tell either if Jake is kidding or not.

"What do you think?" Jake straps on his shoulder holster, as Annie hands him his coat.

"I just don't know."

Mrs. Weigel

"Making your acquaintance is very nice, Helen," Jake's mother says to Annie, when they meet at Mrs. Weigel's apartment in Boston. Annie is up for the weekend, Will back in New Jersey with a sitter. Helen was Jake's second wife, and when Jake corrects his mother, she just waves her hand as if to fend him off. "Helen, Annie, Annie, Helen . . ." she begins, then walks into the living room. She is a short woman, less than five feet tall and in her late seventies. Her tiny blue dress has white stars on it.

"Well," she says, sitting down on the edge of one of her massive upholstered chairs. "You drop by. What's the purpose?" She looks like a doll; her feet just barely graze the carpet. The small lace doilies on the back and arms of each of the chairs further exaggerate their size. Mrs. Weigel's eyes show no humor. Her thin-lipped mouth is similar to her son's.

"Ma, don't be so unfriendly." Jake walks over to her and covers her hand with his. Her fingers curl.

"Why do you bring her by? What am I supposed to do?"

"But I wanted you to meet her."

"Okay, so I'm meeting her."

"Ma . . ."

"Okay, sit down." Jake sits. His smile takes in both his mother and Annie. It is hopeful, like a child's. Annie is amazed at the transformation.

"So, are you thinking of getting married?" Mrs. Weigel suddenly asks.

"I've been married," Jake offers. "It didn't work out."

"As if you have to tell me." She turns to Annie. "You know, right after it goes sour, both times, he moves in here. A grown man, living with his mother," she says, with more fondness than indignation.

Annie, who has been assured by Jake that his mother is quite a gal, is determined to win her over. "It must have been nice, though. For you, that is." Mrs. Weigel raises an eyebrow. Her powdered face is as white as the doilies, her neck still smooth but speckled with liver spots. "Nice to have the company."

"Company? The guy was out almost every night of the week. This one, then that one, then this one. Now, if I were younger . . ."

Jake interrupts. "Do you have something to offer us, Ma? A sweet, or something?"

"Nothing," she says, but gets up anyway and walks to the kitchen.

"She means well," Jake assures Annie, putting his hands on her shoulders from behind and pinning her to the deep chair.

"I'm sure she does," Annie says.

"No, really. She didn't mean to hurt your feelings."

"That's all right," Annie insists, "I'm tough. I can take it." And while she feels she can—take anything—there is something inside her—the image of a skater spinning on a single blade, arms drawn tighter and tighter to her body, twirling ever faster.

"That's my girl," Jake declares. He sits down, absently stares at the walls, furniture, waiting for his mother to return. Every few seconds he looks at Annie and smiles. Once he winks, and she winks back. In the kitchen a garbage disposal clatters.

The kitchen door swings open and Mrs. Weigel stands on the

threshold. "Jake," she says, "I need you." Jake jumps up. Annie tries to overhear what the two of them are saying in the kitchen, but can't. Perspiration builds up along the backs of her calves where her stockinged legs touch the scratchy fabric of the chair. She tries to get up, but the size of the furniture, and Jake's hands having pulled her so far back into the chair, make it hard to stand, make her feel small too.

Presently Mrs. Weigel emerges from the kitchen with a small, open pink pastry box and a single cup of coffee, which she hands to Annie, then looks quickly away, placing the pastry box on a table some distance away. "The disposal," she says, to explain Jake's absence. Annie nods. "He's a very difficult man, my boy," she suddenly offers. "Very difficult. Take it from me." Mrs. Weigel sits again and leans toward Annie as if they are confidantes.

"I know," Annie says, deciding to try once more with the woman.

"How so?" She seems disappointed by Annie's agreement.

"I mean, he's very unique. He does things his own way."

Mrs. Weigel raises her eyebrow again. "And that's what you like about him?" She is talking faster now, as if the time for secrets is running short.

"One of the things," Annie says, warily.

"What else?" Mrs. Weigel demands.

"He seems very capable," Annie ventures.

"Very. His father's son."

"No doubt his mother's as well."

Mrs. Weigel glares at Annie. "Listen, sweetie, don't try to get on my good side. I hate that."

Just then Jake reappears. "What do you put in your sink, Ma? Nails?"

"Sometimes. Sometimes just cans," she says offhandedly. Jake reaches down, pulls her up by her thick waist and gives her a hug.

"What did I tell you? Quite a gal, eh?"

"It's fixed?" she asks when he finally puts her down. She straightens her dress, which has gotten twisted in his embrace.

"Fixed."

"You should be going then," she says, looking at her watch.

"Right," Jake says, offering Annie a hand and pulling her from the chair.

Mrs. Weigel stands on her tiptoes and kisses him on the cheek, then closes the pink pastry box and walks away into the kitchen, leaving Jake and Annie in the living room. "Once you get to know her," he says, escorting Annie out the door, "and she accepts you, you'll see. She'd cut her right arm off for you."

The Lodge

The radio in Jake's Hudson plays mostly static. He keeps it on, he says, because he likes the small light it casts across their laps. Outside, blowing snow, which fell earlier, dusts the green, ovoid car. The wiper on Jake's side doesn't work, and occasionally he reaches out the wing window to wipe the windshield with his gloved hand. Entering the rotary approach that will put them on the bridge to Cape Cod, he tells Annie that three of the Army Corps of Engineers who built the span fell into the forms as the cement was being poured for the east anchorage supports.

"And?" Annie asks, hopeful of some satisfactory end.

"And, they just kept right on pouring." After observing what seems like a moment of silence, Jake fiddles with the radio, "for a weather report," he claims. It is New Year's Eve.

In the drone of the heater fan, the light crackle of static from the car radio, and the occasional squeak of Jake's hand on the windshield, Annie wonders what kind of mother she has become. She told Will they would go to Times Square to be part of the crowd that watches the golden ball fall to ring in the new year. But then, Jake called in the middle of the afternoon. He'd booked the flight, he'd pick her up at Logan, 9:00 p.m. It was the first time he'd called in weeks. "I'll make it up to you," she said to Will, as she packed his overnight things in a small duffel. He'd spend New Year's Eve with neighbors. "You'll see." That her leaving didn't seem to bother Will at all pleased her then, upsets her now.

"Why do you think . . ." she begins aloud, then stops. She knows Jake doesn't want to hear any of this.

"Think?" Jake turns. The light from the radio illuminates the bottom of his jaw; the rest of his face remains in full shadow, as if in a cowl. The image startles her, and Annie hopes for a streetlamp or the lights of an oncoming car to soften it, but nothing does.

"Please watch the road," she says, and when he turns, she switches off the radio.

An hour later, at the junction where the small, rural road meets the driveway to Jake's lodge, he stops the car. Snow has formed a drift six feet high that blocks the entrance. It eddies at Jake's feet as he goes to the trunk to get a snow shovel and boots, swirls lightly in the beams of the headlights. Seconds later, Jake's energetic shoveling sends snow flying in every direction like a blizzard. Peering through it, Annie stands at the passenger door and tries to make out the lodge.

"What's the hurry?" Annie asks, coming up behind him. She puts her hands on his back. Suddenly he turns, drops the shovel and gives her a powerful hug. He kisses her, rubs her nose with his.

"I want to be there, with you, for the new year," he says. "So leave me shovel."

Annie retreats to the car to stand at the passenger door again. At one point, Jake calls to her to move the car to shine the lights onto the drift. Annie gets in the car and maneuvers it until the headlights illuminate Jake standing by the drift, which is now less than four feet high. "Keep it running," Jake calls out, "keep it warm," then assaults the drift again, this time with greater focus, like a determined convict digging his way out of prison. Between where the car idles and where Jake shovels is a slight downgrade, and Annie has to engage the emergency brake to keep the car from rolling.

After Jake has made considerable progress, he calls out to Annie to bring the car closer. Annie pulls back on the emergency brake until its teeth disengage, then gradually eases her hold on the handle. The car rolls faster than she expects and is only inches from Jake when she is finally able to stop it. Jake holds his hand out like a traffic cop. "Perfect," he declares, master not only of his own life, but of everything surrounding it. In the warm car with the heater blasting, Annie feels a chill.

"Thinking about running me down?" Jake says, suddenly back in the car, pushing her to the passenger side. Giving the car gas, he lets go the emergency brake and the car pushes through what is left of the drift and plows fifty yards or so along the driveway, where the snow is far less deep. "End of the line," Jake announces, as the car fishtails. He throws open his door, grabs Annie by the hand and urges her toward him along the seat and into the snow, where they both stand leaning up against the side of the car. "The lodge," he gestures, sweeping his hand before them.

Lit faintly by the stars, the small crescent of moon and the light reflected off the snow, Jake's house looks benevolent, expectant even, as if awaiting their arrival. It is set at the base of a steep, wooded hill and overlooks a pond, now frozen and ringed with small trees and bushes, their branches weighted with snow. The lodge is not at all what Annie expects from the travel folders of Cape Cod she has seen, with their prim, two-story New England saltboxes. Instead, Jake's house is, indeed, a lodge—sprawling and shingled, with a peaked roof, and a facade consisting largely of windows. There are two stone chimneys, one anchoring a wing of the structure extending back into the hillside, the other, massive and commanding, at the lodge's center. Two glass-paneled front doors, one on either side of the central chimney, provide entry from a long, raised flagstone porch that runs the length of the building. A wide, welcoming apron of stone steps leads up to the porch and extends to where Annie and Jake stand.

They do not enter through the front, however. Instead, Jake hustles Annie to the side of the lodge and pushes open an unlocked door. He flicks on a light and stamps the snow from his shoes, urging Annie to do the same. They are in a good-sized kitchen dominated by a black range with a grill and a half dozen burners, with a black hood above. Facing the pond are four curved floor-to-ceiling picture windows that define a semicircular dining area.

Jake opens the refrigerator, removes a can of coffee and goes to the sink for some water, but none comes. "Sonofabitch," he says when he realizes the pipes are frozen. "Someone's going to pay for this." He tramps past the range, Annie's hand in his.

At the threshold of the room marked by the two front doors and the massive chimney, Jake switches on a light, a chandelier made from an old wagon wheel, four feet in diameter, with a hurricane lamp at each spoke, and suspended from the open-beam ceiling with chains. The stone fireplace at the room's center is nearly as tall as Jake, and twice as wide as it is tall. There is a long, oval oak table close to where they stand, surrounded by high-backed baronial chairs. Otherwise, the furnishings in the room are sparse—two worn red leather couches, two more tufted wingback chairs, a low-slung coffee table made of a coarse wooden slab and standing on what looks like tree stumps, and a huge cabinet with carved wooden doors. On the far wall, leading into another wing of the house, is a moose head with a bemused, avuncular expression.

"Stuffed it myself," Jake says, following Annie's gaze. "Very messy. My first and last moose." The lodge is as full of surprises as Jake is, Annie thinks. Growing used to the light, which is not really adequate for the room, she sees a half dozen small stuffed birds and squirrels on the mantel. Caught in alert, lifelike poses, they appear on the brink of escape.

"Well," Jake says, "ready to spend the rest of your life here?" Annie cannot even guess at the rest of her life. As for where she'll spend it, she cannot imagine it will be here, in a house so different from any she has ever been in.

In the master bedroom, Jake bends to build a fire before he turns on any light. The kindling catches in seconds, and in a minute a pleasant blaze warms the room and fills it with flashes of orange light. As the fire brightens, stuffed birds emerge from the room's darker shadows. Annie turns once, twice, before she has seen them all—on the mantel, on bookshelves, on small platforms at either side of the mirror above the built-in dresser.

"Eleven forty-six," Jake announces, "let's get into bed and welcome in the new year." He takes off his coat, helps Annie with hers, then unbuckles his shoulder holster and hangs it on a peg next to a bed built into a corner of the room. It is the largest bed Annie has ever seen. It is not until Jake is in his undershorts and Annie is under the mountainous comforter that she is finally comfortable. Lying on her side facing him, she recalls Jake at *South Pacific* and the pleasure he took in the performance.

Tonight, unlike past times, their lovemaking is slow. Jake seems to be in no hurry to get anywhere, not even to sleep, and it is well into the new year when he finally turns from her and she hears the squeak of his condom as he pulls it off.

Much later, she tries to imagine Will, sleeping on his back at the neighbors', arms outstretched and trusting. But the image fails her again and again, replaced by that of the men entombed in the bridge that crosses the canal—arms and legs splayed, their expressions fixed forever in surprise.

Cape Cod, 1955

The Move

It is an early evening in May, still light outside. Annie and Will are in the Chrysler somewhere in Connecticut. Up ahead is Jake in his Hudson, towing a long, open trailer that holds Annie's furniture from the house in New Jersey. Because of the loaded trailer, Jake drives slowly—so slowly that in the gathering darkness Will can see lightning bugs in the green-black foliage along the side of the road. He is twelve years old; his voice is changing, and he hits so many notes in a single sentence sometimes that Jake has nicknamed him "The Human Accordion." To Annie's surprise, Will seems to like the name.

Jake's strategy for the move was to sneak onto the gently contoured, no-trailers-allowed Merritt Parkway and take his chances on being stopped. Less than ten miles along the parkway, he was—pulled over by a state trooper who cut between the Chrysler and the trailer. Annie stopped some distance beyond them and walked back along the shoulder to where Jake stood face to face with the trooper. When she was still a dozen or so yards away, Jake reached into his coat, and for an instant it looked to Annie as if he were pulling out his gun, though it was only his wallet.

"Looks like we're going overland . . ." Jake announced when Annie was in earshot. He had a ten-dollar bill in his hand. ". . . though I tried to convince the officer otherwise." Map on the hood of the Hudson, Jake plotted a new route as Annie and Will looked on.

The year before, not long after David's business failed, the alimony checks stopped coming. At first, David called to apologize, promising to send money as soon as he had any. One night, when he came for Will, it was no longer in the woman's fancy convertible, but in a beat-up old Chevrolet, much like the car Ann and David owned when they were first married. The woman was still with him, though.

Another night, a month later, David didn't show up at all. When Annie called his apartment to find out what had happened, the phone was disconnected—David had left the country, Jake later found out. "To go where?" Annie asked, even before she thought about how she would survive without David's support. "I thought America was a land of second chances."

Jake thought about it for a moment. "America *was* his second chance," he pronounced, "and he blew it."

At first, Annie tried to make enough for her and Will to live on by taking on more piano students. But it was undependable money, at best. Students came and went, and not one of them seemed to care about the music. Besides, every time she sat at the keyboard, she remembered Nathan Pearl, and that he had loved her better than anyone ever had.

So when Jake offered her free room and board at the lodge and threw in a Smith-Corona to learn to type on so that she could eventually become his secretary, Annie thought, why not?— though she knew the arrangement was unconventional, scandalous even. But he professed to be crazy about her, and maybe "crazy" was what she was about him. Being with Jake, watching him operate, was the most exciting thing she'd done in years, though he often confounded her as much as he pleased her. And while she was intimidated by his power at times, she knew he possessed enough for the two of them, and that if she took him up on his offer to be his "weekend gal," as he put it, he might even share his power with her.

"Just figure it out," Jake said when she wondered aloud what she would do on the weekdays when Will was in school and Jake was in Boston, "just figure it out and we'll make it happen."

It was Annie, not Jake, who suggested the typewriter.

Now, on a steep downgrade on an unlit rural road, Annie, at the wheel of the Chrysler, can barely make out the trailer up ahead. Its single red taillight flickers like a beacon before her, more hypnotic than pleasing. Will, stretched out in the back seat, has fallen asleep. Having been up all night packing the night before, Annie wishes she could do the same. Suddenly, the trailer picks up speed, the red light starts weaving from left to right, left to right, left to right in ever-widening arcs. Then, just as suddenly, it disappears. Annie switches on her high beams, sees the trailer and then the Hudson. The trailer is on its side, its contents mingling with the tall shrubs and grasses lining the road. The Hudson is up ahead, separated from the trailer and lying on its roof.

Annie jams on the brakes, stopping a few feet behind the Hudson, as Will rolls off the back seat and onto the floor. "Jake!" Annie calls out. But even as she opens the door, Jake emerges from the wreck, scratching his head.

"Sonofabitch!" he says, already past the Chrysler and making his way to the trailer, lit red now by the Chrysler's taillights. Annie checks quickly to see if Will is okay, then catches up with Jake. "Are you all right?"

Jake looks himself over theatrically, then stands stiff for a mock inspection. "I look all right, don't I?" Annie puts her arms around him. "So I guess I am."

asdfjkl;

Jake sets up the heavy black Smith-Corona on a small table in front of the semicircular kitchen windows. Rummaging through the four-car garage adjacent to the house, he locates an old gooseneck lamp which he attaches to the table, then fashions a holder out of some heavy-gauge wire to prop up Annie's new book of typing drills. "Ready for action," he declares.

Sitting on a kitchen chair, a cup of coffee next to her and more coffee percolating on the huge black stove, Annie teaches herself to type. For a few weeks it is almost as satisfying as her earliest exercises at the piano, which now she is able to recall distinct from everything else that happened at the Skodagasse. She remembers the pleasure of forming the notes, of hearing them, precise and separate when she wanted them to be, legato when it was melody she sought—*asdfjkl;, asdfjkl;, asdfjkl;*.

Of course, she knows it isn't the same, not at all, but still, there is the pleasure of becoming proficient at something again. As the drill book suggests, she gives herself typing tests using Jake's egg timer to check her proficiency. "20–30 words per minute, good; 30–50 words, average; 50–70 words per minute, above average; 70–90 words per minute, superior."

When, halfway through July, Annie times herself at 82 words per minute, she closes the drill book and looks out over the pond. The water is deep green, without a ripple. Occasionally, the reeds along the pond's perimeter stir as a frog jumps in from the shore or a small fish swims by. From where she sits, she cannot see any of the other houses on the pond. Will is off somewhere on the large hill behind the lodge with Jake, the two of them having left a few hours earlier. She kissed them both as they went out the door.

"Don't wait up for us," Jake joked.

Now at the typing table, Annie closes the drill book and lays it flat. She pulls the paper with her typing test from the platen. It makes a satisfying whirr as it releases the page. Again, she looks out at the pond. She can barely believe she is here—at Jake's lodge—barely believe the events that have brought her to this point. What now? she wonders. Tentative about indulging herself in this not altogether comfortable place, she lets a few memories flicker by, like the newsreels she watched when she was living in Manhattan—she and Cybelle in bathing outfits at the alpine lake they visited one weekend; Herr Hartmann walking the mongrel dog he had found, strutting along with him as tall and proud as the Kaiser; Mama, impatient with Jung for not revealing her future; Papa in his study, day after day, filling his yellow pads, writing . . . writing . . . writing.

Just then a breeze redolent of salt and pine slices through one of the open windows. Of course, Annie suddenly realizes. She takes a piece of paper from the stack, turns the knurled knob that feeds it into the machine until the page presents itself on the platen—clean and perfect. The keys beckon. The black and red ribbon between them and the paper is nearly new, replaced only yesterday. Without another thought, she begins.

Rafts

Nearly every weekend, Jake arrives from Boston with a different car; once a handsome old black-and-white Packard, another time an ancient, faded green pickup truck with a single headlight Jake has rigged to the bumper, still another time a swank yellow Lincoln convertible. In recent weeks he's come in a black Cadillac Meteor, a hearse he took in payment from a mortician he represented who went bankrupt.

Sometimes, Jake arrives alone. At other times he is accompanied by one or two men—"bums," he calls them—whom he picks up on the streets of Roxbury or Dorchester and rehabilitates for the weekend in exchange for their help on odd jobs and projects that usually involve either building something or tearing it down. Alone or otherwise, he always arrives in the dark, most often after midnight. During their first month at the lodge, it becomes a ritual for Annie and Will to wait up for Jake—Will eager to hear about whatever scheme Jake has up his sleeve, Annie anxious about a new set of strangers.

Lately too, Annie has grown anxious about Jake's temper, about the tightly wound skein of anger that seems to propel him from project to project. When she saw him less often, Annie construed Jake's drive as energy, plain and simple. But now, living with him two or three days of every week, it seems there is much more at play.

Tonight, Friday, it is nearly eleven when Will spots the headlights in the trees at the far end of the lodge opposite the entrance to the driveway that circles the house. A second set of lights trails the first, the beams dancing crazily in the woods as the cars jostle up the rough surface of the unpaved drive. First to appear is the hearse, towing a loaded flatbed trailer covered with a tarpaulin. Behind the trailer is the yellow Lincoln convertible, top down, and driven by a small man whose head barely clears the steering wheel. The hearse groans on its springs as Jake brings it to a halt on the gravel parking area next to the lodge. He kills the engine, but leaves on the lights. The beams penetrate some distance into the sparse pine woods and eventually disappear. Behind the hearse, the trailer still extends into the driveway where the Lincoln has stopped.

When Jake steps out onto the gravel, Will is already there, waiting. "There's work to be done," Jake says, tousling Will's hair.

"I know," Will says.

Annie hangs back by the kitchen door. Jake waves to her, then walks back to the Lincoln, where he says something to the man at the wheel. When Jake doesn't get the response he expects, he yells, "I said back it up!"

Meanwhile, a tall, thin man wearing a plaid shirt and dungarees and carrying a small duffel bag emerges from the passenger side of the hearse. Without acknowledging the action around him, he walks to the edge of the woods, opens his fly and urinates.

"Put it away," Jake says, catching the man midstream. The man turns his head. In the light of the full moon, it looks to Annie as if he only has teeth on one side of his mouth. "Just where the hell do you think you are?" Jake demands.

A minute later, on the lawn halfway between the kitchen door and where the hearse is parked, they all rendezvous: Jake, Will, Annie and the two men. The short one, who looks like a weasel with his small, pinched face and slightly pointed ears, is Joe—

"Joe, I can't pronounce his last name, Poleski," Jake jokes. The tall one, with teeth only on the left side of his mouth and with long, silky black hair that he constantly sweeps out of his face, is Soupy, Soupy Campbell.

"Tell her what happened to your teeth," Jake demands.

"V-A benefits run out," Soupy says. Jake laughs. Soupy extends a hand for Annie to shake, but Jake slaps it away.

"Are you kidding! You were just holding your dick with that!"

Annie is embarrassed for Soupy, but he, evidently, is not. He grabs his crotch and adjusts himself.

"A class act," Jake pronounces. He embraces Annie, kisses her on the lips, pulls her to him with one large hand as Will wanders over to the trailer.

"Jake," Annie says, as Joe and Soupy both look on, "please." Most disconcerting is that she finds Jake's touch here in the moonlight, with the others looking on, oddly arousing—she cannot imagine why. She blushes, escapes Jake's embrace.

Back at the hearse, Will peeks into each window. "What are you looking for?" Annie asks. The night is temperate; there is only a slight hissing sound as the pine needles vibrate in a breeze off the pond.

"Someone dead," Will jokes. He has come to resent Annie's affections and concerns lately, accusing her of always trying to run his life.

"How are you doing, fella?" Jake asks, as he and Soupy unhook the trailer from the hitch.

"Good," Will says. "What's on the trailer?"

"Rafts." Just then, Joe pulls off the tarp to reveal four monolithic gray rectangles, stacked in piles of two.

"Rafts?" Annie asks. "What for?"

"For swimming to," Jake says. "Now, in the house. You too, Will. Keep your mother company."

Annie knows that Will resents his assignment, and offers to let him help Jake instead, claiming she doesn't need company, but Jake tells her it's a "done deal." There is no argument.

Will and Annie watch from inside the house as Jake pulls the hearse around the driveway and backs it up to the rear of the trailer. Soupy fastens the first life raft to the hearse's bumper with a rope, then gives Jake the all-clear to pull ahead. The raft hits the ground with a solid thud, then gouges out huge divots from the front lawn as Jake drags it behind the hearse. The process is repeated until all four rafts are free of the trailer. The rafts are made of canvas-wrapped balsa, each about two feet tall and hollow, with a slatted wooden platform suspended by an intricate web of ropes at its center. Lying willy-nilly on the lawn in the moonlight, they look like giant waffles.

When the task is complete, the three men join Annie and Will in the kitchen. Annie makes coffee as Jake, Will, Soupy and Joe sit at the kitchen table. When Jake leans forward on his elbows, the others do as well, and in the faint yellow light, the foursome look like mobsters planning a heist. For all she knows about Jake, she realizes, they might well be.

The next day, the rafts are launched. Will unknots the ropes that attach the free-floating wooden platforms to the rafts' inner perimeters. Using a power saw, Joe and Soupy take turns cutting the lumber for the new stationary platforms that will span each raft's surface. Jake nails the boards together and devises a way of fastening them to the rafts' balsa skeletons. Then the four of them push the rafts to the water, row them out to the middle of the pond and anchor them. It is late afternoon when all four workers jump off the last raft and swim to shore. Annie watches from the kitchen, where she writes about the odd turn her life has taken.

Hull

One night in early October, Jake arrives at the lodge in the Lincoln. Though it is cold and past midnight, the top is down, and Annie, awakened from an uncomfortable sleep, can see that Jake is not alone. Since it is Thursday, a school night and not a Jake night, Will sleeps.

Annie pulls on a robe, and in her bare feet crosses the cold slate living-room floor to the kitchen. Jake refuses to use either of the lodge's two front doors, declaring them a design error, his, and not worthy of use. Tonight, Jake wears an army greatcoat and carries a suitcase in one hand, a pair of large cast-iron andirons in the other. As he walks up the path, the andirons clang against each other, creating a clear, bell-like sound. Behind him on the path is another man, Jake's passenger, wearing only a denim shirt and khaki trousers, and carrying a handsome, worn leather valise in each hand. Annie holds the door open for the two men, who walk past her through the kitchen and into the living room, where Jake drops the suitcase and andirons heavily to the floor.

"Hull Caldwell," Jake's voice suddenly booms, "this is Annie Green, the woman I love." Annie wishes she could match Jake's exuberance with her own, but cannot, and instead just gives in to his theatrical embrace, which bends her backwards and causes her robe to fall open.

"I want you to know," Hull says, "this embarrasses me." He has a slight Southern accent.

"I thought you were a good ol' boy," Jake says, his arm still around Annie, who refastens her robe. "I thought you believed in true love."

"I believe in it. I just can't bear to watch it." The man's teeth are chattering, Annie notices. He is fine-featured, with grass-green eyes and pale skin tinged slightly gray. His thick, strawberry blond hair gives him a boyish air, though the deep wrinkles around his eyes reveal him to be near sixty—Jake's age—maybe older.

"You like him, Annie?" Jake asks, pulling her closer. Hull looks at her eagerly, as if he is counting on her acceptance. She nods. "Well guess what," Jake announces brightly. "He's dying of cancer, the poor sonofabitch."

"Horsepucky," Hull says, then dredges up a cough from somewhere deep inside him that rattles his ribs and brings tears to his eyes.

"You should have a coat," Annie insists. "You must be freezing." Jake picks up the andirons and carries them over to the cavernous fireplace.

"Cold?" Hull seems amused by the suggestion, as if the cold of night in an open car is nothing to bear, though his teeth still chatter. Suddenly, Annie feels the cold herself and cradles her own arms for warmth.

"Give Hull the room next to Will's," Jake calls, kicking the ashes off the old andirons in the fireplace and pulling them out onto the hearth.

"Good enough," Hull says. "Come on now, better not keep the good Mr. Weigel waiting." Though he has no idea of his destination, he drops one of his valises and extends his hand to Annie, who takes it. She is startled to feel how thin the skin of his fingertips is, like the onionskin paper she once used to write to Mama on.

"Who are you?" Annie asks, out of Jake's earshot.

"The architect."

"For what?"

"Don't you worry, now, Annie," he says, when they are in his room. "I'll be the ideal houseguest. I don't have any habits at all, bad or otherwise," he assures her. His drawl is gentle, comforting, save for a slight cunning it cannot quite mask.

"I'm not worried," Annie says, "just surprised." It's the first she's heard of an architect, or that Jake has a scheme in mind that will require one. "Just surprised," she repeats.

"No," Hull insists, "worried. I know worry when I see it."

"The only thing to worry about," Jake says as he appears in the room with Hull's suitcase, "is that the bastard croaks before he finishes the job." Jake gives one of his theatrical winks, then slaps Hull on the back.

"I could grow to love this SOB," Hull declares. "He has absolutely no heart."

"I'll admit it," Jake says, pointing to his chest. "I'll admit it." Everyone laughs.

"Be Happy, Go Lucky"

Jake's plan is to build three dozen small vacation apartments on the hill behind the lodge, then use the lodge and the other outbuildings as a common area. Joe and Soupy, now living full-time in the apartment above the garage, are to clear the trees and the brush from the property. Hull is to design the buildings, draw up the plans, then build a scale model of the development to show prospective buyers. Jake calls the project "Twin Oaks," after the local phone exchange, though there isn't an oak on the property.

Except when Jake is around, Joe and Soupy fix their own meals in the garage apartment kitchen, and the only time Annie sees either of them is when they make their way up the hill carrying chain saws. A few minutes later, she hears the saws cough into life, then buzz incessantly in varying keys. Every so often, too, the saws fall mute and she hears Soupy ordering Joe around. At dusk, they reappear, phantoms emerging from the woods— Joe, with his pointy face and ears, as feral as a wildcat, and Soupy, with his half-dentured mouth hanging open, like a bear in search of water.

In the first month of Hull's residence at the lodge, he eats voraciously, more than Annie has ever seen anyone eat, and, for a time, grocery shopping and cooking for him and Will helps her get her mind off the confusion of being with Jake. But by November, Hull stops eating almost altogether and starts, instead, to chain-smoke Lucky Strikes. His plan, he says, is to flush out the cancer with fire, a therapy he augments with large yellow pills that he bought months earlier on a weekend visit to a Mexico City clinic. Occasionally, he'll pop one into his mouth while Annie is watching, to make a show of how delicious they are, how tasty it is to save your life.

"How about eating?" Annie urges, still cooking for him and piling the food high on his plate. She sits and watches him through dinner, then covers the food with waxed paper and puts it in the refrigerator. Days later she throws the food away.

"These are better than food," he says of the pills, made of an extract of apricot pits. "They're so nutritious, food only gets in the way." He lights a Lucky. "L.S.M.F.T.," he recites, blowing smoke rings as Annie and Will look on. He holds the cigarette deep in the crotch of his second and third fingers, the others open in front of his face, masking it. Along with Luckys and yellow

pills, he also takes garlic capsules, which will cure him of arterio-
sclerosis, if it happens to come along. He takes great pleasure in
telling Annie and Will this, delighted to have them agree or
disagree, and they soon become friends.

To Annie's surprise, Hull's therapy seems to work. Though it
is difficult to tell whether he is losing weight under the bulk of
his sweaters and on his already gaunt face, by late November,
Hull's cough has disappeared. Encouraged, he borrows one of
Will's sweatshirts, and twice a day he trots along the driveway that
encircles the lodge. After about a dozen laps, he comes back into
the kitchen where Annie is typing. He huffs and puffs and beats
his chest—partly show, Annie guesses—then goes back to the
living room, to the drafting table that Jake has set up for him in
the corner of the room below the moose head. After only a few
days of this regimen, Hull's cheeks take on the exaggerated high
color of a young girl first experimenting with rouge.

Though he doesn't eat, Hull still comes to the table to regale
Annie and Will with his "architecting" stories, as he calls them—
about the mansion he designed for a man in Alaska to evoke a
Southern fantasy, and about a soccer stadium in Montevideo ("I
just thought, what would Nazis like?"). Once he talks about the
time he was married ("No one liked anyone"), urging Annie to
tell him about her past as well, but she demurs. "So maybe you'll
write about it," he offers, pointing to the growing pile of manuscript Annie works on every morning, "and I'll read about it
then."

"Maybe."

The other thing they don't talk about is Jake, but it becomes
quickly clear that Hull has little liking for him. And the more time
Annie spends with Hull, the more it occurs to her that maybe she
feels the same. Indeed, the very things that attracted her to Jake—
his confidence, his power and his unpredictability—are, now that
she is dependent on him, what she has come to mistrust, even
fear.

But then, come Saturday when Jake returns, he'll toss her one
of his heavy coats, walk with her down to the pond and together
they'll row around its perimeter in a small wooden rowboat.

Once, they put in at the dock of a deserted summer place and explored the property, peeking into the curtained windows; then later back in the boat, Jake spins out his fantasy of the lives spent in the rooms they have just peered into.

Still, by late November, as ice begins to form on the pond, Annie considers leaving, recollecting as she does Jake's remark about David—how he had his second chance and blew it. Certainly, Annie thinks, she's had many more chances than that. Vacillating, she finally decides, no, she'll stay. She won't let Jake's eccentricities get to her as she did Mama's. No, she'll simply make a better go of it than she has over the past few months. Besides, where would she go?

A week later, Hull's cough returns, and worse than ever, making it hard for Annie to face him, ashamed that she bought him the Lucky Strikes, that she didn't force him to eat—and worried about Will, who shouldn't have to concern himself with another disappearing man. In fact, the only one in the house who seems untouched by the downturn in Hull's health is Hull himself, who gives Will back his sweatshirt after washing it out and drying it with a small, hand-held dryer he has to speed the setting of the glue on the model he has yet to begin. And Jake, of course, who has never believed in Hull's cure for a moment.

Cape Cod, Spring 1956

The House Call

In late April, Annie comes down with a cold. When after a week she starts running a fever, Jake insists she call the local doctor, Dr. Eisenberg—coincidentally, also from Vienna. He arrives at the lodge in a comical little car with headlights like bugs' eyes, a Volkswagen, he says in response to Will's question.

Eisenberg is a large, square-chested man with a small, pinched nose and enormous eyeglasses. The examination goes slowly. Eisenberg's wide, flat hands are cold and somewhat clumsy; his interest in Annie's symptoms seems perfunctory. When he is finished, he sits at the dining-room table, elbows on a placemat, his hands now clasped beneath his chin.

Eisenberg's thin lips form a restrained smile. "You know what I miss most of all?" he says without preamble. "The Nachtmart. I miss the hams, the sausages, the fish from Yugoslavia, from the coast, those big silver ones. And those tiny, tiny little berries. Now that was food, no?"

Annie doesn't recall the market. Also, she is somehow put off by the question, by Eisenberg's assumption that his earlier clinical intimacy with her gives him license to ask even more of her, to take more. But then again, her fever has made her lightheaded, she feels enervated, terrible—maybe it's not Eisenberg at all. He looks to her eagerly for an answer.

"Yes," she says finally, still feeling that by responding, she has been compromised. Eisenberg gives her a penicillin injection, prescribes liquids and bed rest, and within a few days' time, her symptoms disappear.

But as the ice that had frozen the rafts helter-skelter in the middle of the pond that winter thaws, as the last small patches of snow melt, unburdening the boughs of trees and bushes and revealing promising green shoots, Annie continues to feel sick, odd—not herself, in any event. Instead, with the onset of spring, she becomes increasingly aware of the details and flaws of her skin, the way her bones are joined, the feel of her fingers on objects. Her fixed nose, fine for five years, suddenly feels strange, and her auburn hair—dyed blond for Jake in February—seems parched and dying at the roots. It has been some time, too, since she has been able to sleep through the night without awakening with every movement of the house, or branch brushing against a window.

On the nights when Annie awakens and Jake is not there, she pulls on her robe, walks from room to room, checks on Will, on Hull, listens to herself talk, breathe. On the nights when Jake is there, she often sits up in bed next to him as he sleeps on his side, and in the moonlit room gazes at the eerie pinnacle formed by the white sheet draped across his broad shoulders.

Helen

One night in May, when Jake is snoring gently beside her, Annie awakens to the sound of a car coming down the driveway. Its headlights create a crazy quilt of light and dark in the bedroom. For an instant, the stuffed and mounted birds and animals are flushed out of hiding, then disappear back into shadow as the car passes.

"Jake," she says. But he is already reaching for his pistol. A car door opens, then closes.

"Are you in there, you bastard?" a woman yells. Her voice sounds shredded, guttural.

"Who is it?" Annie whispers.

"Nothing," Jake says, "nobody." He pulls on his robe, moving the gun from hand to hand as he draws on first one sleeve, then the other. As Annie sits up, he puts his hand on her shoulder. "Don't worry. It's nothing."

"I know you're in there, you skinny-dicked bastard," comes the voice from the driveway.

"Goddammit!" Jake says, and stalks out of the room. Annie waits for a moment, pulls one of Jake's flannel shirts over her nightgown, and follows him to the living room, where he watches from behind one of the front doors. The car has stopped in front of the house, its engine still running, its headlights shining into the woods. The woman stands some distance from the rear of the car, one side of her illuminated by the red taillights, the other side falling off into shadow. She has long hair, is heavyset.

Jake flicks on the front light, catching the woman full face. She puts up her hands to fend it off. She wears shorts and a halter. Her large breasts sag toward her belly. Annie stands next to Jake.

"Go back to bed," Jake tells Annie. "I told you there was nothing to worry about." He puts his arm around her, but his attention remains on the woman, who now retreats to the car and leans against the fender. Annie looks at the gun in Jake's hand.

"You don't need it," she says, "it's only a woman."

Surprisingly, he hands it to her. "You're right. Now, go on back to the bedroom."

"Show yourself, you sonofabitch," the woman yells. But already her voice has lost its edge. It sounds now merely weather-worn, beaten.

Jake opens the screen door and steps out onto the porch, into the balmy night. The smell of jasmine fills the room. "Go home, Helen," Jake says. Annie recognizes the name, and now the face of the woman by the car: Jake's second wife, the alcoholic. Oddly, even drunk and ten years older, Helen looks less ragged than in the photographs Annie has seen of her when she and Jake were together.

"You!" Helen suddenly wheels and points at Jake as she fixes on him standing on the porch.

"Yes, me," Jake says quietly. "Who were you expecting?" When she doesn't respond, Jake starts in her direction. "Now just get the hell out of here." The closer he gets, the more she shrinks before him. "Out," Jake demands, when he is standing only a few feet from her, "back to where you belong."

"I belong here," she says, both hands behind her on the car.

"The hell you do. Now, out!" As Jake raises his hand, Annie, without thinking, raises hers as well—the hand with the pistol—pointing it not at Helen, but at Jake. The next instant she thinks she hears a shot, but there isn't one. It's a slap. Helen falls. A few seconds later, Jake is back in the living room, looking into the barrel of the pistol that Annie still holds, arm extended.

"It's okay," Jake assures her. "It was only Helen, my ex." Outside, Helen gets up, walks slowly around the car to the driver's door.

"I'll take the gun," Jake says, lowering Annie's arm for her. Will is also standing next to her.

"What's going on?" he asks. He is wearing only pajama bottoms. His slender chest reminds Annie of David the first time she saw him in his bathing suit on the beach in Florida. "What's happening?"

"Nothing," Annie says, the gun still in her hand. "Go back to sleep." He looks to Jake to have the order countermanded. "Now!" Annie commands, startled by her own conviction. Just then, Helen accelerates the car around the driveway, kicking up dust and gravel. She makes a complete circle around the house, returning to the front, then leans out the window to yell something lost in the rattle of the engine.

"Your mother said to go back to sleep," Jake says. Will takes one more look at the car, then turns toward the bedroom. Annie watches his pale back disappear into the darkness.

"Will." She wants to console him, take him in her arms as she did not so long ago, tell him, "Will, it won't always be like this. I'll make it better. You'll see." But Jake has hold of her elbow.

"I'll go talk to him," he says.

"What will you tell him?" Jake smiles, taking the gun from Annie and putting it into the pocket of his robe.

"The truth. What else?"

Ten minutes later, he is back in the bedroom. "Now tell *me* the truth," Annie says. "Everything about what happened with her."

"You saw the truth. She's a boozer. She's crazy. There's nothing more to say." Jake puts the gun back in the holster.

In Miniature

Hull is coughing again this week as he puts the finishing touches on the scale model of the vacation complex. Now that it is spring and he no longer wears his cable-knit sweaters, it is possible to see how thin he has become—like someone mummified. From the kitchen, where Annie writes about watching Papa trim his beard and Herr Sonnenabend's lessons, she can hear Hull puttering, lighting cigarettes, clearing his throat.

"Are you expecting Mr. Wonderful tonight?" Hull asks, appearing in the kitchen doorway. He props himself up with one hand on the frame. It is only Thursday, not a Jake night. "You've got on the outfit he bought you."

Annie is wearing the black toreador pants, the tight red short-sleeved sweater. "Only rehearsing," she says, just recently aware of how off balance her lack of sleep and Jake's constant surprises make her feel.

"You know," Hull says, pouring himself a cup of coffee, "except for Will, I'm just about the only friend you have." He produces a pill and some lint from his pocket. Ever since Annie's cold, Hull has been making disturbing pronouncements that she would rather not hear. When she tells him so, he says he doesn't have time anymore for courteous bullshit.

"You don't think that Mr. Wonderful is my friend?"

"Be serious," he says. He walks around the kitchen table, coffee cup in hand, and stops when he is behind Annie, with a view of the page she is writing, and beyond that of the pond, today a perfect mirror. Annie puts her hand over the page, though she feels there is little she can hide from Hull. He has seen so much over the past months, he probably knows her better than she does herself.

"Come on," he urges, "I'll show you the latest."

The model is off in the corner of the living room. It is four feet square, and illuminated by drafting lights at each corner. Annie studies it hard, looking for what was different since she saw it last, when Hull installed the tiny patio railings.

"Well?" he asks.

Annie is frustrated by being unable to pick out the changes. She is certain that if she could only sleep again, she would be able to get a clearer fix on things. Recently, things have begun to blur, sometimes in the middle of the day, as if someone has drawn gauze before her eyes. But just as she is about to make an appointment with the eye doctor, the gauze disappears, and if anything, she can see more clearly than ever. "Well, I give up," she says to Hull. "What this time?"

"For someone who watches so much, you certainly don't see a lot." Suddenly his hand is on her wrist, his face very close to hers. Annie shudders. She can see the gold fillings in his mouth, the stain of coffee on his tongue. His face is gaunt, a skull with skin. She pulls away.

"Didn't mean to scare you," he says, leaving Annie wondering what he did mean. With a tweezer he reaches into the model, plucks a tiny person, no more than a quarter of an inch tall, from one of the patios, and places it in Annie's hand. It is a perfect replica—a man wearing a bathing suit, smiling and waving his hand.

"There are places you can buy things like this?" Annie asks.

Hull is amused by her delight, claiming there are places where one can buy virtually anything. As he says it, the entire population comes into focus—men, women, children, dogs. Some walk, others run, sit on deck chairs. A solitary woman sits on a raft in the middle of the pond.

"Done," Hull suddenly announces, indicating the completed model with a sweep of his hand. "A few weeks more on the drawings, and I'm gone." Annie asks him where he is headed. She cannot imagine what it will be like in the lodge without him working in the next room, they have grown so comfortable to-gether—sometimes. Hull says he has no plans, maybe he'll just check into a friendly hospital. "How about you?" he asks.

"You know as much as I do," Annie says.

"More," Hull says gently, though it still rankles. For a mo-ment, it occurs to Annie that perhaps he does know more, some quite specific piece of information entrusted to him by Jake.

"Like what?"

"Like I haven't the faintest idea," he says, pointing to himself to absolve himself of any complicity. "Still," he goes on, clicking off the drafting lights and avoiding Annie's eyes, "still, if I were you, I'd take my boy and git."

"Meaning?"

"Meaning, git. This is not the place for you, no more than it's been for me. And as for what Jake has to offer . . ."

"That's easy for you to say," Annie interrupts, "but you don't understand, you don't know what . . ." She stops, unable to finish the thought. Instead, she peers at the darkened model, at the woman on the raft. "I think maybe," she begins, aware of the irony of saying it to someone in Hull's condition, "I'm too tired to git anymore, I've done all the gitting I can. I think maybe it's just too late."

"And that, my dear friend Annie Green, Anna Moser, com-ing from you, is the dumbest thing I've ever heard." He walks across the living room and into his bedroom and slams the door.

Dr. Eisenberg

Annie tells Dr. Eisenberg about her difficulty sleeping. It's her fourth visit to his office since the house call. She doesn't like the man, but he is the only doctor in town, the only one in the area where Jake has an account. Eisenberg writes out a prescription for sleeping pills. Instead of handing it to her, however, he stands, paces his office, looks out the window. "You know," he begins, still looking out the window, "your friend telephoned me."

"My friend?"

"He's concerned. He's a very concerned man."

"Jake?"

"Of course." He busies himself with his stethoscope, which dangles from the pocket of his long white coat; he studies the earpieces. "But I'm not that type of doctor," he admits, "and frankly, I'm not sure who I could recommend out here in the wilderness." He lets out a broad, braying laugh that Annie has never heard before. Noticing that she is not caught up in his humor, but merely sits, watching him, he stops abruptly. "Serious business, hah?"

He touches her cheek solicitously, but she pushes his hand away.

"Do you think so?" she asks, feeling betrayed by Jake, when perhaps she should feel grateful for his concern.

"I told you, I'm not that type of doctor. But this pain and that pain, the not sleeping . . . well, who knows what could be really going on, right?" Annie draws her lips together tightly as she nods her head. Who knows? Her symptoms, she concedes, are not common.

As she stands to leave, Dr. Eisenberg kisses her hand, the first time he has done so. Feeling his large hand on her far smaller one, she realizes that this is no courtesy, but that he is one of those patronizing Viennese men with their false, gracious manner whom Mama always disdained.

Furious, Annie takes the prescription to the drugstore to have it filled.

Will

One afternoon a few days later, Annie is a little tipsy from a glass or two of Cointreau. When she hears the school bus stopping at the top of the hill, she stops her typing, puts away the bottle, and rinses out the sticky glass. She is surprised at how blurred the ridges of the drainboard seem. It is because she has no tolerance for alcohol, she thinks. "I'm just not a drinker."

Will enters the house through the kitchen door, walking past her as she stands at the sink. "Hi," he says, his voice surprisingly deep, no longer the Human Accordion. After a few seconds, Annie hears him shut the door to his room—his indication that he does not want to be bothered. Annie thinks of all the times Will had bothered her when all she wanted was to sit back and read—or think, or savor some memory. The fact is, she would like to bother him now. Now that Hull is about to leave, that Jake is about to arrive from Boston.

It's unfair, she knows, to burden a thirteen-year-old with her problems. She is already certain that Will's distance is her doing, that in the time after David left and before Jake appeared, she confided in him too much. But who was she to talk to? "Every mother makes mistakes," she finally consoles herself, though she is certain that her mistakes are of greater consequence than those made by the mothers she left behind in New Jersey.

She knocks on Will's door. "In a little while," he says.

"Why not now?" She detests her insistence—it is all wrong, she knows, yet she seems perversely driven to it. "Why not right now?"

"I'm busy."

"Busy with what?"

"Things."

Annie tries the latch, but the door is locked. "I'll be out soon," Will says.

In the kitchen, Annie takes a sponge and some cleanser to clean the walls. It has been weeks since she has done so. Standing on a chair to get nearer the ceiling, she feels dizzy, so she concentrates on the lower regions. After the walls, she starts on the black hood over the stove. The cleanser leaves white streaks that she has to go over again and again with a clean sponge. After another small glass of Cointreau, she cleans the glass cabinet fronts with newspaper and water, as Jake has instructed, but today the newspaper leaves little shreds. To pry the dirt out from between the seams of the Formica countertop, Annie uses one of Jake's double-edged razor blades, carefully folding a piece of cardboard over one edge to protect herself. On her hands and knees, she also uses the blade along the baseboards after she has mopped the linoleum floor.

"What are you doing?" Will asks.

She looks up to see him in his striped polo shirt and dungarees. He looks like David. He always looks like David, she thinks. But also like I do, she notices for the first time in a long while. The revelation disconcerts her, and she is now worried for him more than ever. She stands and embraces him. He is taller than she is. "How can I tell you how much I really, really love you?" she says. At first, Will just stands there; then he closes his hands behind her back, and they rock together gently.

"You smell funny," he says, loosening his grip.

"Like soap? Like cleanser?"

"Like booze," he pronounces, "and you know how Jake feels about booze." It is less an admonition, Annie senses, than a warning.

"Are you afraid of him?" she asks, feeling emboldened by the Cointreau. "Are you afraid of him too?"

"Come on, Mom . . ."

"No, really, because if you are, I'm sorry, really sorry. In fact, maybe I . . ."

But Will is already out the door. Maybe I what? she wonders, as the screen slams once, then a second time behind him.

Later that evening, Will joins Annie in the living room. He is in his pajamas. The sun is setting over the pond; the water is so unnaturally red it looks like an amateur's painting. The pajamas have a clock pattern. Annie cannot remember buying them, or even having seen them before.

"I'm sorry," he says.

"Sorry for what?"

"About this afternoon." There are no lights on in the living room, only the light of the passing day to illuminate them. "I know what you want," Will says quietly.

"You know?" It surprises Annie, who feels it is something that she herself can no longer articulate.

"You want me to be your little boy again. You want it to be like the time when Papa wasn't there, and we were alone."

"But that's impossible," Annie says, seeking once to say the right thing. She has not had any Cointreau since the afternoon, and her head aches. "You're older now, and can't be my little boy any longer."

"No," Will says, "but I want to be. I liked it that way. Living in our own house. Back then."

"Better than here? Better than with Jake?" They sit on one of the couches, Annie's hand on his shoulder. Annie cannot see in the dim room, but senses that Will is about to cry.

"Can't we just go back there?" he asks, wistfully.

"There isn't any 'back there,' " she says. For a few moments it is unnaturally quiet in the room. Then from somewhere in the house, Hull clears his throat, and from somewhere else, the plumbing shudders.

"I shouldn't have said it," Will suddenly says. "I'm being stupid."

"No," Annie begins, wanting to reassure him. Just then, Jake's hearse pulls into the driveway, and behind it, the Lincoln.

Breakfast

Annie awakens the next morning with an odd, bitter taste in her mouth from the sleeping pill she took the night before. She hears sounds from the kitchen. To her chagrin, she has fallen asleep completely dressed in the living room, on one of the couches. Both front doors are open, as are most of the windows, and the smell of pine mixes with that of food being prepared. Standing, she feels groggy, and sits back down. Finally, she makes her way to the kitchen.

Jake is at the stove, where he is grilling steaks. He wears an unstarched chef's toque whose crown keeps flopping in his eyes. Next to him is a crock of scrambled eggs. "Ready!" he yells, and in a moment Will, Joe and Soupy stand next to him with their plates. As he is serving them, Jake notices Annie.

"Back in the land of the living?" he asks. "Are you eating?"

Will hands Annie a clean plate, smiling as he does. "Sure," he urges.

"Best thing in the world for you," Jake proclaims. He puts a steak on Annie's plate. "You okay?" he asks, handing her a glass of orange juice. Drinking it relieves some of the bitter taste in her mouth.

"Yes," she says. But Jake is already at the table assigning the chores for today's auction, the latest of his projects. Standing next to the grill, the plate with her breakfast in her hand, Annie has the sensation that the day is happening without her.

When breakfast is over, Jake cleans the grill with oil and a large carbon brick, and soon the grill takes on a fine, metallic sheen, though he has spattered oil on the wall and on the splashboard behind the stove. Soupy washes the dishes in the sink, places them unrinsed on the drainboard. Then, putting his thumb over the faucet, he sprays a stream of water in their general direction, wetting the floor and the nearby cabinets.

"Do you have to do it that way?" Annie asks. Soupy glares at her from the sink as Jake looks up from the grill, the carbon brick in his hand.

"Are you talking to me?" Jake asks, like a thug itching for a fight.

"No," Annie says, pointing at Soupy, "to him."

"You know a better way?" asks Soupy.

"How about just rinsing them in the sink?"

"Yes, boss," Soupy says, then laughs. Jake tells him to watch himself.

"Uh-oh," he says to Joe, who is wiping off the table, clearly satisfied at being a bystander. "You hear that," Soupy goes on, "he said I better watch myself." Joe looks up for a second, then back down at the table. "I'm watching, boss," Soupy says, "I'm watching." Presently, both of them leave the room.

"You see what I have to put up with?" Annie says to Jake, although aware that it is Jake with whom she has her complaint, since Soupy and Joe are never in the house except on the weekends.

"Oh, sure," he says. "Sometimes, I even think about it from your point of view." He pauses, as if he is doing so right now. "It's tough," he concludes, "especially when you're under a strain. Not enough sleep, worry, things like that."

Annie recalls his talking to Dr. Eisenberg and mentions it.

"Guilty as charged," he confesses. "I guess I was out of line, but I had to do something."

Annie watches him as he says it, knowing how many times he has faced a jury, convinced them of his client's best intentions.

"Why?" she asks.

"Why? Because you're still my Nellie. No matter what. Now, come on, let's the two of us take a shower."

"You know what I could go for?" he says as he towels himself off after their shower. Annie nods. He is already hard. "You too, huh?" He strokes himself, closing his eyes with pleasure.

Annie tries to imagine making love, but can't. Then again, she has difficulty imagining what else she might do today.

"How badly do you want it?" he says, fixed on his goal, nothing else.

"Let's just talk first, then maybe . . ." Annie begins, going to the medicine cabinet for a prophylactic.

"Without it," Jake says. "It's okay. I've probably been shooting blanks for years."

Annie moves away from the medicine cabinet and leans with her back against the sink.

"Right here," Jake insists. "Take your pants down."

She does as he asks, and to her amazement she is aroused and ready for him. She cannot believe how readily her body betrays her, how even her face in the mirror conspires to tell Jake one thing when, in fact, it is not at all what she feels. Even her climax—it is all a betrayal.

"Good," Jake pronounces as he pulls away from her. He has his hand over his heart, as if anticipating a coronary.

"Everything okay?" Annie asks.

"Are you kidding!" Jake pulls on his clothes, urging Annie to do the same. "Just what the doctor ordered, eh, Annie?"

The Auction

Will sits in the back seat of the Chrysler as Jake drives to the Old Town Hall. In the past, Annie has taken Will's taciturnity as a way of distancing himself from her, but today, as he stares out the window, she imagines he is plotting his escape. She turns to her window, sees the same horizon.

The Old Town Hall is a large building sitting on a dome of earth, as squat and fat and imposing as a paddle wheeler. It has a clumsy front portico with two white pillars on either side of a wide, wooden double door. Though substantial, the building's skinny clapboard siding gives the impression that the entire structure is about to burst. Off to one side, a green canvas tent has been erected, open to the street. Rows of folding chairs face a stage on the far side. A banner above the entranceway to the building reads "Auction Today. 3:00 p.m."

Initially, Jake bought the former town hall as a place for him to relocate his law practice and for Annie to put her typing skills to use. When he tired of that idea, he decided instead to open an antique shop in the building for Annie to manage. She tried to picture herself working there, and was at first comforted by the thought of being a purveyor of someone's old, valued possessions, imagining it as a type of trust. But when it was clear that the furniture and bric-a-brac Jake was bringing to the Cape every weekend in the hearse was largely junk, she told him that she didn't think she was the woman for the job. So he decided to auction the merchandise he had already bought, along with a few other pickup-truck loads.

Now Annie and Jake stand in the room that was to have been the shop. Chairs are stacked to the ceiling, mattresses are lined up against the walls, headboards are wedged in between couches and desks and standing bookshelves. Bowls, decorative table lamps, metal and glass knickknacks are in a heap in one corner; electrical cords snake through the pile.

Using an electric saw and a sledgehammer, Soupy has just finished cutting a huge opening into the side wall adjacent to the tent. Sawdust and plaster are suspended in the air.

"Who's going to pay money for this crap?" Soupy asks, emerging from the rubble he has created. He examines a table with three legs sitting atilt on the floor.

"You'd be amazed," Jake says. "People will amaze you every time. Everybody wants somebody else's junk. It's the American way, buying something, fixing it up. We're catering to patriots here."

Soupy looks out over the room. He is dubious. "Huh?" he says, scratching his head. Annie is about to express similar doubt, when suddenly Jake grabs Soupy by his shirt and pulls him to him so that they are standing nose to nose.

"Listen, Campbell, you've been an asshole since you got here. When you work for me, you work for me. I don't pay you for your opinions." He lets Soupy's shirt go, pushing him back slightly into the room.

Soupy stumbles, then regains his balance. There is no trace of the sly smile on his face. "Yes sir," he says, not a hint of irony.

As Will and Soupy clean up the mess Soupy has made burrowing through the wall, something familiar catches Annie's eye—her old sectional sofa with the nubbly green fabric. It is one of a number of pieces that survived the crash of the trailer, and, according to Jake, is supposed to be in storage in Boston.

When she asks Jake why the sofa is here and not in storage, he says, "Face it, it isn't worth keeping," then goes off to examine the stage, where the auctioneer is to stand. Annie pushes her way through the room with the furniture and soon discovers a number of other familiar objects including a carton holding, among other things, Oma's cookbook. Shoved up against one wall, nearly hidden by mattresses, is the old Mason and Hamlin.

"How long has it all been here?" she asks, catching up with Jake. "Was it ever in storage?"

"What's the difference?" he says.

"One way it's a lie, the other way . . ."

"It *was* in storage, but here—all right?" Annie wonders if he will grab her as he did Soupy.

"And now what?" she says. "Does it go up for auction?"

"It's entirely up to you. It's your furniture." Again he walks away. Will is doing something at the tent's periphery when Jake orders him to segregate his mother's old furniture. Watching him try to move the old sofa by himself, Annie goes to help him, then suddenly breaks into tears.

"Jesus Christ, Annie, what is it with you?" Jake takes her arm and escorts her to the back of the tent.

"It's just that it was my furniture . . ."

"Yes. Yes? Your furniture, and what?" He has stepped in front of her, and Annie senses he is trying to hide what happens between them from Soupy and Will and the cars that drive by on the street.

". . . and I like it. I want it."

"Goddammit, Annie, we can't just set up a little house with your furniture so you'll feel like you felt fifteen years ago. Time passes," he says.

"I know." He is right, Annie acknowledges. "I guess it was just the surprise . . ." she begins.

"It was in storage for months," he says, "and I've got the receipts to prove it. But we can't go on spending money on this stuff. Unless you've got some hidden mine we can tap."

"You know I don't," Annie says, recognizing how deftly he has cut to the very heart of the matter. "You know I don't," she repeats.

By midafternoon, the time the auction is to begin, the tent is nearly full. The auctioneer whom Jake hired has not arrived, however, and, sensing the crowd's impatience, Jake decides to assume the role until the real auctioneer arrives. Doing so, he forgoes his job as shill, and turns that task over to Annie. He hands her a list of the minimum prices he believes each item is worth. If the minimum is not met, Annie is to bid on the object, and buy it back for the house.

Annie studies the list. As agreed, her furniture is to be among the items auctioned. It is a warm day, though Annie feels a bit cool. Putting on a thin sweater, she feels hot. Soupy walks by as she is about to take a seat in the tent. "I don't know whether I'm hot or cold," she says to him without preamble.

"Hot," he says, pinching her rear end.

A few minutes later, Jake takes the stage, introduces himself, and explains that he has never done this before, so that if things go slowly, to please be patient. The crowd seems pleased by his candor. Most are summer people, though Annie recognizes a few locals. "How about this vase here?" Jake begins, picking up what looks like a large jelly jar. He flicks a finger at its surface, as he has seen other auctioneers do, and the sound rings dully through the tent. "Could be Waterford," he says, "who knows?" Annie checks her list. The minimum is two dollars, but the bidding is already at three, accelerates quickly to ten, and the vase sells for twelve. Annie rechecks the list to see if there was a mistake. No, it says, "Glass jar/vase, $2." She checks it off.

The temperature inside the tent rises as piece after piece is put up for auction and bid upon. Soupy and Will perspire as they haul furniture first onto the stage, then off again, after it has been sold. About a half hour into the auction, it is clear who the afternoon's major players are: a cunning-looking man who is involved in virtually every bid, and who smirks when he passes up an item, as if he has just put something over on the winning bidder; and an obese woman in a pea-green dress who stands as she bids, looking out over the crowd for approval each time she is victorious.

"An antique mahogany headboard," Jake goes on. As the auction progresses, his voice assumes more timbre. An attractive young woman bids $50. "The lady intends to put the bed to good use. Any of you older folks still looking for a headboard of this ilk to witness your copulations?" The heavyset woman bids $60. "Sixty dollars to bed the lady in green." The crowd chuckles. "Any more takers?" The young woman with the opening bid raises the ante to $70. Annie cranes her head to get a look at her. The woman is slight but confident. Her eyes are fixed on the headboard, as if she will buy it at any cost. Meanwhile, the man sitting next to the heavyset woman jumps the bid to $100.

"Now we're talking," Jake pronounces. "Let's see what happens when the man of the house takes charge." "One hundred and ten dollars!" the young woman bids. "One hundred twenty," the man responds. "One-thirty," the young woman counters, but weakly, as if this may be her last bid. Sensing victory, the obese woman takes the measure of the crowd, her eyes focusing on every face that looks back at her. "One-fifty," she says, going for the definitive bid, "one hundred and fifty dollars." It is quiet in the tent. "One-fifty going once, one-fifty going twice . . ."

Desperate, Annie looks at the young woman, who still peers only at the headboard. Then, without any change in her expression, the young woman announces evenly, "I'll take the headboard for one hundred seventy-five dollars." So unexpected is the $175 bid that the large woman collapses onto her folding chair, nodding her head in amazement. "One hundred seventy-five going once, one hundred seventy-five going twice, one hundred seventy-five going three times, sold." The winning bidder raises both hands in triumph as the audience cheers.

Annie joins in as tears course down her cheeks. Jake glares at her. Quickly, she checks her list for the mahogany headboard. It was sold out of order, before, rather than after, the pine headboard, which had a $100 minimum. The mahogany headboard's minimum, however, was $200. She looks back up at Jake, who has pulled Soupy aside. Annie thinks to go up to the stage to explain about the mistake, but knows doing so would give her away. "I'll just have to be more careful," she thinks, trying to indicate this with her expression to Jake when he finally looks up again. He smiles, winks at her. The event is already forgotten.

Just then, Will, Joe and Soupy haul the first of Annie's furniture onto the stage—six dining-room chairs, followed by the table. "What can I say about this dining-room set?" Jake begins. "Belonged to a lady in New Jersey who barely ever ate . . . which is not to say that she didn't drink." The crowd is amused. Annie looks around, trying to guess who the victorious bidder will be. The heavyset woman confers quickly with the man next to her and stands. "Two hundred seventy-five dollars," she pronounces, already exceeding the $250 minimum on Annie's list. The cunning-looking man counters with $285, and quickly, in ten- and fifteen-dollar increments, the bid rises to $380.

Annie is surprised and pleased by the bidding at first, as if finally Jake is being given an impartial measure of her value. But then—picturing either the man *or* the woman sitting at her table, perhaps on the very chair David sat on when he still came home early from the factory and Annie made him pot roast and creamed spinach; or even on the chair where she sat playing solitaire when she was alone and Will was asleep—Annie is furious. "Four hundred dollars," she suddenly calls out. Everyone in the tent stares at her; the heavyset woman turns red. The cunning-looking man, momentarily caught off guard, regroups, bids $410. "Four-twenty," ventures the heavyset woman. Annie doesn't dare look up at Jake. "Five hundred," she pronounces. And in the silence that follows Jake's "Five hundred once . . . five hundred twice . . ." Annie calls out, "Five-fifty."

"The lady must be confused," Jake explains, more exasperated than angry. "Sold for five hundred dollars."

It is assumed by those at the auction that Annie's final bid of $550 for the dining-room set is an aberration. But she quickly proves them wrong as she continues to bid for her furniture, sometimes beginning the bidding well over the minimum, other times raising her own bid. "This is not junk," she thinks, amazed at how cold it has become in the tent, though the others fan themselves with their programs. "These are not discards, but come to the auction block by a mistake of fortune."

As a succession of pieces goes to Annie, the audience becomes restless and disheartened, sensing they are bidding against someone who cannot lose. Some leave the tent, as the facade of good humor and accommodation that marked Jake's earlier auctioneering erodes. At one point, Annie finds herself bidding against the cunning-looking man for a clumsy wooden coffee table she never cared for. Knowing that eventually it will be hers, the man bids along with her, to demonstrate Annie's obvious insanity. When the man replies to Annie's bid of $650 with one of $700, Annie does not respond, and before he can register his amazement, he is the owner of the table.

After that, no one bids, and before long, the once-packed tent is nearly empty, with only Annie and a half dozen curious onlookers remaining. Cars rush out of the lot, raising dust.

"What the hell do you think you're doing?" the cunning-looking man says to her, but Annie refuses to look at him, instead studying Jake in his shirtsleeves, his shirt damp with perspiration. He is talking to Soupy, who stares out at Annie. The auction is over.

Mrs. Goodhue

A few minutes pass and Will comes up to her. "Are you crazy?" She turns to him, her boy. "Who knows?" He throws his hands up in desperation, and before she can reach out to take his hand, he is on the stage with Jake. Annie cannot imagine what they are saying.

After a while, not knowing what else to do, Annie walks up to Jake in the parking lot. "Don't talk to me now," he says.

"I'm sorry," she offers, "but I just had to . . ."

"Later." He gets into the Chrysler with Will. "Later," he mouths through the closed window, as he drives by, only inches from where Annie stands. She sees her reflection in the glass, superimposed over his face. "Later," she repeats. It is as if she had said it to herself.

"Dum-de-dum-dum," Soupy says, when Annie asks him for a ride back to the lodge. "Someone's ass is grass, and for a change, it ain't mine."

Annie sits alone in the back seat of the Lincoln, while Joe drives and Soupy sits up front. For once, the top is up. No one speaks until they are a few miles from the lodge, when Soupy turns and says, "You really showed the sonofabitch."

For a moment, Annie can't decide whether to take Soupy's side against Jake, but then does so gratefully. "What else could I do?"

"No, I mean it. Exactly what you did is how to hurt the guy. Embarrass him." Soupy leans back toward Annie. "You know, I couldn't do it in a million years," he confides.

"I didn't do it to hurt him." Annie mumbles something about "self-defense" that no one hears.

"The hell you didn't."

"Mudderfocker," Joe adds.

"I think if I got him that mad, he'd kill me," Soupy says matter-of-factly.

"He's not going to kill anyone," Annie insists.

"You don't think so?"

"I don't think so."

The tentativeness of her response surprises her and gives Soupy pause. It is dusk; the pine trees lining both sides of the road have been transformed into a hazy green wash, broken only by the sudden gray vertical of a power pole. "Would you like to make this interesting?" Soupy suddenly offers.

Annie feels a slight shiver, like a sliver of ice lodging at the base of her spine. "What do you mean?"

"I like what you did back there. It was real ballsy . . ." Soupy begins, this time keeping his eyes focused on the road. Annie wonders what his expression is. Joe's face is sallow, waxen. "You know, I run errands for him . . ." Soupy continues. Annie knows he is talking about Jake. ". . . pick him up, drop him off, you know . . ."

"And?" Could it be pleasure that she feels at already knowing what she is about to hear—the same uncomfortable pleasure she once felt watching David and the woman in her convertible? It mystifies her to think it may be so.

". . . and the place that I drop him off the most is this house in Waltham, is this lady's house, Mrs. Goodhue, a widow, something like that."

Annie rocks slightly on the seat. "I know."

"You know?"

"No, no," she says, "I don't really. What else?"

"Well, what else *is* there?"

"About the house?" Annie suggests.

"The house?"

"Everything." Annie leans forward, grabs Soupy's shoulder.

"That hurts," he says.

"Everything," she repeats.

The Offer

Dinner tonight is in the dining room. Jake has prepared the food, put a white cloth on the enormous table, and set it with the crystal and china from the sideboard. Six tall candles provide the light. He has also loaned Joe, Soupy, Hull and Will neckties to wear, though his own shirt is open at the collar. "Chef's prerogative," he says, when Hull asks Jake where his tie is.

"You certainly have a lot of prerogatives," Hull says. No one looks up except Annie. First at Hull, who is smiling, and then at Jake, who seems preoccupied with his salad, pushing the lettuce leaves around on his plate.

"As for the auction," Jake suddenly says, "overall I was pleased, highly pleased." Annie stares at him, incredulous. He looks back at her evenly, cordially. "Though I'm not sure whether we'll have another. How about it, boys?"

Joe, Soupy and Will agree they are not sure there will be another.

"What about Frank Lloyd Wright here?" Jake asks.

"Frankly, I could care less," Hull says.

"I like a man . . . or a woman who speaks their mind. Yes, I do." Jake drinks the wine in his glass, refills it, drinks it down, offers the empty glass in toast to the others at the table, then stands. Annie waits for what comes next. The veins in Jake's neck throb. She grasps the table with both hands, ready. If before she was cold, now she feels hot, though it is evening, and a breeze cuts through the open windows, causing the flames on the candles to flicker. "There is so much to say," Jake says, as if in preamble, "so much," he continues, his face flushed from the wine, "but, you know, tonight I'm just too pooped to pop. Period." He gives Annie a quick wink and is gone. Annie loosens her hold on the table. She feels ambushed by Jake's sudden disappearance.

"You know," Annie begins when she and Hull are the only ones left in the room. The candles have burned down and only one remains to illuminate the whole room. Sitting next to each other, the china and the crystal before them, they look like old lovers. "You know," Annie goes on, "he has a woman in Waltham."

She expects Hull to be surprised, but instead he asks, "Soupy tell you that?"

"You knew about her?"

"I didn't. Don't know anything about anybody." Hull's gaunt

face looks macabre in the candlelight. "I just imagined he must." When he sees Annie's hand fidgeting with her napkin, he touches her wrist. "What are you going to do?" he says.

"Tell him I know." Annie tries to picture the scene, the confrontation, but can't.

"Then what?"

"I'll ask him to make a choice."

"And when he does?"

"What do you mean, 'when he does'?"

Hull's voice has dropped to a whisper. "You know, when he chooses either you or her."

Just then the last candle flickers out, leaving only the moon to cast a silvery light on them, now both apparitions. Annie lets out a nervous laugh. "I leave in a few weeks," Hull says. "You and Will can come along with me. I have some money, a house in Atlanta. I can make sure that . . ."

"No," Annie interrupts, not wanting to hear any more, at the same time wishing that her energy hadn't run out, that she hadn't used up her chances. Besides, even if she hadn't, she couldn't bear to watch anyone else die. "Anyway," Annie goes on wistfully, "everything is not so very definite, not so very definitely lost here."

"My dear Annie," Hull turns to her, his hands on her shoulders, "everything here is definitely, definitely lost. Worse, it may never have even been here in the first place."

"No!" Annie says sharply.

"Annie!" He squeezes her shoulders, shaking her. He is smaller than she is, weighs less, but at this moment seems incredibly strong. "Don't you see, this is your best offer. Take it!" He loosens his grip. "No," he adds gently, "your best offer would have been to leave by yourself, but you're not about to do that."

"He could choose me, you know," Annie says softly. "You know, it could happen that way."

"I suppose it could." Hull seems defeated.

"I'll think about the offer, though," she says.

"Do that." He gets up from the table with his coffee cup.

Annie waits for him to come back so that she can thank him, but instead she hears him open the side door. Seconds later, she can see his meager outline striding across the driveway outside the living room and heading toward the pond.

Cape Cod, Summer 1956

Friday

Jake has invited over a hundred people to the lodge for a party the day after tomorrow, on Sunday. "Political friends," he has said, people he needs on his side. The featured guest is to be Elmer O'Leary, the governor of the state when Jake was attorney general. Jake is bringing the comestibles, as he calls them, for the party from Boston—of note, a haunch of steer meat called a "steamship round" that he intends to roast, then carve to order. Annie's chore is to shop locally for the staples.

At the market, she is uncertain about what quantities to buy. One hundred people. She puts items in her cart, takes them back out again. The Cointreau makes her a bit woozy. It would help if she had slept.

Arriving back at the lodge, Annie is surprised to see the hearse parked next to the garage. Its single large rear door is open wide, revealing the cavernous, wine-colored interior. It is far too early for Jake, although, not wanting to be caught off guard by him, she calls his name the second she opens the kitchen door. When no one answers, she calls for Hull, for anyone to explain the appearance of the hearse on a Friday morning. She knocks on the door to Hull's room, then opens it. Hull's handsome valises sit open on his bed, but he is not there. Will is also missing, and as Annie moves from room to room looking for the driver of the hearse, she feels perspiration form at the small of her back. Walking across the living room toward the master bedroom, she calls Jake's name again, expecting him to appear at any moment—alone, with someone, who knows?

At the threshold to the bedroom she stops, opens the door slowly, revealing first the small stuffed and mounted animals on the bureau, a quick reflection of herself in the mirror, the fireplace, then finally the king-size bed, where a thin, pale young man is sleeping. He lies on his back, a slender arm with a large wristwatch dangling off the side of the bed. He is wearing a white T-shirt, washed-out dungarees. His breath rustles his blond hair, which has fallen partially over his eyes. His features are fine, feminine, his eyelashes long and flaxen. Sun streams in through the open window, superimposing a near-perfect rectangle of light onto his form.

Beautiful, Annie thinks, not certain whether to awaken him or not. Feeling slightly dizzy, she sits down on the corner of the bed, as far from the young man as possible. Just then, he sits up with a start, and rubs his hands quickly in his eyes. "Annie?" he asks.

"Annie," she acknowledges, with little conviction.

"Is this your bed? I didn't know. I thought it might be Jake's, Mr. Weigel's." He stands. He is even thinner standing than lying down; his T-shirt and pants look baggy on him. His eyes are gray-blue, like the color of the flagstone on the porch. "Georgie Cooper," he offers. "I'm up for the weekend. To help out." He puts his hands behind his head and stretches, then lets them fall back to his sides.

"Well," he says, "how are you?" Before Annie can answer, though, he sticks his hands in his back pockets and declares, "This is your room; I'm in your room." Annie tells him that it is. "Wouldn't you know it," he begins, as if he is about to tell her that mix-ups like this are already the story of his young life. But he doesn't go on, instead turns and walks out. "Sorry," he calls from the living room.

"It's all right," Annie calls back. And it is, she supposes, in the world of Jake Weigel, of which she is a part—a world where Jake gives complete strangers the keys to his car and his house and the name of his mistress. If she accepts this—as she has come to do—certainly she cannot begrudge Georgie Cooper picking the wrong bed to sleep in.

Much later, after dinner, and after getting Georgie settled in the room next to Will's, Annie returns to the kitchen, where Hull is at the table smoking a cigarette. She pours some Cointreau into a coffee cup and joins him. Outside, the air is thick. The ever-present smell of pine has turned sickly sweet, corrupt. It is nearly dark; there is no light on in the kitchen; the smoke from the cigarette twists to the ceiling. Annie thinks of it curling inside him, insinuating itself deep into his body, coating his insides gray, cutting off the last of his chances.

Suddenly he turns. "Like I said, Annie, now's the time to git." Then, holding his long, thin arms out, he says, "Sunday is my last day. The offer stands."

Sleep covers Annie like felt—dense, textured, uncomfortable. When the first lights search through the room, she lifts her head out from under it. Cars go by on the driveway, stop at the garage. Doors open; there is talking. Jake. Annie tries to pull herself out of her sleep, but it has a potent hold on her. She shakes her head, rubs her eyes. Still drowsy from the sleeping pill she took earlier, she makes her way through the darkened living room and turns on the front light.

Outside, Jake stands, one foot on the bumper of the old Packard, holding what appears to be a rifle. Soupy paces nearby, hands on his hips, while Joe dances around nervously, looking into the lodge for the person who has turned on the light. Annie pulls back from the window, then after a few seconds returns. The two men join Jake, who now swings open the back door of the hearse. The rifle is really a walking stick that Jake props up against the side of the garage. "That sonofabitch," Jake exclaims. "I told him to put this goddamn thing on ice." Jake climbs into the hearse and drags a shapeless package, half as large as he is, to the threshold. The package is wrapped in white paper, nearly pristine save for a deep reddish purple blotch on one side. When Joe and Soupy offer to help, Jake glares at them. "Get the other stuff," he demands.

Just then, Annie feels a hand on her shoulder. It is Hull. "I've come to give you moral support," he says.

"I don't need it," Annie insists, though she can't imagine what it is she does need. "Where's Will?" she asks, slipping out from Hull's grasp. "Is Will awake?"

Will is already outside, however, standing next to Joe at the trunk of the Packard, ready to help. Wearing only his dungarees and a pair of boots, he looks so vulnerable, Annie thinks, so much less substantial than the others.

Jake spots Will and, momentarily abandoning the white package at the rear of the hearse, calls, "Will, go wake up the kid. And you in there," Jake calls out in the direction of the lodge, "put on some coffee."

In the kitchen, Annie asks Will if he'd like to put on a shirt, but he ignores her. As Annie strikes a match to turn on the gas, Jake lumbers into the room, noting Hull near the kitchen table. "Are you still alive?" he asks.

"Yep," Hull says. "Sorry."

Suddenly a scream cuts through the lodge, followed by a thud, then footsteps. Seconds later, Georgie runs into the kitchen. Jake grabs him. "Whoa!" he says, standing Georgie up against a cabinet. "Hold on!"

"Scared the bejesus out of me, Mr. Weigel. I thought the little bastard was trying to kill me."

"If he doesn't, I just might," Jake says. Georgie grimaces as a knob from the cabinet digs into his back. "Didn't I tell you to put the meat on ice?" Jake loosens his grip on Georgie, leaving neat fingerprints on both his arms. Georgie rubs them with his hands.

"Oh, yeah," he says. "Yeah, I remember." Georgie turns so as not to have to look Jake in the eye, but Jake keeps grabbing him and turning him back.

"No more crap out of you, Georgie, or it's back to Roxbury,

back to your AA meetings, and back to that bad, bad boyfriend of yours."

"I'll do it now," Georgie insists, looking out over Jake's shoulder to where the hearse is parked. "Right now." He feints and dodges as if he can somehow elude Jake, who finally just lets him by.

"Ready for some poker?" Jake says to Hull, who has been sitting with Annie in the kitchen while the cars are being unloaded, the steamship round put on ice. "Or am I interrupting something?"

"I'm amenable," Hull says, surprising Annie. "I just want to take the sumbitch's money if I can," he confides, when Jake is gone to get the cards.

Joe, Soupy, Georgie and Will sit around the dining-room table, waiting for Jake. Each has his hands folded in front of him, as if obeying Jake's instruction on how to sit. Hull joins them, folding his own hands. "Jake Weigel and his trained seals," he says to no one in particular. Soupy lets out a small bark, just as Jake arrives with the cards and a small lazy Susan stacked with poker chips.

"Some little thing on your mind, Campbell?" he asks, then, not expecting an answer, starts dealing the first hand. The table is so large that Jake has to stand to distribute the cards.

"What are we playing for?" Soupy asks. "Who's got any money?"

Jake reaches into his pocket and pulls out a roll of bills.

"Tell you what. I'll stake you all." He finds the twenties and hands one to everyone but Hull. "Twenty bucks a pop. You win, you owe me back the twenty, plus two bucks for the loan. You lose, you don't owe me a thing."

"Besides the interest, what's in it for you, Shylock?" Hull asks, taking his wallet out of his back pocket and putting out a half dozen twenties of his own.

"I'll play for the entertainment value. And to whip your ass," says Jake. He exchanges the twenties for chips.

Annie sits nearby on one of the wingback chairs. Earlier, Will walked by her as if she weren't there. In the shadows of the room, and hidden by the chair's sides, she feels that perhaps she isn't. And what of it?

Jake deals the first dozen or so hands. Everyone wins at least one, except Georgie, who bets carefully, folds early. With each completed hand, his fortune diminishes. From where Annie sits, it is Georgie's face she can see most clearly, and she studies it carefully. Each hand, it seems, is of personal importance to him, and every loss a lessening of his worth.

"Tomorrow," Jake announces, as he relinquishes the deal to Soupy, "tomorrow I want you, Campbell, working for Will here, getting the house squared away. Understand?"

When Soupy grumbles something in response, Jake reaches in the direction of his holster, which hangs on the back of his chair with his coat, then stops. "He's my boy, and if I say you work for him, you do."

"Sorry," Soupy says, "yessir," then starts dealing the cards.

Will looks down at the cards he has been dealt, while Jake looks over to Annie. She gazes coolly back at him. The hand lasts longer than any of the others. No one folds, not even Georgie, until Hull increases the bet to $100. He has four spades showing, and three down cards, one shy of a flush. Jake shows two pair, and raises Hull another $100. Hull calls him. "You got it?" Jake says, a slight raggedness to his voice. Hull turns over the fifth spade. "Your lucky day," Jake says. "Your lucky nine months," he adds. "Free food, free bed . . . even free woman."

Hull ignores him as he stands gathering his winnings. Jake's last $200 comes in tens and twenties, which Hull distributes to the others. "No strings, interest-free," Hull declares, as Joe eyes the money warily.

Everyone but Georgie uses Hull's gift to buy more chips and the game continues. Now Jake has a run of good hands, and eventually the pile of chips builds in front of him, along with nearly $1,000 of Hull's cash. Jake can barely suppress a grin as Hull goes back to his wallet again and again. Annie watches, half awake; the sound of the cards as they are dealt, the click of the chips tossed on the pile on the table, are soothing, soothing. Her view of the game has become distant, abstract. Five men and a boy late at night. Little talk.

Soupy excuses himself and returns a few seconds later with a bottle of Johnnie Walker Red. "You don't mind?" he asks Jake. Soupy puts the bottle to his mouth and takes a swallow.

"Mind?" Jake says. Soupy offers him the bottle. Jake accepts it, and takes a long swig himself. "Hell, no." He passes it to Joe, the only other player to drink from the bottle. Hull takes his from a coffee cup. Georgie and Will don't drink at all, though Georgie looks longingly at the bottle each time it goes by.

With the liquor, Jake gets sloppy, losing more often than winning, staying with losing hands, thinking his bravado will carry him. At one point he finds himself in a face-off with Soupy, all the others folding early. Soupy has three queens and an ace showing, Jake nothing—a seven, a four, a ten, a two. Still, Jake continues to raise him. Hull leans forward. "Stay with him," he says to Soupy. "I'll back you as far as he'll take you." Jake glares at Hull.

"Keep out of this. This is between Campbell and me."

When it is Soupy's bet, he studies his cards, then looks over at Jake and watches his thick fingers drum the table. "Too good for me," Soupy suddenly declares, turning his up-cards face down and throwing them into the pot. Jake looks up, surprised, then gathers in the chips proprietarily, as if he has won on the strength of his cards.

"Jesus Christ," Hull pronounces, "that was pathetic."

"You have a problem?" Jake asks. Joe and Soupy and Will get up from the table. The commotion rouses Annie. Georgie continues to sit, beating his fist into his hand, studying the gesture intently.

"Let's just cut the deck," Hull offers, "for whatever you've got there. Plus this." Hull produces four $100 bills from his wallet.

"What the hell for? Besides, you don't need money where you're going."

Hull assures him that they charge for cigarettes in the hereafter, then adds, "I just want to know what you're made of, that's all."

"Well, at least I'm not made of tumors." Jake looks around to the others for laughter, but there is none.

Suddenly, Hull sweeps the table in front of him with his arm, dumping his chips to the floor at Jake's feet. "Here, take them," he says. "You're the big winner." Hull walks off to his bedroom.

Jake looks quickly at Annie, then at Georgie, the only ones remaining in the room. "You," he addresses Georgie, "pick up the chips." The bottle of scotch, one-quarter full, is on the table. Georgie's lips are set; he perspires freely. "Pick them up!" He looks down from the bottle to Jake and back again. Finally he gets to his knees, scrapes up the chips and puts them on the table. "All right," Jake says, "now get to bed."

When he is gone, Jake turns to Annie. "Are you coming to bed?"

"I don't know."

"I would like it if you did." He walks over to her, holds her hand. "There's no reason, you know, we can't go back to what we had when we first met. No reason."

Annie thinks about what she knows. About Mrs. Goodhue. About Jake. With the single lamp behind him, he throws her into shadow. "What if I leave?" Annie suddenly dares, uncertain whether she has said it aloud or not.

"Don't threaten me," he says, letting go of her hand, as if it were his last conciliatory gesture. "Don't you dare threaten me."

"It's not a threat," Annie calls to his back. "It really isn't." For some reason, she follows him to the bedroom and watches him undress. "I don't want to lie next to you," she tells him when he holds the comforter up for her to get under.

"Fine." He lets the comforter drop. "Fine."

Annie walks out of the room. She thinks to check on Will, or Hull, or Georgie, to go to her typewriter, but doesn't. Instead, she returns to the wingback chair and, while the lodge and its occupants breathe and the ship's clock on the mantel ticks forward toward daylight, she lies bluntly awake in the room and listens—listens to the sound of her own pulse gradually losing its beat to the sighs of the room and the passage of time.

Much later, a car engine starts. Getting up quietly, Annie sees

Georgie drive by the living-room window in the hearse, lights doused.

Saturday

The next morning, though it is obvious the hearse is gone and Georgie with it, Jake says nothing. Instead he makes breakfast, humming as he mixes pancake batter. He still hums as he cuts slices of fresh apple into the batter. There is no talk at the kitchen table where Joe, Soupy and Will sit, toying with silverware, glancing occasionally at the spot where the hearse was parked the night before. Of Jake's anger, there is no question. It is as palpable as the bright Hawaiian shirt he wears beneath his apron. When Annie joins the others at the table, Jake hums louder. Annie wants to tell him to stop, to mete out the punishment for Georgie's departure and be done with it. Her confidence fails her, however, leaving her uncertain again.

"Vee go back to Boston tomorrow?" Joe suddenly asks almost loud enough for Jake to hear.

Soupy looks up, surprised. Joe rarely talks. "Yeah," Soupy nods, putting his finger to his lips, "tomorrow."

"Good." Joe's weasel face twitches. "I'm no like it here too good."

"Right," Soupy says, trying to end the conversation before Jake gets wind of it.

"Mudderfocker," Joe observes. He laughs his high-pitched laugh, then says it again. Jake looks up at him from the griddle where the oil for the pancakes sizzles.

"Listen," Soupy says quietly, "why don't you just shut up?"

"Vat? Piss you off?"

Soupy puts his hand to his head to indicate his frustration. "Don't you get the message, pal?"

Joe jumps up. He is wearing a loose white dress shirt, streaked yellow with age. "Hey," he says, striking a boxer's pose. "Big man, big man!"

"All right!" Soupy stands, grabs Joe by the shoulders and

pushes him back onto his chair. "You dumb bastard, you want to get us all killed?" Joe sits, contrite.

"Will," Jake suddenly calls from across the room, not looking up from the griddle. "Will," he repeats. Annie puts an arm around the chair where Will sits.

"What, Jake?" he asks. "What?"

"You know what time Georgie left?"

"No."

Jake has stacked the first batch of pancakes on a platter. "Does anybody know what time he left?" He points with his spatula in the direction of the table where everyone sits. Annie feels suddenly exhausted by the prospect of having to answer Jake. She cannot remember whether she slept or not, whether she actually saw Georgie leave or dreamed it. Besides, sleeping time, waking time, it has all begun to feel the same.

"Do *you* know, Annie?" Jake asks quietly, as if not to disturb her.

Annie blushes. Unable to muster the energy to lie, she reports hoarsely, "Yes." Hull is suddenly standing near her.

"I wish," Jake begins, all reason and restraint, "I wish you would have woken me up, because I might have been able to do something about it. But now . . ." He stops to take the last of the pancakes from the griddle.

Annie watches the muscles across Jake's back as he works. I should have awakened him, she thinks now. But at the time, there was something about the larceny that was so provocative: the doused headlights, the gentle warble of the big Cadillac Meteor's engine, the car whisking by, and Georgie's delicate features in the moonlight. Certain that Georgie's transgression would push Jake further than she'd ever seen him pushed, she let him sleep, hoping his anger would lead her to something, some sort of resolution.

As they are eating breakfast, Jake asks them all how they like their pancakes. The consensus is they are delicious. "Best goldurned flapjacks I ever et, Cookie," Hull says, then barks like a seal. Jake eyes him suspiciously. "No, really," Hull insists.

"You reedy little bastard, you're on my list."

"Uh-oh," Hull says, "I'm on his list."

Jake changes the subject. "Annie, you just about ready to go?"

"Go?"

Jake looks around the table, then at Annie. "You know, to see Ma. Like we arranged last week."

Annie cannot remember any such arrangement, and wonders if Jake is trying to confuse her. Before it is settled, however, Will excuses himself.

"You going somewhere?" Jake asks.

"No," Will says, "I just . . ."

". . . you just wanted to do the right thing, right?" Jake adds, embracing Will in front of the others. "You're a good man," Jake says. "And your mother did a fine job raising you." He holds the embrace a few more seconds, then lets Will go.

"I mean it," Jake says to Annie. And though he seems earnest, Annie sees the compliment as yet another trick, another of Jake's gestures to catch her off guard. She feels as much rebuked as pleased.

Later, as Annie dresses for the trip to the sanatorium where Mrs. Weigel, following her breakdown last year, now lives, Jake comes up behind her and puts his hand on her shoulders. "You don't sleep enough," he says. "That's why I knew you would know about Georgie. I was sure you would either be awake or wake up. I even know why you didn't wake me."

"You do?" Annie's heart raced.

"Sure. You don't like scenes, confrontations. And you knew damn well that's what it would have meant. Now, am I right or am I right?" Jake smiles a self-congratulatory smile.

"You're right," Annie admits.

"And don't you worry," he says, chucking her under her chin. "That boy will be back with that car and a whole hearseful of apologies. Mark my word."

Annie imagines herself as Georgie, navigating a stolen hearse through the streets of some town. Twenty years old, no future in sight, not even a drink to take for solace—and of course, no money. Jake is probably right. Enervated by the conclusion, she first sits, then lies back on the bed, looking up at him.

"You in the mood?" he asks.

"I'm really not," she says, aware she has already disappointed him twice today—by forgetting about the visit to his mother and by not awakening him when Georgie left.

"That's fine," Jake says.

"Really?"

"Really. What do you think I am? Some sort of sex fiend?" He takes off his shirt, revealing his chest, as bare of hair as a baby's. Annie imagines him doing the same in Mrs. Goodhue's bedroom. Her eyes glaze over. Tears, she thinks, but for what?

"You know what I wish?" he says, walking into the bathroom and turning on the taps at the sink. "I wish we could go to see *South Pacific* again." He returns to the bedroom, wiping his face with a towel.

"You loved me then. Is that what you mean?"

"Don't be ridiculous," he says. Annie hears the soft drone of an airplane. Jake dabs on some Bay Rum.

"I know I'm not what you hoped," she tells him, the tears coming so fast she can barely see through them.

"Don't be ridiculous," he says again. His back has been to her, but now he turns. "Are you sure you're not in the mood?"

Outside, waiting for Jake to finish talking with Soupy, Annie sees Will some distance from the lodge. He is working with a sledgehammer and wedges, splitting logs. The dust in the air irritates Annie's eyes, already bloodshot. Will sees her approaching, and brings the sledge down onto one of the wedges with a resounding clink, driving it deep into the log. "What?" he says, breathing heavily.

"You don't have to work so hard," she says. "You're only thirteen." She watches his face for signs. Of what? Love?

"Mom," he begins, setting the sledge down at his side. "You're just going to have to leave me alone," he goes on patiently, "that's the only way I'm going to do okay here. Understand?" Annie brushes a chip of wood from his cheek. "Understand?"

"I just wanted to say that . . ."

"Please," Will insists. He lifts the sledge again and brings it down, so hard that the wedge cleaves the log neatly and the very ground on which Annie stands shakes.

"I hate it that she's here," Jake says suddenly as he and Annie walk up the front steps of the sanatorium he has chosen for Mrs. Weigel. The two visitors are reflected in the polished brass hardware on the door, a quick blur of color and features misshapen and golden. "But what else could I do?" There is a slight whine to his voice. Annie does not respond, has said little on the half-hour trip to the handsome brick home.

Mrs. Weigel pads around her room wearing scuffs and a flannel nightgown whose pattern has faded to a near-solid cream color. The machine-made lace at the sleeves and collar has frayed. "I don't get dressed anymore," she says, without expression. "My clothes are trying to kill me."

"Come on, Ma," Jake says, "be a trooper."

"*You* be a trooper," she accuses, pointing at him. "You."

Jake looks at Annie for commiseration, but she is looking out the window to the bench where the three of them sat, only last year, before Mrs. Weigel got worse. Back then, the green-painted wooden bench trimmed in wrought iron, the green lawn rolling before them, the courteous way people visited, how slowly and decorously everyone moved, reminded her of the Stadt Park in the summer. Now from the window, watching the others visit with the sanatorium residents, Annie remembers her own stay at the hospital following her gesture for David. She cannot believe what she has done for love.

"Are you sure, Ma, you wouldn't just like to get dressed and walk down the hall?" Jake opens the closet to find a dress for her. He pulls out a navy-blue one with white triangles on it. "Annie would be glad to help you put it on."

Mrs. Weigel looks over at Annie and cringes, then clicks on the television. A soap opera flickers on. "See him," Mrs. Weigel says suddenly, with spirit, indicating a bland-looking man on the screen, "he tried to murder her."

"Really?" Jake asks.

She gets up and changes the channel. A woman advertises refrigerators. "Put the kids in one of those and they'll shut up," Mrs. Weigel declares, "oh, yes."

Jake turns off the television. "That's enough," he says, as one orderly, then another, rushes past the partially open door.

"Let's go for a walk to the lounge," Mrs. Weigel says, brightening for no apparent reason.

"You'll get dressed, then?" Jake asks.

"Don't you try to trick me," she says.

Jake holds her hand as she scuffs around the lounge. She is still in her nightgown. The television is tuned to another soap opera, and Mrs. Weigel tells him who is trying to murder whom and for what reason.

"They can't all be trying to murder someone," Jake finally says, exasperated.

"Hah!" she says.

Annie follows close behind, wondering what separates her from Mrs. Weigel and the other residents here and their vision of the world. An event in the past misconstrued? The accretion of too much memory? Chemicals in the body, in the brain? They have lost their perspective, she decides, simple as that. In realizing it, she realizes she has not lost hers—only hope, the energy to act.

Back in the car, Annie confesses to Jake, "I don't know what it is. I can't sleep, or at least it doesn't feel like sleep anymore. I can't think what I've just done, or what I'm going to do next."

Jake drives fast, though he gives the impression of total calm. With each of Annie's statements, he depresses the accelerator harder, as if daring her to continue. When she is silent, he asks, "Is that all?"

"I suppose so," Annie says, oddly relieved.

"Fine," he says, "fine." Then suddenly he bangs on the steering wheel and the car shudders. They are traveling at nearly ninety miles per hour. "Well, what about Ma?" he yells. "What about *her*?"

Annie has been so absorbed by her own situation, she has completely forgotten about Mrs. Weigel. "I'm sorry," she says, not finding anything else to offer.

"You're *sorry,*" Jake says ironically. "Sorry. I'll say!" Jake is about to go on when he sees a patrol car behind him, red light flashing. "Wouldn't you know it?" he says, pulling off to the shoulder.

When the officer appears at the window, Jake opens the door, nearly knocking the man over. He is in his late twenties, possibly younger. The officer asks Jake for his license. But when Jake reaches into his coat for his wallet, the officer quickly draws his gun.

"Hold it," he demands. "Get your hands out of that coat and up into the air."

"Don't be an asshole," Jake warns, though he raises his hands. "I'll have your goddamn badge." The officer spins Jake around and shoves him against the side of the car. Annie can see his chest pushed up against the driver's window, sees the officer reach around and pull the gun out of Jake's shoulder holster.

"Expecting trouble?" he asks.

"You're the one that's got the trouble," Jake informs him.

"Think so?" The officer orders Annie out of the car and has her stand next to Jake, both of them with their hands up and pushed up against the side of the car.

"I have a permit to carry this gun, cowboy," Jake says.

"Sure," the officer says. He pushes Jake's face down onto the top of the car. "And don't call me 'cowboy,'" he insists, "cowboy!"

As Jake's face makes contact with the warm metal, Annie experiences a slight flicker of pleasure. Yes, she thinks.

Just then a second patrol car arrives, and a second officer, an older man with a pockmarked face, gets out. He walks up to where Jake stands, grabs his shoulder and spins him back around. "Jesus Christ," the older officer says when he sees Jake. "Do you know who this guy is?"

"Who?" the younger officer asks, sounding suddenly confused.

"Your former attorney general, that's who."

Unsure what to do, the young man puts his gun into his holster. "Well, how the hell was I . . ."

"I'll have his ass," Jake says, dusting himself off and pushing back away from the car. "Now give me back the gun." Annie, in the meanwhile, turns.

"You heard him," the older officer says. The younger officer hands the gun back to Jake, who makes a show of inspecting it. He twirls the chamber, looks into the barrel, then takes a bead into the greenery along the edge of the roadway. A shot rings out, then echoes through the woods.

Annie is lying awake next to Jake when she sees the headlights, then hears the hearse pull into the driveway. Georgie is at the wheel, the same moonlit apparition he was the night before— his blond hair snow-white, his face like a mime's.

"What is it?" Jake mumbles in his sleep.

"Nothing," Annie assures. When she can't locate her own robe, she puts Jake's on and walks through the living room into the kitchen. Georgie is already there.

"I'm scared," he says, suddenly on his knees in front of Annie, his hands around her waist. "I'm so goddamn scared."

Annie rubs his hair, touches her cool palms to his temple. "It's okay. Nothing is going to happen. The car is back."

He holds her tighter. "I don't know. I don't know." Annie feels his body quaking. He is so frail. She gets on her knees in front of him and strokes his face. "I don't know," he says again.

"I understand," she tells him, knowing everything about not knowing. What she can't understand is why Georgie has returned. "Why did you come back?"

"I had to. I had Mr. Weigel's car."

"You had it last night. Why didn't you keep it?"

"I told you," he insists loudly, "I don't know."

"Shhhhh!" Annie embraces him. She feels his tears on her cheeks.

Suddenly the light goes on. Jake, wearing only his boxer shorts, stands at the kitchen threshold. "What's going on?" he demands.

Georgie jumps to his feet, leaving Annie on the floor. "I'm sorry, Mr. Weigel. I don't know what got into me. I came back, you know. It's like I was never gone." He is frantic, trying to explain every side of his lost argument.

"Let him go to sleep," Annie says, getting to her feet.

"Let him go to sleep, my ass!" Jake pushes Georgie against the stove. His head bangs sharply on the hood. "Let him go to sleep!" Jake slaps him across the face with his open hand, and Georgie stumbles sideways into the open china cabinet, shattering plates, cups and bowls. Jake pulls him to his feet. "You stupid bastard! Don't you even know when someone's doing you a favor?" Annie is at Georgie's side. She touches his cheek, which is red from where Jake slapped him.

"I brought the car back," Georgie insists, still crying, trying to catch his breath.

"As if that were the issue," Jake sneers. He punches Georgie in the stomach, and when he doubles over, Jake cracks his knee against Georgie's chin. He passes out cold onto the broken china.

Just then, Will appears from his room, Joe and Soupy from the garage apartment. "Go back to bed, fella," Jake tells Will. "And you two, get this scumbag cleaned up and out of here. No more free nights." Will is already gone when Joe and Soupy stand Georgie on his feet. He is still dazed, so they carry him outside. When it is just the two of them, Annie says to Jake, "You had to do that, didn't you?"

"What were the two of you doing on the floor?"

"The same thing you and Mrs. Goodhue do in Waltham." Jake stares at Annie, lost in his large wine-colored robe. Then a smile cracks his stony expression. He bends to pick up a piece of china.

"Well?" Annie insists.

"Well, if we talk about it now, a lot of things will be said that we'll both regret. Let's talk about it in the morning." Jake goes back to cleaning up.

"And if I want to talk about it now?"

Jake stops. "Then," he stands and walks past Annie, "you'll have to talk about it alone." He traverses the living room, shuts the bedroom door behind him. When she can't find the Cointreau, Annie pours herself a glass of scotch.

* * *

"Mudderfocker!" Annie hears. She lifts her head from the table where she fell asleep to see Joe run by the kitchen window in the dark. Right behind him is Soupy, then Georgie, limping slightly. All three are in their undershorts. They circle the lodge once, then again, their movements herky-jerky in the moonlight. It is like a chase in a silent movie, save for Joe's occasional expletives and Soupy's exaggerated shushings. Annie watches, listening for sounds from the master bedroom. There are none.

Now the three men are wrestling on the ground, their three pale bodies merging into a single roiling phantasm. Annie fears, even as she hears their exertions, sees them clearly not twenty feet away, that this is a dream—her new way of dreaming, where the dreamer is awake and troubled, and everything around her is dreamlike. The three men continue to tumble around, then suddenly separate, each on his hands and knees, staring directly at Annie, watching from the kitchen window.

The tableau of the three of them staring persists for a few seconds, when Annie cinches the belt of Jake's robe tighter around her and walks out onto the lawn where they are kneeling.

"Uh-oh," says Georgie.

"Shhhhh, shhhhh!" Soupy commands, putting a finger to his lips. "Hide." The three men scamper away as Annie approaches. Until her eyes become accustomed to the dark, she cannot see them, but then she discovers Soupy next to the lamppost, and Joe behind the oil tank. She cannot see Georgie, but hears someone vomit near where the cars are parked.

"Go on upstairs," Annie says in an exaggerated whisper. She walks over to Soupy, who still hides next to the lamppost, holding his breath. "Get them upstairs," she implores. Soupy lets out his breath, filling the air with the reek of alcohol. "You're drunk," she says. "Georgie too."

"You are too," Soupy whispers. "So what?"

"Upstairs," Annie repeats. "Now!" She grabs Soupy's hand and pulls him toward Joe; then the three of them go to find Georgie. "All of you, to bed!" When she sees first Joe, then Soupy, stumble on the stairs to the garage apartment, she helps them up. Inside the small room, she sees them each to a cot. "No more of this," she says, as she closes the door behind her.

The words, her own, reverberate through her skull, as she walks back toward the lodge. She opens the kitchen door, walks through the kitchen, the living room, and finds herself suddenly in the master bedroom. She is out of breath; her legs ache for no reason. She flicks on the light.

"Jake," she yells. He puts a pillow to his face. She tears it away. "You bastard!" He sits up on the bed, tries to get his bearings. Annie knows that for once it is she who has surprised him. She flicks the light on and off, on and off. He jumps up, grabs her around the waist and pushes her back on the bed.

"What's going on?" he demands.

"What are you trying to do to me?" she counters. "Are you trying to drive me crazy? Is that what? I mean, what's going to happen next?" she screams.

"Quiet, quiet." Jake puts his wide hand over her mouth. Annie tries to tear away from him, but he is far, far too strong. "I'm not going to let you go until you are quiet," he says calmly, at the same time extending his hand to cover her nose as well. Not being able to breathe is like a large, black blot suddenly extending from behind her ears forward to her eyes and forehead. Annie grabs frantically at Jake's wrist with both her hands, but the harder she fights with her whole body, the more strength he seems to gather in the hand that covers her face. "Stop, and I'll let you go," he says evenly.

Lost either way, Annie gives in to him. "All right," he says. "All right? You tried to kill me," she hisses at him.

"Don't be ridiculous." He props himself up on the bed next to Annie, who still wears his robe, though it is open and torn. She covers herself with a blanket. "Now what the hell is the goddamn problem?"

"You don't know?"

"I know, I know," he says dismissively. "What if I told you that the situation was purely platonic? Just friends. No fooling around."

"I'd say you were a liar."

Jake laughs. "My word against your intuition, then. And we'd both be better off with my word."

"You mean *you'd* be better off with it." Annie is still trying to regain her breath, find some equilibrium.

"Your intuition stinks," Jake pronounces. "You bought back that goddamn furniture, and now it's going to sit in that garage and no one is going to get anything out of it. No use, no money, nothing."

"It was mine. I wanted to keep it." Annie senses she sounds like a sulking child, but knows that about this she is right.

"Nothing is yours. Face it. Face facts," Jake pronounces.

"My own life, to do with as I like," Annie declares.

"That's right," he says. "You *do* have that." He gets up, turns off the light, then lies down on the bed facing away from her. "You do have that."

Sunday

Sunday, late morning, the sun beats down mightily on the pond. The gray-painted rafts are bleached the color of bone. Drawing on her robe, Annie hears voices in the kitchen.

"Well, good afternoon," Jake says when Annie walks in. On the counter next to the stove is a tray with eggs and bacon, coffee, juice and toast. "I was just about to bring you breakfast." He winks. He is wearing checked chef's pants, a double-breasted white cook's jacket, and a tall, starched toque. "Sleep well?"

Will sits on a kitchen chair, peeling potatoes. Joe and Soupy shell peas from a large pile on the table. Georgie looks up from the silverware he is cleaning. He smiles sheepishly, and then waves. His face is swollen, one of his eyes is blackened—the only trace of the night before.

"Just one big happy family," Jake declares. The sun is everywhere, glinting off the china in the cabinet, the large sieve Jake is using to strain something, Annie's typewriter, the water-filled pot where Will throws the peeled potatoes. Though she has slept well, Annie can't quite rise to the intensity of the morning. At the table, she makes a show of eating, but everything tastes slightly off—the eggs a bit metallic, the bacon way too salty.

While Annie tries to eat, Jake gives the day's assignments. Soupy and Will are to be waiters; Joe, the bartender; and Georgie will park cars. "That doesn't mean you'll take them for a ride, either. Right, Georgie?"

Georgie nods. "Right, Mr. Weigel." His face is so swollen, it is difficult for him to manufacture the words. Jake pats him gently on the shoulder. Just then, Jake's toque, which had been standing a good ten inches above his forehead, flops down before his eyes. Everyone laughs.

"Think that's funny, huh?" Jake says, sweeping the fallen crown to the side. The laughter stops. "Well, it is!" he proclaims. "It is!"

A half hour later, when only Jake and Annie remain in the kitchen, he asks, "Are you all right?"

"Sure," Annie says. She has left most of her breakfast. "Sure," she repeats, almost flippantly, yet as she does, sadness levels her like a harrow.

"I'm just not sure what I'm supposed to say." He looks up at her questioningly. "You know, like 'I'm sorry,' or what?"

"No, nothing, fine," Annie says. "I'm sorry too." Standing behind her, Jake rests his hands on her shoulders, massaging them softly. The sun has lost a bit of its intensity, and Annie feels the first traces of a chill. She turns her head to let her cheek rest on Jake's left hand.

"You know," he suddenly begins, looking beyond her out the lodge windows and to the pond, his expression wistful, "you take a morning like this, and you feel on top of the world." Annie tries to imagine it—being on top of the world, alone, levitating just a few feet above it while it spins. The notion is oddly satisfying. Just then, Jake bends and kisses her gently. "I'll make it better," he declares. "You just wait and see."

Jake whistles "There Is Nothing Like a Dame" as he opens the oven to baste the steamship round in the black roasting pan.

Carrots and onions tumble off the roast onto the floor and Annie, now dressed in the slacks and top Jake likes best, bends to pick them up. Will is there first, however, and tells her to move away, he'll do it.

"Fine," she says, trying to get Will to look at her, but he won't. No one will, it seems, not even Hull, who appears in the kitchen wearing the same lightweight khaki slacks and denim shirt he had on the night he arrived. Annie recalls the scene: the chill night, the andirons, Jake's exuberance, Hull's courtly manner. Back then, he looked as if he were only a few good meals away from having his clothes fit him. Now, Hull's shirt hangs from his shoulders as if he were made of cardboard, his belt stretches nearly twice around his waist. He carries a valise in each hand.

"Can anyone give me a lift to the bus depot?" he asks.

Jake looks up from the roast as the oven door slams shut.

"What, not staying for the party?"

"I'd rather not," Hull says softly, "I'm just not in a party mood, don't you know." He affects lightness, but it fails him. Annie winces to see him so beaten down.

"Everybody's busy," she says, "I'll take you. Let me just get the keys." As she moves by him, Hull holds his hand out and touches her elbow.

"I'd rather you didn't," he says, gracious and distant.

"I'll get Georgie to take you then," Jake offers. Grabbing a large French knife from the counter, he lumbers to the side door to find him. "Georgie," he calls from the stoop.

"Is it something I did?" Annie asks Hull quickly.

"It's something you didn't." Across the way Annie can see Georgie emerging from the garage apartment, Jake meeting him halfway.

"You really mean to say I should just pack up and leave with you? Is that what you want?"

"That's what I recall asking you to do, yes." Jake turns back to the kitchen.

"But how could I . . ." Annie implores, "how could I leave again? Start again . . . again, all over . . ." The idea exhausts her, saps whatever energy she gained from sleep.

The kitchen door opens. "We'd talk about it later," Hull says, urgently. "But the time is now. Do you understand?"

"All set," Jake announces. Georgie backs the Lincoln out of the space at the side of the lodge. "Will, give him a hand with his bags." Will takes the valises from Hull's hand. When suddenly Hull stands in full profile, Annie is shocked to see that he has virtually no dimension at all. "We're all settled up moneywise, aren't we?" Jake asks.

"Just about," Hull says, his voice smooth and dulcet again. He moves toward the door, then stops and turns, as if to wave. Before he can, Annie embraces him, drawing him to her. Fearing she might crush him, she lets him go, kisses him once, then again.

"Well, well, well," Jake observes, "if I didn't know better, I'd say you two had a little something going after all." Will, who has returned from the Lincoln, looks mortified.

"I wish," Hull says.

"Well, you're forgiven," Jake says, "right, Annie?" Jake looks to her for a response, but she cannot fabricate one for him and quickly leaves. A few moments later, from the living room, Annie watches the Lincoln drive past. She waves, but Hull is on the far side, and she is certain he can't see her. Still, she can imagine him, as she has seen him dozens of times before, looking bemused, sad and disappointed. Unsure what to do after the yellow car sweeps past the last of the trees, Annie turns to the model that Hull labored over. It is still perfect and real in every detail, though the only one of the miniature people that so enchanted Annie that remains is the woman on the raft.

Annie sits at the typewriter, imagining it to be a piano. She is typing nonsense syllables, but takes pleasure, nonetheless, in the bend of her wrist over the keyboard, the curl of her fingers over the keys. She can sense music in her body, feel her shoulders tense as the coda nears. A perfect triptych comes to mind: listening to her play the piano at the Skodagasse is Papa, in his dark suit sitting in the old chair in the corner, a cup of coffee poised in a saucer balanced on his knee; Mama, sitting gracefully on the Persian carpet, legs bent beneath her, wearing a demure gray silk dress trimmed with black lace; and Oma, standing, so intimate with Anna and the music that it is as if there were no piano save the one the two of them share in their imagination. When the music is over, Papa carefully places the cup in its saucer and claps, Mama rises and hugs Anna, and Oma blows her a kiss. Outside, the day is gray, but in that parlor filled with overstuffed sofas and chairs covered in velvet and chintz, suffused by the glow of family and the coals through the isinglass window of the enamel stove, it is warm, close.

"Tonight," Jake says matter-of-factly, coming up behind Annie, "make sure you behave yourself."

When Annie returns to Hull's model to see if perhaps he has stowed the miniature people somewhere for her to find, she sees Soupy and Will at the far end of the room, sitting next to each other at the dining-room table.

"Come on, come on," Soupy says, "give me some competition." Annie walks over. "Arm wrestling," Soupy informs her. He positions his elbow on the table as Will does the same. Will looks serious and determined, moistening his lips with his tongue just as David did when about to essay a difficult task. The two combatants lock hands. Soupy calls, "Ready, set, go," makes a show of straining against Will's strength, then takes him down easily. "You gotta do better than that," Soupy tells him. "He's got to do better," he says, turning to Annie. "Life is a bear, and you've gotta wrestle it down."

"For Christ's sake, I'm trying," Will insists. Annie recognizes Jake's inflection, then watches as Will rubs his wrist to strengthen it for the next go-around. He is clearly disappointed by the obvious ease with which Soupy took him down. She wants to console him, but knows he will resent it. Instead, she suggests Soupy pick on someone his own size.

"You're my size," he says. "Why don't you take me on?"

"That's not true. I'm more *his* size," she says, indicating Will.

"Fine, then. Take *him* on." Soupy steps away from the table, offering Annie his chair with a mock bow. Soupy sees Will wince. "What? You afraid to fight the old lady? Put her down?"

Seconds later, Annie and Will sit, forearm to forearm. It is true, Annie is his size—their forearms, wrists and hands almost identical.

"Ready . . . set . . . go!" Soupy calls.

Will exerts pressure immediately, and Annie's inclination is simply to concede, be done with it. But to her surprise, she meets his pressure with her own, realizing suddenly that even with all his log-splitting, she is still stronger, much stronger even. Will strains, bites his lip.

"Come on, come on," Soupy urges. "Put her down, kid." It is meant to encourage Will. Instead, it makes Annie furious, and without thinking, she pushes Will's wrist nearly to the table.

Soupy puts his mouth to Will's ear. "Come on, kid." Annie sees Soupy's exhortation register on Will's face, feels him redouble his effort. Giving in to it, she allows Will to push her back to the ready position, but then again exerts her strength, amazed at how easily she brings his wrist to within an inch of the table. Tears form in Will's eyes, he wants so badly to win. And then, as Annie lets him do so, lets him arc her wrist nearly 180 degrees to smash painfully on the oak tabletop, she thinks that if only she had gained leverage on Jake and on the rest of them early on, she would have had a better chance.

"Great, Will, great," she says, extracting her hand from his. "You're really strong."

He looks up at her. He is furious. "I wish you'd just drop dead," he says evenly.

Later that afternoon, Annie is awakened by voices from the kitchen. She has dozed off in the wingback chair for a few minutes (hours? seconds?). She ought to help, she thinks, astounded to note that while she has slept, all the living-room furniture, including the chair in which she sits, has been moved. She ought to help, but somehow the preparation for the evening's party has passed her by.

In the kitchen, Jake opens the oven door. The smell of the roast fills the room. It is an intense, masculine aroma, overlaid with that of grease. When Jake pulls out the roasting pan, the cooking juices sizzle and pop. The onions and carrots garnishing it are singed, the roast itself burned black. "Perfect," Jake declares. He is still in his chef's attire.

Will stands nearby, wearing a sport coat and slacks. Soupy, in one of Jake's old tuxedos, looks like a man adrift. At the kitchen table, taking highball glasses out of a cardboard box, is Joe, in a red bartender's coat and an open-necked shirt, black bow tie clipped onto a single collar point. Georgie, it seems, has not yet returned from the bus station.

"Is there something I can do to help?" Annie asks, watching as the roiling cooking juices spatter the floor. No one answers, and for a moment she is uncertain whether she has actually said anything. She repeats the question, and there is still no response, though Soupy does look over at her. "Why doesn't someone answer me?" she insists. And when no one does, she realizes they must be under orders from Jake. But why? Why now, when just hours ago, Jake had promised to make things better? Joe, Soupy and Will walk past Annie and out of the room, leaving her to consider Jake's broad back moving from pot to pot like a sorcerer, laboring over the stove, she imagines, as he has labored over her.

Annie wonders what grand gesture is left for her, what way to make her presence felt again, to reassert some semblance of the power that took her from Vienna to London and back again. Finally, she says hoarsely to Jake, "Please."

"Please what?" he says, turning around.

"Please pay attention."

"I'm paying attention. I've heard every word you said." He recites her request back to her: " 'Is there something I can do to help?' "

"Then please," she interrupts, "just make me feel comfortable." She is begging, she knows—something Jake detests—but it has been so long since she felt comfortable, she thinks she has forgotten how it feels, and worse, that she may never feel it again. "Just please."

"What do you want me to do?" he articulates evenly.

She has forgotten *this* as well, she realizes, standing as close to him as on the night she first kissed him. "Just be nice," she finally offers.

"Okay, I'll be nice," he tells her. "Now why don't you just take a nap or something while I finish cooking." He pulls a large frying pan from the cupboard and walks away, leaving her standing, her mouth open to speak, her hands outstretched as if to grab his retreating back.

When she is alone in the bedroom she screams into her pillow, "No! No. I don't want to. I don't want to take a nap," but no one hears her. Of this, she is certain.

It is dusk. Outside, Georgie parks the cars that Jake's guests leave with him, casually handing Georgie their keys in mid-sentence and walking away. In the living room, Will and Soupy offer canapés from silver trays that Annie has never seen before. Joe stands behind a small bar set up next to Hull's model. An occasional guest studies the perfect little balconies and terraced gardens, but for most, the model, particularly the open areas and the pond fashioned from a mirror, serves as a place to set down half-empty glasses, frilled toothpicks and half-eaten canapés.

Jake stands among a group of florid men. A red bandanna tied around his neck accents his chef's outfit. He smokes a cigar. Annie, wearing the white dress he has bought for her for the party, moves in his direction, but when he sees her approach, she stops. "No, no, come over," he insists, and the circle of men around Jake opens to accept her. "I want you to meet the woman of my dreams," he announces, putting a proprietary arm around her waist.

"So this is what Jake Weigel dreams about?" one of the men says.

"Nice."

"Very nice."

"You're a lucky lady."

The buffet is set up on the dining-room table, covered tonight by a red cloth. Jake stands behind the steamship round, which he has wrestled from the roasting pan to a large wooden tray with a moat-like trough that catches the juices and four large spikes that hold the roast upright. "I hate to start before Elmer gets here," Jake says to the first guest in the buffet line. He carves the man a slab of beef.

"That's right," the next person in line says. "Where's Elmer?" And though the appearance of the roast and the other food is meant to increase the festivity, a sudden pall falls over the room as Elmer's absence is noted—their leader of a decade before. People sit quietly, the sound of conversation replaced by that of silverware on china.

A half hour later, Jake finally concedes to the men he sits with that Elmer is probably not coming. "Heart trouble," he offers by way of explanation. A few guests amble out of the lodge and to their cars. Jake checks his wristwatch, then looks around the room to see if perhaps Elmer has arrived unannounced. Having met the rude, obese, gout-ridden man once before, Annie cannot imagine what Elmer's attraction is, what the disappointment means, particularly to Jake, who never seems to need a thing. She has a glass of Cointreau, and then a second.

A few minutes later, in the void created by Elmer's absence, Annie announces to a small cluster of women standing under the moose head, "I'm Annie. I'm living here with Jake these days." The women look up at her, and instantly she realizes what a fool she has made of herself. She is searching for something to say to rectify her error when suddenly there are lights in the driveway. "Elmer," a dozen of the guests say in unison. Jake looks relieved, happy even.

"That old sonofabitch," Jake pronounces, tramping out of one of the front doors of the lodge to the limousine that is stopped in the middle of the driveway. The driver scurries around to open Elmer's door. Everyone in the house waits. There is not even the pretense of nonchalance. As heavy as he is, Elmer must extricate himself from the back seat, pulling himself up and out with both hands on the doorframe. When he is finally free of the car, he holds up both hands in greeting. Nearly everyone claps. Jake shakes Elmer's hand, then puts one arm partly around his back, as they walk together to the living room, passing Annie at the door.

Once inside, Elmer announces that he has to use the can, and Jake escorts him through the guests into the master bathroom. Emerging with Jake a few minutes later, Elmer suddenly booms, "Where's my little Annie?" The guests, who have been awaiting

Elmer's return, all turn to search her out, as if to deliver her to him. Elmer holds his arms out to her. His open coat reveals his large belly straining the buttons of his shirt. Jake stands beside him and looks at Annie, a desperate expression on his face—like Will's when he wanted to beat her in arm wrestling. The room is absolutely silent. Elmer gestures with a nod of his head for Annie to come to him, and when it is clear that she will not, he closes the distance between them and grabs her buttocks with both hands.

"Now this," he announces, "is a real woman." He kisses her cheek and then quite unexpectedly turns away from her and says he needs a drink. The crowd follows him to the bar.

Some time later, Annie is talking with a woman who it seems has sought her out. She asks Annie how she feels, what she is thinking about. When Annie tells the woman that she is unsure about all these things, the woman pats her arm and says she understands, then quickly disappears into the crowd.

"Well, what did you think?" Soupy says, coming up to Annie.

"Of what?"

"Of Mrs. Goodhue." Annie feels undermined, tricked.

When she asks Jake what Mrs. Goodhue is doing here, he says, "Nice woman, don't you think?"

"You didn't say she'd be here tonight." Jake nods, as if it had slipped his mind. "At least you could have told me." She knows that others overhear their conversation, but doesn't care.

"I told you," Jake replies, moving away from Annie. "I told you I wanted you to meet her."

"Mr. Weigel, Mr. Weigel!" Georgie's voice, higher-pitched and more nervous even than usual, breaks over the crowd. Annie stands alone, next to the model, removing half-filled glasses and crumpled napkins, and looking up every few seconds for Mrs. Goodhue, though she is uncertain what she will say to her if she finds her. Still, she just wants to see her, understand what it is that the woman offers that she, Annie, cannot. "Mr. Weigel, there's a lady outside," Georgie announces.

"Well then, bring her *inside.*" Jake's voice resonates from somewhere in the room. Suddenly he emerges to join Georgie by the front door at the left of the fireplace. "She's pretty loaded," Georgie confides.

"All the better," Jake tells him.

The car parked on the flagstones is familiar, though Annie cannot remember where she has seen it before. Its lights are on; its right directional signal flickers feebly. Inside the car, the driver slides across the seat from the driver's side, flings open the passenger door and emerges. It is Helen. She totters slightly in her heels, her uneven progress to the house exaggerated by the flashing yellow light thrown by the turn signals. Once on the porch, however, she gathers her dignity and walks purposefully toward the nearest entrance.

Watching her, Annie feels an odd delight; Helen's arrival could not have been better planned. In the living room, Helen props herself against the wall. She is dressed in an elegant green taffeta gown that reveals her shoulders and trails nearly to the floor. An evening purse dangles from a strap at the crook of her elbow. Just then, Soupy walks by with a tray of champagne glasses. She grabs one, and in the process her purse hits three others, which topple from the tray and crash to the floor.

" 'Scuse me," she says. A man Jake's age with stringy white hair and large bulging eyes seems to recognize her, and quickly whispers something to the bored woman standing at his side, who immediately seeks out someone else to whom she tells the news of Helen's arrival. Sashaying away from the couple, Helen bumps into another woman who has been gazing into the mirror of her compact.

"Pardon me," the woman says, not looking up.

"Screw yourself," Helen tells her. She makes her way to the room's center, barely outpacing the rumors of her arrival. Spotting Elmer O'Leary's huge back, she drives her hand under his suitcoat and into his pants. Elmer yelps. "Stop it. I love it!" He turns. "Helen! Helen Weigel! As I live and breathe!" For a moment, he is as eager as a youngster given a long-awaited gift. The saddlebag-like pouches that form his cheeks flush red, and his small mouth hangs open in excitement and surprise. The next instant, however, he is out of breath, jubilation slipping away, replaced first by concern, then fear, as he is helped by his driver to the side of the room. Annie watches, a feeling not unlike pleasure coursing through her.

"All our old friends, and you didn't invite me," Helen says to Jake, who confronts her off to the side of the room. Beneath her irony, she sounds pouty, crestfallen.

"Leave," Jake demands. "Leave now."

"Leave now? I drove all the way from Foxboro."

He grabs her arm to propel her to the door.

"No, no," she insists. "Elmer wants me to stay." She manages to tear herself away from Jake to rejoin Elmer, who sits, breathing heavily, on one of the couches. His driver hands him some pills. "Don't you want me to stay, Elmer?"

Smiling wanly, he looks up at her. Drawn to Helen's performance, Annie stands nearby. "Let her stay, Jake," Elmer says slowly. He plucks the pills from his palm with his lips.

"See"—Helen brightens—"old friends stick together." Victorious, she attempts to start conversations with the other guests, but no one will speak to her; no doubt, Annie thinks, Jake's orders. Quickly, Helen becomes despondent, then sits down in the wingback chair, where she rubs her arms and elbows. Watching Helen, Annie finally sees Mrs. Goodhue, but pays her little heed. Instead, Annie goes over to Helen and sits on an arm of the wingback chair.

"What are you doing here?" Helen asks, still rubbing her arms.

"I live here," Annie says.

"You?" She looks Annie over. "I don't believe it."

For some reason, Annie finds Helen's surprise amusing. "What were you expecting?"

"A whore!" she says harshly. A couple nearby turns, then turns away again.

"I qualify for that," Annie admits ruefully.

"Hardly." Helen's talk is tough, but behind it, Annie sees the beaten-down woman Jake slapped only a few months ago. To Annie's surprise, up close Helen is actually quite pretty, with small, red, bow-like lips and blond hair done in a permanent wave, now breaking away loosely. Helen bends to rub her knees and calves. "Goddamn circulation," she says, "always cold."

"There you are!" Jake says, standing in front of Helen as she bends. He ignores Annie. "Now get the hell out of here before I call the police. I mean it!" Annie notes the set of Jake's jaw as he says it.

"Come on," Annie says, taking Helen's hand. "Come on, we'll take a walk." When Helen is on her feet, Annie puts her arm around her.

"Does he still have that long skinny dick?" Helen asks. Annie doesn't answer, instead moves with her to the kitchen door. At the threshold, Helen announces to anyone within earshot, "He was going to Dick Academy to see if he could fatten it up enough to be a passable screw."

"Quiet," Annie insists.

In the kitchen, Helen pulls away from her. "What do you want?" she demands.

Annie finds the Cointreau. "Just to talk," she says. From a pile on the kitchen table, she grabs a coat for Helen and one for herself. "You said you were cold." Annie offers to help Helen with the coat. At first Helen objects, but then, considering the gesture, and finally the coat itself, she acquiesces.

"Hmmm, silk," she says, twirling once with the coat when she has it on. "My favorite fiber."

Will comes into the kitchen. "My son," Annie says, holding her arms out to him.

"Don't drink," he says, noticing the bottle back in Annie's hand.

"He lives here too?" Helen asks, tweaking his cheek as he passes her on the way through the room.

Will suddenly stops, registering that both women have coats on. "Where are you going?"

"Just out," Annie says.

"Not in the car, though." His expression is straightforward, earnest, like when he was five. There is a tray in his hand, empty but for a few crumpled napkins.

"Not in the car," Annie assures.

"It's just that I'm worried."

"We'll be all right," Annie says, helping him load his tray with tiny cream puffs shaped like swans and dusted with confectioners' sugar. Helen looks on. When the tray is full, Annie kisses him on the cheek and shoves him gently toward the living room. "Don't worry, we'll be all right."

Outside, Annie and Helen walk arm in arm around the driveway. "He left you?" Annie asks.

"I forget."

"What was he like back then?" They are walking quickly, Annie setting the pace and leading the way. The moon is high; a breeze on the pond disturbs the pine branches nearby.

"The same. He was born a sonofabitch."

"Can that be?" Annie asks, remembering suddenly Mama's words about her own temperament.

"Sure. Of course, he had some help from his old lady. A real prize, she was. She dead?"

"Almost."

"The world will be a better place."

"You think . . ."

"I bet," Helen interrupts, staring guilelessly at Annie, "I bet you used to be a pretty woman."

"Not anymore?" Annie asks, never having considered herself pretty, but thinking she has made herself prettier, first for David with her nose job, and later for Jake by dyeing her hair, wearing all those outfits.

Helen shakes her head sadly. "You just worried all the prettiness away here."

"Well, there have been a lot of things," Annie begins, "before 'here.' "

"You should see yourself," Helen insists, "see yourself like I do, like a stranger sees you." She puts her hands to Annie's face and kisses her lightly on each cheek.

". . . and?"

"And you'd see what I mean. Like your face has two dimensions to it—what it used to be and what it is now."

Helen's touch leaves Annie both sorrowful and confused: sorrowful for what she has lost, and confused by this reversal wherein Helen offers her solace, and not the other way around.

"*I* left *him,*" Helen announces as they start walking again. "The smartest thing I ever did." Annie recalls Hull's offer, only hours old. "They all leave him—wives, mistresses, girlfriends. They're a wreck when they leave, but better for it, believe me. Everyone but Nurse Goodhue has left," Helen pronounces with scorn.

"You know her?"

"I think she gave him a blow job when he was thirteen and he's been forever grateful."

"Really?"

"Annie, you're sweet."

Annie pulls the cork on the Cointreau bottle, takes a swig and offers it to Helen. "I'll pass," she says.

"Come on," Annie says, "there's somewhere I want to go."

She steers Helen in the direction of the pond, and the wooden rowboat tied to a post embedded in the sand.

"What's out here?" Helen asks, sitting at the stern, as Annie pushes them off. Their high-heeled shoes left on the small strip of beach look like four mantises.

"Distance," Annie replies, "rafts." She jumps onto the boat. There is only a single oar.

"I don't know how to swim," Helen says matter-of-factly.

"So what?" Annie says, and for some reason they both laugh.

"What if," Annie says, guiding them in the direction of the rafts—dark undulating shadows off the bow, water lapping gently at their sides—"what if I can't leave?"

"Then pray the boat sinks and that you can't swim either." There is nothing drunk about Helen, Annie notes, wondering whether Helen was drunk earlier or was acting. The Cointreau loosens Annie's limbs, provides her with a familiar comfort.

"No, really."

"Really."

They are a hundred yards from shore. Ahead of them, the rafts are like a mirage in the moonlight. "If I could just prove to him that I'm exactly the one," Annie begins, but Helen interrupts.

"He hasn't the faintest idea what that is. Besides, he doesn't want anything. He just wants you around to jerk off. He jerks off with the world."

Just before the boat makes contact with the nearest of the rafts, Annie takes another swallow of Cointreau. "Gimme some of that hooch," Helen says, making her way to the bow of the boat where Annie sits. The boat rocks dangerously and Helen grabs the gunnels. Handing her the bottle, Annie secures the bowline to the raft, helps Helen aboard, then joins her on the wooden platform. The raft heaves, accepting their weight, then gradually rights itself, and the pond is quiet again; with no one rowing, there is not even the sound of the water lapping.

Helen is the first to sit. "The day I left him was the absolute high point of my life," she says into the quiet. "I just packed and called a cab. He asked me why, and I told him he was a lousy lay. Then he said, 'No, really.' And I told him it was because I hated him and maybe did all along, confusing it with something else that made me marry him. He told me I was crazy, and I agreed. The cab came and I got in."

"That's a gesture," Annie says. The lights from the lodge shimmer.

"That was no gesture," Helen says. "It was a decision. He doesn't respond to gestures," she insists. "Forget it." She finishes the last of the Cointreau, stands and heaves the bottle into the pond as far from the lodge as she can. "So tell me," she says, sitting back down, "what's a nice girl like you doing out in the middle of Brewster Pond on a night like this?"

Annie peers back at the lodge. Where seconds ago it was completely still, now suddenly voices carry over the water to where she and Helen sit. "Do you really want to know?"

Helen puts an arm around her. "Really."

And though it is Annie's intention to start with the night she first met Jake, she goes back further—so much further—beginning with the day she watches Papa trim his whiskers, and how, certain he would leave, she sought to save them.

After a while, Annie grows self-conscious and asks, "Do you want to go back now?" to which Helen replies, "Not now, later," rocking Annie in her arms, her face pressed against Annie's hair.

*   *   *

It is Helen who first notices the ambulance pulling into the driveway; no siren, but red lights flashing, playing into the woods and over the water.

"I hope he croaked," Helen says. "I hope it was Jake and that he croaked. I hope it so much." She clasps her hands, as if in prayer.

Annie pulls the boat onto the shore just as the gurney is being wheeled out of the living room. The huge shape being borne is unmistakably that of Elmer O'Leary. Jake and Elmer's driver stand at either side of the back doors of the ambulance. Walking next to the gurney is Dr. Eisenberg, carrying his small doctor's satchel, his face illuminated by the flashing red light. With some effort, the medics heft the stretcher with Elmer into the ambulance. "I'm coming along," Jake announces, stepping into the crowded van. Just then he notices Annie.

"Where the hell have you been?"

"Is he dead?" she asks.

Before Jake can answer, however, the ambulance driver slams shut the door, gets into the driver's seat and pulls away. Annie watches as the ambulance careens out of the driveway and up the hill. When she tries to find Helen, she too has disappeared.

With Elmer, Jake and the ambulance gone, the guests make quickly for their cars, as if the events of the evening are the long-awaited conclusion to a lingering drama. Those whose automobiles are blocked by others stand at their car doors and shout, "Come on, come on!" Cars back in every direction, headlights slash through the woods, discover random details of the garage, the lodge, the barn, and other cars, freezing drivers and passengers caught in the moment of escape. Someone smashes into the hearse, backs up, and smashes into it a second time.

In the melee, Annie spots Mrs. Goodhue again, but she is gone immediately, not leaving so much as an afterimage. Joe, Soupy and Georgie, without a car, maneuver for one of Jake's, but they are all blocked in. "This one," Soupy suddenly yells, pointing to Annie's Chrysler. In an instant, Soupy is at the wheel, Joe in the passenger seat, Georgie in back.

"No!" Annie yells from the porch. The Chrysler skids around

Elmer's limousine, slows to avoid the lamppost, then stops. Annie
bangs on the windshield. Soupy rolls down the driver's window.
   "Get in!"
   Georgie opens the back door. She can barely see him. "Come
on, Annie," he beckons. He reaches his hand out to her.
   For a moment, she takes it. Then, looking back at the house,
she sees Will standing at the tall kitchen windows, watching.
Annie lets go of Georgie's hand and moves away from the car.
   "Well?" Soupy demands.
   "Come on, Annie," Georgie urges, spotting Will, "we'll pick
him up later." Except for Elmer's limousine and the smashed-in
hearse, all the other cars are gone, even Jake's. "Come on."
   "I can't. I can't because . . ."
   Soupy steps on the gas, the force of the Chrysler's acceleration
swinging the back door shut. Annie stands away, stunned. She
is either hot or cold again, and in the quiet that follows, she walks
around the driveway. Through one of the open windows, she can
see Will brushing his teeth, getting ready for bed. Should she go
back to tell him she is here? She thinks she will, then reconsiders.
Perhaps his appearance in the kitchen window was his benedic-
tion of her departure. Perhaps it would have been better for both
of them if she had taken Soupy's offer, Georgie's hand. But,
Annie thinks, she has already been to so many places, and found
no more in one than in any other. Instead, she walks around the
driveway a second time, and then a third, and then many times
more.

   "I'm back," she tells Will as he sleeps. His light is off, his
breathing even, fluttering the sheet near his face.
   "Oh, hi," he says, suddenly opening his eyes and lifting his
head.
   "I just wanted you to know . . ." Annie begins. But Will's head
has already dropped back to his pillow.

   When Jake returns in Dr. Eisenberg's Volkswagen, Annie is
sitting in the wingback chair, a glass of scotch in her hand. All
the lights in the lodge are off. There is some talk between Jake and

Eisenberg that Annie cannot make out over the sputtering engine; then the little odd-shaped car putters away. Accustomed to the dark, Annie can make out Jake's face as he enters the room. It registers no emotion; there is no way of knowing what has happened, what Jake might feel.

He goes immediately to his desk at the far end of the room, switches on a single lamp and sits down heavily in his swiveling desk chair. For an instant, he cradles his head in his hands; then, with some purpose, he spreads out several pages before him and draws on his bifocals. Annie cannot imagine when he put it on, but he wears his shoulder holster over his double-breasted chef's coat.

Sitting nearly the length of the room away from him, she watches as he writes, watches for quite some time before taking a final sip of scotch and padding barefoot to the desk—never having reclaimed her shoes from the beach. Walking, she feels like a spirit, disembodied, with the ability neither to generate heat nor to feel cold.

"Jake!" she pronounces when she is right behind him, putting a finger to his back.

He spins in his chair, pistol drawn. "All right!"

"It's only me," she declares. She stares at the little, snub-nosed, blue-black gun inches from her breast, then puts her palm to its barrel. He, his gun, are laughable actually, she thinks.

"Well, for Christ's sake, Annie, what the hell are you trying to do? Get yourself killed?" He lays the gun on the desk. "I mean, you've got to *think,*" he goes on, pointing to his temple.

"I'm sorry." But she is not; this she knows.

"Sorry?" he repeats, as if sorry were hardly enough.

"Is Elmer dead?" she asks.

"Not yet," he says. "Soon, tomorrow maybe." He turns partway back to his desk.

"Heart attack?"

"That and a lot else. Now, if . . ." Jake is getting impatient, she can tell.

"Like what? Like what else?"

"Listen," he begins, "I don't want to talk about it, do you understand?"

"Well, what do you want to talk about?" Jake seems to consider her question, then asks suddenly how much she has had to drink.

"Some," she says. "And some more. Why?"

Jake nods, as if everything has suddenly been explained. "So, where the hell were you?" She tells him she was out on one of the rafts. "Are you out of your goddamn mind?"

"I was out there with Helen."

"You *are* out of your goddamn mind," he pronounces. "Go to bed."

"I want to talk," Annie says, knowing that this is not what she wants, knowing she wants only to tap into his anger, coursing ever closer to the surface. The danger she feels is intoxicating. It is the most alive she has felt in months. "I want to talk," she repeats.

"Talk to yourself, then." He turns in the chair and goes back to his papers. Leaving him to do so for a few seconds, Annie then spins the chair until he is facing her again. He looks over his bifocals at her and smiles, as if this is a game they are playing. Then, after a few seconds, he turns back to his desk again. The next time Annie spins the chair back, he stands in a slight crouch, shoulders curled forward like a prizefighter. "I hate you," he tells her.

She slaps him. "Always?"

"No. Only since I've gotten to know you."

"Prove it," she demands.

"I'd just as soon not. And *you*, you'd just as soon I wouldn't either, take my word."

Annie slaps him again, this time with all her strength. "You bastard!" He puts his hand to his face, rubs his cheek, staring at Annie all the while.

"All right," he says quietly. He raises his right hand. Annie gazes at it transfixed, expecting it will strike her. Just then, Jake closes his other hand around her throat and squeezes. "All right." Hand still on her throat, he draws her into the master bedroom, where he loosens his choke hold.

"Now what?" Annie says, hardly able to form the words.

"Now . . ." Suddenly, Jake grabs her dress and tears it off with a single sweep of his arm, then throws her to the floor. The next instant, he is on top of her, pants around his legs, his penis pushing at her underwear. His eyes stare into hers.

She tries to kick him, to hurt him, but he has already pinned her legs with his own, then tears away her underwear. Her hands go to his face, but he grabs her wrists and pins them together over her head, his belly against hers. "Scream," he demands. "Scream. Make it good for me." His penis is now inside her, his buttocks heaving. Holding both her hands with one of his, he reaches down with the other to pinch Annie's thigh. "Scream, I said."

"Never," Annie whispers. "Now that I know that's what you want."

"Scream," he repeats, pushing against her.

"You scream," Annie commands. "You!"

And then he does: a deep, guttural cry that means nothing to Annie, that has no effect. On his knees, he waves his spurting penis at her breasts and belly. After a few moments he rises, and, hobbled by his trousers, he walks to the bathroom. Seconds later he emerges, stark naked.

"Now go to bed," he orders.

Annie is still on the floor. "I'm leaving," she says.

"I'll believe it when I see it." He gets into bed, pulls the covers up over him.

Annie remains on the floor for a few moments more. Then, feeling the coarse grout from the stone hearth where she fell imprinted on her back, she stands, goes to the bathroom to wash Jake's semen from her body. In the mirror she sees herself—drunk, gaunt, ruined—sees only the recent layer that Helen saw, and not a trace of who she once was.

In her closet she finds a white spring dress with flowers and draws it on. Still barefoot, she walks through the living room and out onto the porch. Elmer's limousine is gone. She gets into the hearse, starts the engine, puts it into reverse, but cannot turn the steering wheel; the cars crashing into it have folded the right front fender into the tire. Annie gets out, looks down the road, can see nothing.

Back in the house there is little left for her to do. She walks past Jake, snoring in his bed, thinks briefly about the pistol on the dining-room table, opens the medicine cabinet, grabs the sleeping pills, swallows the twenty or so capsules left, and replaces the cap.

At Jake's desk, where the single light still burns, Annie finds a legal pad and begins to write an apology. To Will, of course. But what to say? What to apologize for? It's not my fault, she thinks. She writes that: "It's not my fault," then crumples up the sheet of paper and tosses it on the floor.

Instead, she thinks, she'll wake Will to tell him. And then what? Will. He'd call an ambulance. Will. She remembers him when he was little, his nose like a nut. Will. No, she cannot drag him into this. He should sleep. He'll need his sleep.

Annie gets up from the desk and walks to the wingback chair. Sitting in it at first, she can think of nothing, but then quite suddenly she recalls what a lovely place she once lived in, what a lovely feeling it was to take the trolley, to skate in the morning. Lovely. The memory, and the others that follow, are all in the most vivid color, perceived by Annie as if for the first time. Gradually, though, a heaviness falls over her, and she must work harder to bring the pictures into focus. The heaviness is like ballast that she drags along with her back into the master bedroom. She falls into bed next to Jake. "I'm leaving," she says, "finally."

He is wide awake. "So I see," he says.

"Won't you please save me?" Annie asks.

"No," Jake says. He moves away from where she lies. "What would be the point?"

"Are you sure?"

"Yes."

"Call the doctor."

"Later."

She hears him say it. "Later . . . later . . . later." The word reverberates, then disappears, and in its place, music—the simplest of pieces, like the preludes she played on the piano that Papa bought for her; then, the Beethoven from her first recital; then, the Bach she practiced on the Mason and Hamlin bought for only $50; then the Scriabin, the Mozart, the Schubert that Nathan Pearl taught her; and finally, finally, the last piece she ever played, the Chopin nocturne, in that torchlit bowl, her third and final encore, when she struck a note so singular that it seemed to have nowhere to go but up, lofted by currents into the comforting, starlit, dark blue sky.

ABOUT THE AUTHOR

Thomas Trebitsch Parker is an author, teacher, business consultant, and an award-winning writer of video, film, and live presentations. His first novel, *Small Business,* won the Commonwealth Club Silver Medal, and his short story "Troop Withdrawal: The Initial Step" was awarded an O. Henry Prize.